Sleepwalk

By John Saul

SLEEPWALK

JOHN SAUL

BANTAM BOOKS
NEW YORK • TORONTO • LONDON • SYDNEY • AUCKLAND

SLEEPWALK
A Bantam Book

Published simultaneously in the United States and Canada

Bantam Books are published by Bantam Books, a division of
Bantam Doubleday Dell Publishing Group, Inc. Its trademark,
consisting of the words "Bantam Books" and the portrayal of
a rooster, is Registered in U.S. Patent and Trademark Office
and in other countries. Marca Registrada. Bantam Books,
666 Fifth Avenue, New York, New York 10103.

PRINTED IN THE UNITED STATES OF AMERICA

Quality Printing and Binding by:
Berryville Graphics
P.O. Box 272
Berryville, VA 22611 U.S.A.

For Lee and Marshall—

So many places yet to go . . .

Sleepwalk

Sleepwalk

Prologue

The woman stood at the blackboard at the front of her classroom, watching her students work on the problem she had laid out a few minutes earlier. Though her eyes flicked constantly over the class, her mind wasn't registering the images her eyes were feeding to it.

The heat of the day was building, which was good.

The hotter the sun beating down on the roof, the less the joints in her fingers and toes, her hands, her feet—even her arms and legs now—hurt her.

That was some consolation, though not much. At least, although the winter's cold threatened to make her totally immobile, she still had the summers to look forward to—the dry, desert summers, when the heat would soak into her bones and give her some tiny measure of relief, a slight easing of the pain her disease brought with it, a pain that grew each month, along with the ugly deformities of her misshapen joints.

She was supposed to be better now. The doctor had promised her the new treatment would work. No, that wasn't actually true, she reminded herself. He'd said he *hoped* it would work; he hadn't promised her anything.

She gritted her teeth, and denied herself even the brief solace of a sigh as a sharp pain shot up from her left ring finger.

Her instinct was to rub the painful finger, but that would only make her right hand hurt more, and already she was barely able to hold the chalk as she carried on her class.

Against her will, her eyes traveled to the clock.

Ten more minutes and the noon bell would ring. Another day of summer school would be over.

She could make it.

* * *

In the fourth row of the classroom the boy stared once more at the problem he'd copied onto the paper on his desk, and quickly computed the solution in his mind. It was right, he was certain, but even if it wasn't, he didn't care.

He put his pencil down and let his gaze wander to the window, where the heat was making the mesa shimmer in the distance.

That was where he should be today—hiking up on top of the mesa or in the cool of the canyon, swimming in one of the deep holes the river had cut from the canyon's floor, working the anger out of his system with physical exercise. He'd had another fight with his father that morning, and the last thing he'd wanted to do was go from the oppressiveness of his home to that of the school.

Perhaps he should just get up and walk out.

He tried to put the tempting thought out of his mind.

He had agreed to go to school this summer, and he would.

But it would be the last summer.

Indeed, these few weeks of school might be the last ever.

He looked up at the clock and sucked in his breath.

Nine more minutes.

Then, as he watched the second hand jerk slowly around the face of the clock, he had a sudden feeling he was not the only one concerned with the time.

He glanced instinctively at the teacher.

As if feeling his glance, her eyes shifted from the clock and met his for a moment, and he thought he saw the beginning of a smile on her lips.

Then she winced slightly and, as if ashamed that he'd seen her pain, she turned away.

The boy wondered why she kept teaching. He knew—everyone knew—how much the arthritis hurt her, how much it crippled her in the winter. Even now he could remember the day, the previous January, when the temperature had been well below zero and he'd seen her sitting in her car in the parking lot. He'd watched her for a few minutes, unable to see her face clearly through the moisture that had built up on the windshield, but still somehow able to sense her reluctance to step out of the warmth of the automobile into the bitter morning chill.

Finally he'd approached the car and asked her if she was all right.

She'd nodded, then opened the door.

Slowly, painfully, she'd eased her legs to the ground, and finally, carefully, stood up, a gasp erupting from her lips as she battled the pain.

He offered to help her, but she'd shaken her head.

He'd turned away and hurried into the school building, but when he was inside he'd turned back and watched her through the glass doors.

She'd moved slowly, every step clearly an agony, her face down in an attempt to hide her pain.

But she'd kept moving, kept walking, not even hesitating when she came to the steps and had to pull herself slowly upward, gripping the iron railing with her gnarled left hand as her right hand clenched against the pain.

She wouldn't give up.

She'd never give up.

She'd keep teaching, and keep browbeating her students to do better and work harder, until the day she died.

The boy smiled slightly as he remembered the last time he'd been subjected to one of her tongue-lashings. She'd called him in after school and flung a homework assignment at him, her eyes fixing accusingly on his as she announced that she was considering failing him.

He'd studied the homework and discovered two mistakes, which he didn't think was so bad. When he'd voiced that opinion, her eyes had only mocked him: two mistakes might be fine for most of the class; from him she expected more. Much more. He was smarter than the rest of them, and the work shouldn't have been a challenge.

He'd squirmed, but she'd kept on: if he wasn't going to try in high school, how was he going to get through college, where there would be a lot of people smarter than he?

That was when he'd told her he wasn't going to college. Even now he wished he hadn't.

Glaring at him, her fist had smashed down on the desk with a force that should have caused her to scream with agony. But he had been the one who flinched at the blow, and she had smiled in triumph.

"If I can do *that,*" she'd said, "then you can damn well go to college."

He hated to think what she would say, at the beginning of his senior year, when she found out he was thinking of dropping out of high school.

But there were other things he wanted to do, things he didn't want to put off.

The teacher glanced surreptitiously at the clock once more. Just two more minutes. She could go home and sit in her back yard, ignoring the shade of the cottonwood trees to bask in the sun, letting the full heat of the afternoon penetrate the pain as she worked on her lesson plans and graded the examinations she'd given the class that morning.

She began straightening up the clutter on her desk.

She frowned slightly as a strange odor filled her nostrils. For a moment she couldn't quite identify it, but then realized what it was.

It was a malodorous scent, like a garbage dump on a hot day.

She sniffed at the air uncertainly, her frown deepening. The dump had been closed years ago, replaced by a treatment plant.

She looked up to see if anyone else had noticed the odor.

A flash of pain shot through her head.

She winced, but as quickly as the pain had come, it faded.

She shook her head, as if to shake off the last of the pain, then looked out at the class.

A red glow seemed to hang over the room.

She could see faces—faces she knew belonged to her students—but tinged with the red aura, seen dimly through a wall of pain, they all looked strange to her.

Nor could she put names to the faces.

The knife inside her head began to twist again.

Just a twinge at first, but building quickly until her skull seemed to throb with the pain.

The reddish glow in the room deepened, and the odor in her nostrils turned rank.

A loud humming began in her ears.

The aching in her head increased, and turned now into a sharp stabbing. She took a step backward, as if to escape the pain, but it seemed to pursue her.

The hum in her ears built to a screech, and the redness in the room began to flash with bolts of green and blue.

And then, as panic built within her, she saw a great hand spread out above her, its fingers reaching toward her, grasping at her.

She screamed.

The boy looked up as the piercing scream shattered the quiet of the room. For a split second he wasn't certain where it had come from, but then he saw the teacher.

Her eyes were wide with either pain or terror—he wasn't certain which—

and her mouth twisted into an anguished grimace as the last of the scream died on her lips.

Her arms rose up as if to ward off some unseen thing that was attacking her, and then she staggered backward, struck the wall and seemed to freeze for a moment.

As he watched, she screamed once more and sank to the floor.

Her arms flailed at the air for a few seconds, then she wrapped them around her body, drawing her knees up to her chest as she rolled helplessly on the worn wooden planks.

The boy rose from his seat and dashed to the front of the room, kneeling down beside her. But as he reached out to touch her, she screamed yet again and scrabbled away, only to collapse a second later, sobbing uncontrollably.

When the ambulance took her away, she was still sobbing, still screaming.

The boy watched the ambulance leave, but even after it had disappeared into the distance, the sobs and screams lingered on, echoing in his memory.

Perhaps the other students who were in the classroom might forget the agony they'd heard and seen that day.

The boy never would.

Chapter 1

Judith Sheffield felt the familiar tightening in her stomach as the final bell rang. All that was left of her day was the walk to the parking lot, accompanied, as always, by the prayer that today the tires on her car would still be inflated and none of its windows would be smashed. The day itself hadn't been too bad. Both her classes had gone well, which, she ruefully reminded herself, meant only that the disruptions had been minor.

At least today no fights had broken out in the classroom. After two years of teaching in East Los Angeles, Judith regarded that as a victory. But still, teaching during the summer session had been a mistake. She should have taken the summer off to relax, to rejuvenate herself and prepare for the far worse chaos of the regular school year. But she'd let herself be tempted by the extra pay, and conned herself into believing that the summer students would be more motivated than the regular term crowd.

The truth—which she knew perfectly well—was that the summer session students were there because they thought summer school would be a snap. Eventually they'd turned out to be right, for as Judith's energies had slowly drained through July and into August, she'd begun to slip, ignoring assignments not turned in, and skipping her regular morning quizzes. As the heat and smog of the Los Angeles summer closed in, she'd even begun dismissing her second class early, eager to return to her tiny apartment in Redondo Beach, strip off her clothes, then spend the afternoon lying in the sun on the beach, listening to the surf and trying to pretend that teaching in Los Angeles would get easier as she gained more experience.

It was getting harder to pretend.

The bell rang, and the kids poured out of the classroom into the halls like an overflowing toilet. Judith chided herself for the cruelty of the simile, then decided she didn't care—she tried to be a good teacher, tried to take an interest in the students, but if they didn't care, why should she? And what, really, could she do about it?

She could try harder.

And she would.

For the next six weeks she would relax, and by mid-September she would be ready, searching for new ways to capture the kids' interest, combing through the school's budget for the money she would need for new books. Perhaps this fall she would even organize a painting party to make her classroom a little less drab. She could hustle some plaster from Bobby Lansky's father—after all, it was Bobby who had hurled the desk that had made the hole in the wall—and she herself would spring for the pizzas she'd use to bribe some of the better students into participating.

She waited until the last of the kids' babble had died away, finished straightening the papers on her desk, then left her room, locking the door behind her. Warily, she glanced up and down the corridor, but it seemed deserted, and she told herself that today there would be no problems—it was the last day of summer session, and even the worst troublemakers would have been eager to get out of the building.

But as she moved toward the back staircase, she thought she heard a faint shuffling sound. She froze, listening.

A snicker, echoing maliciously, drifted through the hall.

She turned and started toward the main staircase at the other end of the hall.

Her step quickened and she instinctively clutched her heavy leather bag tighter, one hand gripping its shoulder strap while the other hovered protectively over the purse's flap.

A low whistle sounded behind her, and she steeled herself against the urge to break into a run.

Another whistle, slow and seductive, echoed in the hallway, and Judith felt her face turning scarlet.

She should be used to the wolf whistles by now—she heard them every day. Most of the time she simply ignored them.

But today, in the deserted third-floor corridor, the sound held an ominous note.

She hesitated at the top of the stairs, refusing to glance behind her, peering down the stairwell itself.

Empty.

She started down, moving quickly, one hand on the banister. She had made the first turn, and started down the fifteen steps to the second-floor landing, when suddenly she heard another whistle.

Two boys she didn't recognize stepped into the wide opening provided by the double doors on the landing below. They gazed up at her, smiling mockingly.

Though Judith knew they were no more than seventeen or eighteen, their eyes seemed much older, and they slouched in the doorway with a dark malevolence.

Judith paused as the familiar fear reached out to her once more. Her fingers tightened on the strap of her bag, and she slowly continued her descent.

One of the boys whistled again, while the other let his fingers stroke suggestively at his groin. "Got something for you, pretty teacher," he said. "Wanta see it?"

Judith said nothing. She came to the bottom of the stairs and took a tentative step toward the next flight.

The larger of the two moved to block her. "Want to have a good time?" he asked, his voice lilting with menace.

Judith's mind raced. She could scream, but there was no one to hear. And if someone heard her cry, would he rush to help?

Not likely.

She could try to flee back up the stairs, but a display of fear would only spur the boys on, turning what might have been a game into something far worse.

She moved forward again, focusing her mind on the lessons she'd learned last summer, after her first year of teaching here. "If you'll excuse me," she said, willing her voice to remain steady, "I'd just like to get to my meeting." There wasn't a meeting, but at least the boys might think she was expected somewhere.

The second boy reached out to her. "I got something wants to meet you."

As his hand came close to her, Judith spun around, slipping her bag off her shoulder and swinging it hard. She completed the turn, and the bag slammed into the boy's head, the weight of the ten rolls of quarters she always carried in its depths lending it enough force to knock the teenager against the wall. As her would-be attacker howled in pain and his friend stared at Judith in open-mouthed surprise, she broke into a run, dashing down the stairs, grabbing at the banister to steady herself.

"Get her!" she heard one of them shout as she came to the first-floor landing. Footsteps pounded in the stairwell. She ran into the corridor, turning left toward the side door that led to the faculty parking lot. By the time she reached the door she could hear her pursuers racing down the hall after her. She burst out the doors, praying that someone—anyone—would still be around.

There were a few cars in the lot, but no one in sight.

She stumbled down the steps, fumbling in the bag for her keys, then made a dash for her car. She jammed the key into the lock just as her assailants exploded from the building, twisted at it frantically, then managed to pull the door open. Scrambling inside, she jerked the door closed and pushed down on the lock just as the boys reached the car.

As she put the key in the ignition, the boys began rocking the car—a tiny Honda Civic she'd had for five years.

The ignition ground for a moment, then caught, and she stamped hard on the accelerator, racing the engine.

The boys were laughing now, and the car was rocking wildly. Saying nothing at all, Judith put the car in gear and released the brake. The Honda shot forward and her attackers jumped back. Judith turned sharply, heading for the parking lot gate, and suddenly the boys were running to another car, a low-slung Chevy painted a brilliant candy-apple red. As Judith pulled out of the parking lot and turned left toward the freeway a mile west, the Chevy fell in beside her.

They were going to follow her home!

Thinking quickly, Judith made a quick right turn, drove two blocks, then made a left, and another right.

The red Chevy stayed behind her, so close she was certain they were going to hit her. But then, as she made one more turn, her tormentors must have realized where she was going.

A block ahead was the low-slung building of the precinct station, a few patrol cars sitting in front of it. At the next corner the Chevy turned and disappeared into the traffic along Whittier Boulevard. Shaking, Judith pulled up in front of the police station, put the car in neutral and sat for a few minutes as her breathing returned to normal and her fear began to ease.

At last, when her hands could grip the wheel without trembling, she put the car in gear again and started home. But as she turned onto the freeway and started toward the beach, she realized what was happening to her.

Though she was barely twenty-six years old, she was already beginning to feel burned out. She no longer cared about her students; she couldn't even be bothered to report what had just happened to the police.

The traffic inched along the broad expanse of the Santa Monica Freeway. In the distance, where she should have been able to see the hills surrounding the Los Angeles basin, there was today only a thick brown veil of smog, as heavy and unpleasant as her mood. Every day, for the next six weeks, she would dread that first day of school more and more.

She'd set out to be a teacher, not a warden.

An hour later she pulled her car into the garage under her building a block from the beach and let herself into the small apartment. She'd intended it only to be temporary, but it was fast looking as though she would spend the rest of her life here. On her salary, there was no way she would ever be able to buy a house in Southern California, and rents everywhere were skyrocketing—only her lease was protecting her now, a lease she would renew this week in the hope that next year rent control would come to her area. If it didn't, and her rent went up again, she would have to find a roommate, maybe even two.

She unlocked the sliding patio door and dropped her heavy purse onto the coffee table. As she entered the kitchen in search of a Coke, the phone began to ring, and she decided to let the answering machine handle it. Probably it was the boys who'd been following her, calling her up now to continue their harassment.

She made a mental note to have her phone number changed, with the new number unlisted.

But a moment later, as her message tape ran out and a voice she hadn't heard in years began to speak, she snatched up the phone.

"Aunt Rita?" she asked. "Is it really you?"

"Judith!" Rita Moreland exclaimed. "I thought you weren't there. I was just going to leave a message."

"I just don't answer the phone anymore until I know who's calling," Judith said. Propping the receiver against her shoulder, she opened the refrigerator and pulled out a Coke. "I'm afraid it's been a rough day."

"Oh, dear," Rita Moreland murmured apologetically. "If it's a bad time, I can call back—"

"No!" Judith protested. "It's just that it was the last day of summer session, and something happened." Twenty minutes later, with the Coke finished and another one opened, Judith realized that she'd just unburdened herself of all her problems to a woman whom she hadn't seen in nearly ten years. Though she'd called Rita Moreland "aunt" all her life, the Morelands were really not relatives at all, but old family friends. "I'm sorry," she said. "I guess I really needed to talk to someone just now, and you happened to call. And I didn't even ask you why."

Rita Moreland laughed softly, an oddly tinkling sound that transported Judith back to the childhood that seemed so long ago and so far away. "Actually," Rita said, "perhaps it's providence that made me call today. I have a problem, and I'm getting desperate. And I thought of you. If you want to say no," she added in a rush, "believe me, I'll understand completely."

Judith frowned, mystified. "What on earth is it?" she asked. "You know if there's anything I can do for you and Uncle Max—"

"Oh, no," Rita broke in. "It isn't us. It's the school. We have an opening for a math teacher. Poor Reba Tucker's been hospitalized. . . ."

"Mrs. Tucker?" Judith said, surprised. Reba Tucker had once been her teacher and she remembered her fondly.

"I know it's awfully late in the year," Rita hurried on, "and you already have a job, but we're having a terrible problem finding someone." Rita Moreland talked on, but Judith was only half listening to what she was saying. Finally, Judith interrupted her.

"Aunt Rita?" she asked. "What's Borrego like now? It's been so long since I've been back."

Rita Moreland fell silent for a moment, then, once again, her bell-like laugh came over the line. "It's about the same," she said. "Things out here in New Mexico don't change very fast, you know. We're pretty much the way we've always been."

In that instant Judith Sheffield made up her mind. "I'll take the job, Aunt Rita," she said.

Jed Arnold slouched in the driver's seat of his ten-year-old Ford LTD, his fingers drumming impatiently on the steering wheel. The radio was blaring, tuned to the single station with a signal strong enough to reach from Santa Fe up to Borrego. It played country and western music twenty-four hours a day, but he supposed it was better than nothing at all.

"Maybe Jeff's not going to show up," Gina Alvarez said, reaching out to turn the volume down. She was curled up on the seat next to Jed, her head cradled against his shoulder. The remains of a hamburger and a shake were balanced on the dash, and when Gina felt a slight pressure on her shoulder, she reached out, picked up the last of the fries and stuck it in Jed's mouth.

"He'll be here," Jed told her, munching on the fry. "He was gonna get some beer."

Gina stiffened, then sat up and moved to the far side of the car, her eyes flicking to the backseat, where Heather Fredericks was necking with Randy Sparks. "You didn't say anyone was bringing beer," she said, her voice taking on an accusatory tone.

Jed grinned at her, that cocky, half-mocking grin that never failed to quicken her heartbeat. "If I had, you wouldn't have come, would you?"

Gina hesitated, then shrugged. "Maybe," she temporized. "Maybe I would, and maybe I wouldn't."

"You wouldn't," Jed declared knowingly. "You'd have given me one of your lectures on the evils of alcohol, and then shut the door in my face."

"I would not!" Gina replied. "How come everyone always acts like I'm some kind of goody-goody?"

"Because you are," Heather Fredericks replied from the backseat, squirming loose from Randy's arms and buttoning up her blouse.

"I am not," Gina protested. "But what happens if we get caught?"

Jed sighed in mock exasperation. "We're not going to get caught," he told her. "All we're gonna do is go out and drag the highway for a while, then go up into the canyon and have a couple of beers. What's the big deal?"

Gina thought it over, and decided that maybe he was right—maybe it wasn't a big deal. Almost all the kids she knew—certainly all of Jed's friends —got a couple of six-packs practically every weekend and went up into Mordida Canyon. And it wasn't as though they did anything really wrong. They just went for a swim, then sat around on the beach, listening to the radio and talking. And if she didn't go, all she'd wind up doing was sitting at home with her little sister, watching television.

Her mother would be furious if she found out, but it was Friday night, and she'd be working at the café until at least one in the morning. By then Gina would be home in bed, asleep.

A pair of headlights swept across the ugly orange walls of the A&W stand in front of them, and a horn blasted as Jeff Hankins pulled up next to the LTD in his ancient Plymouth. He revved the engine threateningly, then called to Jed, "Still think that piece of junk can take me?"

Jed snickered, and switched on the Ford's engine. "Only one way to find out, isn't there?" he yelled back. As he dropped the transmission into reverse, the car jerked backward with enough force to throw Gina against the dashboard. She shoved herself back onto the seat and pulled the seat belt around her waist. "What's the matter?" Jed teased her. "Think I've forgotten how to drive?"

"I think if you roll the car over, I want to stay where I am," Gina told him.

They were out of the parking lot now, and a moment later Jeff Hankins pulled his Plymouth up next to the LTD. "The canyon?" he asked.

"You got it," Jed replied. "Anytime you're ready."

Jeff nodded, then suddenly popped his clutch, and the Plymouth, its tires screaming, shot forward. A split second later Jed jammed his foot onto the LTD's accelerator. By the time he was ready to shift into second gear, he'd come abreast of the Plymouth, but as he shoved the gearshift up into second, the Plymouth pulled ahead of him again.

"Shit," he yelled. "What the hell's he done to that thing?"

"Stuck in a new carburetor," Randy said from the backseat. "I got a buck that says he beats you."

Jed gunned the engine, then shifted again, but the Plymouth was far ahead of him now, its taillights mocking him as Jeff raced out of town. The road ran straight for a mile, then turned right for another mile before coming to the canyon turnoff. Jed broke into a grin as he spotted a side road ahead. "You're on!" he shouted, then hit the brakes and spun the wheel.

The LTD slewed around, then left the pavement and shot onto a dirt track that angled off from the main road.

Randy Sparks jerked around to see the Plymouth disappearing into the distance. "Hey, what the hell are you doing?" he demanded.

"Cutting cross-country!" Jed shifted down and tightened his grip on the wheel as the Ford lumbered along the rough track.

"Are you nuts? You'll tear the pan out."

They hit a bump and the car thudded as its suspension hit bottom. Then a roaring filled the night.

"Oh, Christ," Jed muttered. "There goes the muffler."

The car lurched down the rutted road, its undercarriage slamming hard every few seconds. In the distance Gina could see Jeff Hankins's Plymouth making the turn on the main road. Jed saw it too, put the LTD into a lower gear and gunned the engine. The roar from the unmuffled manifold rose, but the car shot forward.

When he hit the main road again less than a minute later, Jed was only ten yards ahead of the Plymouth. He spun the wheel once more and skidded across the road. The tires on the right side of the car left the pavement, hit the gravel along the shoulder, and finally dropped into the ditch next to the road. The steering wheel wrenched loose from Jed's grip and spun around.

The car flipped, rolled over, and came to a stop upside down, its wheels spinning slowly. There was a sudden silence as the engine died, then a screaming of tires as Jeff Hankins braked to a stop.

A moment later Jeff and his girlfriend, JoAnna Garcia, were in the ditch, staring numbly into the ruined LTD.

"Heather!" JoAnna screamed, finally finding her voice. "Gina! Oh, my God. Are you all right?"

"Get the door open," Gina mumbled. She was still strapped to the seat, suspended upside down, her head brushing against the roof of the car. She fumbled with the seat belt for a moment, got it loose, and dropped in a heap onto the roof itself. JoAnna struggled with the wrecked door. One of its hinges already broken, it squealed in protest, then fell off into the ditch. A moment later Randy Sparks managed to force the rear door open too, and the four teenagers began creeping out of the wreckage.

Heather Fredericks had a cut on her right arm and a bump on her head, and Randy Sparks's left hand was bleeding, but otherwise they seemed uninjured.

"What the hell were you doing?" Jeff demanded, as his relief that his friends were all right gave way to anger. "You could have killed yourself and everybody else, too!"

Jed Arnold hardly heard Jeff's words. He was staring dolefully at the wreckage of his car. Already he could hear his father yelling at him. His father hadn't wanted him to buy the car at all, and now . . .

His thoughts were interrupted by the distant wail of a siren. He looked up to see the flashing red and blue lights of a police car coming toward them through the night.

Jed sat alone in the little police station in the basement of the City Hall, waiting for his father to come and pick him up. His friends had left an hour ago, Randy Sparks, Gina, and Heather having been escorted to the hospital to have their injuries taken care of, Jeff and JoAnna sent home.

But Jed was still waiting. His father was working the swing shift at the refinery and wouldn't get off until midnight. Jed had done his best to talk Billy Clark into letting him go, but the deputy had only looked at him coldly.

"You damn near killed yourself and three other kids tonight, you damn half-breed." Jed's eyes had blazed with cold fury at the term, but he'd kept silent. "You really think I'm just going to let you go?" the cop went on. "You've been making trouble around here long enough, but this time you're not getting off." He'd fingerprinted Jed, taken mug shots, then locked him in the station's single holding cell while he'd written up a report and a citation against Jed for reckless driving and endangerment of human life.

In the cell, Jed waited silently until his father finally showed up a little after midnight.

With no words exchanged between them, Jed signed for his things, and showed no emotion at all as his father led him out of the police station and drove him home.

He listened equally silently as Frank Arnold lectured him on the stupidity of what he'd done and told him he could forget about getting the car fixed.

At last Jed went to bed, but he didn't sleep.

Instead he lay awake, remembering Billy Clark's words, and knowing Clark was only saying what nearly everyone else in Borrego thought.

He, Jed Arnold, wasn't white, and he wasn't Indian.

He was something else, something halfway in between.

Sometimes—like now—he felt as if he didn't fit in anywhere.

It was at times like this, late at night, when he was all alone, that all the fury contained within him would threaten to erupt to the surface.

It was at times like this that he wondered if someday the rage might overflow and he might actually kill someone.

Or maybe even kill himself.

That, as he well knew, was always an option too.

Chapter 2

A week after Rita Moreland's phone call, Judith Sheffield was on her way to Borrego. Immediately after the conversation, there had been a moment of panic as she wondered whether she'd been rash to accept the offer, but by the next morning, when for the first time in months she'd awakened with a sense of actually looking forward to the day, rather than dreading it, she knew she'd made the right decision.

For the next five days she dealt with the details of making the move.

It was surprisingly simple. Her landlord was actually relieved when she told him she'd changed her mind about renewing her lease—he had three people willing to take the apartment at a rent far higher than Judith would have paid. And the new tenant, anxious to move in as quickly as possible, instantly agreed to buy whatever furniture Judith left behind.

She left all of it, packing only her clothes and personal belongings into the foot locker she'd been using as a coffee table, and shipping her books and records ahead.

The moment she dreaded most—the moment of telling Floyd Morales that she wasn't signing the contract for next year—turned out to be almost as easy.

"Well, you're certainly not making my life any easier," the principal had commented. "But I can't say that I blame you. There've been plenty of times when I've thought about getting the hell out of here myself."

Judith's brows had risen, but Morales had only shrugged. "What can I do? I grew up here . . . my family lives here—maybe I feel like I owe them something." But then his gaze had drifted to the window and the littered playing field, fenced in like a prison, that lay beyond his office. "I don't know," he'd mused. "Sometimes it feels so hopeless." At last he'd straightened up and taken on his usual briskness. "But there are still kids who want an education, and deserve one. So I guess I just can't give up and go away."

Judith felt the sting of his words. "Is that what you think? That I'm giving up? Cutting and running?"

Morales had apologized immediately. "Of course not. In fact, you're doing exactly what I did when I came back here after college. You're going home, and helping them out. Nobody can condemn that." He'd offered her his hand. "They're lucky to be getting you. You have a way with the kids."

Judith had grinned ruefully. "I wish that were true."

"It is," Morales had insisted. "I know it's been rough, but you've had less trouble with the kids than most of the teachers. And you've turned at least half a dozen of them around. Kept them in school when they were on the verge of dropping out."

"Half a dozen," Judith had repeated. "Out of how many hundred? Somehow, it doesn't seem like much to me."

Still, as she'd left the school for the last time, she felt a sharp pang of regret. There were a few students—not too many, but some—to whom she wished she'd been able to say good-bye.

The next morning, when she read an account of a gang fight the night before and found that one of her best students hadn't survived it, the last of her regrets evaporated.

Now, as she drove the final fifty miles north from Interstate 40, up into the neck of land between the Navajo reservation to the west and the Apache lands to the east, she was still certain she'd done the right thing.

The New Mexican sky, an immense expanse of brilliant blue that seemed —impossibly—to have grown even larger than she remembered from her childhood, spread above her, dwarfing even the mesas that rose from the desert floor in the distance.

She was tempted to turn off the highway for an hour or so and pay a short visit to the vast ruins at Chaco Canyon, but as she came to the turnoff, she changed her mind, suddenly eager to see Borrego once more. Borrego.

The town she'd grown up in, but never, until last week, expected to come back to.

She came over the last rise in the gently rolling desert floor and pulled over to the side of the road, parked the Honda on the shoulder and got out of the car. She perched on the hood, staring out at the town in the distance.

Borrego could have been beautiful: sprawled at the foot of one of the mesas, it lay near the mouth of Mordida Canyon, a deep, narrow gorge that, though only the tiniest fraction of the size of the Grand Canyon to the west, had a unique beauty all its own, its flat bottom dotted with cotton-woods, a gentle stream flowing through it year 'round.

The town hadn't been built on the river, for the Mordida, like all the other streams in the region, could turn into a raging torrent within a few moments, fueled by the torrential rains that could pour out of the desert sky with no warning at all.

Not that the Mordida was a threat to the town any longer; indeed, the river had been safe from flash floods for more than fifty years, ever since a small dam had been constructed across one of the canyon's narrows, gener-ating the electricity needed to power the refinery that old Samuel Moreland had built when he discovered oil in the area.

For that was what Borrego really was—an oil town. But not a boom town like the bonanza towns of Texas. No, Borrego was only a tiny service village, a place for the refinery workers to live, along with the drillers and the crews who looked after the dam. As the oil reserves around Borrego had always been limited, so too had the prospects for the town, which had reached its peak shortly after the dam and refinery had been constructed. Ever since, it had slowly been declining. The Sheffields had moved from Borrego to Los Angeles for just that reason, when Judith was sixteen. Now, squinting against the glare of the sun, she could just make out the worn buildings that made up the town.

A layer of dust seemed to lie over Borrego, a layer that even the violent desert rain squalls could never quite seem to wash away. It was almost as if the town had deliberately ignored the expansive red, orange, and brown landscape that surrounded it, and become afraid of the limitless cobalt-blue dome of sky above. Borrego appeared to huddle defensively against the ground, many of its old adobe buildings long since replaced with a collec-tion of cinder-block structures whose metal or asphalt roofs absorbed more of the summer heat than they reflected.

Judith's gaze shifted to the top of the mesa, and for a moment she imagined she could actually see the little Kokatí Pueblo. That, she hoped, was still unchanged, but after her visit to the Hopi mesas yesterday, when she'd seen the same tin-roofed, cinder-block houses that so many of the Indians had moved into—leaving their beautiful pueblos to begin crum-bling in the weather—her hope had faded. It was certainly possible—even probable—that the Kokatís had also abandoned the old village for some-thing that was not better, but was only new.

She climbed back into the Honda, started the engine, and drove the last few miles into Borrego. A mile and a half out of town, set back from the road, the oil refinery stood exactly as she remembered it—a maze of pipes and towers, with a small tank farm behind it. Then there was the cutoff to the canyon—still unpaved, little more than twin ruts leading off across the desert floor toward the cleft in the mesa.

At last she came to the town itself, its boundary marked by the squat, ugly orange building that was the A&W stand. Not one of the new ones— bright and airy, with tables and a fast-food counter—but the old style, with a walk-up window and a couple of teenage carhops wearing outdated uniforms, lounging at a picnic table at the edge of the deserted parking lot.

Judith wondered if the A&W was still the place where the kids met in the evening, shouting back and forth between their cars, then racing off into the night, going nowhere, only to return to the drive-in a few minutes later.

The main street was unchanged. The same two competing markets stood facing each other, one of them flanked by the dry goods store, the other by a drugstore and the post office. Beyond them were a few new shops that Judith didn't recognize, and some of the old ones were gone.

Two blocks down, opposite the small movie theater that was now boarded up, stood the Borrego Building—a four-story brick structure that housed the bank on its main floor and the offices of Borrego Oil Company on the floors above. When it was built, it had been intended to be the first of many multistoried buildings in what everyone had hoped would become a small city.

But Borrego was still nothing more than the little town it had always been, crouched in the high desert, all but bypassed by the development along the interstate to the south.

Yet Judith found she was glad so little change had come to the town. She felt oddly comforted to recognize some of the people who stood chatting in front of the tiny post office, their faces weathered by the desert climate, but their features—like the town's own—essentially unchanged, only more deeply ravaged by time and the elements than they'd been a decade ago.

She left the town behind, driving east for a mile, then turned up the long drive that led to the foot of the mesa and the big house—a bastard-Victorian structure that stood defiantly at odds with its environment, not quite a mansion, but by far the largest home in Borrego. Old Samuel Moreland had built it for his wife at a time when no one else was building such things. His son Max, and Rita Moreland, still lived there.

Surrounded by a grove of large cottonwoods that sheltered it from the sun and screened the most ornate of its gingerbread details from the viewer, it had a look of solidity and permanence to it that Judith admired. Tall, and somewhat narrow, it seemed to peer out at the desert with a spinsterish disapproval, as if eyeing its surroundings with thinly-veiled distaste. Judith pulled the Honda to a stop in front of the house, then stepped out into the cool shade of the cottonwood trees. Even before she'd mounted the steep flight of steps to the porch, the big door opened and Rita Moreland stepped out, her arms spread wide in welcome.

"Judith? Is it really you? I hadn't thought you'd be here until tomorrow!"

Judith rushed up the steps and into the older woman's embrace, then pulled away to get a good look at the woman who'd been the closest thing to a grandmother she'd ever had.

"You look wonderful, Aunt Rita."

It was true. Rita Moreland, at seventy-two, looked no more than sixty. She still held her tall, somewhat angular frame perfectly erect, and she was dressed in the sort of simple linen skirt and blouse she had worn as long as Judith could remember. Around her neck was an antique silver and turquoise squash-blossom necklace, and her wrists held several bracelets, most of them modern Hopi designs. Her hair, snow white, was rolled up into an elegant French twist, held in place by a silver comb. Only her eyes, alight with pleasure, belied her look of cool composure.

"Well, you've changed," Rita replied. "All grown-up, and just as pretty as your mother. Although," she added, cocking her head speculatively, "I think perhaps your hair's starting to darken a little."

Judith grinned. "It's called aging, Aunt Rita. Is Uncle Max here?"

Rita's eyes clouded for just a split second, then cleared as she shook her head. "Oh, no—always at the office, or the plant. You know Max—he'll work till he drops, even though he keeps promising me he'll slow down. Now come on, let's get you inside." Before Judith could protest, Rita had darted down the steps and pulled one of Judith's bags from the backseat of the Honda.

Upstairs, Judith gazed with unabashed pleasure at the room Rita had chosen for her. It was a large chamber in the corner—almost two rooms, really, since the tower that rose at the southwest corner of the house was incorporated into it. There was an immense four-poster bed, and in the tower itself, a cushion-filled love seat and a large easy chair. Five windows were set into the curving wall of the tower, and the view, framed by a pair of cottonwoods, was a panorama of desert and mesas, with the town no more than a small collection of buildings in the foreground.

"You can see almost fifty miles from up here," Rita told her, reading her thoughts. "Of course, it would be even lovelier without the town and the refinery, but without those we wouldn't be here at all, would we?" She lifted one of the suitcases onto the bed and snapped it open. "Let's get you unpacked. By then Max should be home and we can all have a gin and tonic."

Judith firmly closed the suitcase. "I have an even better idea," she said. "Let's leave the unpacking for later, and you and I can have something right now. It's been a long drive."

Long, she thought as she followed Rita back downstairs, but worth it. All her doubts were now gone.

She was glad to be home.

Stretched out on a chaise under one of the cottonwoods, sipping slowly at her second drink, Judith felt a sense of ease and comfort she hadn't experienced for years. Rita had filled her in on most of the news of the last decade, what there was of it. Many of the kids she'd grown up with were still here, married now, most with at least one child. Laura Sanders, to whom she'd promised to write but never had, had come back five years ago, graduating from nursing school and taking a job at Borrego High.

The one piece of news that had truly upset her was Rita's recounting of the death of Alice Arnold four years ago.

"How did Jed take it?" Judith asked. In her mind she pictured the little boy—only five or six when she'd last seen him—with his Kokatí mother's dark skin and jet-black hair, and his father's brilliant blue eyes. She remembered Jed as a happy child, interested in everything he saw, full of questions, always eager to go exploring in the canyon or up on the mesa. Judith had baby-sat for him many times, once or twice taking care of him all weekend while Frank took Alice away, hoping to break her strange melancholy with trips to Santa Fe, or up into the Utah canyon lands. Judith had loved those weekends, taking care of Jed, riding up into the canyon with him perched on the saddle in front of her, or up to the mesa to visit his grandfather in Kokatí. Jed, his bright eyes darting everywhere, talking constantly, asking questions, urging her onward to explore.

To have lost his mother, when he was still only eleven . . .

"It was hard for him," she heard Rita saying. "It was Jed who found her. He came home from school one day, and there she was . . ." Rita's voice trailed off, and both the women were silent for a moment.

"How is he now?" Judith asked. "It's such a terrible thing for a child that age."

"It's hard to say," Rita replied. "In so many ways he's so much like his mother. I'm afraid there's a part of him no one will ever know. It's almost as if he's closed part of himself down." Her eyes met Judith's. "It's very difficult for him, you know, being half Indian out here."

"But not as difficult as it must have been for Alice, trying to live in Borrego after growing up in Kokatí. After she married Frank, her father barely spoke to her."

"I know," Rita sighed. "In their own way, the Indians can be every bit as prejudiced as we are."

They talked on for a while, and finally Judith turned to a subject she'd been avoiding—the reason she was back in Borrego.

"What about Mrs. Tucker?" she asked. "How is she?"

Again, as when Judith had asked about Max, a troubled cloud passed over Rita Moreland's eyes, but this time it didn't pass. "I think maybe you should save that question for Greg," she began.

"Greg?" Judith exclaimed. "You mean Greg is here too?"

Rita stared at her. "You mean you didn't know?" she asked. "You had such a crush on him ten years ago, I thought that might have been one of the reasons you came back."

A crush, Judith thought. The first great love of my life, and all it's remembered as is a crush.

But of course infatuation was exactly what it had been.

Greg Moreland—Max and Rita's nephew—had spent all his summers in Borrego, coming home from his boarding school each spring, impressing all the local girls with his blond curls and dimpled chin, as well as his sophistication, then leaving them each fall with broken hearts as he returned to New England, first for college, then for medical school. During the summer before his last year at Harvard Medical School it had been Judith's turn to fall for him. Not that he'd even noticed her, of course, except to take a turn with her once or twice at the weekend dances at the union hall.

But it had been enough to make her fall in love with him—or at least develop a major crush—and when he'd left, she was sure she would die.

Not only hadn't she died, but she'd quickly developed another crush on someone else—someone even more unattainable than Greg—and hadn't even thought of Greg for the last five years.

"But what on earth is he doing back here?" she asked. "Somehow, I always pictured him opening a terribly successful Park Avenue practice in New York."

Rita chuckled appreciatively. "Well, I can't say I didn't see pretty much the same thing myself. But it turned out we were wrong. He did a residency in Boston, then came back here for one more summer to think things over. And he never left." Rita beamed with as much pride as if Greg were her own son, instead of her nephew. "He started dropping in on Bob Banning at the clinic every now and then, just helping out when there was an emergency, and at the end of the summer he decided to stay until Christmas. That was six years ago, and he's still here."

"Does he live here?"

"Oh, no," Rita replied. "He has a little house in town—nothing special, considering what his tastes used to be."

Judith frowned. "But he has plenty of money, doesn't he? Why hasn't he built something terrific?"

Rita smiled cryptically. "Why don't you ask him yourself?" she asked. "He'll be here for dinner tonight."

Judith stared at Rita for a moment, then cocked her head. "Is this part of a plan?" she asked archly.

Rita's smile faded. "I wish it were," she said softly. "But I don't think I would have gone so far as to put poor Reba in the hospital."

Judith's laughter died on her lips. "I'm sorry," she said. "I didn't mean—"

"Of course you didn't," Rita assured her.

Judith said nothing, but lay back, relaxing in the warmth of the sun that was now beginning to drop toward the western horizon.

A lot in Borrego hadn't changed at all.

But a lot else, she suddenly realized, had.

Unbidden, her thoughts returned to Alice Arnold, and she made a mental note to call Frank the next day.

So many things had happened here, so long ago.

And now she was back.

"How are you feeling?" Greg Moreland asked as he carefully unwrapped the gauze from Heather Fredericks's arm.

Heather winced as the bandage came off the wound, then relaxed as she realized there was no pain at all. Still, the cut looked ugly, with its coating of dried blood and the four stitches the doctor had taken a week ago. "Okay," she said. "Is there going to be a scar?"

Greg turned on his best reassuring grin. "Would I leave a scar on a girl as pretty as you?"

Heather blushed with embarrassment at the compliment, and shook her head.

Greg carefully began cleaning away the dried blood, and was pleased to see that the cut was healing nicely. There was none of the puffiness that might have indicated an infection setting in, and the raw edges of skin were knitting perfectly. In another week there would be nothing left except a hairline, and that too would be gone within a month.

"What do you say we get the stitches out?" he asked.

Heather shrugged, but her face screwed up with anticipation as Greg carefully clipped the threads, then worked them loose with a pair of tweezers. When he was done, he re-covered the cut with a piece of surgical tape, then replaced the old bandage with a new one.

"How about your head?" he asked when he was finished. "That was a pretty nasty bump you got. Any headaches? Blurring of your vision?"

Once again Heather shook her head. "I took aspirin for a couple of days, but there was hardly even any swelling."

"Okay," Greg said, making a couple of notes on Heather's chart. "Then I guess that's it till next week, when you should be able to get rid of that bandage."

Heather made a sour face. "Who cares about the bandage? My mom won't let me go out for two more weeks anyway. And none of it was even my fault."

Greg leaned back in his chair and gave Heather a speculative look. Perhaps, in this case at least, Heather was right. She'd been in the backseat of Jed Arnold's car, and hadn't been drinking. But then he remembered the two six-packs of beer that had been found in Jeff Hankins's car. "And I suppose you weren't going to drink any of the beer either, were you?" he asked.

Heather's expression tightened into a pout. "Maybe I didn't even know it was there."

"Maybe you didn't," Greg agreed. "But I'll give odds you did, and I'll give even better odds you would have had more than your share of it if you'd all gotten up to the canyon." He leaned forward and the lightness disappeared from his voice. "It hasn't occurred to any of you kids how lucky you were, has it?" he asked.

Heather shrugged sulkily as she realized she wasn't going to be able to con Dr. Moreland into talking her mother out of grounding her. "Can I go now?" she asked.

Greg opened his mouth as though to say something else, then changed his mind. He nodded, told Heather to make an appointment for the following week, then watched as she left the room.

A girl, he thought, who was heading for trouble.

Just like so many of the kids in Borrego.

Not much to do, and not much to look forward to.

For the most part they'd wind up like their parents, getting married too young, having too many kids, then living out their lives in trailer houses, or ugly little concrete blocks, like the ones they'd grown up in.

Every day Greg saw it—saw the discontent and unhappiness of the parents, saw the boredom and disinterest of the children.

That, perhaps, was why he'd returned to Borrego.

He wanted to change what he saw there.

But some days, like today when he tried to talk some sense into kids like Heather Fredericks, he wondered whether he was simply wasting his time.

Kids like Heather and her friends just never seemed to listen to him, never seemed to learn.

Still, he couldn't stop trying.

He sighed, glanced up at the clock, then began clearing off his desk. In another hour he was due at his aunt and uncle's house. If he hurried, he'd have time for a quick shower, and maybe even half an hour of sleep.

Even if Judith Sheffield was still as pretty as he remembered her from ten years ago, it was going to be a long night.

Chapter 3

Judith sat quietly in one of the large leather-upholstered club chairs that flanked the fireplace in the Morelands' living room. She was finally feeling the exhaustion of the long day on the road, and though she supposed she should have excused herself an hour ago and gone upstairs to bed, she'd lingered on, listening to the talk between Max and Greg.

It was apparent to her that Max was proud of his nephew, and Judith could understand why. Greg seemed to her to have lost the hard edge of sophistication he'd affected in his college days, and the almost artificial perfection of his features had softened slightly as he'd matured. Now, in his thirties, his darkening hair was no longer as perfectly combed as it had once been, and his dark eyes had taken on a new depth. Though he was still remarkably handsome, he no longer seemed to be either conscious of his good looks, or impressed by them. Rather, he seemed far more interested in his work than in anything else, although she noticed he had listened intently when she'd asked Max about his own plans for the future.

Max, she reflected sadly, had not aged as gracefully as his wife over the last decade. His brow was deeply furrowed, and the flesh of his face seemed to have lost its tone—folds of loose skin hung at his jowls, and his eyes had sunk deep within their sockets. And, beneath his obvious pleasure in seeing her, she thought she could detect a certain strain, as if he were worried about something but didn't want to dwell on it, or cause anyone else to share his concerns. She'd pressed him, though, after dinner, and finally he'd admitted that there were some problems at the refinery. Though he'd done his best to make light of the situation, she gathered that the last few years, when oil prices had suddenly dropped, had been difficult for his company. There was a large debt load to support, and the refinery itself was becoming more obsolete each year.

"But it'll be all right," he'd finally assured her. "The oil business has always had ups and downs, and it always will. Hell, if everything ran smoothly for a couple of years, I'd probably start feeling useless and go do something else." Then, as if to emphasize his wish to change the subject, he'd waved toward Greg. "Now, if you want to hear something really interesting, ask him about what he's doing up in the canyon."

"It's not much," Greg said. "Uncle Max tries to make it sound like I'm the best thing since Mother Teresa, but I'm afraid it doesn't compare at all."

"What doesn't?"

"Well, you remember the old farm up there?"

Judith nodded, remembering it clearly. When she'd been a little girl, it had been one of the most popular haunts around for her and her friends. Far up the canyon, only half a mile below the dam, there had been an abandoned farmhouse, with a few outbuildings including an old barn and a bunkhouse. Legends about the farm abounded, old ghost stories that she and her friends had never tired of telling. The farm, long uninhabited and nearly in ruins, was off limits on the grounds that it was unsafe, and therefore a favorite spot for adventurous ten-year-olds.

Judith could still remember the delicious feeling of forbidden adventure that creeping up into the creaking hayloft in the barn brought—praying the floorboards wouldn't collapse under your weight, shuddering as you heard small unseen creatures scurrying about, and later bragging about your exploits to the younger kids, as you told them what a terrifying place it was. "So what have you done with it?" Judith asked.

"He's turned it into a sanitarium," Max announced proudly.

Judith cocked her head uncertainly. "A sanitarium?" she echoed uncertainly. "I'm not sure I understand."

Greg shook his head. "It isn't really a sanitarium at all," he said. "It's more of a hospice, but since I also take a few rehab patients who have no place else to go, everyone around here has started calling it a sanitarium. Even," he added, feigning a glare at his uncle, "Uncle Max, who should know better. It's just a place for people who need some medical care—nothing too major, of course—but don't have much money or insurance."

"It's a hell of a lot more than that," Max declared, turning away from his nephew to face Judith. He was fairly beaming, and as he talked, all the old zest and enthusiasm Judith remembered came back to his voice. "That old place was just sitting there rotting away, and Greg figured out what to do with it. He's got some nurses and physical therapists up there, but if you just wandered into the place, you'd swear you were in a resort. Everybody has private cabins, and they bring you your meals if you need it. But he figured out how to do it without making it too expensive. It's a great place for people who are too sick to stay home but can't afford a hospital or a nursing home."

"It just seemed that there was a need for something in the middle," Greg said, his expression serious now. "A nice environment for people who were either going to get better pretty fast or were really beyond treatment and just needed a comfortable place to live out their last few days or weeks. So I set it up as a foundation, and conned Uncle Max into donating the land and the buildings."

"And you put in a lot of your own money too," Rita Moreland said, her voice reflecting the same pride in Greg as her husband's had a moment earlier.

"Not all that much," Greg replied. "Actually, I've been spending a lot of time rustling up grants, and it's working out pretty well. I guess," he added, suddenly sounding shy, "what I've really done is build the kind of place I'd like to be in myself."

Judith sat silently for a few moments, then a thought came to her. "Is that where Mrs. Tucker is?" she asked.

It was Rita who nodded, her expression somber.

"What happened to her?" Judith asked Greg.

He spread his hands helplessly. "It was one of those things you can never predict. She had a stroke. It surprised me—I'd been treating her for arthritis, and monitoring her pretty closely. Her blood pressure was fine, and except for the arthritis, she seemed to be in great condition." He looked at his uncle, his features taking on an exaggerated cast of disapproval. "She wasn't like some people I could mention, whose blood pressure is far higher than it should be, and whose arteries are totally clogged up from eating the wrong things for seventy-five years, and who are stroke victims waiting to happen."

"Doesn't sound like anyone I know," Max growled, and poured himself another shot of bourbon from the bottle sitting open on the coffee table in front of him. He held the glass up and grinned at his nephew. "Thins the blood, right?" he asked, and drained the slug of whiskey in one gulp.

Greg rolled his eyes in mock horror. "Anyway, Mrs. Tucker seemed to be doing fine, and then one day last month she had a massive stroke. It happened during one of her classes, and I guess it was pretty bad for the kids. They didn't know what had happened, and there was nothing they could do. She was teaching them one minute, and the next she was on the floor, caught up in a seizure. Now . . . ." His voice trailed off and his hands spread in a bleak gesture of helplessness. "There just doesn't seem to be anything I can do for her except make her comfortable."

The conversation had drifted on, but Judith was only half listening, most of her attention focused on the plight of her former teacher. She tried to imagine what it must be like to be trapped the way Reba Tucker now was, unable to take care of herself, unable even to communicate.

Her whole life reduced to a small cabin, in which she waited to die.

In such circumstances, Judith imagined, a person must pray for death every moment of every day. Long ago she had come to realize that sometimes it was easier to die than to go on living.

Heather Fredericks lay in her bed, staring up at the ceiling. She wasn't certain how long she'd been awake, wasn't even certain what it was that had awakened her.

All she knew was that she felt perfectly relaxed—even the pain in her arm, a lingering throbbing that had been bothering her when she'd gone to bed earlier that night, seemed to be gone.

Her mind drifted, her thoughts floating lazily, vague images appearing now and then, then fading away again.

And then, from somewhere outside, she heard a voice.

"Heather."

Just the single word; nothing else.

She lay still, her eyes fixed on the ceiling, waiting.

A few seconds later she heard the voice again:

"Heather, come outside."

Without thinking about it, Heather pushed the covers aside and stood up. She was wearing nothing except a pair of flannel pajamas, but she didn't stop to dress or even put on a robe before obeying the voice she'd heard. She simply left her room, padded barefoot down the hall and through the kitchen, then went out the back door, leaving it standing open behind her.

When she was outside she stopped, waiting.

A few moments later the voice came again, as though from nowhere.

"Follow me."

Heather gazed around, not questioning the command, only looking for the person who might have spoken the words.

The moon was high, and nearly full, and the desert was illuminated with a pale silvery light. For a moment Heather saw nothing, but then a form appeared out of the deep shadows behind the garage. It stood watching her silently, and a moment later turned and walked away, crossing the backyard and opening the gate in the Fredericks's back fence.

The house, on the very edge of the town, was separated from the desert only by the fence, so as Heather crossed the lawn and stepped through the gate herself, she immediately left the village behind.

She was alone in the desert, following a shadowy form.

Yet she was not afraid.

The figure ahead of her kept a steady pace, moving quickly, and Heather had to struggle to keep up, but in her mind she didn't question what she was doing, didn't wonder why she was doing it.

She only knew she had to obey the instructions she'd been given. Indeed, obeying those instructions was all she wanted to do.

She walked for nearly an hour, her bare feet moving steadily across the sand and rocks of the desert.

She stepped on a broken bottle, the sharp fragment of glass slashing at her foot, but she neither felt the pain of the cut nor noticed the blood that oozed from it. Her attention remained focused on the dark figure ahead as it led her steadily across the desert.

The path they walked began rising, then turned into a series of switch-backs as it led up to the top of the mesa. But even as she climbed, Heather felt no tiredness in her muscles, no shortness of breath. Even her heartbeat remained steady.

They came eventually to the top of the mesa, but still the figure moved onward, not speaking, not pausing, not even looking back.

And Heather followed.

At last the figure stood motionless.

"*Stop.*"

The word was uttered softly, but its effect on Heather was no less profound than if it had been shouted directly into her ear.

Instantly, she too came to a halt, then remained perfectly still, waiting to be told what to do next.

"*Turn left,*" the voice said.

Heather turned.

"*Walk forward ten steps.*"

Heather began to move, silently counting. When she reached ten, she stopped again.

"*Look down.*"

Heather's gaze shifted, and she peered downward.

Only a step ahead of her the wall of the canyon dropped away, falling nearly a thousand feet straight down. At the bottom of the canyon, barely visible, she could see the stream glinting faintly in the moonlight.

"Jump," the voice commanded.

Without thinking about it, without hesitating, Heather Fredericks stepped off the edge of the abyss and plunged silently into the depths of the chasm.

The shadowy figure waited a few moments, staring down after her until she disappeared, then silently began retracing its steps, moving steadily back toward the town.

At last, after all the years of preparation, the time had come.

Jed Arnold was sprawled out on the worn Naugahyde couch in the living room of the house he shared with his father. The television was tuned to a rerun of a show Jed had already seen and hadn't much liked in the first place. Not that he was watching it; more than anything else, it simply served as background noise, filling the silence.

He'd been grounded for two weeks, and he still had a week to go—seven more long evenings, with nothing to do and no one to talk to.

A car pulled up in front, its engine racing noisily for a moment before suddenly dying. Jed heard two car doors slam, then a loud pounding on the front door. Rolling off the sofa, he opened the door to find Randy Sparks and Jeff Hankins grinning at him.

"Come on," Randy said. "Jeff's got some beer, and we're going up to the canyon. We'll do some skinny-dipping and get smashed."

Jed started to shake his head, then changed his mind. After all, it was only eleven-thirty. His father had gone to work an hour ago, and wouldn't be home until a little after seven-thirty in the morning. By then he'd be back home. And even if he went ahead and had a few beers, his father would never know.

But what if his dad called to check up on him, as he had last night?

There was an easy answer to that one, Jed thought—with the phone off the hook, he could say he'd been talking to friends, and his father would never know the difference.

His mind made up, he went into the kitchen, removed the receiver and laid it on the counter. Then he went to his own room and pulled his leather jacket out of the pile of clothes on his chair.

Leaving the television and the lights on, he glanced guiltily at the house next door, but was almost sure the neighbors had gone to bed an hour ago.

By the time he was in the backseat of Jeff's Plymouth, crouched down for the first few blocks so no one would see him, he was certain he was going to get away with it.

"It's okay," Randy said from the front seat a few minutes later. "We're out of town."

Jed sat up, peered quickly out the back window, then relaxed. There were no other cars in sight, and even the glowing lights of the A&W stand were barely visible in the distance.

"Your dad still pissed at you?" Jeff asked as they came to the cutoff that led up the floor of the canyon. There were still faint skid marks from the week before, when Jed's own car had spun across the road and rolled into the ditch.

"Oh, yeah," Jed replied. "Every single day he gives me another lecture on responsibility. It's like he never made any mistakes at all when he was my age."

"Maybe he didn't," Jeff suggested. "My mom says he was always a real straight arrow."

Jed rolled his eyes. "That's what they all say they were, isn't it? But it's a bunch of bullshit, if you ask me."

"Yeah, but nobody asked you," Randy said, switching on the radio and turning the volume up as high as it would go.

They turned up the canyon road, a cloud of dust rising behind the car as its wheels dug into the dirt. Jeff pressed down harder on the accelerator, shooting the plume even higher. The Plymouth shot across the desert toward the mouth of the canyon.

Five minutes later Jeff parked the car at a bend in the canyon where the stream had dug a deep hole next to the canyon's south wall, leaving a gently sloping beach lined with cottonwoods on its northern bank. There was still a little light from the moon on the north wall of the canyon, but the stream was shrouded in deep shadows, and the night air had turned chilly. While Randy Sparks wedged the two six-packs of beer into some rocks a few yards upstream, so the water itself would keep it cold, Jed and Jeff stripped off their clothes and dove into the river.

The water was cold here, much colder than the surface water in the lake two miles farther up, for the water pouring through the turbines of the dam came from the bottom of the reservoir and wouldn't warm up again until it reached the Colorado, a hundred miles away.

Jed's body sliced through the water as he swam upstream, pacing himself against the current so that he could keep swimming as long as he wanted but never move from where he'd started. Finally he rolled over onto his back and let himself float, feetfirst, toward the point fifty yards downstream where the riverbed narrowed, coursing through a cluster of boulders worn perfectly smooth over the centuries. The water raced through the rapids— known to generations of Borrego kids as the Chute—turning and twisting for a hundred yards before coming into the next pool, and Jed sensed the familiar rush of excitement as he felt the current strengthen. The rapids could be dangerous—indeed, during the spring, when the spillways at the dam were wide open to release the floodwater from the melting snowpack in the mountains to the north, they were deadly. By September, though, even some of the more adventurous of Borrego's junior high school kids were trying their courage against the Chute.

Tonight the current seemed a little stronger than usual, which meant the dam was probably operating at full capacity. If he got into trouble . . . For a moment he almost changed his mind, but the sound of Randy's voice galvanized him.

"What's the matter?" his friend shouted. "Is the half-breed chicken?"

Randy's words struck him like stones. His first impulse was to swim away from the entrance to the Chute, to go ashore and shove the epithet back down the other boy's throat. But a moment later the decision was out of his hands as the current grabbed him, hurtling him forward. He braced himself for the first turn. Here, you had to push off with your left foot at just the right moment, or risk becoming wedged between two huge rocks. That part wasn't really dangerous, but it ruined the ride—once stopped, there was no way of getting back into the current, and you had to climb out, scramble over the rocks to the pool upstream, and start over.

He felt his foot touch the boulder, allowed his knee to bend, then shoved hard. His body twisted in the water, and he pointed his toes, using his feet almost like the bow of a tiny skiff. He knew every inch of the Chute, knew where to push off with his feet, where to use his hands instead.

He was getting close to his favorite spot now—an immense boulder with a deep cleft in it. Hollowed out by the river over millennia, it had become a perfect natural water slide. He felt the current strengthen even more, then was into the slide, his skin rubbing against the slippery rock, the water cascading over his body. He picked up speed, then shot over the final lip of the Chute and into the pool below.

And struck something unfamiliar, something that had never been there before.

He paused, treading water, then dived down to feel in the depths, to try to locate the strange object.

His hand closed on something, and then his feet found the bottom and he pushed upward.

When he came to the surface, he strained his eyes in the darkness to see what he held.

It was a mass of soggy flannel, and inside it was the broken body of Heather Fredericks.

Chapter 4

The slowly spinning lights on the roofs of the two police cars and the ambulance shot a kaleidoscopic pattern of reds and blues up the canyon walls, creating a strangely hypnotic effect on Jed. He was still sitting numbly on a rock a few yards from the spot where he'd found Heather Fredericks's body nearly an hour before. Randy Sparks had stayed with him while Jeff raced back into town, and although no more than half an hour had passed before the squad cars and the ambulance had roared up the canyon, their sirens wailing mournfully in the night, to Jed it seemed as if hours had ticked by.

He had no memory at all of having pulled Heather ashore; the memory that stayed in his mind—and, he was sure, would stay with him the rest of his life—was the image of Heather's face, her eyes open, staring at him lifelessly in the silvery moonlight.

He'd been only barely conscious of the arrival of the police, and as the medics had moved Heather's broken body onto a stretcher, Jed had sat staring at the activity, his mind playing games with him, so that several times he was almost certain he saw Heather move. Listening, concentrating, he even imagined he heard a low groaning sound—the longed-for moan that would tell him she wasn't dead after all.

It was the silence—the absence of the siren's wail as the ambulance disappeared back into the night—that told Jed the girl he'd known all his life was truly dead, that what was happening was not simply a nightmare from which he would awaken to find himself back on the sofa in his living room, the television still droning in the background.

"You ready to talk about what happened?"

Jed looked up to see the two policemen, Billy Clark and Dan Rogers, standing on the riverbank, watching him. Clark switched his flashlight on, shining it directly into Jed's eyes, and the boy's arm went up defensively as he turned away from the blinding glare.

"We need to know what happened, boy," Clark growled.

Jed shook his head, trying to clear it, but the image of Heather refused to go away. "N-Nothin' happened," he said, his voice barely audible. "I went through the Chute, and when I got to the bottom, there she was."

Billy Clark's lip curled. "Oh, sure. You and your punk buddies weren't doin' a thing, right? Just came up for a little swim, and there's your girlfriend, drowned. You think anyone's gonna believe that? Now, why don't you tell us what really happened?"

Jed swallowed nervously and glanced around. A few yards away, sitting in the front seat of the Plymouth, Randy Sparks and Jeff Hankins were watching him worriedly. "But that's what happened," Jed said. "Didn't you ask Jeff and Randy?"

"I'm asking you, boy," Clark growled. "And I can tell you right now the coroner's going to be going over that girl, looking to find out what happened to her. And if he finds out she had sex tonight, he's also gonna find out who it was with. You understand me, *breed*? The best thing you can do for yourself is tell the truth, and tell it right now."

Jed felt the familiar tight knot of anger begin to push the shock out of his mind. With narrowed eyes, and fists clenched against the desire to strike out against the insult, he said: "Come off it, Clark. If you're gonna arrest me, go ahead and do it, and then call my dad. But if you want to know what happened, I'm trying to tell you."

Clark seemed about to say something to Jed, but Dan Rogers interceded. "Come on, Billy. Everyone in town knows Jed goes with Gina Alvarez, and even if Heather had been his girlfriend, it doesn't make any difference." He turned to Jed, his voice friendly. "No one's saying you did anything, Jed. We just want to know what happened."

Slowly, almost hesitantly, Jed repeated what he'd said before, beginning with the moment Randy and Jeff had showed up at his house shortly after his father had gone to work. When he was finished, he looked up at Billy Clark, his eyes challenging the policeman. "It's the truth," he said. "I swear it is."

Clark stared at him silently for a long moment, but finally, almost reluctantly, nodded his head. "All right. It jibes with what your buddies said. And the medics seemed to think she'd been in the water for at least an hour."

Jed closed his eyes and felt a little of the tension drain out of his body. "Wh-What happened to her?" he asked.

It was Dan Rogers who answered him. "Don't know. It looks like she might have fallen off the top, or gotten pushed. We'll have a lot better idea after we find out what she was up to tonight." He turned to Clark. "Billy, why don't you call a couple of the day guys and go see Heather's folks. I'll take the boys back to the station and get statements from all of them."

Clark seemed about to argue, then apparently changed his mind. Wordlessly, he went back to one of the squad cars, and a moment later disappeared into the night.

"You want to ride with me?" Dan Rogers asked as he walked back toward Jeff Hankins's Plymouth with Jed at his side. "I figure you must be feeling a little shaky."

Jed nodded, then went to wait in the police cruiser while the cop spoke to Jeff and Randy. Rogers slid behind the wheel and started the engine.

Jed, preoccupied with what had just happened, didn't look back as they drove out of the canyon, Jeff following close behind.

He knew he was in trouble again, but not for something he'd actually done.

He was in trouble simply because of what he was.

Reenie Fredericks stared at the three policemen blankly. "That's not possible," she said. "Heather's in bed, sleeping." But the look on Billy Clark's face made her turn and race from the doorway to Heather's room, where she gazed in stunned silence at the empty bed.

Heather's clothes were still scattered on the floor in the haphazard manner that sometimes threatened to drive Reenie crazy. Now she simply stared at them in dismay. If Heather had decided to sneak out, surely she would have dressed . . .

She started back toward the front door, then felt a draft. Turning, half expecting to see Heather coming in the back door, she saw instead the kitchen door was standing open, a gaping hole leading into the blackness of the night and the empty desert beyond the fence. As she gazed vacantly at the door, the truth of what Billy Clark had just told her struck home. A wail of anguish rose from her throat.

"But she wouldn't have just gone out like that," Reenie said twenty minutes later when Billy Clark had explained to her that when she was found, Heather was wearing nothing but a pair of pajamas. "If she'd gone on her own, she would have dressed!"

And yet, searching the house, the policemen found no signs of a struggle, and even her mother admitted that she couldn't imagine sleeping undisturbed in the next room if Heather had been fighting off an abductor.

It was nearly one-thirty in the morning when one of the policemen brought a dog in and the tracking began. The scent was fresh, and the dog had no trouble picking it up. Sniffing eagerly, it moved steadily through the desert. After fifteen minutes the flashlights the men carried began to pick up spots of blood, still clear on the hard-packed earth of the desert floor.

At last they came to the top of the canyon, where the trail came to an abrupt end at the very edge of the precipice.

"Jesus," Billy Clark said softly, staring down into the dark chasm. "What the hell happened up here?"

He and his men studied the terrain carefully, searching for any sign of struggle, any sign at all that Heather had not been alone. But there was none.

Only a set of bloody footprints, a dark outline on the windswept sandstone of the precipice. Heather seemed to have been walking normally; there was no sign that she was dragging her feet as if someone were forcing her toward the edge, nor was there any hint that she might have been running and seen where she was going too late to stop herself.

At the very edge of the cliff there were two prints, side by side, as if she'd stood there, staring into the abyss.

Stood there for a few seconds, then jumped.

"Jesus," Clark said once again, shaking his head slowly. "What the hell would make a kid do something like that? Doesn't make sense."

One of the other men shrugged. "Who knows?" he asked. "Maybe she was drugged up. Kids these days do all kinds of crazy things."

They stood silently at the edge for a few moments, looking down, then finally turned away and started back toward the town. They moved slowly, unconsciously putting off the moment that they would have to tell Reenie Fredericks that her daughter, an ordinary kid with no seemingly extraordinary problems, had committed suicide.

Frank Arnold said nothing as he drove his son home from the police station for the second time in the space of a week. He sat stolidly behind the wheel of the truck, his jaw set, his eyes fixed unwaveringly on the road ahead. But the tension in the heavy frame of his body was an almost palpable force within the confines of the truck's cab. Jed, his face drawn, sat silently in the passenger seat next to his father, staring out into the night, oblivious to his father's silent anger, still seeing Heather's dead eyes staring at him. When Frank finally turned into the driveway of their small house on Sixth East and switched the engine off, Jed made no move to get out.

"We're here," Frank said, opening the door on his side and jumping out of the cab. For a moment he wasn't sure his son had even heard him, but just as he was about to speak again, the other door of the truck opened and Jed slid out.

They walked down the driveway, entering the house through the back door, and Frank flipped on the kitchen light. Going to the refrigerator, he pulled out a beer. He thought a moment, then pulled out a second one and held it up toward Jed. "Want one? Or would you rather have a shot of brandy?"

Jed looked at his father uncertainly, and Frank managed a wry grin. "I'm still pretty damned mad at you, but I'm not so mad I don't have any idea what you're feeling right now. If you're old enough to pull a corpse out of a river, I guess you're old enough to have a shot of brandy to take the edge off it."

Jed hesitated, but shook his head. "I think maybe I'll just have a Coke," he said.

Frank waited until Jed had opened the soft drink and sat down at the table across from him before he spoke. After his son had taken his first long drink of the soda, Frank pulled at his beer, then set the bottle on the table. "You okay?" he asked.

Jed started to nod, but then shook his head. "I don't know. I just keep seeing her, looking at me. I—" His voice trembled, and he fell silent as his eyes welled with tears.

"What the hell were you doing out there, Jed?" Frank said quietly, staring at the bottle in front of him. "Didn't you think I meant it when I grounded you?"

"I didn't go out there to get in any trouble—" Jed began, but his father cut him off.

"Bullshit! Kids like Randy Sparks and Jeff Hankins don't go out and get drunk in the middle of the night without intending to get into trouble."

"They weren't drunk," Jed protested. "They'd had maybe one beer apiece when they came over here, and—"

"And nothin'!" Frank exploded, his fist slamming down on the table with enough force to knock the beer bottle over. He snatched it up just as the beer itself began to foam onto the table, but ignored the puddle as he glared at his son. "What the hell's going on with you, Jed? You're twice as smart as those jerks, but you keep on letting them get you into trouble. Why the hell don't you start listening to yourself for a change, instead of those two assholes?"

"They're not assholes," Jed flared, his own anger rising in the face of his father's wrath. "There's nothing wrong with them, and they don't make me do anything I don't want to do. I didn't have to go with them tonight! I could have sat home by myself, just like I did last night, and the night before, and the night before that. But why the hell should I? You're either sleeping or at work or at some goddammed meeting or something. What am I supposed to do, sit around talking to the walls all the time? And when I do see you, all you ever do is yell at me!"

Frank's eyes narrowed angrily and a vein in his forehead stood out. But then, taking control of his anger, he bit back the furious words on his lips and found himself slowly counting to ten, just as Alice had always insisted he do when his temper—almost as quick as his son's—threatened to get the best of him.

When he reached ten, he started over again.

By the third time through, his rage was back under control, and he finally began to think about what Jed had just said. For the last four years, ever since Alice had died, he'd tended more and more to let Jed raise himself. Part of the problem was the simple fact of his shift work, that his schedule matched Jed's only once every three weeks. During one of the other weeks he was just going to work as Jed was getting home, and the third week, he was just getting up, still groggy from the restless sleep that was all he was ever able to get when he came home from the graveyard shift. And Jed had a point about the meetings too. But what could he do? He was the president of the union local, and no matter how hard he tried to organize his schedule so he could spend as much time as possible with his son, there always seemed to be something in the way.

Recently, for the last six months, there had been a series of rumors that Max Moreland was finally going to have to sell the refinery. Max insisted there was nothing to the talk, but it had long been Frank's experience that when gossip was as plentiful as it was now, there was something to it. And so, ever since last winter, he'd involved himself in union business more than ever before, working with a group of lawyers and accountants in Santa Fe to see if an employee buyout of Borrego Oil might be possible.

Which meant that Jed was alone even more than usual, for too often Frank found himself spending most of his waking hours driving back and forth over the 150 miles between Borrego and Santa Fe. And, if he was honest with himself, he knew that Jed's problems—the problems Frank had been doing his best to ignore, or attribute to nothing more serious than typical adolescent angst—had increased in these last six months.

During the spring semester of school Jed's grades, which had never before been a problem, suddenly took a nosedive. Before Frank had even become aware of the situation, it was too late. It had been a failing grade in geometry that had sent Jed to summer school.

He and his son had a terrible row about that. Only Frank's threat to take Jed's car away from him had finally convinced the boy that he had no choice.

In the end, Reba Tucker had suffered a stroke, putting a quick end to the summer school session, and now Jed was without his car anyway.

"Look," he said at last, slumping in his chair and wondering why conversations like this always had to take place in the small hours of the morning rather than at a more reasonable time, "I know things have been tough for you lately. But they haven't been easy for me either. Sometimes I feel like I'm trying to do everything, and I guess I tend to let you take care of yourself too much. But up until recently, there's never been a problem."

Jed's eyes clouded. "There's always been a problem," he said, his voice taking on a defiant note. "If there hadn't been a problem, Mom would still be alive, wouldn't she?"

Jed's words hit Frank like a blow. He stared at Jed mutely, trying to decide whether what his son had said was only caused by his momentary anger or if this was something that had been eating at him for months, even years. And yet, as he studied the pain in his son's eyes, he knew the words had been prompted by something the boy had been harboring for a very long time.

"Is that what all this is really about?" Frank asked quietly. "Your mother?"

Jed's expression hardened. "Well, it's true, isn't it?" he asked, his voice taking on an almost childish petulance. "Isn't that why she's gone? Because you treated her the same way you treat me?"

Fury welled up in Frank and he rose to his feet, towering over his son. "No, God damn it!" he roared. "What happened to your mother had nothing to do with me at all. I loved her, as much as I've ever loved anybody in my life, and she loved me too." And yet even as he spoke the words, Frank knew deep within himself that it was that very love between them that had, in the end, been at least partially responsible for her death. For Alice, despite the love they had shared, had never been able to make a place for herself in Borrego. Part of her always longed to be back in Kokatí with the people she'd grown up with. She hadn't talked about it often, but there had been times, particularly during the last months, when she'd curled in his arms late at night. "Nobody here likes me," she'd whispered, her arms tightening around him. "I can tell by the way they look at me. They think I'm stupid, and they don't think I hear the things they say about the Indians."

"But they don't mean to hurt you," Frank had told her. "It's because they don't even think of you as being an Indian anymore that you even hear those things."

But Alice hadn't been convinced. In the last weeks she'd spent more and more time by herself, walking in the desert.

That last day, she'd been gone before dawn, and Frank had nearly taken the day off to go look for her. But in the end he'd decided to leave her alone.

And at half-past three that afternoon Jed had called him, sobbing and hysterical. The boy had come home from school as usual, and opened the garage door to put his bicycle away.

And found his mother's body, hanging from the rafters, a thick rope tightly knotted around her neck.

Until this moment, though, he'd never known that Jed blamed him for what had happened to Alice. Now, keeping his voice as steady as he could, he tried to explain to his son what had really happened. Jed listened in silence, not interrupting until he was finished. Then, after several more minutes had passed, he nodded his head slowly.

"So Mom felt just like I do," he said. "Like she didn't fit in anywhere, like nobody really liked her."

"But it wasn't true," Frank insisted. "Everyone in town loved your mother."

Jed stared at him bleakly. "Did they?" he said. "I wonder. After all, she was an Indian, wasn't she? And don't give me any bullshit that everyone in town loves the Indians."

"But your mother was different—" Frank began, then realized the words had been a mistake.

"Was she?" Jed demanded. "She was never part of anything, not really. She wasn't part of this place, and up in Kokatí no one ever trusted her after she married you."

"That's not true," Frank replied. "She never said anything—"

"She didn't say anything to *you*," Jed broke in, his voice filled with anguish. "But she told me."

Frank wished he could shut out what he was certain was coming, but knew he had to hear it. "All right," he said, his voice choking. "What did she tell you?"

Jed's jaw tightened and his eyes reflected the pain deep within his soul. "That sometimes she wished she'd never had me," he whispered. "She said that sometimes she thought it would be easier for me not to exist at all than to spend my whole life never fitting in anywhere, never feeling like I'm really part of anything."

"But you are part of something," Frank protested. "You're my son."

"I'm your *half-breed* son," Jed said bitterly. "And that's all I'll ever be."

"Now that is bullshit," Frank replied. "If that's the way your mother really felt, I'm sorry. Because she was wrong. You're still you, and you can be anything you want to be. If you don't like it here, you can leave. And after you graduate from high school, you will leave. At college you'll find out that no one cares where you came from or what your background is. The only things that will count are your brains, and your talent. And you've got a lot of both."

"Yeah," Jed growled. "Except that I'm not going to college."

Frank stared at his son. "What the hell are you talking about? Of course you're going to college. Your mother and I—"

"The hell with Mom," Jed shouted, rising to his feet. "Can't you understand that she's dead? She killed herself, Dad. She didn't love you, and she didn't love me. So who the hell cares what she wanted? She didn't even care enough to stick around and help me! So all I want is to get a job and earn some money so I can get the hell out of here. Okay?"

Before Frank could say anything, Jed wheeled and stormed out of the kitchen. Frank sat staring at the beer bottle for a few moments, then silently drained it, tossed it into the trash, turned out the lights and headed for his bedroom. He paused outside Jed's door, his hand on the knob, then changed his mind.

Right now, in the hours before dawn, he suddenly felt as if he hadn't the slightest idea who his son was, nor did he have any idea what to say to him.

As he lay in bed a few minutes later, trying to go to sleep, he felt more lonely than he had in all the years since Alice had died. Until tonight, he'd always felt that he at least had Jed.

Now he was no longer certain he even had a son.

Greg Moreland walked into the hospital at eight o'clock the next morning and smiled a greeting to the duty nurse, Gloria Hernandez. "What's

going on?" he asked. "Another quiet night?" His smile faded quickly as
Gloria looked up at him, her expression haggard.

"I wish it had been," she said. "But we got a body in about one o'clock
this morning. Dr. Banning's downstairs with it now."

The last vestige of Moreland's grin faded away. "A body? What happened?"

"It looks like a suicide," Gloria told him. "It's Heather Fredericks."

Greg nodded perfunctorily, then went into his office, slipped into a white
smock, and went downstairs to the morgue beneath the hospital. He found
Bob Banning in the single small autopsy room, nodded a greeting, then
made himself look at Heather Fredericks.

Her body lay on the metal autopsy table, her abdomen slit open from the
groin all the way up to her chest. Her organs, carefully removed from the
thoracic cavity, lay where Banning had placed them, small samples of each
cut away for testing by a lab in Santa Fe.

Greg turned away quickly, instinctively avoiding looking at Heather's
face. It was the one thing about being a doctor he hated—he'd never gotten
used to seeing corpses, never developed that clinical detachment most doc-
tors managed in the face of death.

For him, a corpse was still a person, and though he knew it was irrational,
he sometimes felt that even after death, a person might still be able to
experience pain.

He picked up the clipboard that held Bob Banning's notes, and scanned
them quickly. From the first gross examination, death appeared to have
been instantaneous, and caused by severe trauma.

Nearly every bone in Heather's body seemed to have been broken in the
fall: both arms and legs, her hips, her back and neck, as well as her collar-
bone. Her cranium was fractured as well, and there were severe lacerations
on her back.

After he'd finished reading the notes, numbed by the shock of what had
happened to his patient, he finally managed to speak to Banning. "Jesus
Christ—how did all this happen?"

Banning shrugged, his eyes never leaving his work. "She fell over a thousand feet, and hit a rock in the river. She's broken up like a bunch of
matchsticks."

"And it was definitely a suicide?"

Banning nodded. "As far as I can tell. I'll have to wait for the lab analyses
before I can make a final report, but apparently she just walked from her
house up to the rim of the canyon—barefoot, and wearing nothing but a
pair of pajamas—and jumped off. No sign of a struggle—her mother didn't

hear anything. She just went to bed, then got up a couple of hours later and went out and killed herself. Unless she was doing drugs—"

Greg Moreland's brows knit into a deep frown, and he shook his head. "Not Heather," he said. "I'd been treating her for that accident a week ago, and if she was on drugs, believe me, I'd have spotted it. I saw her yesterday, and she was just fine. Her wounds were healing, and the biggest problem she had was that her mother had grounded her. But you'd hardly think something like that would be enough to make a kid kill herself."

Banning stretched his aching muscles, and yawned against the fatigue that clouded his mind. "I don't know," he said, almost echoing Gloria Hernandez's words of a few minutes before. "I guess we've been pretty lucky around here. This kind of thing seems to happen every day now. Kids who seem fine just suddenly give up. It's as though the world has become too complicated for them, and anything seems better than having to cope with one more day." He moved to a sink, and began washing up. "By tomorrow we should know for sure. But if her blood comes up clean, I'm going to call it a suicide."

Later, back in his office, Greg found himself still thinking about Banning's words.

And he also thought about Heather Fredericks. He'd liked Heather, even though she had often been a bit manipulative, trying to get her own way about everything. But no one, he was sure, thought she was the kind who would commit suicide.

Perhaps, after all, they would find something indicating that it hadn't been suicide at all.

Sighing heavily, he picked up the phone and rang the front desk.

"Gloria? When the lab reports on Heather Fredericks come in, make sure I get a copy, will you?"

"Of course, Doctor," Gloria replied. "I'd have done it anyway. She was your patient, wasn't she?"

"Yes, she was," Greg agreed, then hung up.

But all that day, and into the next, he kept thinking about Heather, and wondering what, if anything, the lab would find.

Chapter 5

The funeral for Heather Fredericks took place three days later, on the kind of perfect summer day when the New Mexican skies are deep blue and cloudless, and even the heat of the desert is made bearable by the dryness of the air. But as Judith Sheffield stood with Max and Rita Moreland in the cemetery next door to the old Methodist church she herself had attended as a child, it seemed to her the atmosphere was wrong. Though cloudy skies would have been a cliché, she still thought they would have been more appropriate.

Ted and Reenie Fredericks stood gazing blankly at the coffin that contained the remains of their only child, as if they hadn't yet quite grasped what had happened. But as the minister uttered the final words of the service, and the coffin was slowly lowered into the ground, an anguished wail of grief suddenly welled up out of Reenie's throat, and she hurled herself into her husband's arms, burying her face in his chest. Judith, embarrassed to witness Reenie's unbearable pain, averted her eyes, letting them run over the crowd.

She was surprised by how many of the mourners she recognized, many of them people she'd grown up with. Now, as she identified them ten years later, she found herself unaccountably bewildered that they were no longer the teenagers she remembered. Most of them had children, ranging in age from ten downward, and as she watched them she couldn't help wondering what they were thinking. Were they, like her, wondering which of the other teenagers in the crowd might be considering following the course Heather had taken? Were they wondering if, in a few more years, or tomorrow, it might be their own child in that casket? Every face she studied wore an expression of shock—shock mixed with apprehension.

Heather's friends seemed to have clustered together of their own accord, taking up a position close to the casket but separated from Heather's parents by the casket itself.

Amazingly, Judith found she even recognized some of the dead girl's classmates, though they had been only five or six years old the last time she'd seen them.

Randy Sparks and Jeff Hankins were there—apparently still the inseparable friends they had been since they were little boys. But something about both of them had changed. Judith watched their faces—Randy's narrow and vaguely hollowed, in contrast to Jeff's tendency to chubbiness, which gave him a slightly baby-faced look—and realized, sadly, that their eyes, indeed their whole appearance, had lost any semblance of innocence. They stood together, their posture slouched as if to send a signal to whomever might be watching that even here, at the funeral of one of their friends, they were still cool, still somehow detached from it all. With them were two girls, one of whom Judith was certain was Gina Alvarez. Still as pretty as she had been as a child, Gina's dark eyes seemed to sparkle with life, and her chestnut-colored hair framed a face that already had matured beyond the prettiness of a little girl and into the beauty of a young woman.

Next to Gina stood a boy Judith recognized at once. Indeed, she would have recognized Jed Arnold by his eyes alone—those incredibly bright, almost turquoise-blue eyes, made even more remarkable by the crisp planes of his face and the bronze skin he had inherited from his mother.

Those eyes were his father's. Judith scanned the crowd, searching for Frank Arnold himself. A moment later she saw him, standing alone, staring at the coffin almost as if he weren't entirely certain he should have been at the funeral at all. Was he remembering another funeral, when it had been his wife whose remains were being consigned to the ground?

She was about to look away when Frank abruptly glanced up, as if he'd felt her eyes on him. His expression seemed puzzled for a moment, but then his eyes met hers and he shifted his weight slightly, straightening up to his full height. He offered her a small nod of recognition, and Judith felt herself flush, all her childhood memories of him flooding back to her.

She turned away, falling in with Rita and Max Moreland as they made their way toward the Frederickses. As they came to the head of the receiving line, Judith extended her hand to Reenie Fredericks.

"I'm so sorry," she said. "You might not remember me, but—"

"Of course I remember you," Reenie said, taking her hand firmly. "You used to be Judy Sheffield!"

"I still am," Judith replied. "Except it's Judith now. I never did really like 'Judy.'"

"I know," Reenie said, her faint smile fading as her eyes wandered to her daughter's grave. "Heather hated nicknames too. She even wanted me to start making everyone call me Renée." For a moment she seemed about to dissolve into tears once more, but then took her emotions under control. "Well, I'll remember to call you Judith. I can certainly do that for Heather, can't I?" Her voice trembled, but then the person behind Judith spoke, and Reenie turned away, once more forcing herself to smile, determined not to break down again.

Judith let herself drift away, moving through the crowd, stopping to talk briefly to some people, nodding to others. In a way, it was almost as if she'd never left Borrego at all. The same people were still there, doing the same things they'd been doing a decade ago.

No surprises.

An incredible feeling of familiarity.

And then she came face to face with Frank Arnold.

He was still standing by himself, but she hadn't seen him approach until he put out a hand and turned her around. "I suppose everyone's telling you you haven't changed a bit, but I'm not going to," he said.

Judith felt her heartbeat speed up slightly, and prayed it didn't show. "You mean you didn't recognize me?" she asked, then wished she hadn't. She'd never thought of herself as a flirt, and didn't intend to turn into one now. "That was a stupid thing to say," she went on without pausing, "since you nodded to me earlier."

"Oh, I recognized you all right," Frank replied. "But you've grown up. What are you now? Twenty-five?"

"Twenty-six," Judith told him.

Frank's brows rose slightly in a dismissive gesture. "Same difference," he said. "It's not like when we were kids, and a couple of years' difference in age put us into different worlds." His eyes darkened slightly. "Have you seen Jed?"

Judith nodded, but there was something in his tone that told her the question was more than just casual conversation. "I haven't talked to him, but he's certainly just as handsome as ever. With your eyes and Alice's features and skin, he ought to be in the movies."

Frank smiled, but it seemed forced, and when he spoke, there was an edge to his voice. "Maybe you ought to suggest that to him."

Judith stepped back, abashed. "I'm sorry. I didn't mean—"

"Hey," Frank said quickly, "don't you be sorry. It's just that I'm having a rough time with Jed right now." He managed a crooked grin. "They don't give you a book of instructions when they give you the kid, and right now I guess I'm feeling a little inadequate. But I shouldn't take it out on you. I apologize."

Judith let herself relax a little, but when Frank reached out to squeeze her arm reassuringly, she felt something very like an electrical shock run through her. "It's all right," she assured him. Then she thought she understood what Frank had been talking about. "It was Jed who found Heather, wasn't it?"

Frank nodded. "It was pretty bad for him, but that's not really the problem." He seemed about to say more, then apparently changed his mind. "And I sure don't have any call to bother you with my troubles, do I? I hardly know you."

A twinge of unexplainable panic ran through Judith as Frank started to turn away. This time it was she who grabbed his arm. "Not so fast, Frank," she said, doing her best to keep her tone bantering. "You've known me all my life, and Jed was my favorite kid when I was a baby-sitter. Also, I happen to be a high school teacher, which is supposed to make me some kind of an expert on teenagers. Tell me what the problem is."

Frank eyed her appraisingly for a moment, then finally came to a decision. "All right," he said, matching her bantering tone on the surface, but making no attempt to cover the deep worry beneath. "He says he's going to quit school and get a job so he can get out of here. He thinks no one here likes him because he's half Indian, and he thinks his mother killed herself because she was an Indian and didn't think anyone here liked her either."

Almost to her own surprise, Judith's eyes met Frank's squarely, and she asked the first question that came into her mind. "Is he right?"

Words of denial immediately sprang to Frank's lips, but when he spoke, the words that came out were not the ones he had intended. "I don't know," he said softly, his pain clear not only in his voice, but in his eyes as well. "Maybe he is."

Judith said nothing for a moment, having to fight an urge to put her arms around Frank's broad-shouldered body and comfort him. "I-If there's anything I can do . . ." she began, then let the sentence hang, feeling suddenly awkward.

Now it was Frank who was silent for a moment. Then he grinned at her almost shyly. "Maybe you could come over for dinner some night," he suggested. He hesitated, and reddened slightly. "Jed always liked you."

Again their eyes met, and this time the look held for several seconds.

"Tonight?" Judith heard herself ask.

Plainly flustered, Frank managed a nod.

* * *

Max Moreland peered up at Judith over the rims of his half glasses, an almost comical expression of surprise giving him the look of an old Norman Rockwell *Saturday Evening Post* cover. "Frank Arnold invited you to dinner?"

Judith eyed him quizzically. "Is that so strange? We've known each other for years—I used to baby-sit for Jed, remember?"

Max ignored the second question, choosing to focus on the first instead. "Well, I don't know what you call strange, but Frank hasn't invited any woman anywhere since Alice died."

Judith felt a warm glow in her face, and hoped it didn't show. "It's hardly like a date," she said, but could see that Max didn't believe her. "It's just for dinner."

The old man's eyes gleamed with wicked humor, and Judith turned to Rita Moreland for support. "Aunt Rita, will you tell Max there's nothing to this, please?"

"There's nothing to this, Max," Rita parroted, not even looking up from the pillow she was working in an incredibly complex needlepoint design. "Do you believe me?"

"No," Max replied comfortably. "How about you?"

"I don't believe me either," Rita replied, then glanced fondly up at Judith. "Will you be home tonight?"

Now Judith's blush turned scarlet. "You're both terrible!" she exclaimed, but bent down to kiss each of them before she left. And yet, as she drove into Borrego the thought she had been suppressing all afternoon rose once more into her consciousness. What if her spending the night was exactly what Frank Arnold had in mind?

How did she feel about it?

The truth was, she didn't know, or at least wasn't yet willing to deal with what she did know, which was that she was definitely attracted to Frank, and was almost certain he was equally attracted to her. Part of her still thought of herself as that sixteen-year-old baby-sitter she'd been ten years ago, and of Frank as a mature man far older than she.

Now, though, nine years didn't seem like so much.

The Arnold house wore a coat of fresh white paint, and Judith smiled as she remembered: Frank and Alice had painted their house every year, refusing to abandon it to the weather the way most people in Borrego did. And apparently even without Alice, Frank was still determined to keep the house as fresh-looking as it had been the day he bought it.

She parked the Honda, hurried up the path that cut through the well-tended lawn in front of the little house, and knocked on the door. After a moment it opened and Jed Arnold stood facing her, his expression all but unreadable, as if he'd made a conscious decision not to let anyone know what was going on in his mind.

"Jed!" Judith exclaimed. "I'm sorry I didn't get to talk to you at Heather's funeral, but—"

"It's okay," Jed replied, stepping back from Judith's outstretched hand, but holding the door open so she could come into the house. "There were a lot of people there." He closed the door behind her, then stood where he was, as if uncertain of what to do next. "Dad's in the kitchen," he finally said, a small grin beginning to play around the corners of his mouth. "He's trying to cook a roast, but it doesn't look like he knows what he's doing." Jed's grin broadened. "Maybe you'd better go in and see if you can pry him loose from the roast before he wrecks it." Then, as Judith started through the living room toward the kitchen, he spoke again. "What am I supposed to call you?"

Judith turned and stared at him, then remembered her own embarrassment when she'd reached the age at which she felt foolish calling her parents' friends Mr. or Mrs. So-and-so, but hadn't quite dared to call them by their first names. There had been a couple of years when she simply hadn't called them anything at all. Now she shrugged. "I don't know," she said. "As long as it isn't Judy, which I hate, or Miss Sheffield, which makes me feel like an old-maid schoolteacher."

Jed's expression turned impish. "But that's what you are, isn't it?"

Judith eyed him for a moment, her lips pursed. "And I suspect I hate that term almost as much as you hate 'half-breed.' Right?"

Jed's mouth dropped open in shock, and for a split second his eyes glittered with anger. But a moment later he recognized her point, and his grin —the same one that had never failed to enchant Judith when she'd been a teenager—crept once more across his face. "You can play rough, can't you?" he observed. "Jude. That's what I'll call you. Like in that old song Dad's always playing—you know, the Beatles?"

"The patron saint of lost causes." Judith sighed. "Well, I suppose it's better than 'old-maid schoolteacher.' And is 'Jed' all right with you?"

"It's better than 'half-breed,' " Jed offered, and finally put out his hand. Judith took it, then impulsively pulled him closer and hugged him.

"I really am glad to see you again," she said.

Jed hesitated, then returned the hug. "I'm kind of glad you came back too," he said. "I remember when I was a little kid, I always had more fun with you than with practically anybody."

Frank appeared in the kitchen door. "What's going on out here?" he asked, glancing almost anxiously at Jed.

"Nothing at all. We're just talking about the old days. Jed tells me your cooking hasn't improved over the years."

For a moment Frank looked stung, but then burst out laughing. "Well, if that's the way you two feel, why don't you cook dinner, and I'll watch the end of the football game." He peeled off the apron he was wearing, and tossed it to Jed.

A look passed between the father and son, a look Judith couldn't quite read. In the tense silence that followed, she was afraid Jed might hurl the apron to the floor and walk out. He had stiffened for a moment, the apron held uncertainly in his hand. Then, as if making a conscious decision, he gripped the cloth tightly and returned his father's grin. "You're on," he said. "Maybe for once we can have a decent meal around here."

It was nearly midnight when Judith finally started back to the Morelands' house, and before she left, she'd agreed to come back two nights later. The evening, after a strained beginning, had turned out all right, except for the uneasy feeling she'd had that somehow Alice Arnold was still in the house, watching them. The three of them had sat at the table talking long after the meal had been finished, at first hesitantly, then with increasing ease. Judith had formed the distinct impression that Frank and Jed spent little time talking to each other. Indeed, the two of them were almost like strangers living under the same roof, two people living such completely separate lives that they barely knew one another.

A tense moment had come when Judith suggested to Jed that the two of them go horseback riding the next day. Jed's eyes had lit up, but then his excitement had faded.

"I don't think I can," he'd said. "I'm grounded for a couple of weeks."

But Frank, after eyeing his son speculatively for a moment, had shaken his head. "It seems to me when I handed that grounding down, I meant to keep you away from some of your friends for a while. But I don't see how it applies to Judith. If you want to go, I don't see why you shouldn't."

Only after Jed had finally gone to bed and she was alone with Frank had Judith brought the subject up again. "I didn't mean to interfere between you and Jed," she said. "If you want to keep him home tomorrow, it's all right with me."

Frank shook his head. "No, it's okay. In fact, I'm not sure the punishment was the right thing to do in the first place. I have a feeling he'd take off as soon as I went to work anyway. You just can't control kids the way you used to. Something's changed. I worry about him, Judith. I worry about all the kids around here. It's not just Jed—it's all of them. There's something about them—they just don't seem very happy."

Judith thought back to the kids she'd been teaching—or at least trying to teach—for the last couple of years. Troubled, suspicious young people. Certainly they had not seemed happy. "The world's a much more complicated place now, Frank," she said softly. "When you were a kid, you pretty much knew what was going to happen when you grew up. You'd get married, have kids, get a job, and life would go on just as it always had. But what do these kids have to look forward to? Jobs are getting scarcer and scarcer, even for the ones who graduate from college. And they might get married, but where are they going to live? How much does a house right here in Borrego cost now?"

Frank shrugged. "I don't know—forty, maybe fifty thousand."

"And what did you pay for this one?"

"Seventeen five," Frank admitted. "And I had to borrow the down payment."

"And the kids know all that," she told him. "They know what things cost, and they know they're probably never going to be able to afford the things their parents have. So life doesn't seem fair to them. And you know what? They're right!"

"So what do you propose to do about it?" Frank had asked. They were outside by then, and she was already sitting behind the wheel of her car.

"I don't know," she'd replied.

Now, as she left the town behind and drove out into the desert, then turned left on the narrow track that led to the Morelands' house at the foot of the mesa, she reflected on her own words.

Every year, it seemed, the problems of the teenagers seemed to grow steadily worse.

And every year, no one seemed to come up with a solution.

Except that, unknown to Judith, there was one person in Borrego who *had* come up with a solution.

Indeed, that person had already applied that solution to Heather Fredericks.

And her death had finally proven that the solution worked.

Chapter 6

Judith and Jed rode in silence for a while the next morning, Judith relaxing in the saddle as all the old pleasures of riding through the desert came back to her. The morning was still cool, and the air, redolent with sage and juniper, filled her nostrils, reminding her once more of the difference between the air here and the smog-choked atmosphere she had left behind in Los Angeles. She was still lost in her reverie when Ginger, the mare she was riding, suddenly shied, uttered a frightened whinny, then rose up on her hind legs. Leaning forward and clutching at the horse, Judith held her seat, then spotted the rattlesnake, coiled tightly in the partial shelter of a rock a few feet ahead, its tail held erect and buzzing menacingly while its wedge-shaped head weaved dangerously back and forth.

Its tongue, flicking in and out of its mouth, looked almost like a living antenna, searching for its prey.

"Easy, Ginger," Judith murmured, her head close to the horse's ear. "Just take it easy."

The horse twisted, then came down on all fours once again. Judith allowed it to skitter off to the right, away from the snake, then brought it to a halt. When she looked again, the snake was gone.

"You okay?" she heard Jed ask.

"I'm fine. I guess I wasn't looking where I was going." She scrutinized Jed carefully. "Didn't you see it? The snake?"

Jed looked puzzled, and shook his head. "Why? Should I have?"

Judith opened her mouth to speak again, then changed her mind. Taking Ginger's reins firmly in hand, she brought the horse around, then urged it into a reluctant trot until they reached the foot of the steep trail that led up the mesa. When Jed caught up, she held her own horse aside until Blackie had passed, then let Ginger fall in behind the gelding.

Moving slowly, picking their way carefully over the rocky path that in some places had all but eroded away from the face of the mesa, the two horses moved steadily upward. Only when they reached the top did Judith allow herself the pleasure of turning to look out over the vista below.

The buildings of the town looked tiny from the mesa; indeed the town itself seemed almost lost in the vast grandeur of the desert that spread below, its expanse seeming to go on forever, broken only by the mesas dotted across its broad reach and the gullies of the washes that snaked aimlessly across it. Far in the distance an enormous rock rose up out of the desert like a watchtower, impossibly slender, standing alone in regal isolation.

"Did you ever climb it?" Judith asked.

Jed cocked his head, then grinned crookedly. "You remember everything, don't you?" he asked. But before Judith could reply, he shook his head. "I guess I sort of forgot about it. Anyway, I don't think I want to try it anymore. I'm not really crazy about heights."

"You?" Judith asked. "You used to run up and down the edge of the canyon as if it were only an irrigation ditch. It scared me half to death. I was always afraid you'd fall, and I'd be the one who'd have to tell your folks what happened."

Once again that odd cloud passed behind Jed's eyes, and now she made up her mind. "Come on," she said, pulling Ginger's head around and guiding the horse along a trail that cut straight down the middle of the long mesa. "I've decided where I want to go."

Half an hour later they came within view of the ancient village of Kokatí, and Judith reined Ginger to a halt. "Thank God," she breathed softly as Jed drew up abreast of her. "I was afraid they'd done to Kokatí what they've done to the Hopi towns."

Jed glanced at her questioningly, and she told him about the collections of squalid tin-roofed tarpaper shacks that had sprung up behind the villages that had stood for centuries on the rims of the three Hopi mesas. "I was afraid it might have happened here too," she finished. "But it hasn't. It looks just as I remember it."

With obvious distaste, Jed regarded the village in which his mother had grown up. "This is where you wanted to come?" he asked, his tone revealing his disbelief.

Judith nodded. "I love it," she said. "I always have. Even when I was a little girl I used to love to come up here. I always used to think there must be magic in the pueblo."

"The only magic would be if everybody smartened up and moved out,"

Jed groused. "I don't see how they can live up here at all—they have to haul water up from the lake, and they don't even have electricity."

"But that's their choice," Judith replied. "If they wanted to, they could bring power up from the dam. Max says the offer's been good since the day his father built the dam, but they've always turned it down."

"Stupid . . ." Jed mumbled.

"Maybe. But maybe not. Did you ever stop to think about what this place would look like if they took Max up on the power?"

"Sure," Jed replied. "They could have a decent life—real kitchens and bathrooms, and television, and everything else people have now."

"But what would it look like?" Judith pressed. She turned to gaze at the ancient structure once more. It spread along the rim of the mesa, a series of two- and three-storied stone, timber, and adobe structures, each of them built around a small central courtyard. The walls were thick—nearly four feet on parts of the lowest floor, and the roofs were flat. The only concession to the modern world the old pueblo seemed to have made was the installation of windows in some of the rooms; worn wooden casements with small panes, which even despite their own age, looked oddly out of place in the primitive adobe construction.

"Well, I guess it would have to look kind of different," Jed finally admitted. "I mean, you'd have to do some remodeling to get plumbing and wiring in—"

"You'd have to start over again," Judith told him. "You don't just start remodeling something like that. The pueblo's more than six hundred years old; at least parts of it are. You really think they should start tearing it apart just for some plumbing and electricity?"

"But what about the weather?" Jed asked, instantly wishing he hadn't, since he knew just as well as Judith that there was practically no better insulation available than those thick walls.

Judith didn't bother to respond. "Shall we see if your grandfather's home?" she asked instead.

Now Jed looked distinctly uncomfortable, and refused to meet her eyes.

"How long has it been since you've seen him, Jed?"

Jed shifted his weight in the saddle, but finally looked up, chewing uneasily at his lower lip. "I don't know," he mumbled almost inaudibly. "A while, I guess."

"Five years?" Judith asked, making a guess she was almost positive could not be far from the mark. Jed shrugged, but didn't deny it. Judith sat silently for a few moments, taking in the graceful beauty of the Kokatí pueblo and the lake that flooded the canyon on whose lip the pueblo sat.

Finally she gazed out into the distance. Though the town of Borrego was invisible from here, the signs that it existed were scattered everywhere over the desert. "Look around, Jed," she said softly. "Look around the way you used to do, when you were a little boy, and tell me what you see. Tell me what looks right and what doesn't."

Jed cocked his head slightly, his eyes taking on a puzzled look, but Judith kept her face impassive, determined not to give him any clue as to what was in her mind. At last Jed's eyes shifted away from her, and as she watched, he began scanning the landscape around him. "I guess maybe the pueblo looks okay," he finally, reluctantly, admitted. "Except you have to wonder why anybody would want to live in it. But it sort of looks like it's part of the mesa."

"What else?" Judith pressed.

Jed grinned sourly at her. "What is this? A test?"

"Maybe. But there aren't any grades. Just look around some more."

Jed began to scan the landscape once more, finally focusing on the lake. "I don't like the lake," he said at last. "I like the part of the canyon below the dam, where the cottonwoods grow along the stream and there are all kinds of birds and animals." A memory stirred inside him, something he hadn't thought of for a long time. "Grandpa always said the lake looks too much like the sky, and the sky doesn't belong in the canyon. I never really thought much about it, but maybe he's right. Look . . . ." He pointed down into the narrow chasm that held the lake. "See how the water's eating away at the sandstone? And there're stains running up it from the surface, where more water's soaking in. The whole damned thing's going to crumble some day. But of course it won't matter, because the whole canyon will be filled up with silt from upstream long before the walls start caving in. It's kind of stupid, when you think about it—I mean, to wreck the whole canyon just so you can get electricity for maybe a hundred years."

"What else?" Judith asked.

Jed's eyes moved on, roaming over the broad expanses of the desert. Once, three years ago, he'd ridden up here late in the afternoon and come to the top of the mesa just in time to see the sun setting in the west as the full moon rose in the east. Around the horizon, five separate thunderstorms were raging, so far away that even as the lightning bolts shot out of the sky, the thunder itself was a barely audible rumble. He'd sat down on a rock and just watched the sky for nearly an hour, until the sun had finally disappeared and the storms moved on, fading away past the horizon until only the glowing light of the moon illuminated the desert, casting long black shadows from the mesas in the distance. The night noises had begun, and he'd listened to them for a while, leaving only when the lights in the oil field and the refinery came on, wrecking the whole thing.

"The refinery," he said now. "And the oil wells and tanks. Sometimes I wish I could see the desert the way it used to be, before there were roads and power lines."

"But that's what you like, isn't it?" Judith asked. "I mean, without the oil, you wouldn't even be here, would you? There wouldn't be any reason for Borrego to exist at all. Not," she added, "that that would make much difference to you. I understand you're not too crazy about Borrego."

Jed's eyes glowed sullenly. "Why should I like it?" he demanded. "It's ugly, and there's nothing to do. It just sits there, and nobody cares about it. I mean, have you ever really looked at it? Jesus, everytime someone needs a new place to live, they just build another one of those crappy cinder-block houses, or drag in a trailer." His voice took on a scornful edge. "The trailers are the worst. They only last a few years, and then people just move out of them and leave them sitting there to rust. And there's junk all over the place—Randy Sparks's dad must have ten wrecked cars sitting around their yard. But he doesn't ever do anything with them. He's always claiming he's going to fix them up, but everyone knows he's not!" His gaze shifted from Judith back to the pueblo. "Then you look at the Indians. At least they don't have a bunch of crap around they're never going to use." He snickered as another thought came to him. "Shit, they hardly have *any*thing!"

Judith spoke quietly. "Is that why you don't come up here anymore?" she asked. "Because you don't think there's anything here?"

Jed shrugged. "Maybe," he mumbled. "But it isn't just that. You know how the Kokatí are—if you're not one of them, they don't want to have much to do with you."

"But you are one of them," Judith reminded him. "At least your mother was, and your grandfather still is."

Jed shook his head. "You think that matters?" he demanded, making no attempt now to keep the anger out of his voice. "Mom's grandmother never even spoke to her again after she married Dad."

"Her grandmother was a different generation," Judith reminded him. "I used to come up here when I was a little girl." She fell silent for a few moments, remembering.

She'd been about eight the first time she'd come to the pueblo alone, riding the horse her father had given her for her birthday. Some Indian kids had been playing a game of baseball—work-ups—and she'd just watched for a while. Then one of them had asked her if she wanted to play, so she'd tied up her horse and joined the game. She'd started in right field, and slowly worked her way up to the point when she would be next at bat when someone had called the children home for lunch. It hadn't really occurred to her not to go with them, and a little while later she was in one of the courtyards, eating the grayish pita bread the Kokatí women still made the old way, grinding the corn with their mortars and pestles, then mixing the coarse flour with water and frying it on a hot stone. No one had suggested she shouldn't be there, and after lunch she'd gone back to the game with the rest of the kids, not getting home until late afternoon. When her mother had asked her where she'd been, she just told her she'd been up on the mesa, playing with some of the Indian kids. Her mother hadn't told her not to do it again, so a week later she'd gone back. From then on she'd always gone up to the pueblo at least once a week, and soon she knew practically everyone there.

"So they let you come and play with their kids," Jed told her. "What's the big deal?"

Judith shrugged. "Maybe *that's* the big deal," she replied. "As far as they were concerned, I was just another kid. And I came to play with the other kids, not to stare at them. How would you like it if people were always coming up and staring at you, and asking to take your picture, as if you were some kind of exhibit?"

Jed's expression took on a cynicism that was beyond his years. "Okay," he agreed, obviously reluctant to give her even that much. "But did any of them ever come down to Borrego and visit you?"

Judith nodded. "Sure. Why wouldn't they?"

Now Jed stared at her in utter disbelief. "Oh, come on—you know what most of the people in town think about the Indians."

"They think a lot of stupid things," Judith replied. "And most of them just don't apply to the Kokatí. Sure, there's a lot of Indians who spend too much time getting drunk, but there's plenty of white people in Borrego who do the same thing. Nothing to do is nothing to do, whether you're Indian or white. And I think maybe that's why the Kokatí have always stuck so close to the old ways. They have a lot to do in the pueblo. They're still farming their fields the old way, still hauling their water up from the canyon, still doing everything else just the way they've always done it. They don't have time to go out and get drunk, and they won't even accept any money from the Bureau. Of course," she admitted, "they're a lot luckier than most of the tribes. They still have almost all their old land, and they were never displaced."

Jed's expression reflected his scorn. "If everything in the pueblo is so great, then how come my mother didn't stay there?" he asked.

Judith held Jed's eyes with her own. "It seems to me," she said, "that maybe that's a question you ought to ask your grandfather."

Jed was silent for a moment, and when he spoke, his voice was hard. "All right," he said. "Let's do it."

Digging his heels into the flanks of the black gelding, he clucked to it, slapping the reins gently against the horse's neck. Immediately the big animal broke into a fast trot, and Jed guided it directly toward the pueblo.

They slowed the horses to a walk as they approached the pueblo, finally dismounting when they were still fifty yards away, tying the reins to a rail where five mules stood, their ribs showing clearly through their skin. They were work animals, nearly worn out from years of climbing up and down the steep trails that led from the mesa to the desert floor, their backs deeply swayed from the heavy weight of the ollas they carried as they hauled water up to the pueblo. They whinnied softly as Jed and Judith tied the two horses up, and shied away from the bigger animals, as if resenting their presence. For their part, Blackie and Ginger ignored the mules, choosing instead to begin munching on the straw that was strewn around the hitching rail.

Jed and Judith skirted the edge of the pueblo's ancient cemetery, then made their way down a narrow alley between two of the main structures of the pueblo. The alley opened into a plaza after fifty feet, and they paused to look around.

In the decade since Judith had last been here, nothing seemed to have changed at all. A few women were working in the courtyard, constructing pots out of coiled ropes of clay. A little girl, no more than two, was playing with a wad of the soft clay, already trying to imitate the actions of her mother, rolling the clay between her tiny hands, looking almost surprised when bits of it dropped away into the dust in which she sat.

For a few moments the women didn't seem to notice them at all, but finally one of them looked up and smiled. "Jed! You finally decided to come up and see us again?" Then her eyes shifted to Judith and suddenly lit up. "Judy Sheffield!" She began speaking fast in Kokatí, and a moment later Judith was surrounded by five women, all of them asking questions at once.

Jed watched the warm welcome Judith was receiving, and wished he hadn't agreed to come here at all. Once again he felt like an outsider, while Jude, who wasn't one of them at all, was being treated like a long-lost relative. One of the women turned to him. "Are you looking for your grandfather?"

Jed felt himself flush slightly, but nodded his head.

The woman tilted her own toward another of the narrow alleys. "He's in the kiva." Then she turned her attention back to Judith, and a moment later Jed, feeling as if he was being watched from every dark door and window in the pueblo, crossed the plaza and stepped into the shadows of the narrow passageway.

He followed the alley, emerging onto the wide apron that lay between the pueblo and the rim of the canyon. Midway between the pueblo's wall and the lip of the precipice, a low dome rose up a few feet. From its center a ladder emerged from a hole in the dome, along with a steady wisp of smoke from the small fire that almost always burned within the kiva. Jed paused, uncertain what to do, gazing at the mouth of the kiva. Since he'd been a little boy, it had always seemed a dark and forbidding place. It was in the kiva that the Kokatí men gathered to carry out their spiritual rites. It was the place from which they emerged on festival days, wearing their elaborate costumes to dance in the courtyards.

But it was also the place they went to be alone, to chat quietly among themselves without the distractions of their wives and children, or to just sit and think, or commune with the spirits who resided beneath the kiva's floor.

Could he really do it? Simply walk up to the hatch in the roof and climb down inside? But he was only a boy, not even a member of the tribe.

And then he remembered.

He was sixteen, and among the Kokatí that made him a man. Taking a deep breath, he started toward the kiva.

He hesitated as he came to the hatchway, then took one more breath and descended the ladder into the chamber below. It was circular, some fifty-odd feet in diameter, and had been hacked out of the sandstone of the mesa centuries earlier. Around its perimeter there was a stone bench, and a circle of heavy posts formed a smaller ring midway between the walls of the kiva and the firepit in the center. As Jed stepped off the ladder onto the floor of the kiva, his eyes began to burn from the smoke of the fire. For a few moments he could see nothing in the gloom beneath the low ceiling. But after a while his eyes began to adjust to the darkness, and finally he spotted his grandfather.

Brown Eagle was sitting alone on the bench, facing eastward, his eyes closed, his body held perfectly still. Jed approached him almost warily, half expecting the old man's eyes to open and fix accusingly on him. But Brown Eagle seemed not to be aware of his presence at all. When Jed sat down on the bench next to him, the old man never so much as moved a muscle.

Jed sat nervously at first, feeling the hardness of the stone beneath his buttocks, gazing around curiously. He studied the construction of the dome carefully, examining the peeled tree trunks that extended from the walls of the kiva inward to the heavy beams that had long ago been laid on the tops of the posts, and the smaller logs that lay crosswise above the main stringers. There was a geometric orderliness to the dome, and a sense of timelessness that came from the blackened patina of the old wood. Except for the patch of sunlight that shone through the hatch, moving slowly across the floor as the sun moved across the sky above, there was little clue to what was happening beyond the confines of the kiva, and as he sat next to his grandfather, Jed found his own mind begin to drift in strange directions.

His eyes fixed on the fire and he began to imagine he saw shapes dancing in the flames.

A drowsiness came over him, and he began to feel his eyelids grow heavy. When at last he opened his eyes again, the patch of sunlight had moved far across the floor.

"How do you like it?" he heard his grandfather ask.

"I—I don't know," Jed murmured. "I guess I must have fallen asleep."

Brown Eagle regarded Jed with deep and impenetrable eyes. "You didn't go to sleep. It's something else that happens here. Something you won't understand for years. Some people never understand it." He stood up, stretched, then glanced down at Jed. "What do you say we go outside? Whatever happened to you is over now."

A moment later, as they emerged into brilliant daylight, Jed blinked, then glanced at the sun. "Jesus," he said. "I must have been in there almost three hours."

Brown Eagle shrugged. "It happens." Then he eyed Jed appraisingly. "You've grown. Not as big as your dad, but a lot bigger than any of the kids around here. Still, I see your mother in you."

Jed's voice took on a note of belligerence. "How come people can't just look like themselves?"

Brown Eagle's brows rose slightly. "What's wrong with looking like your mother?" he asked mildly. "She was a beautiful woman, my little girl." Then a flicker in Jed's eyes made the Indian frown. "Is that why you came up here? To ask me about your mother?"

Jed felt nonplussed, as if his grandfather had looked right inside him. "I —I don't know, really. You remember Judy Sheffield?" Brown Eagle nodded. "I rode up with her this morning. We got to talking about the pueblo, and the tribe, and . . ." His voice trailed off as he began to flounder over his own words.

Brown Eagle ignored Jed's discomfort. "I remember her. I remember the first day she came up here. She started playing with some of the kids, and before you knew it, she was acting as if she'd been born here. She's the kind who will always fit herself in anywhere she happens to be." His voice changed slightly, taking on a wistful tone. "There's other kinds of people too," he said. "Just the opposite of Judy Sheffield."

"She likes to be called Judith now," Jed broke in.

Brown Eagle's head tipped slightly in acknowledgment of the boy's words, but his penetrating eyes fixed on Jed's own. "It's your mother you want to talk about, isn't it? Not Judith Sheffield."

Jed's breath caught—how had his grandfather known what was on his mind? But then his grandfather had always seemed to know things without being told. He nodded.

"Your mother was one of those other people—people who can never be happy," Brown Eagle said. "No matter where they go, or who they're with. She always had the feeling that everyone else was part of something, but that she was an outsider." He stopped, placing a hand on Jed's shoulder. "I think that's why she did what she did, Jed. I think she finally figured out she wasn't ever going to be happy—whatever that means—and just gave up."

Jed glared angrily at the old man, shaking off his gnarled hand. "I don't believe you," he said. "It was a lot more than that. It was because of Dad, and everyone else down there."

Brown Eagle shook his head, but refused to respond to Jed's anger. "I'm not saying it was her fault. It was just the way things were. She was never happy here, and she was never happy in Borrego. And there was nothing anyone could do about it. Not me, and not your father. It was her nature. She wasn't of the world, so she left it."

Jed kicked at the dust beneath his feet, suddenly feeling frightened. His thoughts tumbled over one another as he recognized himself in his grandfather's words about his mother. Was the same thing going to happen to him too? Was he going to wake up some morning and just decide, to hell with it?

And then the specter of Heather Fredericks rose up in his mind once more, and with it a thought—one he voiced without even meaning to. "Maybe that's what happened to Heather too."

Brown Eagle's eyes narrowed. "The girl who died in the canyon a few days ago?"

Jed nodded. "She killed herself."

"Is that what they're saying down in Borrego?" Brown Eagle asked. He shook his head. "It isn't true. She didn't jump because she wanted to."

Jed eyed his grandfather suspiciously.

"No," Brown Eagle went on, speaking almost to himself now. "She didn't want to jump at all. Someone made her do it."

Jed's brows drew together angrily. "That's not what the cops said," he challenged.

Brown Eagle shrugged. "It doesn't matter what they said. I was in the kiva when it happened. I saw it."

Now Jed stared at his grandfather with open incredulity. "Come on," he said. "If you were in the kiva, you couldn't have seen it."

Brown Eagle gazed at his grandson impassively. "Is that what you think?" he asked. "Well, perhaps if you came up here more often, and found out just who you are, you might think otherwise."

Half an hour later, as they made their way back down the mesa, Judith finally decided the silence had lasted long enough.

"Well? What did you find out?"

Jed glanced at her. "From my *grandfather*?" he asked, his voice harsh, almost mocking. "Oh, I found out a lot. But not about my mom—about him! You know what? He's nuts. Stark, raving nuts."

Judith stared at him. Something, obviously, had happened. But what? Before she could ask him, Jed told her.

"You know what he said? He said Heather didn't kill herself at all. He said someone killed her, and that he saw it. He was in the kiva, and he saw it. Don't you just love it? Shit, the old man's a complete whacko!"

Spurring his horse, he shot ahead, leaving Judith staring after him.

Chapter 7

Jed glared angrily at his father. It was the morning after he'd been up to Kokatí with Jude. By the time he'd returned the day before, his father had already gone to work, and when Frank finally got home a little before midnight, Jed had already gone to bed. So it hadn't been until a few minutes ago that he finally told his father what had happened in the pueblo. And now his father was angry at him again, as he had been nearly every other day lately. "I don't see what the big deal is," Jed muttered, staring into his coffee. "All I said was that Grandpa's nuts. So what?"

Frank's jaw tightened. "You don't know your grandfather, and you don't know a damned thing about the Kokatí."

Jed looked up now, his scornful eyes meeting his father's. "Jeez, Dad, it doesn't take any brains to figure it out. How the hell could Grandpa have seen what happened to Heather if he was in the kiva? What have they got? Some kind of TV monitor down there?"

Frank shook his head. He remembered the day Alice had died, and something that had happened, something he'd never told his son before. "You remember when your mom died?" he asked. The look in Jed's eyes, a sudden opaqueness that came into them, spoke more than any words Jed could have said. "Brown Eagle came down here that day," Frank went on. "He told me what had happened. He said he'd felt funny when he woke up that morning and had gone into the kiva." His voice dropped, turning husky. "And while he was down there, he saw Alice kill herself." He fell silent for a moment, then went on, his voice trembling now. "That's why he came down here that day, Jed. He was hoping he was wrong. But he wasn't."

Now it was Jed who was silent, his eyes narrowed to no more than angry slits as he stared at his father. "That's not true," he whispered. "If he really thought something was wrong, he'd have come down earlier. He'd have stopped her. But he didn't, did he? So then he claims he saw what happened—"

The phone rang, a harsh jangling that cut through Jed's words. He fell silent as Frank reached over and picked up the receiver. "Arnold," he said. He listened for a few moments, grunting responses every now and then. "Okay. I'll be there right away." Putting the receiver back on the hook, he stood up. "I've got to get out to the plant," he told Jed. "They've got a problem, and they're shorthanded."

Jed opened his mouth to protest, then shut it again. What the hell good would it do? His father wasn't going to listen to him anyway. "Great," he muttered to himself as Frank disappeared out the kitchen door a few minutes later, dressed in the gray overalls that were his work uniform. "Start talking about Mom, then just walk away." He slammed his fist down on the tabletop, the coffee in his cup slopping over into the saucer. "Well, who cares?" he shouted into the now empty house. "Who the hell cares?"

Frank arrived at the refinery five miles out of town and swung into his accustomed parking spot outside the gate. But instead of going directly into the plant, he crossed the street and stepped into the superintendent's office. As soon as he saw the frown on Bobbie Packard's normally sunny face, he knew something else had gone wrong. He glanced past the secretary into Otto Kruger's office, half expecting to see Kruger's face glowering with unconcealed rage, but the plant superintendent was nowhere to be seen. "Where's Otto?" he asked. "Out in the plant, making more trouble than they already have?"

The secretary shrugged. "They called him into town for a meeting in Mr. Moreland's office," she said. "It sounds like Max might finally be getting ready to sell out."

Frank felt a surge of anger rise up from his gut, but quickly put it down. It couldn't be true—it had to be just talk. The rumors had been flying for months, ever since the first feelers from UniChem had begun. But so far Max had insisted that he had no intention of selling the place out, and that if he ever did, it wouldn't be to some huge, impersonal conglomerate. It would be to the employees of Borrego Oil. So Frank put his brief spate of anger aside and shook his head. No use having Bobbie spreading the rumors all over town. "Take my word for it, Bobbie," he said. "If Max wants to sell, he'll come to us first."

"I don't know," Bobbie sighed. "From the way Otto was talking, it

sounds like Max is almost broke." She winked conspiratorially at Frank.
"And if you ask me, Otto will do his best to get Max to sell out to Uni-
Chem rather than us. He thinks you'd fire him if you ever got the chance."

Frank's lips twisted into a wry grin. "And just how would I get the
chance?" he asked.

Bobbie giggled. "Come on, Frank. You think if the employees bought
this place you wouldn't wind up on the board of directors?"

Frank shrugged noncommittally. "Even if I made the board, I'd only
have one vote," he pointed out.

Now Bobbie was carefully repairing an already perfect fingernail. "And
everybody else would vote right along with you, as Otto well knows."

Frank's grin broadened across his face. "Does Otto know how much you
hate him?"

"Of course," Bobbie said blithely. "But it doesn't matter, because anybody else who was his secretary would hate him too."

Frank nodded absently, but his mind was no longer registering Bobbie's
words. He was already wondering if he should call a union meeting for that
evening. If there was, indeed, any truth to the rumor that Max was on the
verge of selling out, then there was a lot of work to be done.

Months ago he'd found a lawyer and an accountant in Santa Fe and
quietly hired them to begin studying the feasibility of an employee buyout
of the company. It hadn't been a difficult job—Borrego Oil was a small
company, and the same kind of transfer of ownership had been happening
all over the country. He'd been pleased to note that in most cases, the
turnaround of those companies into profitable organizations had been
nearly immediate; when people were working for themselves, they tended
to be a lot more efficient.

More efficient, and more careful, he reflected as he left the office and
crossed the street once more, this time to deal with the problem that had
brought him out here this morning in the first place. He walked into the
loader's shack to check last night's output, nodding a greeting to Fred
Cummings, and picked up the sheet that showed every gallon of gasoline
pumped from the tank farm into the trucks.

He shook his head dolefully as he tried to decipher Fred's chicken
scratchings, and wondered, yet again, why the whole system had yet to be
computerized. But he knew the answer—the same lack of money that
seemed to be strangling Borrego Oil at every turn. Still, oil prices were
slowly rising again, and he'd thought the end of the steady losses was in
sight. But then as his eye came to the bottom of the shipment list, he
frowned.

Fred had stopped loading at four that morning.

"That's when the pump went out," Fred explained. "We tried to fix it, but someone screwed up on parts, and we didn't have any."

Frank scowled. He'd personally reviewed the inventory a month ago and given a list to Kruger. Apparently, the parts had never been ordered. "Okay," he said. "Give me the list of what you need, and I'll call down to Albuquerque. We should be able to get back in operation by this afternoon."

But Fred Cummings shook his head. "Won't work," he said. "I already talked to the supplier, and they say our credit's run out. We want parts for the pump, we pay cash."

Frank's scowl deepened. "Okay, then let's fix the parts we have. Can we do that?" he asked, knowing the answer even before he had uttered the words.

"I 'spose we could fix it," Cummings finally said, avoiding Frank's gaze. "But it'd take an overtime crew, and Kruger ain't authorizing overtime." Still avoiding Frank's eyes, he picked up his lunch bucket and headed toward the door, but Frank stopped him.

"You could hang around a couple of hours on your own," he pointed out.

Cummings spat into the dirt outside the door. " 'Spose I could," he agreed amiably. "But it's not my outfit, and I don't notice Kruger, or Moreland, or anybody else comin' over to mow my lawn on their own time."

As Cummings left, Frank swore softly to himself. And yet the man was right—why *should* he work overtime, knowing full well he wouldn't get paid for his time? But in the long run, Borrego's inability to deliver gasoline, even for a day, would only add to the losses, and bring on more cost-cutting. Soon the layoffs would increase, and in the end the layoffs would only drop production even further.

Cursing again, Frank studied the work schedule, looking for a way to pull enough men off their regular jobs to put together a crew to repair the broken pump.

And when Kruger got back, he'd have a little talk with the man. If they weren't even paying their suppliers anymore, the situation must be a lot worse than anyone had told him.

What the hell was going on?

He picked up the phone to call Jed and explain what was happening. "I'm probably going to be tied up all day," he said. Jed listened to him silently, but as Frank talked he could picture clearly the dark look that would be coming into the boy's eyes, the look of resentment that always came over Jed when he had to change his schedule yet again. But there was nothing he could do about it.

By mid-afternoon Frank's temper was beginning to fray. The broken pump, totally disassembled, lay scattered in the dusty road. Two of his makeshift crew had disappeared after lunch, sent back to their regular jobs by Otto Kruger, who had insisted that the pump would be of little use if the refinery itself had to be shut down because nobody was looking after it. Frank had argued that there had been a general shutdown only two weeks ago, and that every pipe and valve in the place had been thoroughly cleaned and inspected. Right now the plant was quite capable of running itself for a few hours. But Kruger had insisted, and in the end Frank decided the issue wasn't worth fighting about, since his two other men were going to be occupied for the next couple of hours with repairing the broken shaft of the pump's motor.

If they could repair it at all. Carlos Alvarez and Jerry Polanski had insisted they could make the weld easily enough, but Frank wasn't so sure. The shaft looked to him as if it had bent pretty badly when the break had occurred, and he suspected that even if they managed the weld, the pump might tear itself apart again as soon as they reassembled it and started it up.

But now the repair had been made, and Alvarez and Polanski were beginning the process of reassembling the pump. Denied the help of half his crew, Frank pitched in himself, holding the shaft steady while Carlos carefully adjusted the collar that would clamp it to the pump.

"What the hell's going on?" Otto Kruger's harsh voice demanded from behind. Frank waited until Carlos had tightened the last bolt before straightening up. Using the bandanna he habitually wore, which was now hanging out of his rear pocket, he mopped the sweat from his brow.

"Just about got her fixed—" he began, but Kruger didn't let him finish.

"By breaking every union rule in the book?" the superintendent growled. Frank tensed, tightening his grip on his temper. "Alvarez and Polanski aren't part of the yard crew," Kruger went on. "It's not their job to be working on that pump. And you're a shift foreman, right? That means you make sure your men are doing their jobs. It doesn't mean you do the work for them."

Frank felt his anger boiling up from the pit of his belly, but he was damned if he was going to get into a fight with Kruger. Not right here, anyway. "Maybe we'd better go into your office to talk about this, Otto." His voice was even but his eyes glittered with fury. What the hell was the man trying to do? Weren't things bad enough without Kruger making it impossible for him to do his job?

"If that's what you want," Kruger rumbled. He spat into the dirt, then turned his attention to Alvarez and Polanski. "Leave the pump and get back to your regular jobs."

Frank saw Carlos's hand tighten on the wrench he was holding, but he shook his head just enough to tell the man to leave it alone. Without a word, Carlos put the wrench down and turned away from the loading shed. A moment later Jerry Polanski followed him. Only when they'd both disappeared into the plant itself did Kruger turn away and stride across the street to his office. Frank followed him, managing only the tightest of nods for Bobbie Packard as he passed her desk.

Unseen by Kruger, she made a face at the superintendent's back, then gave Frank a thumbs-up sign.

"Shut the door," Kruger growled as he slouched low in his chair and propped his feet up on his desk. "No sense airing our problems in front of the hired help, is there?"

Frank closed the door gently, deliberately depriving Kruger of the pleasure of seeing his anger. "Seems to me we're both part of the hired help around here," he observed evenly, retaining his position by the door, but folding his arms across his chest as he leaned back against the wall. "Now why don't you just tell me what's going on? Our credit with the suppliers is shot, and the last of the yard crew got laid off a week ago. How the hell am I supposed to fix that pump if I don't use men from the plant? And don't give me any shit about it not being my job to work on it, 'cause you and I both know my job's to keep the shift running, even if I have to do it myself."

Kruger averted his eyes. "Those layoffs were temporary. We lost a bundle during the shutdown. The men will be hired back as soon as we can afford it."

"But if we can't move the gas out of the tanks—" Frank began. Once again Kruger didn't let him finish.

"As it happens, we should be getting a new loading pump up here within a week or two," he said. "And since we've got no problem with storage, it looks like all your work was sort of a waste of time, wasn't it?"

It wasn't only Kruger's refusal to meet his eyes that roused Frank's suspicions—it was the smugness in his voice. "What's going on?" he demanded. "Is Max getting a new line of credit?"

Now Kruger smiled, but it was a cruel twisting of his lips. "I 'spose you could call it that," he said, drawling elaborately. "Anyway, by the time we get the new pump, we should be ready to start hiring the men back."

Frank Arnold's eyes bored into Kruger's. "It's a sellout, isn't it?" he asked, but the words came out more as a statement than a question. A cold knot of anger formed in his belly. "Are you telling me Max is selling out?"

Kruger's hands spread noncommittally. "He hasn't yet," he said. His feet left the desk and went to the floor as his chair suddenly straightened and he leaned forward. "But the party's about over," he declared, his eyes meeting Frank's for the first time, "and if I were you I'd start thinking about how I could benefit if someone *does* buy this place."

"Are you telling me that's what's happened?" Frank asked. "Is that what the big meeting this morning was about?"

Kruger shrugged. "Someone wants to do a leveraged buyout, the way I heard it."

"But Max won't do that," Frank protested. "Everybody knows if he sells out, he'll offer the company to the employees first."

Kruger chuckled hollowly. "If you've got that in writing, I'd suggest you call a lawyer pretty damned quick. Because if you don't have it in writing, I think it's a pretty sure thing that by next month you and I will be working for someone else. Which," he added, finally allowing himself a genuine smile, "is just fine by me. How's it suit you?"

Every fiber in Frank wanted to strike out at Kruger, wanted to punch that smile right down the son of a bitch's throat. But that, he knew, was probably just what Kruger was hoping for. There weren't many things Kruger could use as grounds to fire him, but physical violence was certainly one of them. So Frank restrained himself, shoving his hands deep in his pockets, as if it was the only way to hold them in check. But when he spoke, he made no attempt to conceal his rage. "It doesn't suit me at all," he replied. "And there are a few things I *can* do about it." His mind was already working. He'd have to organize a union meeting and put a proposal to buy the company before the membership. That meant weeks of spending practically every waking hour when he wasn't at work dealing with the lawyer and accountant from Santa Fe.

But there had to be a way to counter any offer Max Moreland might already have on his desk.

He turned away from Kruger, jerking the door to the superintendent's office open with so much force it almost came off its hinges. Bobbie Packard, startled by his sudden presence, looked up at him. "What is it?" she asked.

Frank's eyes glared malevolently. "You mean he didn't tell you? Someone's trying to buy Max out. And you can bet they're not going to be interested in the refinery—without a lot of improvements, it won't even break even. And the new takeover people aren't interested in investment— they're interested in fast bucks, which means they'll keep the wells and close down the plant. Pretty neat, huh?" He jerked his head toward Kruger's office. "And I'll bet that son of a bitch has already cut himself a deal to keep an eye on the wells while the rest of us go looking for work that doesn't happen to exist around here."

Bobbie shook her head dazedly. "Mr. Moreland said—"

Frank leaned down so he could look into the secretary's eyes. "Don't you get it, Bobbie?" he asked. "Max is at the end of his rope. He's sunk every nickel he has into this place, but it's not enough. It's old and obsolete, and you can bet no outsider is planning to spend a lot of money out here. All they'll want is the wells."

Without waiting for her to reply, he pushed his way out of the office and crossed back into the plant.

From his office window Otto Kruger watched Frank Arnold disappear into the refinery, and knew exactly what he was up to. He sat quietly for a while, savoring the anger he'd seen in Frank Arnold, enjoying the rage he'd induced in the man. It wasn't often that he got the best of Frank Arnold, and whenever he did, it gave him an intense pleasure.

He'd hated Frank for years, and knew exactly why: Frank knew the refinery better than he did, and had the trust of the men.

Even Max Moreland had more respect for Frank than he had for him, Kruger thought. A year ago, when he'd demanded to know why, if Frank Arnold was so smart, he hadn't been promoted past shift supervisor, Kruger remembered Max smiling at him almost pityingly.

"I need him where he is, Otto," he'd explained. "You can't run an oil refinery without a man like Frank Arnold. Oh, you do fine, overseeing the whole operation. But without Frank in the plant, there wouldn't be any operation for you to oversee."

He, of course, had said nothing in response, but ever since that day he'd hated Frank.

Hated him almost as much as he hated Max Moreland himself.

Finally he turned back to his desk and picked up the phone. He dialed a number quickly, then spoke as soon as the phone was answered at the other end, not waiting for a greeting.

"I just talked to Arnold," he said. "I told him just enough to gauge his reaction, and it's just like I told you. He's going to make trouble."

Then, knowing he'd said enough, and knowing there would be no reply, he hung up, his face wearing a satisfied smile.

Soon, very soon, Frank Arnold would be out of his hair.

It was a thought that gave him a great deal of pleasure.

Chapter 8

Frank Arnold glanced up from his newspaper as his son came into the kitchen, dressed—as usual—in a manner carefully calculated to tell the world he didn't give a damn what it thought. Frank bit back the words of criticism that immediately came to his lips. During the last two weeks, while it seemed he'd spent every waking moment with the lawyers and accountants, the situation with Jed had only worsened. Indeed, over the Labor Day weekend that had just ended, the two of them had barely spoken, except for Friday night, when Judith Sheffield had come for dinner.

That night there had been no question of who would do the cooking. When Frank had come home from work, the house was already redolent with the aroma of a roast in the oven. That night, as on the other nights Judith had spent the evening with them in the little house on Sixth East, Jed had seemed perfectly happy, as though his resentments had magically vanished. But the next morning, with Judith gone, he had retreated again behind his sullen mask, and they had barely spoken over breakfast. Maybe if Judith had spent the night . . .

He quickly abandoned the thought, although there were several nights during the last few weeks when he'd been almost certain she would have stayed if he'd asked her. Every time, he'd lost his nerve, terrified of looking like a fool for even thinking she might find him as attractive as he found her. Yet had Judith only been here this morning, he was absolutely sure things would be better between him and Jed. Everything seemed to be better when Judith was around. She seemed to understand his moods, even to understand the importance of what he was trying to do.

But then, despite the holiday weekend, Frank had had to leave for Santa Fe, for yet another series of meetings which would culminate tonight at the union lodge, when he would finally present to the employees a plan for them to buy the company.

Assuming, of course, that by tonight the company had not yet been sold to UniChem.

And if his plan succeeded, would Jed finally forgive all the time he had spent? Frank wondered. Would pride in his father's accomplishment bridge the chasm between them? Leaning back, Frank folded his arms across his chest, and his eyes settled again on Jed's self-consciously "cool" clothes. Idly, he wondered if Jed was aware that his scrupulous attention to his dress only gave the lie to the message he was trying to project: if he truly didn't care how he looked, why were his jeans always so meticulously torn, why was his black leather jacket inspected for missing studs every day, and why was Jed's hair always greased into total submission to the whim of the moment? Why, if his son truly didn't care what anyone thought, did he constantly do his best to look like a thug and hide the quickness of his mind?

Frank knew the answer, or at least most of it. But aside from the loss of his mother, Jed had weathered more than his fair share of fights over the years—practically all of them having to do with his Kokatí heritage—and had finally built a shell around himself that told people not to mess with him, that warned them he would strike back if pushed too far. Frank supposed the shell Jed had built served a purpose, protecting the boy from things he didn't want to deal with. But now he was almost grown, and in danger of wrecking his life. Frank had seen too many kids like Jed—bright but angry—just give up and drift into a job on the oil field or at the refinery, spending their evenings drinking too much in the bar at the café. And that wasn't what he wanted for Jed. Jed was going to go to college, and get out of Borrego, and do more with his life than he had done with his own. Unless Jed gave in to his image, and decided going to school was no longer cool.

"Hope they're not planning to take the class pictures today," Frank said mildly, pushing the newspaper aside.

Instantly, Jed's eyes began to smolder, as he understood what his father was really saying. "You don't like the way I look?" he demanded.

"I didn't say that," Frank countered. "It's just that on the first day of school—"

Jed cut him off. "What's the big deal about the first day of school?" he pressed. "It's just another day of sitting around listening to a bunch of dull teachers say dull things—"

"That's enough!" The sharpness in Frank's voice made Jed fall silent, and the boy slouched low in his chair. "I know what you think about school, and I'm tired of hearing it."

"I do okay," Jed muttered. "And I don't notice how not finishing school hurt you."

Frank's eyes fixed on Jed. "You think being a shift foreman at the refinery is a big deal? If I'd paid attention when I was your age, I could be managing the whole thing."

"Sure," Jed shot back, his voice dark. "And Mr. Moreland would still own the whole thing. Come on, Dad! I don't care if you'd gotten every goddamn degree they can give you—you'd still be working for Max Moreland. Nothing ever changes—if you don't start out rich, you don't get rich. So why the hell should I keep going to school? What's the big deal if I graduate or not? I'm going to wind up working in the refinery, just like you! In fact," he added, shoving his chair back and standing up, "maybe I'll do it today. Maybe instead of going to school, I'll go down to the company office and get a job!"

So that's what it's all about, Frank thought. That's what he hasn't been talking about. He looked at Jed and knew the boy was waiting for him to explode, waiting for him to start yelling. Controlling himself, he leaned back and shrugged. "Well, if that's what you want to do, there isn't much I can do to stop you. You're sixteen—there's no law that says you have to go to school." Jed's eyes flickered with uncertainty. "I can save you a little time, though—there aren't any jobs at the company. The only reason I'm still working is seniority. So you'd better start checking with some of the stores—maybe they can use some help." He glanced up at the calendar on the wall. "Let's see . . . I guess I can give you a week or ten days, so what do you say we start the rent on the fifteenth? That should give you time to find a job."

Jed blinked. "Rent?" he asked, his voice suddenly hollow. "What are you talking about?"

Frank shrugged again, his arms spreading in a helpless gesture. "What do you expect? If you're going to school, I pay the bills. If you're not, you pay your share." He watched Jed carefully and could almost see the thoughts going through his son's mind, see him calculating how much money he might earn bagging groceries at the market or clerking in the lumberyard. At last Jed finished his coffee, then stood up, his face a mask of belligerence.

"Maybe I'll do it," he said. "Maybe I'll start looking around, and see what kind of job I can find."

Frank nodded affably. "Sounds good to me." He picked up the paper again and pretended to read, but he kept one eye on Jed, not missing the fact that when Jed went out the back door a few minutes later, he was carrying his book bag.

Stuart Beckwith, the high school principal, smiled thinly as Judith Sheffield came into his office. He remembered her well—the blond, blue-eyed girl who always sat in the front row of his social studies class and asked too many questions. And now here she was, back in Borrego, once more looking at him with those bright blue eyes, obviously just as inquisitive as ever. He pushed a stack of folders across the desk, then nervously ran his right hand over his nearly bald pate as if pushing back a lock of hair that had long since disappeared. "So," he said as she took the chair opposite him and began quickly thumbing through the folders, "how does it feel to be back home?"

Judith shrugged, the nervousness she had been feeling earlier that morning dissolving. Ten years ago, when she'd been a teenager, she'd always thought of Beckwith as mean, but now she could see that what had once seemed like petty spitefulness was actually nothing more than weakness. She knew the type perfectly from Los Angeles—the sort of administrator whose prime rule was "don't rock the boat."

She, of course, had always been a boat-rocker, and had no intention of changing. Still, she didn't want to alienate Beckwith on her very first day on the job. "It's interesting," she said carefully. "Actually, the town hasn't changed much. In fact," she added without thinking, "it doesn't even look like it's been painted since I left." She immediately regretted her words, as a defensive tightening pinched Beckwith's sallow face. "I didn't mean—" she began apologetically, but to her surprise, he cut her off.

"Of course you meant it," he said. Judith felt herself reddening slightly, and an uncomfortable silence filled the room until, as if he'd come to a decision, Beckwith leaned forward and rested his forearms on the top of the desk. "I'm afraid I seem to be getting off on the wrong foot, don't I? But I have to confess that I'm still at a bit of a loss. Losing Reba Tucker was very upsetting, and . . . ." He paused then, his lips pursing into what struck Judith as a phony smile. "And I have to confess," he went on, "that having one of my own students return as one of my teachers is making me feel just a little old."

Judith didn't know whether she was expected to laugh, but decided not to. "I was very sorry to hear about Mrs. Tucker," she said, choosing to ignore Beckwith's feeble joke. "She always seemed so—well, strong, I guess."

Beckwith's head bobbed and his expression took on a too mournful cast. "We all thought she was," he said. "And it seemed to come on her quite suddenly. She was teaching summer school, and everything seemed to be fine at first. And then she began to have strange moods, and finally, well . . ." His voice trailed off and he made a helpless gesture, as if there were really nothing else to say.

Judith tensed. Rita Moreland had distinctly said that Mrs. Tucker had suffered a stroke, and Greg, Reba's doctor, had concurred. But Beckwith's implication was something else entirely. "You mean she had some sort of breakdown?"

Beckwith hesitated, then sighed. "I suppose that's what one would have to call it, yes," he said. "Of course, young Greg Moreland says it was a stroke, but it seems to me it was a lot more than that. In the weeks before the . . . episode, she seemed to get listless." He clucked almost like a ruffled hen. "Not like Reba. Not like herself at all." Pointedly, he glanced at his watch, then pushed another folder toward Judith. "At any rate, these are her lesson plans. She used the same ones every year, and I'm sure she'd have no problem with your using them too."

Judith made no move to pick up the folder. "That's very kind of you," she said, "but as it happens, I've got my own lesson plans. As I'm sure you know, I've been teaching in L.A. for the last couple of years, and I think it might be easier for me to do what I know how to do than try to turn myself into Mrs. Tucker."

Beckwith leaned back, his hands folded over his stomach. His lips tightened in a show of disapproval that made Judith suddenly feel as if she had been undergoing some kind of oral exam she'd just flunked. Gathering the folders that contained the records of her homeroom students into a neat stack, she stood up. "If I'm going to go through these before classes begin, I'd better be going," she said.

Beckwith seemed about to let her go without comment, but as if changing his mind, he stood as she turned toward the door and smiled at her, then came around his desk to shake her hand. "Let me welcome you back to Borrego," he said. "I have to confess, I had terrible misgivings about your coming here. I was afraid you might want to come in and start changing everything, modernizing everything, that sort of thing. But we don't have the money to do much, and you know we're just a little backwater high school in the middle of nowhere. If you can deal with that, then I'm sure we'll get along just fine."

Judith hesitated only a moment before taking Beckwith's extended hand. Yet as she left his office she wondered if she had, after all, made the right decision in returning to Borrego and taking this job. The interview had been odd, and Beckwith, once her least favorite teacher, had not become any more appealing now that he was principal of Borrego High. But what troubled her most, what would not leave her mind as she hurried through the building to find her classroom, was his strange description of what had happened to Reba Tucker.

What had he meant? Had what happened to Mrs. Tucker been something other than a stroke?

The house sat at the top of a small rise on the floor of Mordida Canyon, nestled almost invisibly into a grove of cottonwoods. Even during the hottest part of the day, it was always cool here, and as the woman emerged from the building, she felt a slight chill. The sun had moved far enough across the sky so that even without the trees, the house would still be lying in shadows, and it occurred to her—not for the first time—that it was an odd place for a rehabilitation center. How was anyone supposed to get well when they never got any sunlight? Still, the spot was beautiful, and the pay was good, and God knew, the work was simple enough.

She balanced the tray on one raised knee and quickly pushed the door to the little cabin open. There were no lights on, and she groped for the switch, wondering, not for the first time, how people could stand to sit all day in the dark.

Not that this newest patient could do much about it, she reminded herself.

The lights came on, and the woman looked over at the bed.

There she was, sitting by the window, staring out at the canyon just as Reba Tucker had been doing an hour ago, the last time she'd looked in on her.

"Here's lunch," the attendant said, summoning up a cheeriness she knew sounded false, but not really worrying about it, since she wasn't at all certain the woman even heard her.

Stroke victim, was what Dr. Moreland called her.

Just plain old senile, the woman thought.

Still, she had a job to do. She set the tray on the rolling table, then pushed the table around so it swung over the chair in which the woman sat. Finally she eased the patient around so she was no longer staring blankly out the window, and shoved an extra pillow behind her back.

Lifting the cover off the single dish on the luncheon tray, the attendant plunged a spoon into the soft grayish mush, then brought it close to the patient's lips.

"Come on, Mrs. Tucker," she crooned. "We have to eat, don't we? We don't want to starve to death."

The spoon touched Reba Tucker's lips, and, as always, they parted just enough for the attendant to slide the pablum into her mouth.

The woman waited a moment, until she felt Mrs. Tucker's tongue wrap itself around the spoon, removing the food from it so that it could slip down her throat. Then she scooped up a second serving . . .

Slowly, concentrating the small part of her mind that still functioned on the task at hand, Reba Tucker managed to swallow the gruel.

Sometimes, as she did now, she wished she could bring herself to speak. Indeed, when she was alone, she sometimes practiced it, moving her tongue slowly, struggling to form the sounds that had once been so natural to her.

She knew the attendant didn't think she could talk, didn't even think she could hear.

And that was fine with Reba.

Let them all think she couldn't hear, and couldn't talk.

She still didn't know who they were, or even where she was.

All she remembered was waking up and finding herself here.

Except she didn't know where "here" was or what had happened to her.

Panic had set in, and she'd screamed and screamed, but mercifully, she didn't know how long the screaming had lasted, for she no longer had any more sense of time than of place.

There was darkness, and there was light.

And there were the nightmares.

Perhaps, she thought in that tiny corner of her mind that still seemed to work now and then, she should stop eating and let herself starve to death.

She wasn't sure, because sometimes, in those fleeting moments when she could think at all, she thought she must already have died and gone to Hell.

But there wasn't any point to dying again, and besides, if she wasn't dead already, she knew they wouldn't let her die.

If they let her die, they couldn't give her the nightmares anymore.

For Reba Tucker, that was what life had become.

Waiting for the nightmares.

Chapter 9

"Will you please hurry?" Gina Alvarez pleaded, though she knew her words would fall on deaf ears. As far as Jed Arnold was concerned, it was definitely not cool to hurry on the way to a class. The whole idea, in fact, was to look as though you didn't care whether you got there or not. Now she looked up at Jed's face to see his incredible blue eyes twinkling happily at her. She knew he was testing her, knew he was waiting to see if she'd wait for him or hurry off by herself so she wouldn't be late to class. She wrestled with herself, part of her wanting to leave him standing there lounging against his locker, idly passing time with his friends. She didn't even like his friends—they seemed to her like a bunch of jerks who didn't know what they wanted to do with their lives.

Gina knew perfectly well what she was going to do with her own. She was going to graduate with honors from Borrego High, then win a full scholarship to Vassar. Her mother had told her she was wasting her time, that girls from Borrego didn't go to Vassar—they didn't go to college at all, especially when their father was a drunk who had abandoned them, and their mother had raised them by working as a waitress in a rundown café. But Gina didn't care what other girls did. She just didn't want to wind up like her mother, getting married right away, having a couple of kids, and wondering what happened when her husband suddenly took off and she was left to raise her children on whatever she could earn waiting tables.

So Gina went her own way, ignoring the flickering television while she studied every night, and still finding time to be a cheerleader for the football team, serve on the student council, look after her little sister, and maintain her relationship with Jed Arnold.

But sometimes, like now, she wondered why she bothered with Jed. Partly, of course, it was his dark good looks—there wasn't any question that

Jed was the handsomest boy in town. But it was something else too. She'd always had a feeling that there was more to Jed than what he showed to the world, that his tough-guy image was only that—an image. In fact, sometimes when they were alone together, hiking out by the canyon, he changed. He'd sprawl on his back, looking up at the clouds, and show her things he saw in them—fantastic cities in the air, whole circuses of animals and acrobats. Once he'd even told her stories he'd heard from his Indian grandfather, about the gods who lived on the mesas and in the canyon itself, looking after the Kokatí. "It means 'the People,'" he'd explained. But his voice had taken on an almost scornful edge as he continued. "That's what they call themselves, as if nobody else in the world is real. Grandpa says the gods are all waiting right now, but someday soon something is going to happen, and all the land is going to be given back to the Kokatí." She'd tried to get him to explain what he meant, but he'd only shrugged. "How should I know? You know how the Kokatí are—they never tell everything, and they don't trust white people."

"But you're one of them," Gina had protested, and immediately a dark curtain had dropped behind Jed's eyes.

"No, I'm not," he'd protested. "I'm not anything, remember? I'm not white, and I'm not Kokatí."

Ever since that day she'd realized there was a part of Jed Arnold that she barely knew. And so, in spite of his sometimes infuriating manner, she still went out with him, and tried to find a way to uncover what was really going on inside him.

As the final bell for the first class rang, breaking her reverie, she made up her mind. "Maybe you don't care if you're late, but I do," she said. She turned away from Jed and started down the hall.

"We're already late," she heard him say as he caught up to her. "But so what? The teacher's Jude Sheffield, and you know how crazy she is about me. I could walk in thirty minutes late and she wouldn't say a word." Sweeping Gina an exaggerated bow, he held the door to the classroom open and gestured her inside. The rest of the class, already in their seats, giggled appreciatively.

Judith, standing at the blackboard outlining the study program for the semester, turned to see what had caused the ripple of laughter in the room. Gina Alvarez, her face red with embarrassment, avoided Judith's eyes as she slid quickly into an empty seat in the back row. But Jed Arnold, his startlingly blue eyes fixed on her with the same cocksure expression she had seen all too often in East Los Angeles, was strolling nonchalantly toward a desk at the front.

"I'm terribly sorry, Jed," Judith said evenly. "I'm afraid I don't accept tardiness. If I can be here on time, so can you."

Jed stopped in his tracks, then grinned crookedly at the teacher. "Hey, what's the big deal? A couple of lousy minutes?"

Judith nodded. "They're *my* lousy minutes, Jed, and I don't like to waste them. If you'll come back during the next break, I'll give you the homework assignment."

Jed's mouth dropped open. Recovering himself, he asked: "What do you mean, come back? I'm not going anywhere." He made another move toward the empty desk.

Judith's expression hardened. "If you mean you're not going to that desk, you're right," she agreed. "I don't really care where you go or what you do, but please don't expect to come wandering in here any time the mood strikes you."

A tense silence fell over the room, but Judith kept her eyes firmly fixed on Jed. He still stood in the aisle next to the wall, but she already knew she'd won. If he intended to defy her, he'd have taken the seat and challenged her to remove him. But he didn't. Instead, his brows furrowed into an uncertain frown, which he quickly deepened into a deliberate scowl.

But the scowl didn't come quickly enough to hide from Judith the hurt that had come into his eyes. Ducking his head, he turned and strode out of the room.

For a split second Judith felt an urge to go after him, to bring him back into the room, but she put the urge aside, determined that her friendship with Jed was not going to interfere with the discipline of her classroom. As if nothing at all had happened, she turned back to the blackboard. But the silence she'd commanded lingered on, and as the chalk continued to scratch across the board, she heard none of the whispering that had preceded her confrontation with Jed.

She smiled to herself. Now that she had their attention, she could begin the process of teaching them. She reminded herself to find a way of thanking Jed for the opportunity he'd offered her. Unless she'd hurt him too badly. Unless he now felt that she too had betrayed him.

As the bell signaling lunch period rang and Judith watched her last morning class stream out of the room, she smiled to herself—obviously the word was getting around already that Miss Sheffield was not to be messed with. She'd sensed it at the start of the third period, when she'd spotted two potential troublemakers ambling in at precisely the moment the bell rang.

They were Randy Sparks and Jeff Hankins—friends of Jed's. So as they grinned insolently at her, she called them by name and told them to sit by the door. "That way there'll be less disruption when I throw you out," she'd explained with deliberate blandness. The rest of the class had snickered appreciatively, and both Randy and Jeff had reddened. But for the rest of the hour they'd sat quietly watching her, as if trying to figure her out. Since then there'd been no trouble at all.

Her door opened and a face appeared. "You have a date for lunch, or may I escort you to the lounge myself?" Judith's brow rose questioningly, and the man stepped inside. About the same age as Judith, he could have been handsome with his sandy hair and soft gray eyes, except for a tired cast to his face that Judith had seen before. Here, she thought immediately, is a man who shouldn't be teaching. Already, before he was thirty, he seemed to be worn out. "I'm Elliott Halvorson," he said, thrusting a hand toward her. "I thought you might like to meet some of your colleagues."

Judith took the proffered hand, then withdrew it when Halvorson seemed to hold it a little too long. You mean you thought you might make a pass at the new teacher, she thought to herself, more amused than offended. "Fine," she said, slinging her purse over her shoulder. She followed Halvorson out of the room, then turned right, toward the cafeteria. Halvorson reached out and took her arm. "Not that way," he said. "That direction leads only to the zoo."

"The zoo?" Judith repeated.

"That's what we call the cafeteria," Halvorson replied, grinning sourly. "All of us steer pretty clear of it. If you want to enjoy your lunch, the teachers' lounge is the only place."

Judith shook her head. "You go ahead," she said. "I think for at least today I'd like to see what's going on in the cafeteria."

Halvorson stared at her for a moment as if he thought she'd lost her marbles, but then he shrugged. "This," he said, "is going to be worth seeing." He fell in beside her, then paused when they were outside the cafeteria itself. "Tell you what," he offered. "If you last out the hour, I'll pay for your lunch."

Judith smiled. "You're on," she said. "And you might as well pay for it while we go through the line. It'll make the bookkeeping easier." She pulled open the door and was immediately assaulted by the blare of rock music, which almost drowned out the babble of voices as some of the kids tried to talk over the roar of heavy metal.

She glanced around and immediately saw the source of the din. At a table in the far corner, Jed Arnold sat with Randy Sparks, Jeff Hankins, Gina

Alvarez, and a couple of other kids whom Judith didn't recognize. As the ghetto-blaster on their table continued to fill the room with the roar of heavy metal, Jed leaned back in his chair and, using a knife as a catapult, flicked a pat of butter up to the ceiling, where it stuck, one more yellow blob in the midst of an already thick layer of previous shots. She watched in silence as Randy Sparks repeatedly tried to match Jed's achievement, raining butter down onto the surrounding tables. She began threading her way through the tables until she stood over Randy.

Reaching down, she pressed a button on the ghetto-blaster, cutting off the tape. In the sudden silence Randy looked up at her angrily.

"Hey, what do you think you're doing?" he demanded.

"Turning off the music," Judith replied. "In case you hadn't noticed, some of the people in here are trying to talk to each other."

Randy pushed his chair back and rose to his feet, spinning around to tower over Judith. But even as he turned, she expertly grasped his wrist, then twisted his arm back and up into a tight hammerlock. Randy winced with pain.

"Don't ever try to hit me," she told him so quietly only he could hear her words. "I threw Jed out of my class this morning, and I can throw you out of the cafeteria right now. So just sit down and be quiet, and let everyone enjoy his lunch. All right?"

Randy, his arm hurting too much for him to speak, managed to nod, and Judith released him, easing him back down into his chair as her eyes shifted to Jed. "Good trick with the butter," she observed, then gazed up at the ceiling. "If we say two and a half cents a pat, how much do you think all that's worth up there? And don't forget the cost of paint, at six dollars a gallon." All the kids at the table were silent now, glancing nervously at each other.

Judith, knowing she had their full attention, went on talking, keeping her tone almost conversational. "Of course, to get a good match, we'll have to paint the whole ceiling, and I think you can figure about two hundred square feet per gallon. Figure the price of the painter at $12.75 an hour, for, let's say, three and a quarter hours." She smiled at the six kids at the table who were in one or another of her classes. "Any of you who come within ten dollars of the total value of the damage and the repairs gets an automatic A on tomorrow morning's quiz, and I'll be back in five minutes to answer questions." Then, leaving all of the kids at the table except Jed staring at her in dumbfounded silence, she headed toward the cafeteria line, where Elliott Halvorson was waiting for her.

Jed, she noticed, was looking almost smug, as if she'd just done exactly what he'd expected her to do.

Elliott Halvorson, on the other hand, was anything but smug. "Are you out of your mind?" he asked as they started through the line. "Randy Sparks could sue the school for what you just did."

Judith nodded in agreement. "But he won't," she said. "In order for him to do that, he's going to have to own up to exactly what happened. And what's going to happen to his image when he has to admit to everyone in town that a teacher—a woman teacher, no less—took him?"

"But everybody already saw it," Halvorson pointed out.

"Ah, but that's different. If he tells them all he let me twist his arm on purpose because he didn't want to hurt me, he saves face." She loaded up her tray, then, after Halvorson had paid for both of them, started back toward the table.

Randy Sparks refused to meet her eyes, and Jed was no longer at the table at all. For a moment Judith wondered if perhaps she'd been wrong and he'd simply taken off, but then she spotted him.

He was walking along the far wall, carefully pacing off the dimensions of the cafeteria. Saying nothing, Judith sat down at the table and began eating, at the same time beginning her count of the butter pats that were stuck to the ceiling above her. Finally, as she began to work out the formula that would solve the problem she'd set for the kids, she reached over and turned the tape player back on, but with the volume turned so low that only the students at that table could hear it.

Five minutes before the end of the hour, she began collecting the napkins on which the kids had scribbled their solutions to the problem.

At last she looked up, not surprised to find all six of the kids at the table watching her warily. "Okay," she said. "It's not bad at all. It's good enough so everyone except Jed gets an A tomorrow." Her eyes met Jed's. "You want to tell me why your price is so high?"

Jed shrugged. "You forgot something," he said. "You didn't figure in how much it was going to cost for someone to clean up the mess before the painting could start. Paint won't stick to grease."

Judith was silent for a moment, then slowly nodded. "Touché," she said, as she marked Jed's napkin with an A+, then handed it back to him.

As she left the cafeteria a few minutes later with a very quiet Elliott Halvorson at her side, she could feel not only Jed's eyes, but the eyes of all the students, staring speculatively at her.

* * *

Greg Moreland glanced up at the clock, surprised to see that the day was half over. Already this morning he'd been out to The Cottonwoods, where he'd examined Reba Tucker once more. Her condition had deteriorated—she'd been through yet another series of tiny strokes the night before—but still she hung on. Her vital signs were almost as strong as ever, and so far her heart and lungs seemed totally unaffected by what was happening to her brain.

Her brain, Greg knew, was being slowly destroyed, and he couldn't help but wonder how much longer Reba would be able to hang on.

One more massive stroke—the kind she'd had the day she collapsed in her classroom—would do it. Indeed, Greg wasn't sure that such a thing wouldn't be a blessing for the woman now.

Her eyes, as she'd stared up at him that morning, had been terrified, and her mouth had worked almost as if she was trying to speak. But speech had long since become impossible for her; all she was capable of now was a stream of incoherent screams that occasionally erupted from her, screams generated by pain or by terror.

He wasn't sure which, for he knew full well that it could be either one. The strokes Reba had suffered could as easily induce phantom pain as phantom terror. The anguish for Reba would be as great whichever emotion she experienced, assuming she was aware of her condition at all. Greg hoped that Reba's mind was now so far gone that she had no knowledge of her own situation.

In a week—two at the most—she would be dead, and it would, indeed, be a blessing.

He put Reba out of his mind, and picked up the reports on his desk, studying them carefully.

Five minutes later Greg left his office, heading downtown toward the Borrego Building and the last appointment of his day.

It was an appointment he wasn't looking forward to.

Chapter 10

Otto Kruger glanced out the window of the small office in the control building of the dam, far up Mordida Canyon. He didn't need to look at the clock to see that it was almost quitting time—the dark shadow of the descending sun creeping up the canyon's wall told him the time to within a few minutes. Then, uneasily, his eyes went to the rim of the canyon itself, and the lone figure who stood watching there.

It was Brown Eagle. He stood at the canyon's edge, unmoving, his figure imbued with the same unsettling concentration Otto had only seen before in the birds for which the Indian was named. At first, when Brown Eagle had taken up his sentry's stance early in the afternoon, Otto had only glanced at him casually, then forgotten about him. Bill Watkins, the dam supervisor, had told him people from Kokatí often appeared above the dam, looking down at it for a few moments, their faces set in silent reproof at the dam's very existence, then quietly moving off to go about their business.

But Brown Eagle had remained all afternoon, his stance never changing, not a muscle in his lean body so much as twitching. It had finally begun to make Otto nervous, and he'd considered sending someone up to send the man on his way, but Brown Eagle was doing no harm. If the Indian wanted to stand around like a fool, what concern was it of his?

Still, the presence of the Indian watcher was making him increasingly uneasy, as if something in the Kokatí's gaze compelled his attention; as if it wasn't actually the dam the old man was concentrating on, but he himself.

It was almost, indeed, as if the Indian somehow knew why he was up at the dam that afternoon, and was waiting for the same thing he was waiting for.

The hell with him, Otto finally told himself. So they all hate us, and hate the dam. So what? Irritated, he finished reading Watkins's reports of the day's activities and shoved them in the envelope he would drop off at Max Moreland's office on his way home.

Like a damned messenger boy, he thought, resenting once more the extra workload that had been put on his shoulders as the company was forced to lay off more and more people.

But not for long, he reminded himself. The company was losing too much money for Max to hang on much longer. Soon—perhaps even today —Moreland would face up to reality.

His thoughts were interrupted as a red light began to flash on the control panel in front of him. At the same time a bell sounded sharply in the building, while a siren began to wail outside, echoing eerily off the canyon walls.

His pulse quickening, Kruger dropped the reports back onto the desk. A moment later Bill Watkins burst in the door, shoving Otto aside as he began scanning the dials and indicators on the control board.

"What the hell's happening?" Kruger demanded. Watkins didn't answer. The tendons of his neck standing out starkly, he began twisting knobs and throwing switches. He snatched up a telephone and began barking orders into it.

"Get the main diversion valve open now, then close the number-one intake. And get that shaft clear! Shut down the turbine and get it drained."

Otto's eyes widened slightly as the implications of Watkins's words penetrated his mind, and his eyes instinctively left the control panel to gaze out the window at the dam itself. Though nothing appeared to have changed, men were suddenly spilling out of the doorway that led to the interior of the dam. Some of them were sprinting toward the control shack; others were leaning out over the dam, staring down at its concrete face.

Abruptly, as quickly as it had begun, the siren and bell fell silent.

Otto looked back to Watkins, who was now perched on a chair while he studied the array of meters spread out on the control panel before him.

"What was it?" Otto asked again, and this time Watkins replied.

"Something's gone haywire in the main power shaft. Looks like it may have developed a crack."

"Jesus," Otto breathed, turning back to gaze at the dam. "It isn't going to—"

Watkins gave Otto's back a sour look. "It's not gonna come down, no. Far from it. When Sam Moreland built that dam, he did it right." He leaned back in the chair, unconsciously rubbing at the tension in his neck. "What we've got here is what you might call a minor inconvenience," he said in a laconic drawl. "I'd reckon we're gonna have to cut the power to the refinery in about half, maybe more. 'Course, we're gonna have to shut the wells off completely in order to keep the refinery going at all."

Otto swallowed, trying to keep his expression impassive. But it was plain that this was the final blow. Max would have to sell out now. Watkins gazed at him steadily, almost as if he could read Otto's mind.

"Wouldn't have happened if you'd shown some balls about the maintenance program last month," he pointed out.

Otto's eyes narrowed. "We needed to save money," he said, his voice tight. "I was told we could save twenty-five thousand by skipping it, and not sacrifice safety at all. Max approved it." It wasn't quite the truth, for the maintenance reports Max had signed were slightly different from the ones Kruger had placed in the files. For the most part they were accurate; only one page had been changed.

One page, detailing the maintenance work that Kruger had ordered not to be done. But the signature at the bottom of the work order was still Max Moreland's.

"Is that so?" Watkins drawled, his tongue exploring the hollow where he'd lost a wisdom tooth a year ago. "Well, now, it looks like whoever told you that was a little off target, weren't they?" He hauled himself to his feet, then, without saying another word to Otto, left the control shack to go inspect the power shaft personally.

Alone, Otto savored the moment, then finally picked up the phone. He wished he could see the look on Max's face when Moreland understood that it was all over, that he was finally going to have to sell Borrego Oil.

This time, Kruger knew, there were no funds left to repair the damage.

As he waited for someone to pick up the call at the other end, Otto's eyes went once more to the rim of the canyon.

Brown Eagle was gone.

Otto frowned deeply. It was almost as if the Indian had known what was going to happen to the dam, and had been waiting to see it.

But that was impossible—he couldn't have known.

Could he?

A cold chill passed through Otto Kruger's body.

Max Moreland sat behind the huge mahogany desk his father had shipped out to the wilds of New Mexico almost seventy years earlier. His eyes were fixed on the papers laid out neatly in front of him, but his mind kept drifting back over all those years, the years when he'd been a little boy, accompanying his father as the old man wildcatted the area, spending most of his time capping the artesian wells he'd hit while drilling for oil, then moving on to the next likely spot. Finally Sam Moreland had found what he was looking for. First one well, then another and another. He'd borrowed against the wells to build the first small refinery, and gone on reinvesting his profits to drill more wells and expand the refinery, building Borrego Oil into an enterprise large enough to support a town of nearly ten thousand people. Now it looked as if his father's work and his own were all going to crumble away.

Slowly, he looked up from the papers he had been studying. He loved this office, with its softly glowing mahogany paneling, and the perfectly woven Two Grey Hills rug that had covered the floor since the day the Borrego Building had been completed at the corner of First and E Streets, establishing a new center for the dusty village. His eyes swept over the collection of Kachina dolls his father had begun and he had kept expanding. They covered a whole wall now. For some reason he found himself idly wondering if he should leave them where they were or take them with him if he had to vacate this office.

It was becoming increasingly clear that vacating the office was something he was going to have to do. Though part of Borrego's problems lay with the crash in oil prices a few years ago, he also knew that part of the problem lay within himself.

He simply hadn't kept up with the times.

Much of the refinery was obsolete, and there were all kinds of new drilling methods that could conceivably double or even treble crude oil output. He had fallen behind.

But to make Borrego Oil prosper again would take money, and there was no more. He'd spent it all to keep his obsolete refinery operating, then borrowed more.

Yet something in him refused to accept the inevitable. He stared again at the papers in front of him—the papers that would sell the whole outfit, lock, stock, and barrel, to UniChem for what he knew was more than a fair price. He was still having trouble bringing himself to sign them.

All day he'd been looking for a way to keep his promise to Frank Arnold —and a lot of other people—that the employees would have first crack at buying the company if it ever became necessary for him to sell it.

But what would he be giving them?

A pile of debts on an obsolete plant.

And they'd have to take on more debt if they were ever to have a hope of making the company pay off.

If, of course, they could find a lender, which was highly unlikely, given the climate of the oil industry and the net worth of Borrego's assets.

And yet he still kept working, searching for something he might have forgotten, hunting for something that might postpone the inevitable.

But he hadn't been able to refuse to see Paul Kendall, the representative from UniChem who had first approached him with a buyout offer months earlier. He'd instinctively liked Kendall, a large, ruddy-faced man in his mid-forties who vaguely reminded Max of himself at the same age. And Kendall knew how he felt, even taking the time to show Max some of the places where things had gone wrong over the suddenly all-too-quick passing of the last quarter of a century.

"Nobody could ever accuse you of mismanagement, Mr. Moreland," Kendall had assured him. "Lord knows, you did your best, and for a long time it was about as good as it gets. But you were all by yourself out here, and the industry just sort of passed you by. And who could predict what was going to happen to oil prices? It's been years, and they're just starting to recover."

As the weeks went by, he and Kendall had continued bargaining. Max had to admit that Kendall had been more than fair. He and Rita would come out of it with more money than they'd ever need, and UniChem had committed to an immense infusion of new capital into the operation.

Max had been suspicious at first, certain, just as Frank Arnold was, that UniChem would shut down the refinery and simply begin piping the crude to their own facilities farther west. Kendall had insisted that that wasn't the intention at all. He and the rest of UniChem's management projected a strong market ahead, and foresaw a need for more refineries, not fewer. Max had finally called his bluff.

With a stare so intense it chilled Kendall's soul, he asked: "Then you're willing to sign a guarantee that the refinery remains in operation for twenty-five years?"

Kendall laughed out loud. "Of course not," he said. "But I think you'd settle for ten, wouldn't you?"

At that moment Max knew he could not resist much longer.

Now, he focused his attention once more on the papers in front of him, and took up his pen. He was just signing the last page of the agreement when his intercom chimed softly and his secretary informed him that Otto Kruger was on the line.

Tiredly, he picked up the receiver. "Yes, Otto? What is it?"

Across the room, Paul Kendall looked up when the phone rang. He had been sitting at a conference table with Greg Moreland, quietly explaining to the younger man the complex series of documents that comprised the offer for the company, while he let the older man adjust to the inevitable in any way he could. He gestured to the extension on the conference table, and when Max nodded, pressed a button that amplified Kruger's voice so both he and Greg could hear it clearly.

". . . it's going to mean a shutdown of the dam, Max," they heard Kruger saying. "And the wells, and maybe the refinery too." Kendall saw the blood drain from Max Moreland's face.

When the call was over, Paul Kendall faced Max. "If it'll make you feel any better, Mr. Moreland, none of this will affect our offer. The offer stands as it is, and we'll deal with the problem at the dam."

Max said nothing for a moment. His expression grim, he punched at a button on his intercom. "I want the maintenance files on the dam," he said. The color had come back into his face, and his voice seemed suddenly to have strengthened.

Kendall glanced questioningly at Greg, who shrugged but said nothing, as Max's secretary entered the office, carrying three thick file folders. She laid them on Max's desk, then turned to go.

"Take him with you, please," Max snapped, nodding toward Kendall and already beginning to flip through the files. Kendall started to object, but Max silenced him with a glance. "I'm sorry, Mr. Kendall," he said. "I want to know what happened out there at that dam, and until I know, I'm afraid I can't let you sign these papers. For the moment this deal is on hold." He slid Kendall's documents into the center drawer of his desk, then locked it.

Kendall frowned. "But I already told you—"

"I heard what you said," Max interrupted. "And it may not make any difference to you and your company, but it makes a hell of a difference to me. I don't sell shit for the price of fertilizer."

Kendall's brows rose slightly, but he followed the secretary out of the office without another word. When the door had closed behind him, Max looked up again, this time fixing his gaze on Greg. "Something's going on," he said, his voice dropping. "Take a look at this."

Greg crossed to his uncle's desk and leaned over to look at the page that lay exposed in the file folder. The notations on the page were as indecipherable to him as his prescriptions were to his patients. "What is it?"

"The results of the last inspection of the dam, and the orders for repairs that needed to be made. Except that what's here and what I signed are not the same."

Greg frowned. "I'm not sure I understand . . ."

Max's fist clenched angrily. "It means that what I authorized—hell, what

I *ordered*—wasn't done. I may be getting old, but I remember what I read, and what I sign. And what I signed was an order that all the cracks in the main drive flume were to be repaired. But those orders aren't here. Christ, anyone who looks at this would have to assume I'd lost my grip completely!" His voice was rising now and a vein was beginning to stand out on his forehead. "God damn it—look at this! Here's Watkins's report on the damage they found at the last inspection." He picked up the page and began reading it out loud. " 'Transverse cracking at the intake—erosion of the primary casing in the area of the turbine.' Hell, there's ten or fifteen items here, and every single one should have been taken care of. But according to this, I didn't authorize any repairs. Which is a damned lie!" His fist slammed down on the desk and he fairly trembled with rage.

"Now take it easy," Greg said, alarmed by his uncle's fury. "You might be wrong. You might have thought you authorized those repairs but forgot—"

"No!" Max roared. "I don't forget things like that. Not something as important as that dam." He fell silent for a moment, sitting still, his mind working quickly as he tried to figure out what might have happened.

"All right," he said, his breathing slowly coming back to normal as his rage subsided and reason took over. "Here's what we're going to do. You tell Kendall he's going to have to wait until at least tomorrow. And in the meantime I'm going to have a little talk with Otto Kruger. This whole thing smells, and the only thing that could have happened is that Kruger changed the orders after I signed them. And that," he added, "seems to me like a pretty good indication that someone's been paying him off." A cold grin spread across his face and his eyes shifted to the door through which Paul Kendall had passed only a few moments ago. "Now, who do you suppose would have been interested in paying Otto off to sabotage the dam?" he asked. His voice hardened. "If I can pin this on that son of a bitch, we won't need to sell this company at all."

"Even if you can prove it, what difference will it make?" Greg asked. "It would mean a lawsuit, and that would drag on for years. We don't have the time for something like that, let alone the money—"

"We'll find it," Max declared, his voice suddenly stronger than Greg had heard it in years. "I'm damned if I'm going to let them just squeeze me out like this." He picked up the phone and began dialing, then gestured toward the door. "Go on—get rid of Kendall, and don't say a word about these orders. If I'm right, I want to take him by surprise."

Greg, knowing there was no point in arguing with his uncle, stood up and left the office. Paul Kendall was waiting in the anteroom beyond the secretary's office. As he came in, Kendall rose to his feet.

"What's going on?"

Greg shrugged. "Nothing much. He just wants to find out what happened to the dam. I don't think anything else is going to happen until tomorrow."

Kendall eyed Greg shrewdly. "He's not thinking of backing out of this deal, is he? He'll never get a better offer."

Greg shook his head. "That's not it at all," he said. "You just don't know Uncle Max. If the dam's in really bad shape, he'll insist on lowering the price of the company."

"Come off it, Greg," Kendall replied. "If we're still willing to pay the price, why should he accept less?"

Greg's lips curved in a thin smile. "Because that's the way he is. Maybe he's the last honest businessman."

Again Kendall regarded Greg narrowly. "But he'll go through with the deal?" he pressed.

Greg hesitated, then nodded. "Yes," he said. "He'll go through with the deal. He's already signed the papers, and no matter what he thinks, he doesn't really have much choice, does he?" He offered Kendall his hand. "Now, if you'll excuse me, I've got some things I have to attend to at my office."

Kendall grasped Greg's proffered hand, shaking it firmly. "Then I'll see you here tomorrow."

Once again Greg nodded. "Tomorrow."

Max drove slowly, his mind only half concentrating on the road ahead of him. The sun was dropping low, and the sky to the west was beginning to glow a brilliant red, shot through with orange, purple, and magenta. But Max saw none of it. Instead, his mind was whirling. Was it really possible, after all these years, that Otto Kruger had betrayed him?

Of course it was. Kruger was as aware as anyone of the financial condition of the company, and Max had known almost since the day he'd hired Kruger that the man's number-one interest was himself. If someone had come along and offered him a deal, Kruger wasn't the sort who would refuse, particularly when the alternative would almost certainly be to end up working for Frank Arnold.

Frank Arnold.

How the hell was he going to explain to Frank what had happened? How many times had he told Frank that when the time came to sell, the employees would have the first opportunity?

But he'd waited too long, and now selling to the employees, no matter the condition of the dam, would be the wrong thing to do. Despite the bravado of his words, he knew that Greg was right.

He had neither the time nor the money for a long legal battle which, in the end, he'd probably lose anyway.

He was on the mesa now, driving along the dirt road that led up to the dam, and as he finally looked out over the canyon, the last of his cold fury drained away from him. It wasn't just the time and money he was lacking for a fight with UniChem, he realized.

He lacked the stomach for it too.

Better to give it up gracefully, he decided, admit when he'd been beaten. Losing, after all, was losing, whether Kruger had sold out or not. In the end it really didn't matter, for in the end the condition of the dam was his responsibility, not Kruger's. He knew what repairs he'd ordered, and he should have been up at the dam to make sure they were done.

If he wasn't going to do his job, it was time to step down. With a UniChem buyout, at least he could secure the future of all the people who worked for him for another ten years, and none of them would have to live with the constant specter of debt that had hung over him for more than a decade.

It would be all right, once they got over the shock of it.

And he'd be all right too.

No!

He'd be damned if he would be betrayed like this, and just fade quietly away into oblivion.

Never!

He frowned suddenly as a sharp stab of pain lashed through his head.

His fingers tightened on the wheel and he reflexively closed his eyes for a moment, as if to shut out the searing pain in his skull. A noxious odor, rotten and pervasive, invaded his nostrils. When he opened his eyes, his vision was blurred behind a thick red haze.

The pain slashed at his brain again, even more powerfully this time, and his whole body went into a convulsive spasm.

A second later the spasm passed, and Max's own weight pulled the steering wheel around as he slumped over into the passenger seat.

The car veered off the road, lurched toward the edge of the canyon, then struck a boulder.

It jerked to a halt, its front end collapsing under the sudden impact. The engine died almost immediately.

The windshield didn't shatter, and the driver's door swung open, one of its hinges broken from the stress of the impact.

It would have been easy for anyone to have crawled out of the wreckage, unharmed.

Anyone, that is, except Max Moreland.

For Max, at the age of seventy-five, had already died even before the car left the road and slammed into the boulder.

Perhaps he'd died even before that.

Perhaps he'd died in his office when he'd finally affixed his signature to the UniChem documents, giving up the company that had been his whole life.

It no longer made any difference *when* Max had died.

The only thing that would make a difference was *how* he had died.

Chapter 11

The chill of the desert night had already settled in. Frank Arnold lingered in the cab of his pickup truck, gazing at the squat building that had once been the social center of Borrego. Only a few years ago, when the company had been making plenty of money, the union hall had been well-kept, its exterior freshly painted every year, its lawns regularly watered and mowed at least once a week during the summer. Now, even in the shadowed light from a rising moon, the deterioration of the building was visible. The union hall, like the rest of Borrego, was showing the effects of the ill-fortune that had befallen the company. Its paint was beginning to peel away, and the lawns had been allowed to die, slowly becoming overgrown with sagebrush and tumbleweed.

Part of the neglect, Frank knew, was a simple lack of money. As raises had become scarcer—and smaller—but prices had continued to rise, the union's support from its members had begun to dwindle. The negative attitude had grown slowly, but pervasively: What good was the union, if it couldn't win a better standard of living for its members? And so the weekend get-togethers at the hall, the Friday-night dances and the Saturday softball games on the field behind the hall, had slowly dwindled away too, until there were no longer either the funds or the interest to keep them up.

The glare of headlights swept through the cab of the truck as another car pulled into the parking lot and came to a stop a few feet away. Frank stirred, then got out and greeted Tom Kennedy, the attorney who had driven up from Santa Fe to help Frank answer the mass of questions tonight's meeting would surely generate.

Together the two men went inside the hall, and while Frank turned on the lights and heat, Kennedy began setting up a table on the small platform at the far end of the main meeting room.

"How many do you think will turn up?" Kennedy asked as Frank straightened the rows of folding chairs facing the platform.

"Couple hundred, maybe. I should think a lot of the wives would show up too."

But half an hour later, when Frank finally banged his gavel on the table and stood to call the meeting to order, he had counted fewer than a hundred people. It was not surprising, really. A rumor that the company had already been sold had spread like wildfire, and even most of the men who had come to the meeting looked as though they didn't think anything could be done. He knew he had already lost. But still, he had to try. He glanced down at the notes he had put together over dinner that evening, but just as he was about to begin, the door opened and Jerry Polanski stepped into the room, his face pale. He signaled to Frank, but then, instead of waiting for Frank to come to him, he hurried down the center aisle and leaped up onto the platform.

"Max is dead, Frank," he said, bending over the table and keeping his voice so low that no one except Frank and Tom Kennedy could hear him.

Frank stared numbly at Polanski.

"They found him half an hour ago," Polanski went on. "He was on his way to the dam, and his car went off the road."

Frank's hands clenched into tight fists, his knuckles turning white. "Jesus," he breathed, sinking back into his chair.

He struggled against his own emotions for a moment, his eyes moistening as a choking sob rose in his throat. He'd known Max Moreland all his life. He'd both liked and respected the man, and known his feelings had been reciprocated. And even though in recent years they'd often been forced to meet as adversaries, their personal relationship had never changed.

Now Max was gone.

Finally conquering the emotions that threatened to overwhelm him, Frank gazed uncertainly out at the crowd. They were all looking at him with guarded expressions, as if they knew that some new disaster was about to be revealed. His voice shaking slightly, Frank began to speak.

"You all know why I called this meeting," he began. "It was my hope that we could find a way to buy Borrego Oil from Max Moreland, even though he apparently agreed to sell it to UniChem today." He hesitated, then forged on. "Tom Kennedy, here, thought there might have been a way, but . . ." His voice trailed off again, but once more he gripped his emotions in the vise of his will. "But I'm afraid all that is past us now. I've just been told that Max is dead."

There was a moment of shocked silence in the hall, and then a babble of voices rose. Frank banged the gavel hard on the table. Slowly the rumbling began to subside. "I'm afraid we don't know exactly what happened," he went on. "But given the circumstances, I don't see any reason for this meeting to go on. So, if there is no objection, it's adjourned."

He banged the gavel once more, then dropped back into his chair.

Immediately the room came to life. A crowd gathered around the table, and voices shouted questions at Jerry Polanski, who could only repeat what he'd already told Frank. After several minutes Frank leaned over to Tom Kennedy.

"Let's get out of here. I need a drink."

As Kennedy began shoving papers in his briefcase, Frank pushed his chair back and began making his way through the crowd, ignoring the hands that plucked at his sleeve and the voices that shouted questions in his ear. Outside the hall, he paused for a moment, taking a deep breath of the cold night air in a vain effort to wash his mind clear of the ugly suspicions that were already beginning to take form in his head.

An hour later, he sat by himself at a table in the bar at the back of the café. Tom Kennedy, Jerry Polanski, Carlos Alvarez, and a few other men sat at other tables, the faces changing as they drifted from spot to spot. Frank stared at the shot glass in front of him, which contained the first half of his fourth boilermaker. He was looking for numbness in the liquor, a cessation of thought. So far, though, his mind was still clear.

Clear, and functioning all too well.

He knocked back the whiskey, then took three fast swallows of beer, finally banging the stein down on the table with a force that silenced the conversation.

"They killed him," he said, giving voice for the first time to the suspicions that had been roiling in his mind since the moment he'd left the union hall.

One of the recent arrivals—Jesus Hernandez, an electrician from the dam—heard his remark and stared at him, his mouth twisting into a half-drunken grin. "Killed him? C'mon, Frank," he mumbled. "Why the hell would anyone wanta kill ol' Max? He was a good ol' boy." He raised an arm and waved to the waitress. "Hey, Katie. Bring us another round, and come listen to what ol' Frank says."

Katie Alvarez came over with a tray of drinks. After she'd placed glasses on several tables and another boilermaker in front of Frank, she shifted her attention to Jesus Hernandez. "So what's Frank say that I've got to hear?" she asked, feigning more interest than she actually felt. She'd learned long ago that customers left better tips if you listened to their hard-luck stories.

"He thinks the guys from UniChem killed Max Moreland," Hernandez replied, downing half his fresh drink. "Can you believe that?"

For the first time in weeks something a customer said finally seized Katie's attention. "Killed him?" she repeated, echoing Hernandez's words. "Why would they want to do that?"

Frank tossed back his fifth shot of whiskey, chased it with a gulp of beer, then wiped his mouth with his shirt-sleeve.

"Keep him from making trouble," he said, his words slurring now as the alcohol in his blood began to penetrate his brain. "I coulda talked him out of it, and everybody knew it," he went on. "I told Kruger that just the other day. Told him I could figure out a way. So they fixed it so I couldn't even talk to 'im." His eyes wandered over the messy tabletop. "Bastards," he mumbled, only half aloud. "The bastards jus' went ahead an' killed ol' Max."

Katie glanced around the bar nervously. If what he'd said got back to UniChem, Frank would be fired for sure, but no one at any of the other tables seemed to have heard. If she could get him to go home and sleep it off . . . . "Come on, Frank," she said. "You've had too much to drink, and you're just upset. That's crazy talk, and you don't believe it any more than anyone else does." She had a hand on his arm now and was easing him gently to his feet. "Now, why don't you just go on home and get some sleep. Okay?"

Frank shook her hand off, then wheeled around to glare drunkenly at her. He staggered, then braced himself against the table to keep from falling. "I'm telling you," he said. "Somethin's goin' on around here." His eyes narrowed and he searched Katie's face. "What are you, part of the whole thing?" he asked. "You got something goin' with that guy from UniChem —what's his name? Kendall?"

Katie felt her temper rise. She knew what a lot of people in town thought of her; it was no different from what people thought of cocktail waitresses everywhere. But she'd thought Frank Arnold was different. Then she remembered that he was drunk. "Right," she said, forcing herself to grin at him. "I've never even met the man, but I'm screwing his brains out every night. Okay? Now come on." She took his arm again, steering him gently toward the door, and by the time she got him outside, he seemed to have steadied slightly. "You think you can drive?" she asked. "I can get someone to take you."

But Frank shook his head. "I'm okay," he said, taking a deep breath of air, then shaking his whole body almost like a dog ridding itself of water. He pulled open the door of the truck and swung up into the cab. Then he rolled down the window and spoke to Katie once more. "Sorry about what I said in there. I guess maybe I've had too much to drink."

Katie chuckled. "I guess maybe you have," she agreed, then patted his arm reassuringly. "Look, Frank, take it easy, okay? Drive carefully, and don't go shooting your mouth off about Max. If what you said in there gets back to UniChem or Otto Kruger, they might can you."

"Kruger'll try to do that anyhow," Frank replied. "But he can't, 'cause I won't give him any reason to. That's what the union's for, right?"

Katie shook her head in mock despair, but decided to have one last try at reasoning with him. "Frank, you don't know what happened to Max. But if you start telling everyone he was killed, that's libel, or slander, or something, and I bet they can fire you for it."

"They can't if it's true," Frank growled. He slammed the truck into gear, his rear wheels spinning in the loose gravel as he took off. The free-spinning tires screeched in protest when they finally hit the pavement, then they caught and the truck jackrabbited across the road. For a split second Katie thought Frank had lost control completely, but then the vehicle swerved around, straightened out, and took off down the street. She watched him go until he turned the corner two blocks away, then shook her head tiredly and went back into the café. She had a feeling Frank Arnold wasn't the only drunk she was going to have to deal with that night. The bar seemed to be full of them.

Frank rolled both windows down, and the cold air washed over his face, sobering him slightly. He was driving well, keeping his speed ten miles below the limit, and the steering steady. But one more drink and he wouldn't have been able to drive at all.

It was another five minutes before he realized where he was going, although as he turned onto the long gravel drive that led up a rise to the foot of the mesa where Max Moreland's parents had built their great Victorian pile of a house so many years ago, he knew he'd decided to come out here as soon as he'd left the café.

He wanted to talk to Judith Sheffield, wanted her to listen to him, to believe him.

And besides, he rationalized, the least he could do right now was pay his respects to Rita Moreland.

Kill two birds with one stone. The trite words seemed to slur even in his mind.

He pulled unsteadily up in front of the house, slewing his truck in next to

Greg Moreland's worn Jeep Wagoneer. He climbed the steep flight of steps to the wide veranda that fronted the house, then leaned heavily against the doorframe for a moment as a wave of dizziness swept over him. Maybe, after all, he shouldn't have come out here. But then the door opened and Judith Sheffield, her face ashen and streaked with tears, looked out at him.

They stared at each other wordlessly for a moment, then Judith took a step forward. Frank's arms slid around her, and her face pressed against his chest. A single sob shook her, and then she felt Frank gently stroking her hair. Regaining her composure, she stepped back. "I—I'm so glad you're here. It's terrible."

Frank, feeling suddenly sober, nodded. "How's Rita taking it?"

Judith managed a weak smile. "On the surface, better than I am, I guess. But you know Rita—no matter what happens, she never loses her composure. She's in the living room." Taking Frank's hand, she led him into the house.

Rita Moreland, her lean body held erect and every strand of her white hair in place, stood up as they entered. "Frank," she said, taking his hand and clasping it tightly. "I'm so glad you've come. I was going to call you, but . . ." Her voice trailed off.

"I should have called you, Rita," Frank replied. "In fact, I should have come out as soon as I heard."

Rita shook her head. "Don't even think it. Greg is here, and there have been people in and out all evening."

Frank felt a wave of nausea as the alcohol in his blood regained its grip on him, and he swayed slightly. "I—I don't know what to say," he mumbled. "I just can't believe he's dead. Not Max. He was so—" He faltered, unable to find the words he was looking for.

"I know," Rita told him, gently steering him toward a sofa and signaling Greg to pour a cup of coffee from the immense silver urn that stood on a sideboard. "We're all going to miss him terribly, but we're going to go on, just as he would have wanted us to." She perched stiffly on the edge of a wing-backed chair opposite the sofa.

Greg came over and set a cup of coffee on the table in front of Frank. "Looks like you've had a couple of drinks—" he began, but before he could finish the sentence, Rita Moreland's melodic voice smoothly cut in.

"I think I could use one myself, Greg. I think perhaps a shot of your uncle's bourbon might be in order." Though she spoke to Greg, her eyes never left Frank Arnold. "Frank?"

Frank hesitated, then shook his head. "I think I've had enough, Rita. In fact, I probably shouldn't have come out here tonight—"

"Nonsense," Rita replied, letting just enough sharpness come into her voice to let Frank know she meant what she was saying and was not simply being polite. "Outside the family, no one in town was closer to Max than you were."

Frank nodded, then licked nervously at his lips. He knew he shouldn't say what he was about to say, but he also knew he wasn't going to be able to stop himself. And there was something in the way Rita was looking at him that told him she already knew what he was about to say. "I think they killed him," he blurted.

Rita Moreland, hand extended to accept the drink Greg was holding out to her, didn't so much as flinch. Her eyes remained on Frank. "Go on," she said softly.

Frank met her steady gaze. "I don't know what happened to Max, but I can't believe it was just an accident. I think they must have run him off the road or something." He began speaking faster, his words tumbling over one another as they rushed from his mind to his mouth. "Max was a good driver. He would never have just run off the road like that. And think about it—UniChem wanted the company, and Max didn't want them to have it —he wanted to sell it to us, he told me so—"

"Now just a minute," Greg Moreland interrupted. He set the drink on the coffee table in front of his aunt, as Rita's eyes remained fixed on Frank, her face an expressionless mask. Greg glared at Frank. "You've had way too much to drink, Frank, and I don't know what you're thinking, coming in here tonight—of all nights—and throwing around charges like that. You don't know what you're talking about."

"I know what I think—" Frank began, but once again an indignant Greg Moreland cut him off.

"You know what you imagine," he shot back. "If you want to know what happened, I—or even Aunt Rita—will be glad to tell you! It was a one-car accident, Frank. And it wasn't even Uncle Max's fault. He was already dead when the car went off the road."

Frank frowned, as if he couldn't quite put the words together. "I don't—"

"You don't get it?" Greg finished for him, his voice crackling with anger. "Well, maybe if you hadn't gone out and gotten drunk tonight, you *would* get it. He died at the wheel, Frank. He'd just sold the company, which except for Aunt Rita was the only thing that meant anything to him. He was under a lot of strain, and he had a stroke while at the wheel. That's what killed him, Frank. Not the accident. A stroke. He was already dead when the accident happened."

Frank, dazed, sank back into his chair. His eyes fixed on Greg Moreland, but he could see by the anger in Greg's eyes that Max's nephew was telling him the truth. Finally he managed to shift his gaze to Rita Moreland, a wave of shame sweeping over him as he saw the pain in her eyes.

The pain he'd caused her, with his drunken accusations.

"I—I'm sorry, Rita," he said, pulling himself to his feet and managing a single step toward her before collapsing back onto the chair.

His words seemed to trigger something in Rita Moreland, and suddenly she came alive again. "It's all right," she said, the forgiving words coming to her almost automatically. "We've all had a terrible shock today."

"It's not all right," Greg Moreland broke in, his voice cold. "He had no right to come out here and upset you that way, Aunt Rita. I ought to call the police."

But Rita held up a protesting hand. "There's no need for that, Greg. I've known Frank for a good many more years than I've known even you. If you'll just call Jed, perhaps—"

"It seems to me he got out here under his own steam—" Greg began, but Rita shook her head.

"We don't need any more cars going off the road today, Greg. Please, just call Jed."

"You don't need to call him," Judith put in quickly, anxious to calm the situation before Frank's temper might erupt. "I'll take him home, and Jed can drive me back."

Greg seemed about to argue, but a look from his aunt changed his mind. As he stalked out of the room a moment later, he glared at Judith, and for an instant she had the strangest feeling that he was jealous. But why would he be? Since she'd been back in Borrego, he hadn't shown the slightest interest in her. "I—I'll just go up and get my coat," she stammered, feeling as if she had somehow inadvertently made a bad situation even worse.

When Judith too was out of the room, Rita Moreland finally picked up the untouched drink from the coffee table, stared at it for a moment, then drained it. She paused as if waiting for the alcohol to fortify her, once more met Frank's eyes. "I want you to know I understand how you feel," she said gently, her voice now free of the carefully controlled graciousness she had mastered so many years ago that it had become second nature to her. "In fact, the same thought you just expressed crossed my mind too. Max called me just before he died. Something had happened, and even though he'd already signed the papers, he said he had time to back out. And he intended to do it." She shrugged helplessly. "I'm not sure what the problem was—he didn't tell me. But I have to tell you the first thing I thought when Greg told me what had happened was that somehow—for some reason—they'd killed him. But I was wrong, Frank. Greg assures me it was a stroke, Frank, pure and simple. Max was at an age when those things can happen, and Greg had warned him about the possibility for months. It was just one of those things that nobody can predict."

Frank's sense of shame deepened.

He'd come out here to offer his condolences and express his sorrow.

Instead, Rita Moreland was comforting him.

Jed came awake slowly. Darkness surrounded him, yet his room was filled with a strange silvery glow, as if a full moon was somehow shining through the ceiling itself. But when he looked at the window, the night outside was a velvety black.

The glow was somehow coming from within the room itself.

He sat up, then gasped.

Perched on the top rail of his cast-iron bedstead was an enormous bird. It looked like an eagle, but Jed was certain he'd never seen one this large. Indeed, as he watched, it suddenly spread its wings and its feathers filled the room, spreading from one wall to the other. Jed felt his heart begin to pound, and he involuntarily shrank back. But a second later the bird settled down again and its head turned sideways so that one of its eyes fixed on Jed.

It was from the giant bird's eye that the silvery light emanated, a cold radiance that hung in the room, yet did not wash away the darkness. When Jed held up his hand to shield his eyes against it, he found that his hand was invisible. Though he could feel his fingers touching his face, the bird's image remained before him, as clear as ever.

The bird's beak opened, and a single word issued forth from its throat.

"Come."

Jed froze as he recognized the voice that had risen from the maw of the great bird.

It was his grandfather's voice, as clear as if it had been the old man himself standing at the foot of the bed.

The enormous bird spoke the word once more.

"Come."

And then it spread its wings and the room filled with a great roaring noise as the bird rose straight upward. It seemed to pass right through the ceiling, and as it rose higher into the pitch-blackness of the night, Jed could still see the silvery light radiating from its eyes. It hovered in the air for a moment, then wheeled around, and with a great rushing sound as its wings found the breeze, it soared toward the mesa.

As it disappeared, Jed came awake for the second time.

This time he was lying on the sofa, the television droning in the background. In his mind the dream he'd just awakened from was still fresh and vivid.

So vivid, it hadn't been like a dream at all. Even now that he was fully awake, he still felt as if he had actually experienced the presence of the enormous bird.

He had a strange urge to go to the mesa, to Kokatí, right now, and find his grandfather.

His reverie was broken by the sound of his father's truck pulling into the driveway, and a moment later Frank, leaning heavily on Judith Sheffield, lurched through the back door and into the kitchen. Jed stared stupidly at his father for a second, then his eyes shifted to Judith.

"He's drunk," she said. "Help me get him into his room, and then I'll tell you what happened."

Jed took his father's other arm, and between the two of them they managed to get Frank through the living room and down the hall into the master bedroom. He collapsed onto the bed, rolled over on his back and held out his arms toward Judith. "Stay with me?" he asked.

Judith felt herself reddening, and glanced toward Jed. To her surprise, the boy was grinning broadly. "It's not funny," she snapped. "Of all the things for him to say—"

Jed tried to control his grin and failed. "Why shouldn't he say it? He's been wanting to all week. Haven't you seen the way he looks at you?"

Judith's blush deepened. "Jed!"

"Well, it's true, even if he's too drunk to know what he said," Jed insisted. His eyes fixed on her, twinkling impudently. "You want to get him undressed, or shall I?"

"You do it," Judith mumbled, her cheeks still burning. "I'll go make some coffee."

Five minutes later Jed joined her in the kitchen, still snickering. "What happened?" he asked. "I don't think I've ever seen him drunk before. Not like this, anyway. He's really blitzed."

"Max Moreland died this afternoon," Judith told him.

Jed's laughter faded away. "Mr. Moreland?" he echoed. "Wh-What happened?"

Judith explained, then added: "Your father got the idea in his head that someone from UniChem killed Max."

"Oh, Christ," Jed groaned. "What's going to happen now?"

Frank Arnold's voice filled the kitchen. "Now," he said, "I'm going to find out what *did* happen."

Jed and Judith spun around to stare at him. He was standing in the kitchen door, a bathrobe wrapped around his large frame, his face still wet from the cold shower he'd just taken.

"I thought you were asleep," Judith said.

Frank shook his head. "I wasn't asleep, and I wasn't so drunk I didn't know what I was saying." His eyes met hers squarely, and his voice dropped. "And Jed was right—I *have* been wanting to ask you to stay all week."

Once again Judith felt herself beginning to flush, and once again she found herself glancing involuntarily toward Jed.

Jed, realizing that whether or not Judith spent the night with his father was up to him, hesitated only a second. "I think maybe I'll take off for a while," he said, his eyes shifting to his father. "Okay if I take the truck?"

"The keys are in it," Frank replied, his eyes never leaving Judith.

Jed started toward the back door, then turned and winked at Judith. "See you in the morning. And pancakes would be great for breakfast. We haven't had a decent pancake around here for years."

It wasn't until he was a block away from the house that he realized where he was going. When he'd left, he thought he'd drive around for a while, or maybe go see if Gina Alvarez was still up.

But now that he was in the truck, he knew.

He was going to Kokatí, to see his grandfather.

Brown Eagle emerged from the kiva. He'd been sitting on the stone bench facing the firepit for hours, his body motionless, his mind turned outward from his own spirit to accept whatever might emerge from the sipapu in the center of the floor.

He had maintained a silence during his long vigil, listening only to the voices from the underworld. When at last he came back to himself, he discovered he was alone in the kiva. There had been ten others in the holy place when he'd come in so many hours ago, and he had no recollection of them leaving. But that was all right; it often happened to him when he was in communion with the spirits, and when the communion was over he had no memory of where he'd been or what he'd done, much less of what anyone around him might have done.

Indeed, for all he remembered, he might never have been in the kiva at all.

Tonight, as he climbed out of the hatch in the chamber's roof, he had the distinct feeling that this wasn't the first time he'd left the kiva since the vigil began.

Tonight he'd been possessed by Rakantoh, the greatest of all the Kokatí spirits, who had dwelt in the canyon until the dam had forced him to fly away from his home.

Yes, tonight the great spirit eagle Rakantoh had come to him, and they had flown together. Flown, and seen many things; things that he needed, for reasons the spirit had not yet revealed to him, to tell his grandson.

So he strode away from the kiva and went to look out over the canyon and the lake that flooded Rakantoh's ancient home.

He stood at the edge of the canyon, waiting in the darkness, and when, half an hour later, he saw headlights bobbing across the mesa far in the distance, he knew at once that it was Jed.

Rakantoh had summoned him, and he had answered.

Tonight Brown Eagle would introduce his grandson to the mysteries of the kiva.

Chapter 12

It was close to midnight, and Rita Moreland knew she should feel exhausted. Until an hour ago the phone hadn't stopped ringing, and though Greg had argued with her, she'd insisted on taking every call, exchanging a few words with all the people who had offered her their sympathy. After a while the words had come almost automatically, but still she'd listened, and spoken, and been amazed at how much her husband had been loved. For the last hour, though, the phone had been mercifully silent, and she and Greg had sat alone in front of a small fire that had now burned down to no more than a few glowing embers.

"You should go to bed, Aunt Rita," Greg said, rising from the sofa to sweep a few coals off the hearth and place the screen in front of the huge brass andirons that had been in the fireplace as long as the house had stood.

Rita's hand fluttered dismissively. "I wouldn't sleep. I'd just lie there, waiting for Max to come home." Her eyes, their normal curtain of reserve lifted, were bleak and lonely as she gazed at her nephew. "But he's not coming home, is he?" she asked.

Greg made no answer, knowing none was expected.

Rita leaned forward and picked up her glass. A half inch of Max's favorite bourbon still remained, and Rita held it up to the light of the fire, the glowing coals flickering eerily in the amber liquid. "We have to decide what to do, Greg," she said.

Greg nodded briefly and sank back onto the sofa. "The funeral will be on Friday morning," he told her. "I've already made most of the arrangements. It'll be at the old church."

"I wasn't thinking of that," Rita replied, her voice oddly detached, as if she hadn't yet brought herself to deal with Max's funeral. "I was thinking of the company."

Greg's brows rose slightly. "I'm not sure there's anything that needs to be done. Uncle Max signed the sale today—the papers are in his desk."

Rita's lips tightened. "But there was something wrong—he was going up to the dam to talk to Otto Kruger."

Greg nodded. "It was something about the maintenance reports," he said. "There was a problem up there today. Some damage to the main power flume. Uncle Max thought there was some kind of irregularity—"

"Irregularity?" Rita repeated. "What do you mean?"

Greg's eyes shifted to the floor, and when he spoke again he sounded almost embarrassed by what he had to say. "I'm afraid Uncle Max didn't read the last reports very well," he said. "He seemed to think he'd ordered some repairs that weren't made. But he'd signed the report, and the repair orders."

Rita frowned. "I find it hard to believe Max would have let the dam go," she said.

Greg met her eyes. "Aunt Rita, he was getting old. He was already suffering from high blood pressure, and his arteries weren't in the best condition. He should have retired five years ago."

Rita turned the matter over in her mind, hearing again the last conversation she'd had with Max. He'd sounded upset—indeed, he'd sounded furious—but he hadn't told her exactly what the problem was.

At whom had he been angry? Himself, after discovering his own mistake?

Or someone else?

She'd never know.

She took a deep breath. "All right," she said. "I suppose there's no point in trying to figure out exactly what happened. But what do we do about the sale? Max seemed to think it shouldn't go through."

"Not exactly," Greg replied. "He wanted to find out what had happened up at the dam—how bad the damage was. I suppose it would have affected the value of the company."

"You mean UniChem might not want it anymore," Rita translated. To her surprise, Greg shook his head.

"Not at all. In fact, Paul Kendall heard everything Otto Kruger had to say about the dam, and it didn't seem to bother him at all. He's quite willing to let the deal go through with no changes."

Rita stared at him. "But that doesn't make sense. If the dam's damaged badly, the company's not worth as much."

Greg shrugged. "I suppose when you have as much money as UniChem does, whatever it will take to fix the damage doesn't mean much to them.

They just seem to want the company, and they don't seem to care what it costs."

"But why?" Rita insisted. "Max always said that if a deal looked too good to be true, it *was* too good to be true. If they're willing to pay the same price, disregarding the condition of the dam—"

Before she could complete her thought, a loud crash echoed through the house, followed by the tinkling of glass. Rita and Greg stared at each other for a moment, then Greg was on his feet, charging out to the foyer.

On the hardwood floor, amid the shattered remains of the broken judas window in the large oaken door, was a rock the size of a fist. Ignoring the rock, Greg jerked the door open and stepped out onto the broad veranda that fronted the house. But he already knew it was too late. The moon was low in the sky, and the darkness of the desert night surrounded him.

Whoever had thrown the rock had already disappeared into the vast emptiness around the house. Still, Greg left the porch and quickly searched the grounds before going back in and gingerly picking the rock from among the shards of glass.

It was a river cobble, round, flat, and worn smooth from eons of tumbling. But on one of its surfaces a word had been scrawled with a laundry marker.

Bitch

Greg stared at it in puzzlement, then finally looked up at his aunt, who was standing in the wide arched opening of the living room.

"What does it say?" Rita demanded, her voice clear and calm.

Greg handed the rock to his aunt, who turned it over and read the single word. "Why the hell would anyone want to do something like this?" he asked. "And tonight, of all nights?"

Rita shook her head. "I don't know," she said, her voice sorrowful. "Apparently I don't have the sympathy of everyone in town after all."

Greg's eyes hardened. "I'm calling the police," he said. "There's no reason why we should have to put up with vandalism."

Rita took a deep breath, then shook her head. "No," she said, the exhaustion of the long evening finally closing in on her. "Not tonight. I don't want to talk to anyone else right now, Greg. I just want to go to bed and think for a while."

But a few minutes later, when she was at last alone in the large bed she'd shared with Max for almost half a century, she found she didn't think at all.

She fell asleep, and dreamed of Max.

* * *

Jed had no idea what time it was, except that the sun had risen and a bright patch of light lay trapped on the western edge of the kiva floor. The fire still smoldered, tendrils of smoke drifting up to dance for a moment in the rays of the sun, only to climb onward, escaping out of the hatch and riding away on the breeze.

He was still uncertain exactly what had happened last night. When he'd arrived at Kokatí and found his grandfather waiting for him, he had been unsurprised, as if there were nothing abnormal about Brown Eagle having known he was coming. He'd told his grandfather about the dream, and a bemused smile had come over Brown Eagle's face as he listened. "Maybe," the old man had mused when Jed was finished, "your grandpa isn't so crazy after all, eh?"

"But what happened?" Jed had asked. "What did I see?"

Brown Eagle shrugged. "You can see anything in dreams. Some of it is real—some of it might not be. Some of it means something, some of it doesn't." At the look of puzzlement on Jed's face, he continued, "The trouble with your father's people is that they won't open their minds. When they dream, they say everything they see comes from inside their minds. When their eyes are closed, they don't think there's any other way to see. But to the People, sleep is a different world. When we sleep, we see different things."

"I don't get it."

Brown Eagle put an arm around Jed's shoulders. "Why do you have to? If you don't understand why the sky is blue, does it make it another color? Just because you don't know where something comes from doesn't make it less real. Come on." He guided Jed toward the kiva, but as they approached the ladder, Jed hesitated, remembering the strange loss of time he'd experienced when he'd gone into the kiva on his last visit to Kokatí.

"Wh-What's going to happen?"

"Who knows?" Brown Eagle countered. "Maybe nothing. Maybe we'll just sit for a while and I'll tell you stories, like I did when you were still five years old." He nudged Jed forward, and Jed climbed down into the gloom of the subterranean chamber. As always, a fire crackled in the pit, but the suffocating heat that built up in the day had long since dispersed through the hatchway. Tonight, the room held only an intimate warmth, with none of the stultifying closeness that bore in on it when the sun was at its zenith.

"You can learn practically anything down here," Brown Eagle told him as they seated themselves on the bench. "To me, this place is a doorway. I can sit here for hours, looking out at things I can't see anywhere else. If I want, sometimes I can even pass through the door and go to other places." He grinned at Jed. "Tonight, for example. I went with Rakantoh tonight, and spoke to you."

Jed smiled nervously. "Come on, you don't think I'm gonna believe that, do you?" But even as he spoke, he remembered the word that had risen from the bird's throat, a word he had heard in his grandfather's voice.

"Look at the fire," Brown Eagle told him. "Watch the flames. Let yourself drift. Let the fire guide you, and don't be afraid."

Jed leaned back against the stone wall. For a few minutes he looked around the dimly lit chamber, peering into the shadows around its circumference, examining the stones that paved the floor. But soon the fire itself seemed to beckon to his eyes and he stared into the flames themselves.

For a while he saw nothing, but slowly the flames began to take on shapes, and he began to imagine that they had come alive. Amorphous forms began to appear—a brilliantly hued snake slithered among the coals, only to disappear a second later, transformed into a bird which rose up from the ashes, then disappeared as quickly as it had come.

The fire came alive, and a whole new world appeared within the stone ring that surrounded it. Life came and went, strange creatures lived for a moment, then died, or were transformed into something else. Jed felt his mind begin to expand and reach out toward the world within the fire, wanting to explore every corner of it.

The fire grew then, surrounding him, and suddenly he himself was walking among the coals. Yet he felt no fear, no burning of his flesh; and his nostrils, instead of filling with the acrid aroma of smoke, thrilled instead to the myriad perfumes of the desert night—sage and juniper, and the scents of earth.

A bird appeared before him, the same bird he'd seen in his dream, and when the bird spread its wings to soar into the sky, Jed let himself go with it.

He rose out of the fire, drifted like the smoke up through the hatchway and into the coolness of the night sky. The huge eagle rose beside him, and Jed felt as if he could reach out and touch the creature's feathers. He reached out. Suddenly the bird turned on the breeze and soared higher.

As they rose upward, Jed gazed down on the pueblo spread along the edge of the mesa. From the sky it seemed a perfect reflection of the landscape around it. The plazas appeared to wander through the buildings just as the floor of the desert meandered among the mesas that lay scattered across it, and the whispers of smoke that rose from the firepits of the village gathered over it like so many clouds. Seen from the night sky, Kokatí seemed perfect.

Jed wheeled with the great bird and sailed out over the canyon. There was a coldness to the air above the lake, and for a moment Jed felt as if he was going to fall out of the sky and plunge into the waters below. He could stand to look into their black depths for only a moment, for a feeling of desolate loneliness and longing came over him, wrenching at his spirit. Then he was above the ugly concrete scar of the dam, and the canyon spread out before him. Even from the great height at which he soared, he could hear the soft babbling of the stream as it made its way through the rocks, and hear the muted rustlings of small animals scavenging in the night.

The mouth of the canyon opened before him, and the vastness of the desert spread away from the banks of the wash. He breathed deeply, sucking the clean air into his lungs, feeling the rush of the wind against his face.

But a moment later his nostrils recoiled as they were choked with a noxious odor, and Jed realized he was above the refinery now. Like a hideous pit of vipers, the tangle of blackened pipes writhed among themselves, twisting around the furnaces that glowed with the light of Hell and belched fumes into the sky. Sickened, he turned away, only to be faced with the oil fields themselves, the drilling rigs poised like giant insects sucking the blood from the planet's body. Once again that bleakness of spirit overcame him; once more he turned away.

He was above the village now, and in the distance he could see the angry glare of artificial light, far too bright against the darkness of the night, and he flew toward it.

Below him now was the ungainly Victorian shape of the Morelands' house, all its windows glowing brightly, as if its occupants were trying to fend off the night itself.

There was a movement then, and Jed's eyes shifted. A figure was moving through the night, darting across the desert, crouched low to the ground. Jed let himself drop downward, following closely as the shadow dodged among the boulders and trees. Then at last he lost interest, drifting once more on the wind, feeling at one with the sky.

He let his eyes close, let his mind soar free . . .

And now it was morning, and the kiva was already beginning to take on the heat of the sun as well as the fire. Jed blinked and stretched, prepared for the pain he expected to wash over him as he flexed his muscles after the many hours of sitting on the hard stone bench.

But his body felt relaxed, as if he'd been sleeping all night.

Yet in his mind all the images he'd seen as he stared at the fire, and then imagined himself soaring free with the great bird, were still clear.

Nor were they the vague, fleeting fragments of dreams that sometimes caught in his memory for a few seconds upon awakening, only to disappear forever a moment later. No, these were clear memories, as bright and vivid as his memories of riding up to the mesa with Jude; as vivid, indeed, as his ride up the mesa last night in his father's truck.

The memories were not the memories of dreams at all. They were memories of something that truly happened. As the realization hit him, he felt a hollowness in his belly and his heart began to pound. When he turned to his grandfather, his face frightened, Brown Eagle only chuckled softly.

"What happened?" the old man asked. "What did you see?"

Jed did his best to explain the strange thing that had happened to him during the night, but even as he listened to his own words he realized they sounded crazy.

It was impossible, all of it.

But when he was finished, Brown Eagle nodded. "The bird is Rakantoh," he said, his eyes fixing once more on the fire. "He is the totem of our clan. What you felt when you were over the lake was what he feels. His home is there somewhere, under the water, and he tries to go back. But he can't." He laid a gentle hand on Jed's knee. "Maybe he feels the way you do," he went on. "Maybe he feels he has no home and doesn't belong anywhere. But it's not true, of course." Brown Eagle sighed heavily. "His home is still there. Someday he will reclaim it."

Jed made a hollow snorting sound. "Yeah?" he asked. "How?"

Brown Eagle shook his head. "Some things none of us can know." He stood up and moved toward the ladder. "Time for you to go," he said. "Up here time might not mean much, but down in Borrego your father will be worried about you."

Jed steered the truck down the winding road that led off the mesa, then stopped at one of the turns to look out over the desert. In the distance he could see the refinery and the oil fields, something he'd seen all his life. But this morning, after what happened to him during the night, they looked different.

They looked wrong.

Wrong, and somehow evil. He drove more slowly now, looking at all the things the people of Borrego had brought to the area.

The refinery and the dam, and paved roads and electric cables.

Great pipes, shooting straight across the desert like scars made by a surgeon's scalpel.

All the things that were supposed to make life better for the people who had built them. But as he thought about it now, he realized that wasn't quite what had happened.

For the people of Borrego, unlike the Kokatí, had become slaves to what they had built, spending most of their time tending to the machinery that was supposed to take care of them.

The only good thing, he supposed, was that at least most of them didn't know they were slaves.

Idly, he wondered what would happen if they ever found out . . .

"Well," Judith Sheffield said, glancing at the clock and dropping her chalk on the ledge below the blackboard, "shall we all line up and play kindergarten?"

The sound of laughter rippled through the class, and Gina Alvarez grinned. "Maybe we should all pin our permission slips to our shirts," she suggested.

Judith smiled at her. When she'd briefed the class earlier about what was to occur at exactly 8:45 that morning, she'd made no attempt to disguise her disdain of Stuart Beckwith's precise logistical plans. Indeed, she'd hardly listened at the staff meeting yesterday afternoon, when he'd made his laborious explanation of how the distribution of flu shots was to be carried out. It had sounded to her more like a military campaign than a simple inoculation, and as soon as he'd begun repeating himself—which had happened in about the second minute of his presentation—Judith found herself thinking not about the logistics of administering the shots, but of the shots themselves.

After all, it was only last spring that she'd heard that flu shots were no longer going to be administered on a mass basis. If people wanted them, they were going to have to get them privately. Nor, for that matter, had she heard anything about an epidemic sweeping the country, which was the kind of thing that invariably got some mention on the evening news. Finally, out of pique at what she considered Beckwith's wasting of the staff's time, she'd decided to call her doctor in Los Angeles, who was also a close friend. "Actually," Sally Rosen had told her, "there *is* an epidemic going on, a small one, though, and pretty well localized in New England. But there's no inoculation against it. It's some new strain." Judith hadn't made a big deal about it; indeed she'd soon been more interested in hearing about Sally's latest boyfriend. Then, when Greg had arrived at the Morelands' the night before, with the news of Max's death, it had vanished from her mind completely.

This morning, as Frank scribbled his name on the inoculation permission slip Jed had left for him on the refrigerator door—and which was now in Judith's purse—she'd remembered her conversation with Sally, and gone to talk to Beckwith as soon as she'd arrived at the school.

He'd pasted a smile on as she stepped into his office, but it had immediately disappeared when she'd told him she had some questions about the shots the students were to receive that day.

"Really," he'd said, his eyes fixing on her as if he'd just detected a cockroach creeping across the floor of his office. "I hadn't been aware of your medical background, Judy."

"It's not my background," Judith replied. "It's a friend of mine. I happened to be talking to her yesterday. She told me there's no epidemic around here, and even if there were, there's no immunization shot available."

Beckwith's scowl deepened. "I'm afraid you're talking to the wrong person," he said. "It was Greg Moreland who arranged for these shots to be given. If you have a problem, you should take it up with him."

Judith felt her face burning. "It just seems to me that if there's any question—" she began, but this time Beckwith didn't let her finish.

"What you're saying is that you expect me to jeopardize the students' health simply because some friend of yours hasn't kept up with this epidemic."

"If that's the way you want to put it, fine!" Judith replied, then wished she'd been able to keep the anger out of her voice. But it was too late.

"That *is* the way I want to put it, Judy," Beckwith had told her. "And until you're the principal here, I think you'd be well advised to leave administrative decisions up to me. Now, if you'll excuse me, I have a great deal of work this morning." He'd nodded toward the door in a gesture of dismissal that Judith had found infuriating. Still, he was right in one way—the shots were his business, and Greg Moreland's business, not hers.

"Okay," she said now, "let's go." She watched in amusement as the class trooped out of the room, their permission slips neatly pinned to their chests just as Gina had suggested.

Lining themselves up in alphabetical order, they all joined hands like a kindergarten class trooping through a museum. "Do we get cookies and milk if we're good?" someone asked.

Despite herself, Judith laughed out loud. "I'm just hoping none of you embarrasses me by passing out," she replied. Then, deciding that if the class were going to make a joke out of it, she might as well too, she stepped to the head of the line.

Stuart Beckwith was waiting outside the nurse's office, a clipboard in his hand, and Judith had to suppress an urge to snap him a sharp salute. His eyes swept her class, and a flicker of anger crossed his face as he saw the slips pinned to their chests. "Well, at least you're prompt," he observed tightly. "Line them up against the wall. Laura will be ready for them in a moment."

Judith glanced at the class, who, not being deaf, had managed to translate the principal's words for themselves, then moved closer to Gina Alvarez. "You didn't see Jed this morning, did you?" she asked, hoping her words sounded as casual as she intended them.

Gina shook her head. "Maybe he's already got the flu," she suggested.

Or maybe he's upset about me sleeping with his father, Judith said to herself. And yet, when he'd left last night, he'd actually seemed pleased. In fact, she reflected, he'd seemed downright *smug* about it.

Her thoughts were interrupted as the last of the preceding class emerged from the nurse's office. Beckwith, still posted against the far wall, nodded tersely at Judith. She stepped into the nurse's office, and Laura Sanders smiled at her. "All set?" she asked.

"All lined up, just as Beckwith wanted," Judith replied as she handed that morning's attendance report—the space next to Jed's name still blank —to Laura. Then her eyes fell on the boxes containing the disposable syringes, and she frowned as she recognized the bright red UniChem logo emblazoned on each of them.

"Okay," Laura said. "Bring them in."

Judith stepped out into the hall and waved the class inside. The first in line was Gina Alvarez.

Gina unpinned her permission slip, handed it to the nurse, then rolled up her sleeve. Then, as Laura Sanders slipped a needle beneath Gina's skin, Jed Arnold appeared. He waved and started toward Judith, grinning broadly.

Judith glanced back into Laura's office. The shot administered, the nurse pulled the needle out of Gina's arm, but instead of throwing it away immediately, she carefully copied a number from the syringe onto the attendance sheet on the clipboard. Judith frowned. She'd seen inoculations before— dozens of them, in her years of teaching—but she'd never seen anything like this. Suddenly, as all the elements came together, a warning bell sounded in her head.

No epidemic, at least not around here.

No vaccination, even if there was an epidemic.

Needles, supplied by UniChem, on the day UniChem was taking over the town's single major employer.

Judith glanced around. Beckwith was nowhere to be seen. Jed was next to her now, still smiling. "I know I'm late," he began, "but I couldn't help it. I—"

Judith didn't let him finish. "Go back out," she said, her voice an urgent whisper. "Go back outside, and don't come in until the second period bell."

Jed stared at her, mystified. "What?" he began. "What's going on? I got here as—"

"Never mind!" Judith exclaimed. "Will you just do it? I'll tell you later on, at lunchtime."

Jed still hesitated. What was wrong? Was she mad at him or something? Then he saw the look in her eyes and realized that it wasn't anger.

It was fear.

He backed away, then turned and disappeared down the hall.

Only when he was gone did Judith turn back to her class, watching in uneasy silence as the rest of her students received their shots.

She had no idea what the purpose of these inoculations was. But she was suddenly very certain they had nothing whatever to do with the flu.

Chapter 13

With tired eyes Paul Kendall surveyed the three people gathered in the darkly paneled room. He'd been up most of the night; he'd spent most of those long hours here in this very office, the office that only yesterday had been Max Moreland's—and now was his. In a gesture that was not lost on the group gathered opposite him, he moved behind the immense desk and lowered himself into the large leather swivel chair.

Kendall's eyes moved from one face to another as he tried to read the minds of these men to whom he had been a total stranger only yesterday, but for whom, just half an hour ago, he had become of paramount importance. Now that he had countersigned the papers Max had left in the top drawer of his desk, the deal was done. UniChem was in control of Borrego Oil.

The men in the room were gazing at him guardedly now, their expressions half expectant, half apprehensive. Except for Greg Moreland, of course, who had been for the sale right from the start. Indeed, had it not been for the rumors that had begun last night, and continued to fly around the town this morning—rumors that wouldn't exist at all if Frank Arnold hadn't lost control of himself—Kendall's job right now would be much simpler.

He brushed the thought aside, concentrating not on what had already happened, but on what needed to happen now.

Otto Kruger, of course, he already knew. Kruger was mean, and essentially weak, but would do whatever was needed without wasting anyone's time with unnecessary questions.

Ted Whittiker, though, was another story. The mayor of Borrego was a politician, which meant that above and beyond anything else, in the end he would be worried only about his own skin. The impact of UniChem's acquisition of Borrego Oil would matter to him only in terms of votes.

Finally there was Greg Moreland. Though Kendall knew he could deal with the change in management without Greg Moreland's presence, he also knew the transition would be accepted in a far more positive way with Max's sole male heir offering his full support. And that, at least, Kendall knew he could count on. Greg had assured him the papers would be signed today, and indeed they had been. Already, Greg's cooperation had made the takeover much easier.

"Okay," he said, passing each man a folder that contained both a copy of the executed agreement between Max and UniChem, and a copy of the hastily constructed outline of his proposed plan of action. "We all know what's happened, and if the rest of you have heard the same rumors I've heard today, then you all know we've got a problem."

"The only problem we have is Frank Arnold," Otto Kruger interrupted. "It seems to me the first thing you ought to do is fire him."

Kendall's eyes fixed coolly on Kruger. "I'm not firing him or anybody else, Otto," he said. "Frankly, though I wish it hadn't happened, I can understand what must have been in Arnold's mind last night." He could almost hear Ted Whittiker's silent sigh of relief. Nothing would lose a mayor votes faster than a mass firing, even if he couldn't be held directly responsible. "The point of this meeting," he went on, "is for me to find out if I have your support. I intend to put my cards on the table, and I'd appreciate it if you'd put yours the same place. I don't know if there are rumors I haven't heard, but if there are, this is the time and place for me to hear them. I want to answer every question you have, and then, if you're satisfied with my answers"—he grinned encouragingly—"we can get down to the business of getting this company going again." He sat back in the chair, predicting that it would be the mayor who spoke first. He wasn't wrong.

Whittiker shifted in his chair and cleared his throat nervously. "I suppose what concerns us all most is the future of the refinery," he said.

"We intend to keep it going," Kendall promptly assured him. "As you know, it's going to be shut down today, until the problem at the dam is fixed. But . . ."

His words died on his lips as the door to the office flew open and Frank Arnold stormed in. Otto Kruger rose to his feet immediately, but Kendall, sizing up the situation instantly, motioned him to sit down again.

"What the hell's going on?" Frank demanded. His eyes, blazing with indignation, fixed on Kendall. "Judging by the fact that Whittiker's here," he growled, "I'm assuming this is something more than a management meeting. And if it is, it seems to me that I should have been invited, since I'm still president of the union local."

Before he spoke, Kendall shot Kruger one more warning glance. "If you'd gone to the plant this morning," he said, judging the redness in Arnold's eyes and taking a gamble, "Otto here would have brought you along with him. Have a seat, Frank."

Taken aback by Kendall's unexpected welcome, Frank stared uncertainly at the other man, then sank into a chair. Kendall turned his attention back to the group, but as he went on he made certain to address himself directly to Frank Arnold as often as he did to any of the others.

He talked steadily for nearly thirty minutes, outlining UniChem's plans to keep the refinery going and to expand it. There would be a huge investment of capital into Borrego Oil; within four years, employment would at least double.

"It all sounds good," Frank Arnold said after Kendall had finished sketching UniChem's plans. "But it seems to me there's a catch. The hydroelectric plant at the dam is already working to capacity. When," he added, "it's working at all. How are you planning to power this new refinery?"

"Power is hardly a problem," Kendall replied. He tossed a document to Frank. "That's a commitment from the state to run a major line up here."

Frank studied the paper for a moment, then eyed Kendall warily. "How'd you get this? Max Moreland tried for years, and couldn't get to first base."

Kendall smiled. "Shall we just say UniChem is a lot bigger than Borrego Oil?" he said. Not to his surprise, Ted Whittiker chuckled appreciatively. "I also want you all to know," he went on, this time addressing himself almost exclusively to Frank Arnold, "that we intend to fulfill the union contract, and bring the pay in the refinery up to industry standards."

Frank's face turned ruddy. "Are you saying I haven't been doing a good job for my men?"

Kendall held up his hands in a mollifying gesture. "All I'm saying is there's now enough money to pay everyone what he's worth," he said. "Everyone in this room, including me, knows you did the best you could for the workers, given the situation. My company did a lot of research on this outfit before we made our offer. There isn't much we don't know about it, and we believe it's worth every cent we spent, and every other cent we plan to invest." He paused, then went on, choosing his words carefully. "Now, there's one more thing I want to show you," he said, passing each of the men another sheet of paper. "This is the autopsy report on Max Moreland. Greg, here, brought it along this morning." His eyes came to rest on Frank. "I've already told everyone else in this room that I understand what happened last night, and I'm not holding it against you. But this town is going to be going through a lot of changes in a short time, and the fewer rumors we have flying around, the better. So I want all of you to know exactly what happened to Max Moreland. If nothing else, at least we can get that settled here and now."

Frank Arnold took the sheet of paper Kendall offered him and studied it carefully. It had been prepared by the county coroner, a man Frank had known most of his life. And the words were clear. Cause of death: massive cerebral hemorrhage in the region of the hypothalamus.

He absorbed the words slowly, then handed the page back to Kendall as his gaze shifted to Greg Moreland. "I'm sorry," he said, his voice turning gruff. "I was drunk last night, and out of order. I'll call Rita this afternoon and apologize to her too."

Greg Moreland nodded once as an acceptance of the apology, but said nothing.

Paul Kendall stood up and came around the desk as the rest of the men in the room rose to their feet too. "Well, how about it?" he asked. "Do I have your support?"

One by one the men shook his hand and assured him they were behind him.

Finally he came to Frank Arnold. "How about it?" Kendall asked. "Truce?"

Frank hesitated, his lips curving into a thin smile. "We'll see," he said. Then he turned and walked out the door.

Jed stood in the hall outside Judith Sheffield's room, waiting for the corridor to empty out before he went inside. He still wasn't certain how much he was going to tell her of what had happened last night. All morning, since he'd come back down onto the desert floor and the reality of Borrego, he'd been wondering himself exactly what had happened to him in the kiva.

Vivid as they were, his memories were impossible. He couldn't fly—no one could. And he had seen nothing on his journey with Rakantoh that he hadn't seen before—the view from the top of the mesa, of the refinery and the town, was a panorama he had viewed many times. No, he'd simply let the fire hypnotize him, and let his mind drift. His own imagination had conjured up all the rest.

The corridors finally emptied as the students hurried toward the cafeteria, and Jed at last stepped into the room. But when he looked at Judith, he hesitated. Instead of the smile he'd been expecting, she looked angry.

"Where were you last night?" she demanded. "If you think you can just go out and vandalize houses all night, I think you're going to find out you're wrong. When I tell Frank—"

Jed gaped at her. "What are you talking about?" he broke in.

Judith's eyes narrowed. "I talked to Rita Moreland during the morning break," she said, her voice cold. "She told me about the rock." When Jed didn't flinch at the word, but only looked puzzled, she felt the first pang of uncertainty. She had assumed that when Jed had left the house last night, knowing she was about to sleep with his father, he'd felt jealous. And he'd vented that jealousy by throwing a rock through a window of the house where she lived. And yet now, as she faced him, she was suddenly not so sure her assumption was correct. Could he really mask his guilt this well? She chewed nervously at her lower lip, then started over again. "Someone threw a rock through the Morelands' front door last night," she said. "There was a word on it. 'Bitch.' " She watched Jed carefully, but his expression still betrayed nothing more than bewilderment. "I—Well, I guess I simply assumed you did it," she finished.

Jed shook his head slowly, a memory already stirring in his mind. Then it came back to him. It was fuzzy at first, but as he focused in on it, the scene etched itself sharply in his mind.

There had been lights on in the Morelands' house, and he'd sailed closer.

A form, darting away from the house.

Dropping lower, following the running figure.

Suddenly, starkly, like a black-and-white landscape emerging in a photographer's darkroom, the scene came clear in his mind. From the shadows, the face of the figure came into focus.

"Randy Sparks," he said out loud.

Judith stared at him. "Randy Sparks?" she echoed.

Jed nodded. "I—I saw him," he said. Then, slowly, trying not to make the tale sound too unbelievable, he told her what had happened to him the previous night. When he was done, though, he could see that she didn't believe him.

"I see." Her voice was cold. "In that case, I think maybe both of us should go talk to Randy and see what he has to say."

To her own surprise, Randy Sparks looked almost guilty when he saw her, and only reluctantly responded to Jed's beckoning wave. They stood just outside the cafeteria, Randy slouching nonchalantly against the wall.

"What's up?" he asked.

"What's up is that you threw a rock through a window in the Morelands' front door last night," Jed said, fixing as closely on Randy's face as Judith.

Randy shook his head, his eyes averted. "I don't know what you're talkin' about—" he began, but Jed cut him off.

"I saw it, Randy," he said. "I saw you running away from the house."

"Bullshit!" Randy exploded. "There wasn't anybody out there! I made sure—" Too late, he realized his mistake. He swallowed hard, then managed to glare truculently at Judith. "What the hell did you expect?" he muttered. "After what you did to me yesterday . . ."

But Judith wasn't listening. Her mouth slightly agape, she was staring at Jed, her eyes searching his. Finally, impatiently, she turned back to Randy. "You'll pay for the window," she said, "and apologize to Mrs. Moreland. You scared her half to death."

Randy stared at the floor, but nodded miserably. "And you might also be interested to know," Judith added, "I wasn't even there. I was out for the night. So the next time you have a problem with me, make sure you know where I am before you come to—" She hesitated, searching for the right word, then went on, her voice sarcastic: "Shall we say before you come to 'talk' to me about it?"

Randy's head came up. "You mean you're not going to tell Beckwith?" he asked, his voice trembling like a guilty eight-year-old's. "Or the cops?"

Judith shook her head. "Let's just call a truce, okay?"

Randy swallowed once more and nodded. Then his eyes shifted to Jed. "Where the hell were you?" he demanded. "If you were close enough to see me, how come I didn't see you?"

Jed said nothing. A slow, sardonic grin spread over his face. "I'm a half-breed, remember?" he drawled. "Us Indians can sneak around where you guys can never spot us." Leaving Randy staring at his back, he turned and followed Judith back to her classroom.

"So do you believe me now?" Jed asked when the door closed behind him.

Judith dropped into the chair behind her desk, regarding him thoughtfully. "You know," she said, her voice vague, as if she were thinking out loud, "this kind of thing isn't exactly unheard-of." Jed frowned uncertainly. "There's a phenomenon called an out-of-body experience. There are a lot of reports of them from people who have come close to dying. They say they actually leave their bodies and can watch what's going on around them. There are reports of people who almost died in surgery—some of them *did* die, but were brought back to life—who can recount what happened when they died. What was done, what was said—everything. Yet they were completely unconscious at the time."

Jed looked doubtful as Judith fell silent, lost in thought. Then, softly, he asked, "You believe me, don't you?"

Judith sighed, nodding reluctantly. She glanced up at the clock on the wall. "Do you want to get some lunch? We still have twenty minutes."

Jed was about to agree, then remembered the note his third-period teacher had handed him. "I can't," he said. "I have to go to the nurse's office and get my shot." His eyes narrowed quizzically. "What was going on this morning?" he asked. "Why did you shove me out of there?"

Judith's expression hardened. She glanced toward the door as if she expected to see someone standing outside, listening. "I got you out of there," she told him, her voice dropping, "because I don't understand what those shots are all about, and I don't know why the kids are being given them."

"They're just flu shots—" Jed began, but Judith didn't let him finish.

"Maybe. But something is wrong." She told him about the conversation she'd had with Sally Rosen the day before. "The thing that really got to me," she finished, "was the UniChem label on the boxes."

Jed's eyes narrowed. "UniChem?"

Judith nodded. "It just seems strange to me that on the day UniChem is taking over Borrego Oil, they're also giving shots to every kid in town. Especially when someone I trust tells me there is no effective inoculation against the latest strain of flu."

"Jesus," Jed whispered, his tongue running over his lower lip. "What are you going to do?"

Judith shrugged. "I don't know," she said. "In fact, I don't even know what I *ought* to do. But I know I'd just as soon you skipped that shot."

Jed smiled crookedly. "That's okay by me," he said. "The last time I had a shot I passed out."

Together they headed back to the cafeteria, but as Judith toyed with the limp sandwich that was all that remained by the time they passed through the line, she kept thinking about those shots.

By the time her afternoon classes began, she had come up with an idea.

Judith stepped out into the hall, closing the door of the lounge behind her. It was almost four, and the school was nearly deserted, only a few teachers left in the lounge, lingering over gossip rather than work.

Across the hall, the door to Laura Sanders's office stood slightly ajar. Inside, Judith could see the boxes of syringes sitting on the table where

Laura had apparently left them. Laura herself had come into the teachers' lounge a few minutes ago, looking harried and announcing that she intended to take a good long break. "I missed lunch waiting for Jed Arnold," she grumbled, rolling her eyes balefully at Judith, "and he didn't even show up. Can you beat that?"

Judith had shrugged sympathetically, then waited until Laura had settled into conversation with Elliott Halvorson. Certain that she had at least ten minutes to herself, she had finally slipped out of the lounge.

Now she hesitated, glancing in both directions.

The hall was empty.

Quickly, furtively, Judith crossed the hall, slipped into Laura's office and quietly shut the door behind her.

On the table, neatly stacked, were all the class lists of the day, duplicates of her own. Beside each name there was either a five-digit number or a notation that the student had been absent that day. Clipped to each class list were the permission slips that had been collected from the students.

On the floor by the table next to the window, boxes with the UniChem logo were carefully stacked. All but one of them were empty, but on the table itself were two more boxes. The seal on one of them was broken. Judith opened it. The box was nearly full. Good! No one would notice if one of the syringes disappeared. Making up her mind, she took one of the needles out of the box and started to slip it into her purse.

And then she saw the serial number neatly printed on the tube of the syringe.

She frowned, then picked up the class lists once more. Scanning through them, she counted the number of students from throughout the school listed as absent that day.

Twenty-two.

On the table was one box of twelve syringes, its seal unbroken.

The open box had contained ten more, but one of them was now in her hand.

Apparently UniChem had supplied exactly enough syringes to inoculate the entire student body, and had insisted on an accounting.

Judith's sense of unease over the whole inoculation program congealed into fear. Why would UniChem be so concerned about accounting for all the needles?

Still, because of what she'd seen that morning, she was prepared for this accounting system, and now flipped through the lists once more, until she found the one for her own first-period class.

The second name from the top was Jed Arnold's, and the space next to his name was still blank. She breathed a sigh of relief as she realized that, expecting him later in the day, Laura Sanders had not yet marked Jed as absent.

Judith fished in her purse and found the permission slip she'd taken from Frank's refrigerator that morning. Her eyes flitting guiltily toward the door, she added the slip to the stack attached to the top of the class list. Next she picked up a pen, tested it to make certain its ink matched that of the pen Laura had used to fill in the class lists, then carefully copied the number from the syringe she'd taken from the box into the space next to Jed's name.

The handwriting match wasn't perfect, but it was so close that she didn't think anyone would notice.

Leaving everything as she had found it, Judith slipped the syringe into her purse, and moved quietly to the door.

She listened for a moment, but heard nothing from the corridor outside.

Finally she opened the door a crack and peered out into the hall.

It was empty.

Unconsciously drawing her breath in, Judith pulled the door open and slipped through. Leaving it a few inches ajar, just as she had found it five minutes before, she walked quickly away, her mind already fully occupied with figuring out the fastest way to get the syringe to Sally Rosen in Los Angeles. And then she remembered Peter Langston.

She'd dated Peter in Los Angeles for a few months, until he'd moved to Los Alamos to take a position with a think tank. The work was highly technical, he'd explained, and secret. It was, he'd added, the opportunity of a lifetime.

And here was her opportunity: Peter was a chemist—he'd be able to tell her exactly what was in the syringe.

If Judith had looked back at that moment, she would have seen Stuart Beckwith emerge from his office and frown as he saw her disappear around the corner toward the cafeteria, then turn his attention to the open door to Laura Sanders's office.

He stood where he was for a moment, apparently lost in thought, then went to the nurse's office himself.

He scanned the lists carefully, then took his own count of the syringes.

He repeated the process, assuring himself that the number of needles matched the number of students who'd been absent that day.

Perhaps, he finally decided, he'd been wrong.

Perhaps Judy Sheffield hadn't been in Laura's office at all.

Still, as he left the nurse's office a moment later, he made certain the door was firmly closed, and locked it as well.

He made a mental note to reprimand Laura Sanders. Greg Moreland, after all, had made it absolutely clear that the syringes were to be kept under lock and key at all times.

Well, nothing had gone awry, so there was really no point in even mentioning the incident to Greg.

Laura Sanders, on the other hand, was another matter.

He went into the teachers' lounge, already silently relishing the tongue-lashing he was about to give her.

Chapter 14

Frank drove quickly down the narrow dirt road that edged the canyon. Only a fraction of his attention was focused on driving, for the ruts in the road were so deep that the pickup essentially drove itself. His mind kept turning over what he'd seen at the dam.

He still wasn't certain why he'd decided to start poking around after the meeting in Max Moreland's office; he only knew that, despite Kendall's assurances to the contrary, he had not been expected to attend. He'd seen it in Otto Kruger's eyes.

He also knew, regardless of Kendall's claims, that UniChem's plans were not going to be nearly as beneficial to Borrego as Kendall maintained. Over the past two days, despite the hectic schedule of the plant shutdown, he'd still managed to do his homework, and now, on Thursday morning, he knew more about UniChem than Kendall—or anyone else, for that matter—suspected. This morning, with the shifts already juggled so he could attend Max's funeral, he'd decided to drive up to the dam and have a look around.

He hadn't liked what he'd seen.

Everywhere he'd looked, there had been signs of sloppy maintenance.

Greasy rags, which should have been stowed away in a fireproof bin until they were ready to be washed, were scattered haphazardly through the passages.

Valves had been allowed to rust and corrode, some of them so badly they should have been replaced weeks, if not months, earlier.

When he'd finally taken a look at the main flume, the shaft that carried water from the lake down through the dam to power the huge main turbine itself, he'd been downright scared. Cracks had developed in the flume's lining—cracks too big to have developed overnight, or even over a period of days. In fact, they'd been damned lucky they hadn't lost the entire turbine.

If a sizable chunk of concrete had come loose, they would have had a major disaster on their hands.

When he'd asked Bill Watkins why the dam had been let go so badly, the operator had shrugged helplessly. "Otto just kept telling us to make do," he explained. "He kept telling us Max didn't have the money."

Though he'd said nothing, Frank knew that whatever Watkins believed, Otto Kruger had been lying to him. Max Moreland would have closed the dam down before he'd have let it run in the condition he had just observed.

As Frank's anger built, his foot pressed down on the accelerator and the truck shot forward. He knew Kruger would be at the plant, and no doubt Kendall was with him. Whatever they were up to, Frank was not going to let them get away with it.

As he suspected, the two were in Kruger's office when Frank stormed in. Paul Kendall looked up, a smug smile playing at the corners of his lips as Frank spoke.

"I've just been up at the dam, Otto," Frank said, steel in his voice. "And I want to know what the hell is going on. The shaft's ready to blow, and that didn't happen overnight."

"Now just a minute," Kruger broke in, his face livid. "Max Moreland ordered those maintenance cuts, not me—"

He'd given Frank the opening he was waiting for. Staring straight into the other man's eyes, he finished the sentence for him. "And Max, conveniently enough, isn't here to defend himself, right, Otto?"

Though he'd been careful to make no direct accusation, the implication was clear. Without another word, he turned and left the office.

Paul Kendall stared at the door Frank had just slammed, then turned to Kruger. "What's going on with him?" he asked. "I thought you had him under control."

Kruger's eyes fixed malevolently on Kendall. "He's shooting blind," he said. "He doesn't know what he's talking about."

Kendall regarded his plant supervisor darkly. "Well, if that's the way he wants to fight, there's a few things I can do too."

"Listen to Frank," Max said.

Rita Moreland froze. She felt suddenly cold, although above her the sun was blazing down, and she could feel the midday heat radiating from the sandstone boulder on which she sat; her legs, clad in a pair of worn jodhpurs, curled beneath her, her back as ramrod straight as ever.

She wasn't certain how long she'd been sitting there, high up on the mesa above her house, gazing out over the town.

It lay spread out before her, the sun glinting off the tin roofs of its small rectangular houses. Beyond the town she could see the refinery, and even a few of the oil wells. And then, in the distance, the mouth of Mordida Canyon, its sandstone walls sloping gently down to the desert floor, a winding double row of cottonwoods lining the banks of the Mordida wash as it emerged from the confines of the canyon itself.

She knew why she'd come to the mesa; it had always been one of Max's favorite places, indeed the only place where he could stand and gaze out over everything he and his father before him had built.

Gone now, all gone.

Her jaw clenched as she turned to look at Max.

He was standing a few yards from her, his hands on his hips, his eyes fixed on the distance. When he looked up, Rita's eyes instinctively followed her husband's.

High up, almost invisible against the brilliant blue glare of the sky, an eagle soared, its wings outstretched as it effortlessly rode the invisible currents of a thermal over the mesa.

As she watched, the bird drifted lower, and she imagined that it was coming down to look at her.

"He knows," Max said. "He knows everything."

Rita's eyes left the soaring eagle and returned to Max. Now he was smiling at her and his hand was outstretched, as if to take her own.

She stood up and took a step toward him, then another.

But he was no closer, and she suddenly felt a stab of fear.

She took another step, and then another. Then she was running, stumbling toward Max along the rough path hewn out of the mesa's crumbling sandstone. But no matter how fast she ran, Max seemed only to slip farther and farther away from her.

And yet he still smiled, and his hand was still outstretched. Then, so abruptly she didn't realize it had happened, her foot slipped and she lost her balance. She stumbled, fell, slipped over the edge of the path.

"Max!"

And then she was falling, tumbling through the air, and the eagle was swooping down toward her, its talons extended.

"Max!" she cried out again.

This time, as she cried out her husband's name, she woke from the dream.

She blinked in the late-morning sunlight, her whole body still trembling from the memory of the dream. Slowly she regained control of herself. She was all right, she repeated to herself. She was at home, in her bed, and nothing had happened to her at all.

Automatically she reached out to touch Max, reached out to feel his solid strength next to her in the bed.

He wasn't there; would never be there again.

Her hand, feeling suddenly heavy, dropped to the sheet, and for just a moment she wondered if she would be able to get through this day.

In only another hour she was going to bury Max, lay him to rest in the small graveyard on the edge of town, next to his father and mother.

Summoning her will, she threw off the covers and left the bed, moving to the window to close it against the growing heat of the day, but pausing to glance up toward the mesa. Even from here she could see the spot from which she'd fallen in the dream. High up, it was a dangerous place in the path, a place that Max had always warned her about. Even now, fully awake, she half expected to see him there. Almost against her will, her hand came up to wave to him.

But the path was empty, the mesa standing in its placid majesty like some great sentry looking out over the desert. And then, soaring high, she saw the eagle.

Now, in the morning sunlight, it looked exactly as it had in the dream, its wings fixed, circling slowly on whatever faint traces of breeze there might be, its eyes hunting the ground below for prey.

Except that, as in the dream, Rita had the strange sensation that the eagle was watching her.

Shivering despite the warmth of the morning, she closed the window and began dressing. But even as she slipped into the simple black silk dress she would wear to her husband's funeral, she heard once more the words he'd spoken to her in the dream.

"Listen to Frank."

She seated herself at the small vanity in her dressing room, then willed her hands to stop trembling as she began carefully applying the mask of makeup that would hide her emotions. One hour from now she would sit in the church, trying to look at Max's coffin without really seeing it, for she knew that if she let herself truly accept that it was Max inside that dark mahogany box, she might well lose the bulwark of self-control she had so carefully built since the moment she'd been told he was dead.

Finally satisfied with the image she saw in the mirror, she went downstairs, where Greg was already waiting for her in the breakfast room at the back of the house.

He stood as his aunt came into the room, and his eyes seemed to search her, as if looking for a chink in her serene armor. "Are you all right, Aunt Rita?"

Rita managed a slight smile. "I dreamed I was falling this morning," she said, apparently out of nowhere. Greg gazed blankly at her. "And it's odd, but Max was there, trying to help me," Rita went on. "But of course he couldn't, and it seemed I couldn't help myself either." She took a sip of coffee. "Have you ever dreamed you were falling, Greg?"

Greg frowned, trying to puzzle out what his aunt was saying. If there was some hidden message in her words, he couldn't fathom what it might be. "Everybody dreams of falling," he said at last.

Rita's eyes clouded for a moment as she remembered once more the words Max had spoken to her in the dream. "I haven't," she replied, setting the cup back on its saucer. "And I don't think I ever shall again."

An hour later Rita, with Greg at her side, watched the pallbearers slowly lower her husband's coffin into the hard ground of the cemetery. A dense crowd surrounded her, for nearly the whole town had turned out for Max Moreland's funeral, but still she felt alone, even with Greg on one side of her and Judith Sheffield on the other. At last, as the pallbearers stepped back, she moved forward, stooped down, and picked up a clod of earth. She held it for a moment, and then, feeling eyes on her, she looked up.

A few feet away, on the other side of Max's grave, Frank Arnold stood watching her, his eyes glistening with the tears he refused to give in to.

Rita hesitated a moment, and yet again Max's words in the dream sounded softly in her head. Her eyes met Frank's and she smiled at him.

Her fingers closed on the lump of earth in her hand and the clod broke up, sifting down onto the coffin in the grave.

Rita looked up into the sky. There, as if at her command, the form of an eagle appeared, hovering for a moment, then wheeling around, its wings beating strongly. A moment later it disappeared over the rim of the mesa and was gone.

Rita stepped back from the grave, and as if accepting her silent signal, the townspeople began filing past, some of them adding their own small lump of earth to Max's grave, others pausing only to murmur soft condolences to his widow.

Finally Paul Kendall appeared, his face grave, his eyes dark with concern. "Rita," he said quietly. "I'm so sorry."

It was as if she didn't hear him, didn't even see him. Her eyes swept past him as if he didn't exist, and came to rest on another person, a person who seemed to have been waiting silently for the right moment to approach her.

"Frank," Rita said, her voice carrying clearly through the morning as she beckoned him to her side. "Come and stand with me, will you? Help me say good-bye to Max."

Paul Kendall's jaw tightened and his right hand clenched into an angry fist, then relaxed. He moved on, stepping aside so that Frank Arnold could take his place.

A few minutes later Kendall found Otto Kruger in the crowd.

"I've had it," he said, drawing Kruger aside. "I've had it with both of them. Clear?"

Kruger nodded, his lips twisting into a cruel smile. "Clear," he agreed.

At four o'clock that afternoon Frank Arnold wheeled his pickup truck into the dusty lot in front of the refinery gate and shut off the engine. There weren't many cars there—all but a handful of men had been laid off yesterday, and today more would go. It was only temporary, according to Kruger, but Frank didn't believe him any more than he believed Kendall. Why should they start up the refinery again when they could make more money by simply selling off the crude as it was pumped out of the ground?

An eerie feeling came over him as he moved through the refinery. The usual cacophony of hissing steam and clanging pipes was silent now, and there wasn't even the usual racket caused by the rattling out of the pipes during a regular shutdown.

Today the refinery had an atmosphere of death about it, and Frank kept glancing back over his shoulder, as if half expecting to see some strange specter closing in on him. But there was nothing there.

He came finally to the catalytic cracking plant at the far end of the refinery. When it was built thirty-odd years ago, the plant had been Max Moreland's pride and joy. It was a semiexperimental installation back then, and Max had been one of the few men in the country who was willing to take a gamble on the new refining process.

Now, though, it was as obsolete as the rest of the refinery. In the control room, as Frank began scanning the gauges, he wondered if maybe Max hadn't been right in selling out to UniChem. Now, with the deal done, and his own dream of taking the place over gone forever, he began to realize just what an expense it would take to bring the plant up to date. He sighed, but as the crew began drifting in for the afternoon shift, the sigh gave way to a frown.

"Where's Polanski?" he asked Carlos Alvarez.

Carlos shrugged. "Same place as Phil Garcia. Laid off this morning." He forced a humorless grin. "Good thing they're shutting us down, eh, amigo? There's nobody left to run it anyway."

"I've got to tell you," Frank said to Alvarez and the others who had gathered, his voice somber, "I wouldn't be surprised if the rest of the layoffs come today. We should be done by ten or eleven, and if I know Kruger, he'll be out here with the checks and the pink slips, even if it's the middle of the night."

Alvarez spread his hands philosophically. "So what can we do? It's not your fault." Then he brightened. "Anyway, I hear they're gonna move a lot of people up to the dam. Get it fixed right away, huh? Then we'll all be back in business."

Frank nodded, wishing he could believe it.

But that night, exactly as he'd predicted, Otto Kruger was waiting for them as he and the rest of the men came out the front gate.

"Damn it!" he heard Carlos mutter. "Here it comes."

Kruger, an appropriately serious expression on his face, handed out the envelopes, then turned to face Frank, his eyes glowing with malice. "I need to talk to you in my office," he growled.

Frank's eyes narrowed angrily as Kruger turned and fairly swaggered away, then he heard Carlos Alvarez's cautioning voice.

"Take it easy, Frank. Don't let him get your goat. Come down to the café afterward, and I'll buy you a beer."

As Alvarez and the rest of the crew climbed into their cars, Frank headed toward the supervisor's building. Inside, Kruger was lounging in his chair, hands behind his head, legs sprawled across his desk. "Don't bother to sit down, Arnold," he said, a satisfied smirk spreading across his face.

Frank remained where he was, standing next to the door. "You can't lay me off too, Otto," he said. "You're still going to need a mothball crew around here, and I'll be part of it."

Kruger shook his head. "It seems Kendall has something else in mind for you," he said. "He thinks—and don't ask me why—that your talents would be wasted around here."

Frank shifted his weight uneasily. From Kruger's smug look a few minutes ago, he'd been certain that he too was going to be laid off, despite the union rule dictating that his seniority would make him the last man to go. But apparently that wasn't going to happen. "Okay," he said, when it was obvious that Kruger would wait for him to ask about his new assignment. "What is it?"

"The dam," Kruger replied. "It seems Kendall's been studying the union rules, and given an emergency situation, he can assign you to pretty much anything he wants. At least," he added, his smirk broadening into a malicious grin, "for as long as the emergency lasts."

Frank tipped his head in silent concession. It was true, though it hadn't occurred to him that Kendall might use the emergency provision like this.

Kruger's grin spread even wider. "You don't know enough about the dam to be a foreman," he went on, "so you're going to be on one of the labor crews. Chopping concrete, Frank. Working down there in the shaft, where it's cold and dirty and cramped. Breaking up old concrete, and building forms to pour new. How do you like that?"

Frank knew what they wanted him to do. They wanted him to refuse the job and quit entirely.

And it wasn't Paul Kendall's idea at all. It was Otto Kruger's.

Once before, Frank had worked in the pipes. He could still remember the day ten years ago—long before he'd become a foreman—when he'd crept into one of the immense pipes during a shutdown, dragging the rattler behind him, intent on knocking the deposits of coke and sludge from the interior of the pipe.

But he'd panicked, and the pipe had seemed to close in on him, threatening to crush him, strangling his breath until he could barely even scream.

In the end they'd had to pull him out, so paralyzed with unreasoning terror that he couldn't move at all.

Max Moreland had told him to forget about it—that it could happen to anyone.

Otto Kruger, obviously, had not forgotten about it.

So now Frank was faced with a choice.

Accept the new assignment, in compliance with the rules that he himself had helped to formulate, or quit.

Quit, with no prospect of any other job.

He forced himself to keep his face impassive, and met Kruger's eyes. "All right," he said. "When do I start?"

Kruger frowned, and Frank knew his answer had thrown the man off balance. Then Kruger appeared to recover.

"Tomorrow," he said. "And you know what? I think I might just come out and take a look. Should be fun, watching you crawl into those shafts."

As Kruger began to laugh, Frank walked out.

Chapter 15

"Maybe you should quit," Judith suggested early the next morning. She'd spent the night with Frank again. He had called shortly before midnight, and though he hadn't managed to ask her directly to come over, his voice told her how upset he was. Finally, it had been Rita Moreland who convinced her to drive over in the middle of the night.

"Go," the older woman had said. "I don't expect to sleep much myself tonight, and I have to get used to being alone in this house."

So Judith had driven to the house on Sixth East and they had sat up until almost two, she listening and Frank talking. Eventually they'd gone to bed and made love, but when it was over, Frank had lain beside her, his body still tense. "I don't know whether I can do it," he'd said, his voice hollow in the darkness. "Just thinking about those shafts gives me the willies."

"You'll be all right," she'd reassured him once more, but even as she spoke the words, she knew they were meaningless. The rest of the night had been spent restlessly as Frank tossed and turned.

Now he said tersely, "I can't afford to quit."

"I know," Judith sighed. "But if you're—"

Her words were cut off by the shrill jangling of the telephone. Frank picked it up. "Hello?" He listened for a moment, then his brows arched and he held the phone toward her. "For you," he said, puzzled. "A man."

"Judith?" It was Peter Langston. "What's going on? First Mrs. Moreland tells me you're not home, and then a man answers at the number she gives me. May I assume you've thrown me over completely and are now having an affair?"

"Peter!" Judith exclaimed, ignoring the question. "I was going to call you in a couple of hours. Have you found anything?"

The timbre of Peter's voice changed instantly. "I have, and I haven't," he said carefully. "I can't tell you what was in that syringe you sent me, but I can tell you that whatever it is, it's not a flu vaccine."

Judith felt a chill, and the look on Frank's face told her the blood had drained from her own. "Then what is it?" she asked.

"I don't know," Peter went on. "I gave a sample of it to our lab guys, and they were able to determine that it's not a vaccine for flu, or anything else. In fact, it seems to be a simple saline solution, but with some impurities in it."

"Impurities?" Judith repeated, her brows knitting into a deep frown. "What kind?"

"I wish I could tell you," Peter replied. "I'm working on it, but it's going to take a couple of days. Okay?"

Judith managed a wry smile. "Do I have a choice?" she asked.

"I'm sorry," Peter told her. "This place is all tied up with government work, and I just have to work this thing in when I can." He paused, but when Judith said nothing, he continued, "Look—I'll do my best, and get back to you as soon as I know something."

Judith nodded automatically. "Thanks," she said. Then: "Peter? Why would anyone want to inject a saline solution into a bunch of kids?"

There was a silence, then Peter spoke once more. "That's the thing that's got me curious," he said. "I can't think of any reason at all. So whatever the reason, it must have something to do with the impurities in the stuff. Is anything happening to the kids up there? Anything at all?"

"Not that I can see. And believe me, I've been watching. But nothing's happening to the kids at all. In fact, I was starting to think I was wrong about the shots."

"Okay," Peter sighed, his own bafflement clear in his voice. "And who knows? Maybe there *isn't* anything to it."

But as Judith hung up the phone she knew that Peter hadn't believed his own last words any more than she did. You didn't give a whole school full of kids a mass inoculation for no reason at all.

As she was telling Frank what Peter had told her, Jed came in and slid into his chair at the kitchen table, instantly plunging into the business of eating the plate of pancakes Judith put in front of him. As she finished her recounting of the call, her eyes moved to Jed. "What about it?" she asked. "Have you noticed anything about any of the kids? Anything I might have missed?"

Jed shrugged. "They're not dropping dead, or anything like that." He finished off the last morsel of pancakes, then picked up his book bag and headed for the back door. Abruptly he turned back, his eyes fixing on his father. "Dad?"

Frank looked up inquiringly. There was an odd look on Jed's face, and when he spoke again, his voice quavered.

"Be careful today, Dad. Okay?"

Frank felt a sudden tightening in his throat. It was the first time in years —perhaps even the first time since Alice had died—that Jed had exposed his feelings so openly. "I—I will, son," he said, surprised at the gruffness in his own voice. "And you too, right?"

But Jed shook his head. "I'm okay," he said. "It's you I'm worried about. Just be careful."

Before either Judith or Frank could say anything else, he turned and disappeared out the back door. At last Frank turned to Judith. "Do you have any idea what might have brought that on?"

Judith chewed thoughtfully at her lower lip for a moment, her eyes fixed on the back door. "He must have heard us talking last night," she said. And yet just before Jed had left, she'd seen an odd look in his eyes.

The same kind of odd look he'd had as he'd told her about his experience up at Kokatí three nights ago, when he'd seen things he couldn't possibly have seen.

Had he seen something else last night?

Frank Arnold shivered as he stared into the pipe. He hated the dam, hated the total lack of natural light in the narrow winding passages that honeycombed the massive concrete structure; hated the chill of the place, whose temperature never varied from 54° Fahrenheit; hated, most of all, his unreasoning fear of being trapped within the dam's confining spaces.

He'd stood above the dam that morning, looking down at it from the canyon's rim, telling himself it was perfectly safe, that there was no reason to fear it.

But even then his emotions had threatened to betray him, as he began to think about going down into it—not for a brief tour of inspection like last week's, but to spend the next eight hours crawling through its maze of passages.

Brown Eagle had suddenly appeared beside him that morning, seeming to come out of nowhere.

"It is a bad place," he'd said, as if reading Frank's mind. Frank had looked up, startled. He nodded grimly, then managed a grin. "Oh, I don't know. Not really much different from a kiva, I suppose. Dark, and closed in. Seems to me you'd like it."

Brown Eagle eyed Frank solemnly. "The kiva honors nature," he said. "The dam destroys it."

Frank had heard it all before, heard Brown Eagle ramble on for hours sometimes, talking about the patience of the Kokatí, and his faith that in the end the land would be restored to them. Then everything would be as it had been before the white men ever came. But the white men had been around for centuries now, and the dam for more than half of one, and Frank sometimes wondered if the Kokatí ever noticed that their spirits never seemed to do much about the situation. His eyes had drifted back to the dam for a moment. When he'd turned to speak to Brown Eagle again, the Indian was gone, having disappeared back into the desert as silently as he'd come.

Now, as he prepared himself to creep through the access hatch into the pipe that would take him to the main power shaft, opening into it just above the turbine itself, he heard Brown Eagle's words once more and decided he agreed with him. The dam was, indeed, a thoroughly bad place, and right now—if he weren't inside it—he might almost wish that the spirits, whatever they were, would destroy it.

He took a deep breath, hunched his shoulders, and snapped on the miner's light attached to his hard hat. Then he pushed his way through the hatch into the pipe itself.

Instantly, the space seemed to shrink around him, and he felt an almost irresistible urge to draw his knees up, push his back against the tight curve of concrete above him, and try to rise to his feet.

But he couldn't stand up, couldn't even get to his knees. The pipe, barely two feet in diameter, forced him to creep along, using only his fingers and toes to find slippery holds in the algae-covered concrete.

He felt bands of panic tighten around his chest, and stopped moving, concentrating his entire being on fighting the overwhelming urge to thrash himself free from the constrictions of the pipe.

He heard a sound, a crunching noise, and wanted to scream out as he imagined himself trapped inside the pipe as parts of the dam gave way.

No, he told himself. *It's not breaking up, and the pipe's not getting smaller, and I'm not trapped.*

He began talking to himself, whispering silently, giving himself a steady stream of encouragement.

It helped to keep the panic slightly at bay, and after a moment he began creeping forward again, down the pipe's slope.

He had moved no more than a few yards when the light on his helmet
went out and he was plunged into total darkness. Instinctively he clamped
his eyes shut, as if by doing that he could convince himself the suffocating
blackness wasn't real.

Clumsily he pulled the hat off his head and fumbled with the switch on
the miner's lamp. The light came on for a second, then went out again.

Panic was creeping up on him inexorably now. Before, he'd at least been
able to see the pipe stretching away in front of him.

Now there was nothing but blackness around him, and everywhere he
moved, the unforgiving hardness of cold concrete.

Terror loomed up inside him, and he tried to rear up to face it head-on.

The pipe let him move only an inch, then stopped him.

The terror grew, and he felt his mind beginning to give way.

He was going to die here. He knew it. The pipe was going to crush him,
close around him, snuff out his life the way it had snuffed out the dim light
of the lantern.

He felt as though he were going to explode. Finally he gave way to the
panic, thrashing himself against the walls of the pipe, as if to break loose
from the clutches of the concrete.

He knew now what it would feel like to be buried alive, knew the hope-
lessness of it.

He clawed at the concrete, his fingernails tearing and breaking as he
scratched away the algae and gouged at the stone and cement beneath.

Vaguely, he was aware of another sound, a keening wail that echoed
though the pipe like the cry of a tortured animal.

But it wasn't an animal.

It was himself.

And as he understood that the scream was his own, a tiny fragment of his
mind escaped the terror and took hold of him.

He began moving again, but no longer with the mindless churning the
panic had dictated.

Now he was seized with a single overwhelming imperative.

He would keep his mind intact, and escape from the pipe.

He slithered faster, pushing himself along, his eyes still shut against the
terrifying blackness.

He could hear something ahead of him now. He must be near the end of
the pipe, but he dared not stop, dared not even open his eyes to search for a
faint glimmer of light.

He had to get out. Had to escape. Had to keep going.

And then, suddenly, the pipe fell away beneath him.

His eyes flew open and he reached out wildly, searching for a handhold to stop his fall.

It was too late.

His own momentum carried his body out of the pipe, and then he was in the main shaft itself. There was light around him, shining down from above, and he could hear voices calling out to him.

Instinctively he twisted himself around as he fell, so that when he hit the turbine, it was his feet that made contact first.

He thought he heard a distinct snapping sound from somewhere, and then a blinding pain gripped his right leg.

He came to a stop.

"Don't move, Frank," he heard a voice saying.

He couldn't identify where the voice was coming from, couldn't see its source.

But it didn't matter, really. He knew he couldn't move, even if he tried. Blackness closed in around him again, but this time it didn't bring the stark terror of panic with it. This time, it brought only relief from the pain in his leg.

He had no idea how long he'd been unconscious, but when he opened his eyes, he was stretched out on the floor of one of the passages. He tried to sit up, but the pain in his leg stopped him even more effectively than Bill Watkins's restraining hands.

"Take it easy, Frank," Watkins told him. "You're okay, and we've got an ambulance on its way. Shouldn't be more than a few more minutes."

Frank winced against the pain, then forced himself to relax. "What happened?" he breathed.

"You panicked. Came shooting out of the feeder pipe like all the demons of Hell were chasing you. Except when you came out, there wasn't anything to grab onto."

Frank groaned softly. "How far'd I fall?"

Watkins smiled. "Not that far. Fifteen feet maybe." Then his expression sobered. "You were lucky. If you'd hit headfirst, you'd have broken your neck instead of your leg."

There were sounds of footsteps echoing hollowly in the passage, and two men in white uniforms appeared, followed by Greg Moreland. While the medics began unfolding a portable stretcher, Greg himself knelt beside Frank and took a syringe out of a small medical kit.

"What's that?" Frank asked, eyeing the needle suspiciously.

"Morphine," Greg told him.

Frank shook his head. "Forget it," he said. "It doesn't hurt that much."

"Don't be a hero," Greg replied, slipping the needle into a vein in Frank's forearm and pressing the plunger. "It might not hurt now, but when we start carrying you up topside, it's going to hurt like hell."

Frank started to protest once more, but as the drug quickly began to take hold, a feeling of euphoria came over him.

What the hell, he thought. Might as well enjoy it.

As the medics eased him onto the stretcher, he felt his mind begin to drift. Then they picked the stretcher up, and Frank closed his eyes until, a few minutes later, he felt the warmth of the sun on his face.

He blinked in the sunshine.

Overhead, the sky was clear, and an even deeper blue than he remembered having ever seen before. And then, soaring above the canyon, he saw an eagle.

His vision seemed to telescope, and suddenly he thought the eagle's head had changed, and it wasn't a bird at all that was staring down at him from the sky.

For a moment he thought it was his father-in-law, Brown Eagle.

Bullshit, he told himself. It's just the morphine. I'm stoned out of my mind, that's all.

He blinked, and looked up into the sky again.

The bird was gone.

Otto Kruger looked up at the sound of the ambulance siren and smiled with satisfaction. He'd already heard what had happened to Frank. It had worked—Frank was going to be out of his hair for a while. His musings were interrupted by a muffled roar, and he turned to gaze southward. Flying low, just clearing the top of the mesa, a huge helicopter was approaching. Hanging below it, suspended by steel cables, was a large object shaped like an enormous dish.

"Here she comes!" Otto yelled to the crew he'd been overseeing for the last two days.

The five men looked up, shielding their eyes from the sun, then scuttled off the concrete pad whose wooden forms they'd only torn away an hour ago. The chopper came closer, then hovered overhead, the huge antenna, complete with its rotating base, suspended only three feet above its pad. As Otto shouted orders, three of the men moved forward to guide the antenna onto the centering pins that rose up from the freshly hardened concrete.

Two minutes later the antenna settled down and the men quickly freed the steel cables. Otto waved to the pilot, and the 'copter rose once more into the air, swung around, and headed back south.

"Okay," Otto called to the crew as the pounding of the chopper's huge blades began to dwindle, "let's get her bolted down, and then start hooking her up. Kendall wants it in full operation by five o'clock this afternoon."

One of the men threw Kruger a dark look. "Who the hell do you think we are?" he muttered, already beginning the job of sorting out the leads that emerged from a piece of PVC pipe that had been laid into the concrete. A shadow passed over him, and he looked up to see Otto Kruger scowling at him.

"You being paid to talk or work?" Kruger demanded.

The man rose to his feet, towering three full inches above Kruger. When he spoke, his voice held a dangerous edge. "Look, smart boy," he said. "It takes exactly two and a half days to put one of these things in, start to finish. Five guys, two and a half days. This is the sixth one this crew has put in. Everything's on schedule. The pad, the chopper, the pipe down into the canyon. Only thing that's going to hold us up now is you. So why don't you just shut up and let us do our job, huh? Then we'll be out of this dump and you can go back to being King Shit. Okay?"

Kruger glared angrily at the man, but then subsided. Kendall had told him this crew knew what they were doing; in fact, Kendall had told him merely to give them whatever they needed. "Just make sure you get it done," Kruger growled. "If it isn't, it's your asses, not mine."

"Sure," the big man replied, deliberately spitting into the dirt at Kruger's feet. "I'll remember that." Turning his back on Kruger, he went to work. By five-thirty Borrego Oil Company, the newest acquisition of UniChem, would be fully integrated into the company's worldwide communications network.

As if, the man reflected, anybody really cared.

Borrego Oil Company, like its town, was a failing backwater.

In fact, he couldn't imagine why UniChem even wanted it.

What the hell could they possibly do with it?

Judith Sheffield was just about to leave her classroom to go have a cup of coffee in the teachers' lounge when her door slammed open and Jed, his face pale, rushed in.

Rising to her feet, her heart pounding with a premonition of what was coming, she took a step toward him. "What is it, Jed?" she asked. "What's happened?"

Jed leaned against the wall for a moment, catching his breath from the dash up the stairs to Judith's room on the second floor. "It's Dad," he gasped. "They just called Beckwith from the hospital. He's had an accident."

Judith's eyes widened in shock. "Frank?" she asked. "But what—" She cut off her own words. Obviously, whatever had happened, Jed didn't yet know the details himself. "Come on," she said, grasping his arm again, but this time steering him toward the side door and the parking lot. "I'll drive you to the hospital myself."

Chapter 16

Judith pulled the Honda into the parking lot next to the small hospital. A low, single-story building constructed of the ubiquitous cinder blocks, it had an emergency room at the front, with two small wings extending back to partially enclose a tiny courtyard. It appeared that the hospital had been painted green at some time in the past, but most of the paint had weathered away, and now the clinic had a strange speckled look to it, almost as if the building itself had contracted some rare disease. By the time she'd brought the car to a stop in a slot between two battered pickup trucks, Jed already had the passenger door open.

They found the waiting room deserted, but a moment later Gloria Hernandez, looking harried, emerged from the double doors that led to the emergency room. When she recognized Jed, she hurried toward him. At the look on the nurse's face, Jed froze.

"What is it?" he asked, his voice shaking. "What's wrong? Dad isn't . . ." His voice trailed off as he found himself unable even to finish his question.

Gloria shook her head quickly. "He's in the back," she said. "Dr. Moreland doesn't think it's too bad." Then, turning to Judith, she forced herself to smile. "I'm sorry," she said. "When I called the school, I didn't mean for them to make you drive Jed over here."

"It's all right, Gloria," Judith replied. "I—Well, I've been seeing Frank a bit lately. What happened?"

Gloria shook her head helplessly. "I'm not sure. They said he fell—"

She was interrupted by Greg Moreland, who strode into the room, wiping his hands on a white towel which he handed to Gloria. His brows arched slightly as he recognized Judith, and he offered her a quick nod before turning his attention to Jed, who was watching him anxiously.

"Your father's a very lucky man," he said. "It's a clean fracture of the right tibia and fibula, and he may have a slight concussion from hitting his head against the turbine, but given the circumstances, it could have been a lot worse."

Judith's eyes closed for a moment as she heard the words, and she felt some of the tension drain out of her body. "Thank God," she breathed. She stepped forward then, and unconsciously laid a hand on Jed's shoulder. "May we see him?"

Greg spread his hands expansively. "No reason for you not to," he said. "He's a bit groggy, and might not make much sense, but I'll bet he'll be glad to see you. They've just put him in a room . . . one-oh-six, I think."

As Jed moved toward the doors that led to the wing containing the rooms, Judith hung back. "What happened?" she asked when she and Greg were alone.

Greg shrugged. "A freak accident, from what I understand," he told her. "He was working at the dam, and apparently he panicked."

Judith nodded. "He was in the pipes, wasn't he?" she asked, her voice trembling from anger now, rather than from shock.

Greg cocked his head. "I'm not sure what you're getting at."

"He's claustrophobic," Judith told him. "He was afraid of going to work this morning. He was sure they were going to send him into the intake pipes, and he was sure that if they did, he was going to panic. Dear God," she went on, "this isn't the dark ages. There are all kinds of jobs up there. They didn't have to put Frank into a position like that!"

"Stop it!" Greg snapped, his voice commanding her to silence. "You're out of control, Judith," he said, then softened. "I didn't do anything. If you want to get mad at someone, get mad at Kendall or Kruger. They're the ones who sent him up there."

He was right. Judith took a deep breath as she struggled to regain control of herself. "I'm sorry," she finally said. "You're right, of course. I just—" She stopped. She'd been about to tell him that what had just happened to Frank wasn't the only thing on her mind, but then she'd remembered that it was Greg himself who had ordered the shots the other day. "I—Well, I guess I'd better go in and see him," she finished, glancing at her watch. "Damn . . . do me a favor, will you? Have someone call the school so they can cover my next class?"

Without waiting for a reply, Judith hurried toward the doors of the emergency room, unaware of Greg's eyes, still fixed on her, watching her speculatively as she left.

She'd been about to say something else—he'd seen it in her eyes. And then she had changed her mind.

Why?

What was it she had suddenly decided not to tell him?

Judith reached out and gently stroked Frank's brow with the damp washcloth Jed had brought from the tiny bathroom that connected Frank's room to the one next door. For a moment he made no sign that he even felt the wet coolness on his face, but then he stirred in the bed and his eyes opened. He gazed at her blankly, and then his vision cleared. His eyes darted around the room as if searching for something, and finally came back to her. He reached up and gently squeezed her hand.

"Judith?" he breathed, his voice raspy, his throat feeling unnaturally dry.

She picked up the glass of water on the stand next to his bed and held it to his lips, gently raising his head to make it easier for him. "Drink a little water," she urged.

He drank thirstily, then let his head fall back to the pillow.

"Hi, Dad," Jed said, stepping forward and reaching out to lay his hand tentatively on his father's shoulder. Frank looked up at his son, smiled and covered Jed's hand with his own. Then, as if embarrassed by the affectionate gesture, he dropped his hand to his side.

"What time is it?" he asked.

"Almost eleven," Judith replied.

"Jesus," Frank groaned. "It just seemed like a couple of minutes." Then, as his mind cleared further, he shuddered at the memory of what had happened to him.

Once again he glanced suspiciously around the room. "Who's here?" he asked, his voice dropping so it was barely above a whisper.

Judith frowned uncertainly. "Just Jed and me," she said.

"Nobody from work?" Frank asked.

Above him, he saw Judith and Jed exchanging a worried glance. He struggled to sit up straighter, wincing against the stab of pain that shot through his right leg.

"Don't," Judith protested, but Frank ignored her.

Gritting his teeth against the pain, he shoved himself up and back until he rested propped up against the pillows. Then he took Judith's hand again. "What did they say?" he asked. "Did they tell you what happened?"

Judith bit her lip as she nodded. "Greg said you were in a pipe, and panicked," she said. "It was an accident."

Frank was silent for a few seconds, but then his jaw set and his eyes met Judith's. "It was no accident," he said, his voice taking on a belligerent tone, as if he expected to be contradicted. Before either Jed or Judith could speak, he turned to his son and said, "Do you hear me, Jed? They tried to kill me today."

"Aw, come on, Dad," Jed began again, but Frank turned away and fixed his gaze on Judith.

"It was no accident," he repeated. "There was something they didn't tell me. That pipe doesn't go straight across to the shaft. It slopes a little, and then at the end it starts slanting real bad. But there's nothing to hold onto. Even if I hadn't panicked, I'd have fallen. And that's just what they were counting on."

Judith stared at him. "Frank, I can't believe that. It's . . . . well, it's just crazy—"

Frank shook his head. "It's not crazy," he said, his voice taking on a note of obstinacy that told both Judith and Jed it would be useless to argue with him. "They're pissed at all the yelling I've been doing, and they want to get rid of me. And they almost got away with it." He was silent for a moment, then his eyes clouded before he spoke once more. "And they won't stop," he said. "They'll do something else. They're going to kill me, just like they did Max Moreland."

Gina Alvarez glanced over at Jed and wondered once more if her idea of going for a horseback ride that afternoon was a good one. It had seemed like a terrific idea at the time, when she'd found Jed waiting for her after school, his face pale, and his eyes worried. But he'd barely even spoken to her, apparently off somewhere in a world of his own.

"What do you think?" she'd asked as they came to a fork in the trail, the one to the left leading up to the rim of the canyon, the other following the river into the canyon itself. When Jed made no response, she'd made the decision herself, opting to wind along through the cottonwoods, enjoying their shelter from the afternoon heat.

Finally, when the horses stopped to take a drink from the stream, she decided she'd had enough.

"Look," she said. "Either tell me what's bugging you or tell me you're mad at me or tell me to go home. If you aren't having a good time, I'm sorry. Maybe this was just a dumb idea in the first place. Okay?"

At last Jed seemed to come out of his reverie. "I'm not mad at you,

Gina," he said. Then, after a short silence, he added in a whisper, "If I tell you something, will you promise not to tell anyone else?"

Gina's brows creased into a rare frown, and she nodded.

Jed still hesitated, then made up his mind. "Dad thinks the company tried to kill him today," he said.

Gina stared at him, trying to decide if he was pulling her leg, but the look in his eyes told her he wasn't. "Come on," she said. "Why would they want to do that?"

Jed repeated what his father had told him earlier, and Gina listened to it all in silence. When he was done, she shook her head.

"That's nuts," she said. Jed's eyes instantly clouded, and Gina quickly apologized. "I'm sorry. I didn't mean your father's nuts. But it just seems like kind of a crazy idea, that's all. I mean, your dad was probably still in shock, or something, and besides, why would the company want to hurt him?"

"Because he's been making a lot of trouble for them," Jed replied.

"But that's nothing new," Gina protested. "He's always made trouble for the company. That's his job, isn't it? I mean, if the head of the union isn't supposed to make trouble, what *is* he supposed to do? Uncle Carlos says that's what makes him so good at it—he's never been afraid to say what he thinks."

"Yeah," Jed agreed, his voice bitter now. "And with Mr. Moreland, it didn't matter, 'cause they were friends. But it's all different now."

The horses, their thirst slaked, began moving along the trail again, and Gina was silent for a few minutes, her eyes fixed on the clear water of the stream. "Okay, so let's say the company did try to kill your dad," she said. "Can he prove it?"

Jed shook his head. "I don't see how. I mean, even he admitted it was partly his fault. If he hadn't panicked, he would have felt the bend in the pipe and stopped. But he says they were counting on him to panic. He says . . ." His voice faded away, and when Gina turned to look at him, he was looking the other way, across to the other side of the canyon.

Her own eyes followed his gaze. At first she didn't see anything unusual. They were about halfway up to the dam now, near the weathered frame building, nestled against the canyon wall, that had served as the construction headquarters back when the dam was being built. And then she realized what Jed was staring at.

The building, unused for years, had been repainted.

In front of it, several cars were parked, and when she looked up, there seemed to be some kind of plastic pipe—like a water pipe—rising up from the side of the building and snaking up the side of the canyon.

Gina looked at Jed, her expression puzzled. "I don't get it," she said. "I thought that building was abandoned."

Jed nodded. "It was," he said. "Or anyway, it used to be. But it doesn't look like it is now, does it? Come on."

He clucked to his horse and laid the reins over to the left. Obediently, the horse turned off the path, hesitated only a second, then began splashing across the river. Gina, kicking gently at her own mount, followed after him.

The bank was higher on the other side of the river, and Jed's horse stumbled as it searched for footing, then steadied itself, climbed the bank and came to a halt, as if waiting for Jed to indicate where it should go next. Jed waited until Gina caught up with him, then slapped the reins against the horse's neck. It began moving slowly forward until Jed drew it to a halt at the dirt road that ran past the front of the building.

The road, for years nothing more than a pair of nearly overgrown ruts, now showed clear signs of use. And there was a sign on the building:

BORREGO OIL COMMUNICATIONS CENTER
AUTHORIZED PERSONNEL ONLY

"Communications Center?" Jed read. "What does that mean?"

Gina's eyes followed the plastic pipe up to the canyon's rim. "Why don't we go up to the top and see what's there?" she asked.

Jed nodded, and they turned their horses back toward the mouth of the canyon, this time following the track of the old road. "Whatever it is, why would they put it up here?" Jed wondered out loud as they rode. "Nobody's used that building since the dam was built. It's not even safe anymore."

"It looked like they rebuilt it," Gina replied.

"But it's dumb," Jed objected. "I mean, it's stuck way up here in the middle of nowhere."

But when they finally came to the rim of the canyon above the old construction headquarters, Jed thought he understood.

The crew was just finishing up the installation. A six-foot Cyclone fence surrounded the antenna pad now, and the two teenagers stared at it curiously. Otto Kruger, his face florid from the long days in the sun on top of the mesa, jogged over to them. "What are you kids doing up here?" he demanded.

Jed gazed down at him. "We're riding horses, obviously," he said, making no attempt to keep his voice calm. "What's this supposed to be?"

"An antenna," Kruger told him. "UniChem flew the whole thing in this morning. Something, isn't it?"

Jed gazed at the huge machine for a moment. As he watched, it suddenly came to life.

There was a low humming noise, the base of the antenna began to rotate, and the dish itself tipped southward.

The humming noise stopped, and Jed found himself straining to hear the transmissions he was certain were now emanating from the huge dish. Indeed, he imagined he could actually feel them, vibrating through his body. But that was stupid—whatever frequencies they were using would be far out of the range of hearing.

"It's really something, isn't it?" Kruger repeated, his voice filled with as much pride as if he'd designed and built the thing himself.

Jed glared down at him. "Yes," he said finally. "It's something—something really ugly. As ugly as the wells, and the refinery, and everything else that's wrecking this place." Jerking on the reins, he turned his horse away and started back down the trail toward the town. A few moments later Gina caught up with him.

"What was that all about?" she asked. "I know you're worried about your dad, but—"

"But maybe I've just decided I don't like it, okay?" Jed asked. "Maybe I just don't like any of it."

They rode in silence for a while, until the town came into view. As Jed looked at it, after seeing the strange antenna that had suddenly appeared on the mesa and feeling the odd vibrations coming from it, he thought even Borrego itself looked different now.

The space age, apparently, had finally come to Borrego.

Maybe that's all it's really all about, Jed found himself thinking as he let the horse find its own way home, and his mind drifted back to his father.

Maybe it's not that I've changed. Maybe I'm just like dad. Maybe I'm just pissed off because things aren't like they used to be.

Rita Moreland sighed as she stepped out of the heat of the afternoon into the coolness of the house. She stopped in the entry hall, took off her hat and carefully placed it on the shelf in the coat closet. Then, as her eyes fell on Max's three coats, which still hung in their assigned places as if waiting for their owner to come and claim them, she bit her lip.

"I think perhaps it's time I started getting rid of some of Max's things," she said to Greg, but didn't turn to face him, unwilling to let him see the tears she could feel in her eyes.

"There isn't any rush," Greg replied. "You have plenty of time."

Rita's back straightened as she regained her composure, and when she finally looked at him, the tears that had threatened her only a moment ago were gone. "Perhaps I do," she observed. "But one never knows, does one?" She moved across the entry hall and into the library, her thoughts shifting to the hospital she had left only a few minutes before. "Look at poor Frank Arnold," she said. "He could have died today—he was lucky he didn't. And of course Max—" She broke off her own words as once more her emotions welled up within her, and quickly searched for something to take her mind off her husband. On the desk the red light of the answering machine was blinking, and though she often ignored it, she now punched at it hopefully.

But instead of a message of condolence, she heard an unfamiliar voice: "Mrs. Moreland, this is Forrest Frazier, with Southwest Properties in Las Cruces. I have a client who is very interested in buying your house. If you could give me a call, I'd like to discuss the details with you." A phone number followed, then the slightly metallic sound of the machine's synthesized voice as it announced the exact time the call had come in. Rita frowned, and looked at Greg.

"Now what on earth was that all about?" she asked. "What could he have meant?"

Greg shrugged. "Apparently someone wants to buy the place," he said.

"*This* place?" Rita asked. "But it isn't for sale."

"Maybe you ought to at least consider it," Greg said slowly, glancing around the large library. "I mean, given the circumstances."

Rita eyed her nephew acerbically. "You mean because Max died?" she said, willing her voice not to catch as she uttered the words. "Surely you aren't going to suggest that I'm going to . . ." She searched quickly for the right phrase, then: "Rattle around in this big old place," she finished. "Isn't that what they always say when half of a couple is gone?"

Greg swallowed uncomfortably. "I didn't mean that exactly, Aunt Rita," he said. "But in a way, it's true, isn't it? I mean, it *is* a big house, and—"

"It wasn't too big for Max and me," Rita retorted. Regretting the sharpness of her words, she cocked her head, and forced a smile. "Or are you just trying to get your old auntie out of town?"

And then, quite suddenly, Rita thought she understood. "That's it, isn't it?" she said, more to herself than Greg.

"Oh, come on, Aunt Rita," Greg began, but Rita waved his words aside.

"Not you, darling," she said. "I was just making a joke. But let's face it—

there *are* people who would just as soon see me leave Borrego, aren't there? You don't suppose it's UniChem that's making the offer, do you?"

Greg shrugged. "Well, it would certainly be easy to find out. Call up what's-his-name—was it Frazier?—and ask him."

Rita shook her head. "If it were UniChem, they wouldn't be foolish enough to do it directly," she said.

"Oh, Jesus," Greg groaned. "Now you're starting to sound like Frank Arnold!"

Rita's eyes flashed with anger. "Am I?" she asked. "Well, let me tell you something, young man. Your uncle was listening to Frank Arnold long before you arrived on the scene, and he trusted Frank. And I also know what Max would want me to do now, and it certainly wouldn't include selling my house and going elsewhere."

Greg took a deep breath. "Aunt Rita," he said. "I don't know why we're arguing. Nobody's told you to sell your house, and nobody's told you to leave town. All I'm saying is that it's something you should think about. The house *is* big, and it *is* full of memories, and you know as well as I do that Uncle Max often talked about getting rid of it when he retired. You two were going to travel, and he'd even talked about maybe moving to Hawaii." He shrugged as he saw his aunt's eyes narrow. "Anyway, I'm not trying to tell you what to do. If it hadn't been for that phone call, we wouldn't even be talking about it right now. But the call *was* on the machine, and all I'm saying is that maybe you should think about it."

Rita reached out and took Greg's hand, squeezing it fondly. "I'm sorry," she told him. "You'll have to forgive me. None of this has been easy for me, but I shouldn't take it out on you." She moved to the window and stood looking out over the desert. And then, almost unbidden, her eyes drifted up to the mesa, to the spot where she'd been in the dream the morning of Max's funeral.

Once more, she heard Max's words. *Listen to Frank.*

Then, in her mind, she heard Frank's own words, uttered only half an hour before, when she'd sat alone with him in the hospital room.

They tried to kill me, Rita. Just like they killed Max.

She stood still for a few seconds, the two voices echoing in her head. Finally she turned to face her nephew.

"All right," she said quietly. "I've thought it over, and I've made up my mind. I'm not selling my house, Greg. I'm going to stay right here, and I'm going to find out exactly who wants to buy my house, and why, and I'm also going to find out exactly what happened to Frank, and to Max too. Something is happening here, Greg, and I intend to find out what it is. I intend to find out, and put a stop to it."

She showed Greg out of the house, then went to Max's desk. Taking out a piece of his heavy stationery, and picking up his favorite pen, she began jotting notes; notes of what had been happening in Borrego over the past few weeks. She scratched down random thoughts, even impressions. And through it all she kept hearing Max's words from the dream once again: *Listen to Frank.*

She kept writing, kept searching for a pattern in the events she'd noted on the paper.

But there was no pattern, at least not yet.

Still, she was certain that sooner or later a pattern would emerge.

A pattern of death.

Chapter 17

Darkness had fallen and the first chill of the night had set in. Above Judith and Jed the sky was clear, the great swath of the Milky Way glimmering gently against a velvety backdrop. They stood silently for a few moments, gazing upward.

"Are you going to be okay?" Judith finally asked.

Jed nodded absently. "I guess," he said. Then, after a moment or two, his eyes shifted. "What about Dad?" he asked, his voice trembling. "Is he going to be all right?"

"Of course he is," Judith replied. "Why wouldn't he be? A broken leg isn't exactly the end of the earth. He'll be in the hospital a few more days, and then he'll come home." She forced a smile. "Our biggest problem will be getting him to take it easy for a while."

Jed nodded, but Judith could sense that something was bothering him. "What is it?" she asked. "What's wrong?"

Jed took a deep breath, then let it out in a long sigh. "I don't know. I guess it's just that this morning, when I woke up, I had this weird feeling something was going to happen to him today. And it did." He shivered, though the night wasn't that cold. "I keep thinking it was my fault, that I should have told him not to go to work today."

Judith shook her head. "It wouldn't have done any good. In fact," she went on, smiling wryly, "I tried it myself. I even suggested he quit. But you know your father . . ." Her voice trailed off. "Look," she said. "Do you want me to come home with you? I could spend the night, if you don't want to be alone in the house."

Jed considered it for a moment, but shook his head. "I'll be okay—Christ knows, there've been enough nights when Dad was working graveyards."

But later, as he pulled his father's truck into the driveway, he realized that tonight would be different. He let himself in the front door, and immediately felt the emptiness of the place. Always before, even when he'd been alone, he'd felt his father's presence. But tonight, knowing his father wouldn't be home in a few hours, a desolate loneliness seemed to emanate from the house.

He tried to ignore it, switching on the television and stretching out on the couch. But he couldn't concentrate on the TV. Instead of hearing the soundtrack of the movie, his ears kept picking up the sounds of the night outside.

He felt fidgety, nervous.

At last he got up from the sofa, picked up the remote control, and switched the television off again.

Silence closed in on him.

He wandered around the house for a few minutes, his nervousness growing by the second. Finally, making up his mind, he grabbed his leather jacket and went back out to the truck.

The A&W stand.

His friends would be there—it was Friday night. Maybe someone would even have gotten hold of a keg of beer. At least tonight there wasn't any chance of his father finding out what he'd been doing.

There were five of them up on the mesa an hour later. Randy Sparks and Jeff Hankins had already been at the A&W, and a few minutes later Gina Alvarez and JoAnna Garcia arrived on their way home from the movies. When Gina had seen the keg of beer in the trunk of Jeff's Plymouth, her eyes had narrowed ominously, but it had been JoAnna who had finally convinced her to come along. "We can tell my folks we watched the movie twice, and your mom won't even be home till after midnight."

Gina's eyes had shifted over to Jed. "No drag racing?" she asked. "If you wreck your dad's truck—"

"I promise," Jed had replied, putting on his best solemn face and crossing his heart. And he'd stuck to the promise, despite the way Jeff had tauntingly revved the Plymouth's engine as they'd left the A&W and started up toward the mesa.

Now the keg was half gone, and Jed was stretched out on his back, staring up into the sky. Gina was beside him, her head resting on his shoulder, her body snuggled close to his. He'd found an old blanket behind the seat of the pickup, and he was about to pull it over them when he felt something prod roughly at his side. He looked up to see Randy Sparks glaring down at him.

Randy was weaving slightly, and in his hand was a paper cup full of beer. "I wanta talk to you, half-breed," he said, his words slurred.

Jed felt his stomach tighten. When he'd arrived at the A&W, Randy had nodded to him but not said much. Since they'd come up to the mesa and started drinking, he'd noticed Randy eyeing him speculatively, as if he was trying to decide whether or not he could take Jed in a fight. For a while Jed had been on his guard, but when Randy had simply kept drinking, Jed had concluded that nothing was going to happen.

Now Randy's foot jammed into his side once more. "I said I wanta talk to you!"

Gina was sitting up now, one of her hands pressed against Jed's chest. "Come on, Randy," she said. "What's the big deal? You're the one who threw the rock through the Morelands' window, not Jed."

Randy glowered drunkenly down at her. "Yeah, but your Indian boyfriend's the one who told."

Jed thought quickly. The last thing any of them needed right now was a fight. And if they got caught out here with a keg of beer . . . "Look," he said, scrambling to his feet and picking up the blanket. "Let's just forget about it, okay? Maybe I didn't see you at all. Maybe it was just a lucky guess." Taking Gina's hand, he started toward the truck, with Randy staggering after him.

"Whatsa matter?" he shouted. "You scared to fight me? Huh? You a chicken-shit Indian?"

Jed froze, his anger finally beginning to rise, but Gina kept pulling him to the truck. "Don't listen to him," she said. "He's drunk, and he just wants to make trouble. Let's just split, okay?"

They were at the truck now, and Gina pulled the passenger door open, half shoving Jed inside. "Let's go," she pleaded. "Please?"

Randy was still shouting, but now Jeff Hankins was next to him, trying to calm him down. Jed started the engine of the pickup and backed away, then shifted gears. But as he pulled out onto the road, Randy bent down and picked up a rock, hurling it toward the oncoming truck.

Instinctively both Jed and Gina ducked as the rock came at them, and neither of them saw it strike the windshield. But a moment later they both saw the cracks, a spiderweb spreading out from the pit the rock had left in the glass.

"Shit!" Jed yelled, slamming on the brakes and starting to jump out of the cab. But even before the door was fully open, Gina grabbed at his arm, pulling him back.

"Don't, Jed!" she said. "Don't make it any worse! We'll figure out something to tell your father—maybe we can even get a new windshield before he gets out of the hospital."

Jed hesitated, torn. He wanted to jump out of the truck, grab Randy, and throw him down in the dirt. He wanted to make Randy eat his words, and a lot more. And he knew he could do it. He was bigger and stronger than Randy—always had been. And Randy was so drunk he'd barely be able to even throw a punch.

Maybe.

And what would happen tomorrow, when he had to explain to his father where he'd gotten a black eye, or a split lip, or any of the other injuries he'd brought home from fights over the last few years?

Taking a deep breath, he slammed the door once again, venting his anger by jamming the accelerator to the floor. All four wheels spun gratifyingly for a moment before the truck shot forward into the night.

"Slow down, will you?" Gina begged a couple of minutes later as they approached the hairpin turns of the switchbacks that led down to the desert floor.

Still breathing hard, Jed eased up on the gas pedal, then pressed the brakes as he steered into the first of the curves. As he approached the second curve, he slammed on the brakes, at the same time reaching down to switch off the headlights.

"What's wrong?" Gina asked. "Why are we stopping?"

Jed pointed out into the desert. "Look."

Far in the distance a pair of dim lights glowed. It was a car, moving slowly, its headlights extinguished and only its parking lights on. It was heading along the same road Jed and the rest of the kids had traveled two hours earlier.

"You think it's the cops?" Gina asked.

Jed shrugged. "I don't know. But why would anyone else be coming up here at this time of night? And with their headlights off?"

Gina's lips tightened. "I told you we shouldn't have come. If we get caught, Mom's gonna—"

"Just take it easy," Jed told her. Leaving the headlights off, he began carefully steering the truck down the twisting road. A few moments later they were close to the bottom, and Jed brought the pickup to a stop behind a large boulder. "Come here," he said, holding out his arms. "If it's the cops, it'll look like we just came out here to neck. They probably won't even stop."

Gina hesitated, then decided the ruse was at least worth a try. She slid across the seat and snuggled herself into Jed's arms.

The faint beams of the oncoming car's parking lights were brightening now, casting a dim glow onto the mesa's wall. Jed held his breath, knowing the car was approaching the fork in the road. If the twin shafts of light didn't swing away in a moment, it would mean the car was coming up the mesa road.

And then the beams suddenly moved toward them, only to disappear as the car took the turnoff just past the boulder that concealed the truck. Instantly, Jed opened the door and scrambled out of the truck, scuttling around the boulder until he could see the car as it started up the canyon. A moment later he was back, his brows furrowed.

"It's Dr. Moreland's car," he said. "What's he doing going up in the canyon in the middle of the night?"

Gina shrugged. "Maybe something happened up at The Cottonwoods," she suggested.

Jed shook his head. "If it's some kind of an emergency, how come he didn't have his headlights on? The way he was driving, it's like he didn't want anyone to see him."

Gina giggled softly. "Maybe he didn't," she said. "Maybe he's got a girlfriend up there and doesn't want anyone to know about her."

But Jed was barely listening, for he was once more feeling the strange vibrations he'd felt earlier that afternoon, when he and Gina had come across the new antenna UniChem had installed.

Frank Arnold lay in his bed, sleeping peacefully. Then, as midnight came, his eyes opened and he sat up.

Something was wrong.

There was a strange smell in the room, almost as if something was burning. And then the scent grew stronger, and changed slightly.

Garbage.

The air seemed redolent now with the putrid stink of a dump on a hot summer afternoon.

He could even taste the stuff. It was as if his mouth was filled with rotting eggs, and he felt himself begin to gag, then tried to reach for the glass of water on his nightstand.

He missed it, his hand brushing against it, knocking it to the floor.

Suddenly, streaks of light slashed through the darkness of the room, and he saw flickering images of strange creatures lurking in the corners. But when he tried to look straight at them, they seemed to disappear, only to reappear a moment later, coming at him from another direction.

A guttural sound rose from his throat as a wave of pure terror washed over him.

Something was coming at him out of the darkness, and he tried to strike out at it. His arms flailed wildly, and then, as a flash of pain lashed through his head, he tumbled from the bed.

He began screaming then, bellowing out in fear and rage, and a moment later the room filled with blinding light. On the floor, his body writhing, Frank tried to scrabble away from this newest assailant. He cowered against the wall, his arms wrapped around his body.

His mouth filled with the sickening flavor of bile, and then he was retching, vomit spewing from his lips in glutinous streams.

From the doorway Susan Paynter, the night nurse, stared in frozen horror at the spectacle on the floor. Then her years of training took over and she came to life. Pressing the buzzer that would summon an orderly to the room, she dropped onto the floor next to Frank and reached out to touch him. "It's all right, Mr. Arnold," she said soothingly, though she wasn't sure if he could hear her or not. "Just take it easy. I'm here to help you."

As her fingers touched his left arm, Frank screamed out again. His arm jerked convulsively, as if she'd burned him, and he tried to roll away from her.

His head struck the wall, hard. A second later he smashed it against the wall again, and yet again.

Susan heard a sound at the door and looked up. "Get Dr. Banning," she said. "Then call Dr. Moreland and tell him to get over here."

The orderly disappeared, and a moment later she heard his voice on the paging speaker, summoning Bob Banning to the room. Though the sound was barely audible in the room, it seemed to stimulate something in Frank Arnold, and now his whole body went into convulsions.

His broken leg swung around and the cast smashed painfully against Susan Paynter's knee. And then, as if someone had turned a switch inside him, he went limp.

For a split second Susan thought he had died. She seized his wrist, pressed her fingers into his flesh and counted quickly as she found his pulse.

At the same time, her eyes watched his chest begin to move in the slow and steady rhythm of strong breathing.

At last she heard Bob Banning's voice behind her.

"Jesus, Susan. What's happening in here?"

Susan glanced up. "I don't know. I found him like this." She slipped an arm under Frank's shoulders, and the doctor immediately squatted down to

help her. The orderly appeared, and together they managed to get Frank
back into bed.

Banning quickly began examining Frank, double-checking his pulse and
breathing, wrapping the rubber sleeve of a sphygmomanometer around his
arm. But as he began inflating the sleeve, Frank's eyes opened and he stirred
in the bed.

He looked up at the three faces above him, and his mouth opened. "Wh-
What's happening? Is something wrong?"

Susan Paynter stared at him. "Wrong?" she repeated. "Don't you remember what just happened, Mr. Arnold?"

Frank's eyes clouded slightly. "Nightmare," he said at last. "I think I had
a nightmare."

Susan glanced quickly at Dr. Banning, who nodded. "It was a lot more
than a nightmare, Mr. Arnold," she told him. "You started screaming, and
when I came in, you were on the floor. You smashed your head against the
wall, and then you started throwing up."

Frank's eyes widened and his gaze shifted to the doctor.

"You don't remember any of this, Frank?"

Frank shook his head and made a slight movement toward the glass of
water that was no longer there. Susan brought him another from the bathroom, then held it while he drank.

"I—I thought it was a dream," he said. "I woke up, and everything
smelled funny. Then I got this horrible taste in my mouth, and I started
seeing things . . ." His voice trailed off and he dropped back against the
pillows.

"Okay," Bob Banning said, squeezing Frank's shoulder reassuringly.
"Let's just check a few things and see where we are. And how does that leg
feel?"

Frank's lips tightened. "Hurts like hell," he admitted. "Feels like I kicked
something."

"You did," Susan Paynter told him. "Me." Then she smiled. "Don't
worry about it. I have a feeling that in this case, it really *did* hurt you a lot
more than it hurt me."

"Great," Banning commented dryly. "Well, when we're done here, we'll
take him in and X ray the leg again." He peeled Frank's left eyelid back,
examined the pupil carefully, then repeated the procedure on his right eye.
A few moments later he was at the foot of the bed, running the tip of a
pencil up the bare soles of Frank's feet.

Instantly Frank jerked his feet away, then groaned as the flash of pain
shot through his broken leg.

"Serves you right," Banning commented wryly. "Kicking nurses, indeed! Well, your reflexes seem to be in good shape. Other than your leg, how do you feel?"

Frank shrugged uncertainly, then leaned forward so Susan could strip off his filthy hospital gown. "Given what Susan says happened, not too bad, I suppose. But what *did* happen?"

Banning shook his head. "I wish I could tell you," he said, starting to make notations on Frank's medical chart. He glanced at his watch, frowned slightly, and turned to Susan Paynter. "How long ago did the seizure begin?"

Susan's eyes darted toward Frank, then returned to the doctor. "It was strange," she said, her voice muted. "I have my watch set to beep on the hour. And it had just beeped when I heard Frank scream. It was midnight. Exactly midnight."

Chapter 18

It had been more than a year since Brown Eagle had last been in Borrego, and as he left the pueblo at the first light of dawn the next morning, he felt as if he were embarking on a journey into an alien territory. He fell into the steady pace that could carry him across the desert all day if need be, but instead of turning his mind inward to close out the tedium of a long walk, he watched and listened eagerly as the landscape around him changed.

The last rustlings of the night creatures fell silent as they crept back into their burrows, shielding themselves from the heat of the day and the predators that stalked them from the sky as well as on the desert's floor. As the sun rose, Brown Eagle turned to face it, silently welcoming it back to the mesas. His eyes swept the sky, searching for the familiar shape of the bird whose name he bore, but this morning the sky was empty.

Brown Eagle took it as an omen. Today his personal totem had abandoned him. As he continued on his way toward the town, he felt lonely and unprotected.

He paused on the fringes of Borrego, feeling the familiar hostility that seemed to emanate from the town like an invisible sandstorm. During the months he'd stayed in Kokatí, avoiding the town completely, he'd almost forgotten the hostility toward his people that hung over it. But he'd never learned to ignore the way people looked at him, or, more exactly, failed to look at him, acting for the most part as if he didn't exist at all. He'd never grown used to their silent contempt for the Kokatí, and over the years, as his senses had sharpened with age instead of growing dull, he felt the malice clearly whenever he was forced to come down off the mesa. It seemed to reach out to him, as if it were trying to crush him.

He moved on, his head down, the pavement under his feet feeling too hard, the acrid smell of the refinery and the ugly cinder-block houses offending his senses. Finally he came to the house where his daughter had once lived. He walked around to the back door and let himself into the kitchen, sensing immediately that his grandson had not wakened yet.

He sat down at the kitchen table and waited.

Almost an hour later Jed, a bathrobe hanging loosely from his shoulders, came into the kitchen to start a pot of coffee. He stopped short, shocked by the sight of someone sitting at the table, then realized who it was.

"Grandpa? What are you doing here? How long have you been here?"

Brown Eagle grinned at Jed's surprise. "About an hour. I came to find out about your father. Is he going to be all right?"

Jed nodded, but then he eyed his grandfather suspiciously. "How did you know?" he asked.

"I saw them bring him down from the dam yesterday. In fact, I told him not to go into it at all."

Jed scowled darkly. "Great," he said. "I told him to be careful, Jude told him to quit his job, and you warned him not to go in the dam. He really listens to all of us, doesn't he?"

Brown Eagle eyed his grandson dispassionately. When Jed came up to the pueblo to visit him, there was so much of the Kokatí about him that he sometimes forgot the other half of the boy's heritage. But here, in his home in Borrego, Brown Eagle could see the other side of Jed, the side that would forever be alien to the Kokatí, the side he'd inherited from his father.

"Maybe he's as stubborn as you," he said. "It wasn't so very long ago you thought I was a crazy old Indian. Frank probably still thinks so."

There was a knock at the back door, and a moment later Jed let Judith Sheffield in. She put a box of fresh doughnuts on the counter, then noticed Brown Eagle. "I—I'm sorry," she stammered. "I thought Jed was by himself. If I'm interrupting something—"

"It's okay," Brown Eagle told her. "Jed didn't know I was here either." He eyed the box on the counter, and Judith groaned, handed it to him. He bit into one of the doughnuts, then, spoke again. "Tell me about Frank. Is he really going to be all right?"

Judith's eyes darted toward Jed. "I—I'm not sure," she said. "I called the hospital this morning, and they wouldn't tell me much, but I got the feeling something happened during the night. I came over to get Jed so we could both go see him."

Brown Eagle stood up. "We'll all go," he said. "He's still my grandson's father. He might not listen to me, but I care what happens to him."

As they drove to the hospital, Judith glanced at Brown Eagle in the rearview mirror. His face looked odd: his eyes, open and unmoving, seemed fixed on some object a few feet in front of him.

She turned her concentration to the road ahead, but a minute or so later, when she glanced in the mirror again, nothing had changed.

Brown Eagle seemed unaware of his very surroundings, as if he'd disappeared somewhere within himself, some place neither she nor anyone else could follow. Finally she turned to Jed. "Is he all right?" she whispered, nodding toward the backseat of the Honda where Brown Eagle sat, staring sightlessly out the window.

Jed glanced back, then nodded. "He's fine," he said. "He doesn't like the town, you know. So in his mind, he's gone somewhere else. The mesa, probably."

Jed's words echoed in Judith's mind as she continued driving. He'd said them so matter-of-factly, as if there were nothing strange about them at all.

She wondered if he even realized that until a few days ago, when he'd gone up there himself and spent the night in the kiva, he'd never have said such a thing, much less understood it.

Margie Sparks, her ample figure clad in a fading pink housedress, tapped at Randy's door, then let herself in. Randy was sprawled on his back, his eyes closed, and for a moment Margie thought he was still asleep. But when she spoke softly to her son, Randy's eyes opened and he sat up.

Margie eyed him carefully. His eyes were rimmed with red, and his complexion had the same sallow look her husband's always had the night after he'd been out on a toot. "You've got a hangover, haven't you?" Margie challenged, going to the window and pulling the drapes back, deliberately letting the morning sun glare into Randy's eyes. When the groan of protest she'd expected didn't come, she glanced back at Randy, then opened the window itself to air out the stuffy room. When she turned to face Randy again, fully expecting him to have buried his head under the pillow, she was surprised to find him still sitting up in bed, the sun in his eyes, exactly as she'd left him a moment before.

"What's wrong with you?" she demanded. "Don't feel so good?"

Randy shook his head. "I feel fine," he replied.

Margie frowned. Well, at least that was normal: no matter how bad he looked on a Saturday morning, he always insisted he felt fine. And he always lied about drinking, just as if she was blind and couldn't see how he looked. "What were you doin' last night?" she demanded.

"Me and some of the kids went up on the mesa," Randy mumbled.

Margie rolled her eyes knowingly. "And I 'spose you're going to tell me you was just lookin' at the stars, and nobody brought no keg of beer, right?"

Randy said nothing.

"Well?" Margie pressed, her voice taking on a shrill note.

Randy's eyes met hers. "We were just lookin' at the stars," he said. "Nobody brought no keg of beer."

Margie glared angrily at him. "You sassin' me? 'Cause if you are, I'm gonna have to have a talk with your pa. Now you tell me what you was doin'!"

Randy's face remained impassive. "We got a keg of beer, and we got drunk."

"Who?" Margie asked, suddenly suspicious. What was Randy up to this time? she wondered. "Who was with you?"

Obediently, Randy recited the list of names. When he was finished, Margie nodded knowingly. "Well, I might have known that half-breed Arnold kid would be there. He bring the beer?"

Randy shook his head. "I did," he said, his voice almost toneless.

Margie's mouth dropped open in surprise. What was going on? She'd have sworn that no matter how much she browbeat him, he'd never have admitted to having gotten the beer himself. Then she thought she understood.

"You're lyin' again, aren't you?" she prodded.

Randy shook his head, and once more Margie looked at him, trying to puzzle out what might have happened to him. Then she remembered the flu shots they'd given at school the other day. Vaguely, she remembered reading somewhere that sometimes the shots caused the disease instead of preventing it. She laid her wrist against Randy's forehead.

It seemed a little hot to her, but that could just have been the hangover. "You sure you're not sick?"

"I'm okay, I guess," Randy said, his voice still listless. Then he fell silent, staring off into space.

Margie cocked her head. "Randy? Is something wrong?"

Randy slowly turned to gaze blankly at his mother. "No," he said in the same dull monotone as before. "I'm fine."

Margie frowned thoughtfully. How many times had Randy claimed he felt lousy just so she'd let him stay in bed? And now, even looking like death warmed over, and owning up that he'd been out drinking till God knows when, he claimed he was fine. "Maybe you better go wash your face," she said. "It might make you feel better."

Immediately Randy got out of the bed and padded out of his room. A moment later Margie heard the sound of water running in the bathroom down the hall. She plumped up Randy's pillow, then headed toward the kitchen. "You come into the kitchen as soon as you're through in there, hear?" she called as she passed the bathroom door, expecting no reply and already sure that as soon as he finished in the bathroom, Randy would go back to bed.

"Okay," Randy replied.

Margie stopped in her tracks and gazed perplexedly at the closed door to the bathroom.

A few minutes later Randy appeared in the kitchen. He slid onto his chair, then sat still, as if waiting for his mother to serve him. "What's the matter?" Margie carped at him. "Can't you get your own orange juice?" She started toward the refrigerator, knowing Randy would never bestir himself—something he'd learned from his father. By the time she got there, Randy already had the door open and the pitcher of orange juice in his hand.

Margie regarded the boy in puzzlement, then slid a bowl of cereal in front of him as he sat back down at the table. To her surprise, Randy made no move to drink the juice or start eating the cereal. "Well?" she asked. "Aren't you going to drink it?"

Randy stared at the glass for a moment, then picked it up and began to drink. Only when the glass was empty did he put it back on the table.

Margie frowned. "Do you want another?" she asked.

Randy shrugged. "It's all right," he said. "I'm fine."

"Well, you don't seem fine to me," Margie groused, her lips pursing.

Her frown deepened as she studied Randy's eyes. There seemed to be something odd about them—they had a dazed look, as if there were something Randy didn't quite understand. "I think maybe you'd better go back to bed," Margie said at last.

Silently, Randy rose to his feet and disappeared back down the hall toward his room.

For a moment Margie considered calling Dr. Banning, but then changed her mind. Hangovers could do funny things to people. Probably all Randy needed was another few hours in bed.

After all, there wasn't really anything wrong with him, except for that funny look in his eyes. He just seemed totally listless; not at all like his regular self.

Well, for today, at least, she wouldn't worry about it. She'd just keep an eye on Randy, she decided, and if he wasn't better by tomorrow, she'd take him to see the doctor.

* * *

Frank Arnold was sitting up in bed, glowering angrily when Judith and Jed, followed by Brown Eagle, spotted him through the open door to his room. Judith was about to ask him what was wrong, when they entered the room and she saw Otto Kruger standing at the foot of Frank's bed.

"Will you tell him to get out of here?" Frank growled, jerking his thumb at Kruger.

"Now, come on, Frank," Otto said. "I didn't come here to get you upset. I just wanted to find out how you are."

"And I told you," Frank grated, his jaw clenching so that his words shot through his teeth like tiny darts. "I'm going to hire a lawyer, and I'm going to sue. What happened yesterday was no accident. Bill Watkins knew that pipe turned into a chute, and you knew it too. I know what happened, Kruger. They want me to shut up, and they're willing to kill me to do it. So I'm going to sue them. The whole bunch—UniChem, Borrego Oil, Kendall, Watkins, and you. Then we can all find out what's going on. Who knows?" he added. "Maybe we'll even find out what happened to Max!"

Kruger's face flushed angrily. "God damn it, Frank! Will you shut up and listen to reason for once in your life? You think I want to be here? I'm here because Kendall sent me. He says you should have had some kind of safety line if you were going to be in that pipe. UniChem's already agreed to take responsibility for the accident! You're getting all your expenses taken care of, and you'll get a big settlement as well." His eyes hardened and his voice took on a note of scorn. "If it was up to me, you wouldn't get a thing. But it's gonna be our word against yours, Frank. It was just an accident, pure and simple. So why the hell do you have to keep raving about some plot? You're starting to sound paranoid, for Chrissake!"

"Paranoid?" Frank repeated, heaving himself up into an upright position. "You listen to me, Kruger—" he began, but Judith cut him off.

"Stop it, both of you," she demanded. Her eyes fixed on Frank warningly, and she held his gaze for a moment. At last, reluctantly, he let his body relax.

Judith turned to Otto Kruger. "I think you'd better leave," she said coldly. "I don't know what this is all about, but I won't let you upset Frank."

"I'm only trying to reason with him—" Kruger began, but Judith shook her head.

"By telling him he's crazy?" she asked. "Please, just leave. All right?"

Kruger seemed about to argue, then turned and strode toward the door. Frank's voice stopped him just as he was stepping into the hallway.

"You can tell Kendall to get ready," he said. "I'm not kidding about this, Kruger. I *am* going to sue."

Kruger nodded. "I'll tell him," he said, his voice etched with sarcasm. "It's not going to make him feel particularly generous toward you, which I'd think you'd be worrying about right now, but I'll tell him." Then he was gone.

Deprived of his adversary, Frank was silent for a moment, then smiled weakly. "I guess I lost my temper, huh?" he said. "Seems like that's happening a lot lately."

Judith leaned over and kissed him. "Well, the way Kruger was talking, he had it coming. Frankly, I doubt the man even knows what a paranoid is!"

Frank slid his arms around her and gave her a squeeze, then nodded to Brown Eagle. "I guess you were right yesterday," he observed ruefully. "Thank you for coming." His eyes fixed on Jed. "You behaving yourself?"

Instantly, Jed thought of the shattered windshield on his father's truck, but then nodded. "Everything's fine," he said. "Nothing's going on that I can't handle."

Frank frowned slightly. There was something in Jed's eyes that told him the boy wasn't quite telling the truth. He was tempted to press the issue, but then changed his mind. If Jed thought he could deal with whatever was going on, he supposed the boy was old enough to try. He sighed heavily, then let himself sink back onto the pillow. "It seems I might have more of a problem than we thought yesterday," he said, choosing his words carefully. "I guess maybe you'd all better sit down." He glanced up at the clock on the wall. "Dr. Banning said he'd be here at eight-thirty."

Judith felt her knees weaken. "Did something happen last night?" she asked, sinking into the chair next to the bed. "If something happened, how come nobody called me? Or Jed?"

"Now, just take it easy," Frank said. "I had some kind of little seizure last night, that's all. It's probably nothing, but they've been giving me a lot of tests, and—"

"If it's nothing, why were they giving you tests?" Jed broke in. "If something happened, they should have called me. I would have come."

Frank eyed his son sardonically. "Were you home?" he asked.

Jed looked guilty. "I was out for a while," he admitted. "But I was back by eleven."

"And just where were you till eleven?" Frank demanded, unable to set aside his disciplinarian's role, even though confined to the hospital. Jed was spared having to face his father's probing stare by the appearance of Bob Banning. In his hand was a thick sheaf of papers, the results of the tests he'd administered to Frank during the long night. Frank fell silent as Banning began telling them what he thought had occurred.

Paul Kendall's eyes turned cold as he listened to Otto Kruger's report of his conversation with Frank Arnold. When Kruger was done, Kendall thanked him tersely, then sat for a moment, his fingers drumming on the top of his desk. He weighed his options carefully, but even as he conducted the mental exercise, he knew he was only wasting time; he'd made up his mind what he was going to do even as Kruger had been making his report. Finally he picked up the phone.

As far as he was concerned, the problem of Frank Arnold was now solved.

"Unfortunately," Bob Banning finished, "we don't have a CAT scanner up here, and until we can get Frank down to Santa Fe or Las Cruces, we won't know for sure. But he definitely underwent a brain seizure of some kind last night, at about midnight. It might have been a minor cerebral hemorrhage, but if it was, I think we'd have seen something on the X rays. And given the state of his reflexes, I'm more inclined to think it was something involving his nervous system. We discovered a slight fracture in his skull, just a hairline, really, but any blow to the head can cause all kinds of reactions, some of them immediate, some of them delayed."

Judith, her face ashen, stared at Banning. She'd tried to follow him as he reviewed the test results, but she'd been only half listening, her mind occupied instead with an image of Frank writhing in agony on the floor, bashing his head against the wall. "I—I'm sorry," she said finally, her voice barely audible. "I'm afraid I don't understand. Are you saying he had a *stroke?*"

Banning hesitated, then nodded. "I'm saying it's certainly a possibility."

Judith felt her blood run cold. First Reba Tucker, then Max Moreland, now Frank. "I see," she breathed. Then: "Is it going to happen again?"

Banning spread his hands helplessly. "It's hard to say," he said. "Until we know more, I wouldn't want to try to predict anything. But it seems to me . . ." His voice trailed off as Frank's body appeared to stiffen. "Frank?" he said. "You okay?"

"I—I smell something," Frank whispered. Then, as a sour taste began to fill his mouth, he felt a twinge of panic. "It's happening again, Dr. Ban—"

His voice faltered, and suddenly his eyes opened wide as his whole body went rigid.

"Frank!" Judith cried out. She rose to her feet, staring in horror at the figure on the bed. "My God! What's happening to him?"

She instinctively reached out to touch Frank, but as another convulsion seized him, he bellowed in agony and his right arm swung up, his hand smashing against Judith's cheek, sending her reeling against the wall.

As Brown Eagle moved quickly to Judith, and Jed stared at his father in shock, Banning jammed his finger against the signal button, but the instruments wired to Frank's body had already sounded an alarm at the nurses' station, and the door flew open. Two orderlies and a nurse came into the room, surrounding the bed.

Frank was thrashing wildly now, his face scarlet. His spine arched grotesquely and his left leg began twitching spasmodically.

"Get restraints," Banning barked. Instantly, one of the orderlies darted from the room. Frank's voice, his words unintelligible now, rose to an anguished scream, then was suddenly cut off as his body went limp.

"Hold him!" Banning snapped. The nurse and one of the orderlies grasped Frank by the upper arms, and then the second orderly reappeared. Working quickly, he strapped Frank's big body to the bed, attaching the last of the wide nylon straps just as another seizure gripped Frank.

His eyes popped open and his tongue protruded from his mouth. His throat began strangling, cutting off his anguished screams, and he struggled wildly against the bonds that held him to the bed.

"Can't you do something for him?" Judith moaned, her face smeared with tears as she stared helplessly at Frank. "My God, he's going to die!"

Banning spoke quickly to the nurse, and she disappeared from the room. A moment later she returned and handed the doctor a hypodermic.

But instead of plunging it into Frank's arm, he waited, watching.

"My God," Judith screamed. "Can't you see what's happening to him? For God's sake, do something!"

Then, as suddenly as it had begun, the seizure was over. Banning hesitated a moment, then handed the needle, unused, back to the nurse.

Ignoring Judith's sobs, he bent over Frank, checking his pulse and respiration, peering into his eyes.

"He's unconscious," he said. He looked at Brown Eagle, who was standing between Jed and Judith, his arms encircling them both. "You'd better take them out to the waiting room," he said, his voice gentle. "We have a lot of work to do."

Brown Eagle and Judith moved toward the door, but Jed remained where he was. His eyes met the doctor's. "Is he dying?" he asked, his voice eerily calm.

Banning hesitated. "I don't know," he said at last. "But I'm afraid I can't tell you right now that he's not." He saw Jed struggling with his emotions. "I'm sorry," he said. "We'll do the best we can."

Tears welled in Jed's eyes, then spilled over. But he said nothing, silently leaving the room to join Judith and his grandfather in the waiting room.

Chapter 19

The three of them sat quietly in the waiting room, each occupied with their own thoughts.

For Judith, the vision of Frank, his strong body contorted by the horrible spasms, was etched sharply in her mind. But slowly the image changed, and she saw him lying back against the pillows, drained, his eyes closed, all his vitality suddenly gone.

It wasn't fair, losing Frank now, just when she'd found him. She shivered as she remembered the feel of his arms around her body, the touch of his lips on hers. Now she might never experience that again.

No!

She shoved the thought out of her mind. People recovered from strokes —it happened every day. And Frank was strong and healthy. He'd be all right.

For a moment, just a moment, she almost believed her own thoughts. But then she remembered Reba Tucker, and Max Moreland.

And the shots.

Her mind went back to the previous day. They'd given Frank a shot.

No. Not "they."

Greg Moreland had given Frank a shot, just as he'd arranged to give every teenager at the high school shots.

She gasped, then covered her mouth as both Jed and Brown Eagle turned to look at her.

Greg? she repeated to herself.

Was it possible?

Of course not—she'd known Greg Moreland for years.

Except, of course, she hadn't. She'd known him once, ten years ago, when he'd been a medical student. But it had been a full decade since she'd seen him. And yet her mind still rejected her own thoughts. Greg was a doctor—a doctor who truly cared about his patients. He'd even spent a lot of his own money to build a private rehabilitation center. . . .

A rehabilitation center where Reba Tucker still lay, helpless after her own stroke.

But Max?

Surely Greg wouldn't have done something to his own uncle. No. It was simply not possible.

And yet the thought wouldn't let go of her.

She picked up a magazine and began to leaf through it, determined to put the terrible thoughts out of her mind. But her imaginings kept reaching out to her, twisting themselves around her mind like the tendrils of a plant, squeezing at her until she thought she'd scream. And then, when she thought she could stand it no longer, the doors from the back wing opened and Bob Banning stepped through.

For a moment, until she saw the look on his face, Judith felt a surge of hope.

Banning motioned them to stay where they were, coming to perch uneasily on the edge of a chair, his hands clasped together, his eyes grave.

"What's happening?" she heard Jed ask. "What's going on with dad?"

Banning shook his head, and Judith instinctively reached out to take Jed's hand. But Jed, his wary eyes never leaving the doctor's face, barely seemed to notice her gesture.

"I'm afraid the news isn't very good," Banning said. "He's awake again, but he's very groggy, and he's having a hard time speaking. I've checked his reflexes, and they don't look good. He's lost most of his control over his left arm, and he can't move his left leg at all. This time I'm sure of what happened. He definitely had a stroke, and it looks like a bad one."

A tiny wail of anguish tore itself from Judith's lips, but she quickly bit it back, determined not to let herself come apart. Jed, feeling dazed by what he'd just heard, stared anxiously at the doctor.

"But . . . he'll be okay, won't he?" Jed asked, his voice taking on a desperate tone. "I mean, people can get better after strokes, can't they?"

Banning chewed at his lower lip, choosing his words carefully before he spoke. "Yes, they can," he said at last. "And Frank's got a lot going for him. He's comparatively young, and he's strong as an ox." Then, as both Judith and Jed appeared ready to grasp at the straws he'd offered them, he added: "The problem is that we don't yet know how serious his head injuries are. They looked pretty minor until last night, but now I have to tell you that he's in grave danger Apparently he has some blood clots in his brain. We're analyzing the possibilities of trying to relieve the pressure in his head surgically—"

"You can do that?" Brown Eagle asked. "You can operate on him?"

Banning spread his hands helplessly. "We don't know yet. We're trying to lower his blood pressure, and then we'll do another evaluation. But if he should have another hemorrhage while he's on the operating table, it could be pretty serious."

Judith's eyes closed for a moment, as if to shut out the implications of the doctor's words, and suddenly her mind filled with another image of Frank, this time sitting bolt upright in his bed, his face scarlet as he raged at Otto Kruger.

"Kruger," she breathed. "If he hadn't been here—"

Banning held up a restraining hand. "I thought about that," he said. "And of course if I'd known what was going to happen, I wouldn't have let him see Frank. But it isn't necessarily related."

Jed's eyes darkened. "I don't believe that," he said, his voice trembling with anger. "If you ask me, he came just because he knew it would piss dad off—" He cut off his own words, and his shoulders slumped. "What the hell difference does it make?" he asked hollowly. Then his eyes went back to Banning. "Can I see him?"

Banning hesitated, then nodded. "But don't be surprised if he doesn't recognize you," he said. "And don't stay long."

Jed nodded, then stood up. For just a moment his legs threatened to buckle under him, but he steadied himself and pushed through the doors into the east wing. He paused outside his father's room, took a deep breath and let himself in.

His father, lying flat on his back now, with a Levine tube in his nose and an array of wires connecting his body to a bank of monitors on a portable rack next to the bed, seemed to have shrunk since Jed had last seen him. His face was a pasty white, and his arms, lying limply by his sides, looked like the flaccid limbs of a man nearly twice his age. As Jed came in, Gloria Hernandez glanced up at him and gave him an encouraging smile.

"You've got a visitor, Frank," she said, motioning Jed over to the bed.

Jed stared down at his father's sallow face, and his eyes flooded with tears once again. He tried to speak, but his voice failed him. Then he saw that his father was trying to smile, and heard a garbled sound bubble up from his lips.

Jed leaned closer, and Frank's lips worked spasmodically. When he finally managed to speak again, the words came out slowly, one at a time.

"I . . . said . . . I . . . really . . . blew . . . a . . . fuse . . . this . . . morning."

The words seemed to break the tension in Jed. He reached out and touched his father's hand. "Gee," he said, forcing his voice not to tremble, "out there, they told me you were really sick. I guess they don't know what they're talking about, do they?"

Frank's head moved in a tiny nod and he managed to wink approvingly at Jed. "Good boy," he whispered, his words barely intelligible. "Never let 'em see you sweat . . ."

He gasped for breath, the effort of enunciating the words seeming to have drained him. Jed felt a knot of fear grip his stomach, and he squeezed his father's hand. "It's okay, Dad," he said. "Don't try to talk."

But Frank's head moved again, and as his lips began to work, Jed leaned close. "Take . . . care . . . of . . . Judith. . . ." He winced slightly, then strained to speak once more. "They're . . . killing . . . me. . . ." He whispered, his voice all but inaudible. "They're—"

Frank's voice strangled and his fingers tightened on Jed's hand like a vise. Jed's head jerked up and he instinctively looked at Gloria Hernandez just as the nurse roughly pushed him aside.

"He's having another stroke," she said.

But this time it was over almost as soon as it began.

Frank's body went rigid for a moment, and his face twisted into a brief grimace of pain. Then, quite suddenly, he relaxed. His body went limp and his head rolled to one side. Jed, terrified, stared at his father.

"Dad?" he said. *"Dad!"*

The door flew open and Bob Banning, followed by an orderly, rushed into the room. "What's happened?" Banning asked, his eyes scanning the machines.

"Another stroke," Gloria told him. "It didn't last long, but it looked real bad."

"Damn," Banning cursed quietly, his eyes fixed on the monitor that displayed Frank Arnold's brain waves.

The lines running steadily across the screen were jagged and uneven, accurately reflecting the chaos that was occurring in Frank Arnold's brain.

Given what was happening to him, Banning could only believe that it was a blessing that Frank had sunk deep into a coma.

Judith sat in her car, trying to gather her wits together. She still wasn't certain what it was she hoped to accomplish by coming to The Cottonwoods. But as she'd sat waiting for Jed, then heard about Frank's third stroke, she'd known she had to come out here and at least try to find out exactly what had happened to Reba Tucker. Not, really, that she expected much, but at least she felt like she was *doing* something.

She stared at the place, slowly realizing that she'd subconsciously expected to see something quite different; perhaps even something sinister. But there was nothing about it that was out of the ordinary at all. It seemed to be nothing more than an old frame ranch house, together with what had apparently been a stable, a small barn, and a few smaller buildings that might have been guest quarters or bunkhouses, all of them scattered through a large grove of cottonwoods that was nestled against the canyon's northern wall. It was quiet here—birds chirped softly as they hopped among the branches of the trees, and the stream, flowing lazily in its bed along the south wall, was nearly silent; only a faint babbling sound revealed its presence at all.

She got out of her car and walked toward the main building, enjoying the coolness of the canyon. A few moments later she stepped through the front door, and almost immediately a woman she didn't recognize appeared from an office in the rear. The woman greeted Judith warmly enough, but when Judith told her she was there to see Reba Tucker, the welcoming smile was replaced with a small frown.

"Are you a relative?" she asked, eyeing Judith doubtfully.

"No, I'm not," Judith told her. "My name's Judith Sheffield. I—I used to be a student of Mrs. Tucker's." She wasn't sure quite why she hadn't told the woman she had also taken over Mrs. Tucker's job at the school, but something in the back of her mind told her to reveal as little as possible.

"Well, I don't know," the woman mused doubtfully. "Mrs. Tucker doesn't have many visitors . . ."

Judith's nerves, already frayed from the hours at the hospital, snapped. "Is there any reason why I can't see her?" she demanded.

The woman appeared flustered. "Well, no," she began, but Judith, sensing that she was about to qualify her words, let her go no further.

"In that case, why don't you just tell me where she is?"

The woman, looking trapped, glanced around as if hoping someone might appear to relieve her of the decision as to whether or not to allow Judith access to the patient. When no one appeared, she sighed heavily. "She's in Cabin Three," she said. "Just follow the path around the back, then keep to the right."

Moments later, as Judith gazed curiously at the small cabin that was set in a grove of cottonwoods, she realized that from the woman's attitude, she'd half expected to see heavy wire-mesh panels covering the windows of the building, or perhaps even bars. But there seemed nothing odd about the cabin at all. It was simply a square frame building, maybe twenty feet on a side, painted a neutral shade of beige with dark brown shutters flanking the windows on either side of the door. Unconsciously drawing herself up straighter, Judith walked up to the cabin's door and rapped sharply. The door opened and a heavyset woman whose features had all but disappeared into the puffy flesh of her face looked at her suspiciously. The woman wore a rumpled white nurse's uniform, and a badge on her ample bosom identified her as Elsie Crampton.

"I—I came to see Mrs. Tucker," Judith stammered uncertainly as the nurse said nothing to her at all. "Is this the right cabin?"

Elsie Crampton shrugged. "This is it," she said. She held the door open, and Judith stepped into the cabin. Its walls were paneled with knotty pine, and a worn carpet covered most of the wooden floor. A hospital bed sat next to the window on the far wall, and by another window there was a worn chair.

In the chair, staring out at the canyon, sat the huddled form of Reba Tucker. In the ten years since Judith had seen her, the woman had aged terribly, though Judith had no doubt that most of the aging had taken place in the last few weeks.

"Mrs. Tucker?" Judith breathed.

There was no response from the figure in the chair. Judith glanced at the nurse. "Can she hear me?" she asked.

"Hard to say," Elsie replied. "The doctor says she can, but you couldn't make me swear to it. They say she's had some kind of stroke, but if you ask me, she's just gone senile."

Judith felt a flash of anger toward the nurse, but did her best to conceal it.

"Well, I got some things to take care of," Elsie Crampton went on. "If you need me, there's a bell there by the bed," she added, her tone clearly implying that she hoped Judith wouldn't use the bell. Turning her back on Judith, she walked out of the cabin, pulling the door shut behind her.

Judith stood still for a moment, then moved over to the chair by the window. Kneeling down, she gently touched Reba Tucker's arm. "Mrs. Tucker?" she asked again. "It's me. Judith Sheffield. Can you hear me?"

As if from a great distance, Reba Tucker heard the voice speaking to her, and a memory stirred within the fragments of her mind.

This was a voice from the past, not one of the voices she knew from the endless expanses of time since she had awakened and found herself in this frightening place. Concentrating hard, she turned her head slightly, and her eyes examined the face that seemed suspended in front of her.

She recognized the face too. It was from somewhere long ago, before she'd died and gone to Hell. "Judy . . ." she breathed, her own voice sounding strange and unfamiliar to her.

A surge of excitement welled up in Judith. Mrs. Tucker *could* hear her; had even recognized her. "I came to find out what happened to you, Mrs. Tucker," she said, enunciating each syllable slowly and distinctly.

Reba felt her mind drifting, saw the image of the face fading slowly away. She concentrated harder, struggling to keep the image intact and to make sense out of the words Judy had spoken.

"Dead," she whispered at last. "Hell . . ."

Judith's heart sank. Had Mrs. Tucker completely lost her mind after all? "No," she said. "You aren't dead, Mrs. Tucker."

Reba's mind grappled with the words. "Live?" she gasped. Then, her eyes flooding with tears, she shook her head.

"You *are* alive, Mrs. Tucker," Judith insisted. "You're alive, and you got sick, and they brought you here. They're trying to make you well again."

Reba's shattered brain picked at the words, then, once more, she shook her head slowly. "Hurt . . ." she breathed.

Judith frowned. "Hurt?" she repeated. "They hurt you?"

Reba Tucker's eyes clouded and her head moved slightly as she nodded. Then her voice crept forth from her lips again, and her hand reached out to seize Judith's own. "Smells," she managed to say. "Bad. See things . . . Bad . . ." She paused for a moment, then gasped one more word. "Hurts."

Judith felt tears in her eyes as she saw the pain and suffering that was etched in Reba Tucker's face. The woman's fingers, swollen with arthritis, clutched at Judith again, and she watched helplessly as Reba struggled to speak once more.

"Night," she managed to whisper. "Night . . . hurts."

Judith looked at her helplessly, but there was something flickering in the depths of the woman's eyes that told her that whatever had happened to Reba Tucker, she was certainly not senile. She seemed to be trying to reach out, trying to tell Judith what had happened, but finding the task nearly impossible. Desperately searching for something that might help her understand, Judith's eyes scanned the room.

And there, hanging at the foot of Reba Tucker's bed, was a metal clipboard.

Gently extracting her hand from Reba's grip, Judith hurried to the bed and took the clipboard off its hook. Her eyes ran down it quickly, trying to comprehend all the abstruse words and phrases that were jotted there in a nearly incomprehensible medical shorthand. She flipped through the pages, and then her eyes stopped at the last entry. In a sloppy handwriting—a scrawl that Judith automatically matched to Elsie Crampton—was a single word. "Seizure." Next to the word was the time: 12:15 A.M.

Judith's lips tightened and she put the clipboard back on its hook, then went back to kneel by Reba Tucker once again. "You had a seizure last night, Mrs. Tucker," she said. "Can you tell me anything about it? Anything at all?"

But Reba Tucker's eyes had glazed over, and she was once more staring out the window. Judith spoke to her again, then gently stroked her hand.

There was no response from the old woman.

Judith stood next to the chair for a few minutes, trying to think of something—anything—she might be able to do for Reba Tucker. But she knew there was nothing. Indeed, if it hadn't been for that strange, desperate light that had come into Reba's eyes, and the fact that she had spoken the name that Judith hadn't used for nearly a decade, she would have tended to agree with Elsie Crampton's judgment that Reba Tucker had turned senile. But that flicker of intelligence she'd seen had told her that Reba had been struggling to tell her as much as she could, or at least as much as she understood, of what had happened to her. And what had happened to her, as far as Judith was able to see, was that her mind had been destroyed.

Turning away, she moved to the cabin door and stepped outside. She spotted Elsie Crampton standing under a cottonwood tree a few yards away, smoking a cigarette. Making up her mind, Judith walked over to her. "I saw her chart," she said. "I—I hope it's all right."

Elsie shrugged. "It's all right with me," she said. "I don't guess it's any big secret, if they leave it hanging there."

Judith nodded. "I was wondering what happened last night," she said. "I saw that she had some kind of seizure or something."

Elsie took another drag on her cigarette, then dropped it to the ground, grinding it into the dirt with her toe. "She started screaming," she said, her face setting in disapproval. "She went to sleep right after dinner—not that she ate much—and then in the middle of the night she just started yelling her head off. Don't know exactly what happened. By the time I got there, it was all over with."

Judith stared at the woman in disbelief. "You mean she's in there all by herself at night?" she asked. "How can they do that? She's helpless!"

Elsie shrugged. "Don't ask me," she said. "I don't make up the policies around here. I just do what they tell me." But her eyes darted toward the main building and her voice dropped a notch. "If you ask me," she said, "it doesn't seem like anyone around here really cares if the patients live or die. 'Course," she added, "that's the way most of these places are, isn't it? The checks come in, and nobody pays much attention to what happens." She shook her head. "Seems like a crappy way to spend your last years, though, doesn't it?" She looked at Judith. "She say anything? Mrs. Tucker, I mean?"

Judith hesitated, then shook her head. "No," she said. "I'm not even sure she knew I was there."

Elsie Crampton nodded. "Yeah, that's the way she is, all right. Just nothing left of her at all."

Judith nodded absently, already thinking of something else. "The seizure," she said. "On the chart, it said it happened at a quarter after twelve."

Elsie shrugged. "Well, that's what time I got there, I guess," she said. "Actually, I think it hit her just about midnight."

Judith felt a chill run through her.

It was at midnight last night that Frank had suffered his first stroke.

Gina Alvarez stood outside the Sparkses' house, hoping she wouldn't lose her nerve. But why should I? she asked herself. After all, Randy was the one who broke the windshield. Why should Jed have to pay for it? Especially after what had happened this morning.

She'd called Jed earlier, and when he hadn't answered the phone, she'd called the hospital. But when Gloria Hernandez let her know what had happened to Jed's father, Gina told the nurse not to call him to the phone. "I'll come over after a while," she'd said. "There's something I have to do first."

Finally, summoning up her courage, she went up to the front door and pressed the bell. A few seconds later Mrs. Sparks opened the door a crack, looked suspiciously out, then opened the door wider.

"Well, for heaven's sakes," she said. "Look who's here! Come on in."

But her welcoming smile faltered when Gina asked if Randy was home. "Oh, yeah," she said, jerking her head toward the hall. "He's still in bed, sleeping it off." Her eyes narrowed slightly. "You weren't up on the mesa with him last night, were you?"

Gina hesitated, then nodded.

"Hmph," Margie snorted. "Thought you were better than that."

"I—I really need to talk to Randy," Gina said.

Margie Sparks shrugged carelessly. "Suit yourself," she said. "But I warn you—he's acting kind of weird this morning. Not that he's getting any sympathy from me—the idea, a sixteen-year-old kid waking up with a hangover. Well, like father, like son, I always say."

As Margie moved off toward the kitchen, Gina made her way down the hall until she came to a closed door that she assumed was Randy's. She knocked, and when there was no response, tried the door. It was unlocked, and when she opened it a crack and looked inside, she saw Randy lying in bed, his eyes open, staring at the ceiling. "Randy?" she asked.

His head rolled over and he gazed at her blankly.

"It's me," Gina said. She stepped into the room, and Randy finally sat up. "Your mom says you're sick."

Randy shrugged. "I'm fine," he said.

Gina cocked her head. There *was* something weird about Randy today. His eyes looked strange—empty—and his mouth seemed to have lost the sneer he usually affected.

"Well, you shouldn't be fine," Gina said. "Not after what you did last night."

Randy made no reply. Instead he simply sat up in bed, staring at her.

"You broke the windshield on Mr. Arnold's truck, you know," Gina said. "Or don't you remember?"

Randy nodded. "I remember."

It was the tonelessness of his voice that finally made Gina mad. It was as if he didn't even care. "Well, what are you going to do about it?" she demanded.

Randy only seemed puzzled. "What am I supposed to do about it?"

Gina glared at him. What was wrong with him? "Well, the least you can do is pay for it!" she exclaimed. "Why should Jed have to pay for it? He didn't do anything to you."

"All right," Randy said.

Gina stared at him, shocked. She couldn't imagine he wasn't even going to argue with her. Now she eyed him suspiciously. "It costs two hundred and fifty dollars," she said. "I called the Ford dealer in Las Cruces this morning."

She'd expected Randy to start laughing at her now, but instead he got out of bed, stark naked, and went to the chest of drawers that stood against the wall under the window. Too shocked even to speak, Gina simply stared at him. Randy pulled the bottom drawer completely out of the dresser, then reached in and fished out an envelope that had been taped to the inside of the dresser's frame. Opening it, he counted out $250, then replaced the envelope and the drawer. Handing Gina the money, he climbed back into bed.

Stunned, Gina gaped at the money in her hand, then turned to gaze at Randy again. "Wh-Where did you get this?" she asked.

Randy shrugged. "I stole some of it. I made the rest selling drugs at school."

Gina felt her knees start to shake. It was crazy—all of it. She'd expected him to laugh at her—in fact, she'd expected him to flat-out refuse to pay for the windshield. She thought she'd at least have to plead with him, maybe even threaten to tell his mother what had happened.

But she'd never expected what had just happened.

And now Randy was just lying there in bed, as though he hadn't done anything strange at all. "L-Look," she stammered. "I've got to go, okay?"

Randy said nothing. She wasn't even certain he'd heard her. He was just looking off into space again, with the weird, empty look in his eyes. Stuffing the money into her pocket, she hurried out of the Sparkses' house, not even stopping to say good-bye to Randy's mother.

Twenty minutes later she was outside the hospital, wishing there were some way she could avoid going in. She hated hospitals, hated the smell of them, and the whole atmosphere of sick people. She could remember vividly the time when she was only five and her mother had brought her here to visit her grandmother. She had barely recognized the old woman lying in the bed, her eyes—eyes that had always before twinkled so merrily at Gina —now dull and lifeless. Her grandmother had held out a hand to Gina, and though she hadn't wanted to take it in her own, her mother had made her, and finally she'd touched the old lady's damp and clammy flesh, then let go immediately, hiding her hands behind her back. Ever since that day, whenever she had to come to the hospital she remembered her dying grandmother, and felt again her strange, cold touch. Still, she had to see Jed. Taking a deep breath against her apprehension, she pushed open the door and went into the waiting room.

Jed was slumped on the sofa, staring into space, and it wasn't until she sat down beside him and took his hand in her own that he finally noticed her.

"What's happened?" Gina breathed, though she was certain she already knew. "Your dad didn't . . ." Her voice trailed off as she found herself unable to utter the word.

Jed bit his lip, then shook his head. "He's not dead," he said, his voice rough with emotion. Then his eyes met hers. "But he might as well be. He —He's in a coma." Jed's eyes flooded with tears. "He's just lying there,

Gina. He doesn't move, and when you touch him, he doesn't react, or anything."

Gina squeezed his hand, uncertain what to say. They sat silently for a few minutes, then Jed turned to look at her. "Oh, Jeez," he said. "I was going to come over this morning, wasn't I?"

"It's all right," Gina told him. And then she began telling Jed what had happened at Randy's house. "It was weird," she finished, almost fifteen minutes later. "He just did what I told him to do. And when he got out of bed, it was like he didn't even know he was naked."

Jed gazed at her. "You sure he wasn't stoned?"

Gina shook her head. "Uh-uh," she said. "It was like he was dead. It was like something had gotten into his brain and killed it."

Chapter 20

Rita Moreland was upstairs in the room she'd shared with Max, slowly going through the painful process of sorting through his things. The windows were opened wide to catch the afternoon breezes, and when she heard the crunching of tires on the gravel drive, she felt relieved to have an excuse to take a break from her work.

She arrived at the foot of the stairs just as the front door opened and Judith Sheffield stepped in.

"You're home," Rita said, starting down the stairs. But then, as she saw Judith's ashen face, she paused. "It's Frank, isn't it?" she breathed. "Has he died?"

Judith closed the door behind her, leaning against it for a few seconds, trying to gather her thoughts before she spoke. How could she tell Rita what she was thinking? Finally she shook her head. "No," she said. "He's not dead. But he's had a series of—" Her eyes met Rita's then. "He's had a series of strokes, Rita."

Rita froze on the stairs and her face paled, but then she recovered herself. She came to the bottom of the stairs and took Judith by the arm. "You look like you need a drink," she said. She guided Judith into the living room, steered her into a chair, then went to the bar and took out the decanter that contained the last of Max's favorite bourbon. Pouring an inch and a half into each of two tumblers, she handed one of them to Judith. "Drink this," she said. "Then tell me what's happening." Her eyes, clear and unfrightened, fixed on Judith. "There *is* something happening, isn't there?" she asked.

Judith nodded, feeling the tension in her own body easing in the face of the older woman's cool control. She raised the tumbler to her lips. The whiskey burned her throat as it went down, but as it hit her stomach, a reassuring warmth spread through her body, and the chill that had seized her as she'd driven down from The Cottonwoods began to loosen its grip. Slowly, she began to tell Rita everything that had happened, everything she was thinking. The only thing she left out was the single common denominator.

Greg Moreland and his shots.

"I know it sounds crazy," she said when she was finished. "I know I must sound just as paranoid as everyone claims Frank is."

For a long time Rita said nothing. She leaned back in her chair, her eyes leaving Judith to study the glass in her hands, which she began slowly rolling one way and then another. At last, as if she'd come to some kind of internal decision, she faced Judith once again.

"We don't all think Frank is paranoid," she said. "Certainly I don't. But there's something you've left out, Judith."

Judith gazed warily at the elderly woman.

"You haven't mentioned my nephew."

Judith's breath drew in sharply. "I didn't—"

"You wanted to spare my feelings," Rita said, her words clipped. She rose to her feet and began pacing the room. "I keep finding myself wondering at what age it is that people decide they must begin sparing your feelings." She sniffed dismissively, and the fingers of her left hand flicked at the air as if brushing an insect away. "Well, of course it doesn't matter, does it. The point is, you do think Greg has something to do with this, don't you? After all, he was Reba's doctor and Max's doctor. He was also on duty when Frank had his accident yesterday, and I'm certainly well aware that it is Greg who coordinates all inoculations for the school." Judith remained silent, certain that no response was necessary. Rita turned away, and moved to a window, where she stood looking out, her back to Judith. But finally she turned around again. "Did you know I've always found my nephew to be something of an anomaly?"

Judith frowned.

"It's true," Rita went on. "When he was young, he was quite an insufferable snob. Oh, he was smart, and handsome, and had plenty to be proud of, but with him it was more than that. There was an arrogance about him, as if other people only existed to serve him." She smiled ironically. "He thought Max and I were fools when he was young, you know. Every year, after Max's brother died, and Greg started coming out to spend a month or two with us each summer, he used to try to convince us to move away from here. Thought we ought to live in New York, where his mother was, and have a mansion with a staff. 'Clodhoppers' is what he used to call the people around here."

Judith's frown deepened. "But you've seemed so proud of him."

Rita took a deep breath. "Oh, I have been. Ever since he came back that last summer, after poor Mildred died, too. That was the year he stayed. And he'd changed so much. To begin with, I was suspicious of it—I thought he must have some dark ulterior motive. Frankly, I always half suspected that he was trying to make sure Max and I didn't forget him in our wills. But over the last five years, I decided I was wrong." Now her eyes met Judith's. "But perhaps I wasn't," she said, her voice trembling for the first time since she'd begun to speak. "Perhaps nothing about Greg ever changed at all." She fell silent wishing she didn't have to go on, but knowing she did. "There's something about Greg that I've never told anyone before," she continued, her voice barely audible. "When he was a little boy, he—well, he suffocated a puppy once, just to see how long it would take to die, and to find out if he could revive it again."

"Dear God," Judith breathed. For several minutes the two women simply sat staring silently at each other, and then there was the sound of a car pulling into the driveway. A moment later the front door opened.

"Aunt Rita?" Greg Moreland called out.

Rita shot Judith a look of warning. "In here, dear," she called back. "Judith and I are just having a drink."

Greg Moreland appeared in the doorway, his face grave as he faced Judith. "I talked to Bob Banning this afternoon," he said. "I can't tell you how sorry I am about Frank."

Judith gazed at him, trying to read something—anything—into his expression that would give the lie to the sincerity of his words. But there was nothing. His eyes were large and sympathetic, and his smile gentle.

She was wrong—she had to be.

And then she remembered Rita's words of only a few seconds ago.

He suffocated a puppy once, just to see how long it would take to die.

She rose shakily to her feet and managed to force a smile. "Thank you," she said, then set her glass on the coffee table. "If you'll excuse me, I have a few phone calls to make."

Without waiting for a reply from either Rita or Greg, she hurried out of the room.

She imagined she could feel Greg's eyes on her back, watching her speculatively as she left.

Or was it her imagination?

* * *

At ten o'clock, as had been her habit for more than twenty years, Rita Moreland began preparing to go to bed. She moved through the house slowly, locking the doors and windows, following the same routine Max himself had always carried out until the day he'd died. Rita found the ritual comforting, in an odd way. It was almost as if, as she moved through the rooms on the lower floor, Max was beside her, giving her quiet instructions.

"Check the French doors twice," she imagined she heard him say as she went into the dining room. "That lock never worked quite right."

She twisted the lock, then rattled the doors in silent compliance with Max's equally silent instructions. Satisfied, she moved on to the library.

Max's presence was stronger here. His desk was covered with papers— even yesterday, when she'd worked at the desk herself, she hadn't disturbed Max's things. A book still lay open, facedown, on the table next to his favorite chair. Rita paused for a moment, fingering the volume, then abruptly picked it up, closed it, and returned it to its place on the walnut shelves that lined the room.

She crossed to the windows, checked their latches, then pulled closed the heavy damask curtains. When she returned to the door, she paused a moment, looking back into the room before she switched out the light.

A vague feeling of apprehension swept over her, and for a moment she thought she might cry. Resolutely, she flicked the switch, plunging the room into darkness, then pulled the door shut.

At last she went upstairs, but she went through the house on the second floor, opening the windows to let the cool night air drift through the rooms.

Finally, in the master bedroom, she began folding the clothes—Max's clothes—that were spread out on the bed, and packing them away in the boxes Greg had brought her yesterday.

Greg.

She felt an icy chill as she remembered the conversation she'd had with him after Judith had left the living room. She'd done her best to mask her emotions, but she was almost certain he'd known something was wrong.

Still, nothing had actually been said. They'd simply made small talk for a while, and she'd assured him she was doing just fine. No, she wasn't lonely.

No, she hadn't thought any more about selling the house.

Yes, she'd heard about Frank Arnold—Judith had told her.

She'd searched his face as they'd talked about Frank, looking for any sign that would tell her his concern was anything less than genuine. But even as he'd finally said good-bye, he'd spoken once more of Frank. "It's a shame," he'd said, his voice filled with what sounded to Rita like genuine sympathy. "He could be a pain in the neck sometimes, but no one deserves what's been happening to him today."

Rita had searched his eyes as he spoke, but they had revealed nothing. When he left, she went upstairs to talk to Judith again.

"I don't know," she'd sighed, perching on the edge of Judith's bed. "Perhaps we're wrong—"

"We're not," Judith had insisted. "I called my friend in Los Alamos. He doesn't have any answers yet, but he promised to keep trying." She glanced at her watch, then her eyes shifted back to Rita. "Look, I promised Jed I'd meet him at the hospital, then take him out for dinner. Why don't you come with me? I don't think you should be alone here."

Rita had brushed her words aside. "Don't be silly," she'd said. "I didn't say a word to Greg. And I need some time to think about all this. It's just . . . well, it just seems so unbelievable. You go ahead, dear. I'll be fine."

She'd fixed herself a small dinner, but had been unable to eat it.

She'd tried to work on some needlepoint, but her hobby hadn't soothed her either.

In the end she'd spent most of the evening simply sitting in front of an unlit fire, thinking about Greg and the experiment he'd carried out on his puppy.

And suddenly she was certain she knew the truth of what Greg was doing now.

Once again he was carrying on some kind of experiment. Only this time it wasn't a puppy that was dying.

This time it was people.

Tomorrow, she would find a way to stop him.

Tiredly, she put the last of the things on the bed into the boxes, then undressed and put on a robe. She sat at her vanity, pulled the pins out of her hair, then began giving it the hundred brushstrokes it had received every night since she was ten years old.

Usually, the ritual brushing of her hair relaxed her, made her put the worries of the day aside, but tonight it didn't seem to work, and when she was finished with the task, she still felt nervous.

She wandered restlessly to the window and looked out into the night.

The moon was high, and a silvery light danced on the face of the mesa. She could see bats darting through the night, and heard the soft hoot of an owl as it coasted on the breeze, searching the ground for mice.

She was about to turn away when she thought she saw a movement in the shadows outside the house, but when she looked again, there was nothing there. At last she turned away and slid into bed.

She read for a while, but the conversation with Greg kept replaying in her mind, and she had to go back over the pages again and again, the words holding no meaning for her.

At last she drifted into sleep.

She had no idea what time it was when she woke up, but she sensed immediately that something was wrong.

The air in her room was heavy, and acrid with smoke.

She came fully awake, and then she could hear it.

A crackling sound, as if someone were crumpling paper.

She ran to the window and looked out, half expecting to see a brush fire burning in the desert.

But the bright yellow glow that filled the yard was not coming from the desert beyond her property. It was coming from the house itself.

Rita gasped, instinctively slammed the window shut, then snatched her robe from the foot of the bed, shoving her arms into its sleeves as she hurried to the bedroom door.

The hall was choked with smoke. As she pulled the door open, it rolled into the room, filling her nostrils and making her gasp for air. She slammed the door closed again, then ran once more to the window.

No way down.

If she jumped, she would surely break her legs, if not her back.

She thought quickly. If she took a deep breath, she could make it down the stairs and out the front door before she had to take another.

What if she tripped and fell on the stairs?

She put the thought out of her mind.

She returned to the door once more, then steeled herself as she took three deep breaths, holding the last one.

Throwing the door open, she hurled herself toward the top of the stairs twenty-odd feet away.

She could hear the fire roaring now, and almost turned back, but then she was at the top of the staircase. The walls of the foyer were blazing, their ancient hand-carved wood panels crackling and curling as the fire consumed them.

Now it was too late to turn back. She drew the robe tighter around her as she hurried down the marble stairs. Then she was in the foyer itself. The front door was only a few yards away.

She ran to it, twisting at the knob, her aching lungs releasing her breath as they anticipated the fresh air on the other side of the door.

The door refused to open. Rita's fingers fumbled with the lock mechanism, struggling to turn it.

Her lungs expanded and she choked as smoke was sucked into her throat.

Coughing, she twisted at the lock again, then jerked hard on the door.

It gave way slightly, then stuck again.

The chain!

Panic was overwhelming her now, and as she tried to breathe again, smoke gorged her lungs and she felt her legs weaken beneath her. She hurled herself against the door, then tried to reach the chain, but it was too late.

Her legs betrayed her, and she slid to the floor, overwhelmed by the smoke that was trapped in the room.

The fire seemed to close in on her, reaching out to take her in its arms, its flames whispering to her, calling to her.

As her lungs filled once more with the bitter, stinging miasma, she gave in to the beckoning arms, gave herself up to the fire.

And as she passed into the blackness that now surrounded her, she thought she saw Max, coming toward her, his hand held out to her.

That was how they found her when the fire finally died: her hand stretched out as if reaching for help. They thought she was reaching for the door, trying to make good her escape from the flames.

In truth, though no one would ever know it, she had not been reaching for the door at all in those last fleeting seconds of her life.

She had been reaching for Max, and she had found him.

Chapter 21

Night fell in Borrego. High above the town, at the rim of the canyon, there was a low hum of well-oiled machinery.

The huge antenna came slowly to life.

Midnight.

Gina Alvarez was lying in her bed, her eyes closed, a book propped on her knees. She'd fallen asleep earlier that evening, but then awakened when the fire trucks screamed by the little house she shared with her mother and younger sister. She'd gotten up and looked out the window. At first she'd seen nothing, but then, off in the distance somewhere near the mesa, an orange glare had flared up. She'd thought about going outside and trying to get a better look, but then decided against it and gone back to bed. But by then she was wide awake again, so she'd decided to do some reading for her American literature class. The book was *The Deerslayer,* and though she found the story interesting enough, the style seemed kind of old-fashioned to her, and she'd found her eyes growing heavy.

Now she wasn't quite asleep, but neither was she quite awake. She was in that half state somewhere in between, where she was vaguely aware of what was going on around her, but the images of dreams to come were already beginning to sneak up from her subconscious like night creatures emerging from their holes.

A haze of color played around her vision, and she idly wondered if it could be morning already. But she knew it was impossible—her reading light was still on, and she could feel the weight of her book resting on her legs. She toyed abstractly with the idea of moving the book to her night table and switching off the light, but knew the movement itself would banish the sleep that had almost overcome her. Then she would be lying in the darkness, fully awake again, and her mind would start working overtime, going over her schedule for tomorrow, worrying about a quiz in history, trying to think of things she might be able to do to help Jed.

Suddenly, despite herself, she was wide awake again.

Sighing, she picked up her book, stared at its open pages for a moment, then closed it and set it aside.

She snapped off the light, rolled over, and tried to will herself to fall instantly asleep.

Seconds ticked by.

She smelled something.

She frowned slightly and sniffed at the air, then sat up. Something smelled terrible. Like burning rubber. Or garbage rotting.

Gina's frown deepened, but when she drew another breath in through her nose, the strange odor seemed to be gone. She hesitated a moment, then lay down again. She concentrated on making each of the muscles in her body relax, starting with her toes, then working her way up her legs, through her torso, then down her arms to her fingertips. Usually, by the time she was finished, she was almost asleep.

A few minutes later she was almost done. She felt totally relaxed, almost as if she were floating in space. Soft tendrils of sleep stroked at the edges of her mind, and she began reaching out toward them, welcoming them.

Dreams began to form, shapeless images of swirling colors, spinning out of the blackness, dancing in front of her eyes. Then, as she watched, they began to take shape, but just as she was about to recognize what they might be, they would disappear.

And then, quite suddenly, her whole body went into a spasm, every muscle in her jerking in unison.

And she was awake again.

She was sure she knew what had happened. The spasms came over her every now and then, just when she was on the verge of falling asleep. They always seemed to come jumping out at her, taking her by surprise, just when she was most comfortable, just when she had curled in the most perfect position, feeling neither too hot nor too cold. Then she would lie awake for another half hour, having to start all over again with her complicated program of relaxing.

Except that tonight was different.

Tonight, after the spasm hit her, she felt really relaxed. She stretched languidly in the bed for a moment, then yawned.

She had no urge to turn the light back on and read some more, nor did she even feel her usual impatience at the prospect of losing another half hour or so to nothing more productive than trying to go to sleep.

Within the space of a minute she drifted off into a deep, dreamless sleep.

Jeff Hankins rolled over in bed, kicking out at the covers, then jerking awake.

The dream had been vivid.

He'd been on the football field, and he'd just caught the kickoff in the second half. The ball had come into his arms solidly, and he was already on the run.

In the stands he could hear all his friends cheering wildly as he sprinted down the field.

Then, out of the corner of his eye, he spotted one of the opposing players, bearing down on him from the left. He'd feinted, then darted right across the other player's path, feeling the boy's fingers try to grasp his ankle as he went by.

The field seemed to be clear then, and he could see the end zone, only twenty more yards away.

The crowd was going crazy, and the band was already playing a series of fanfares, urging him on as he charged down the field.

Ten yards to go, then five.

And then, out of nowhere, they appeared.

Three of them. Big boys, each of them towering over him, barreling down on him. He tried to turn away, but suddenly there were two more of them, even bigger than the first three, blocking his way.

And then they hit him.

He felt the shock of their weight as they slammed down on him, felt his lungs collapse as the wind was knocked out of him.

He woke up with a start, sitting bolt upright in bed. He gasped for breath, struggling to recapture his wind. Then he realized where he was, and that it had been nothing more than a dream.

Christ, he wasn't even on the football team. In fact, his interest in football went no further than in taking a six-pack to the games and getting drunk under the grandstand with a couple of his friends. Then, after the game, they'd go out and raise a little hell around town until they got bored or the cops sent them home.

And yet, from the way he felt, it sure seemed like he'd been playing just now. The whole thing was clear in his mind, and his head even hurt, just as though someone had kicked him.

He lay back down and his breathing slowly returned to normal. He thought about the dream, even imagined he heard the crowd cheering him on again.

Fat chance of that ever happening. He'd never been any good at team sports—he'd always thought they were stupid. If you couldn't do something your own way, he'd decided long ago, it probably wasn't worth doing.

But now, as he remembered the dream once more and imagined what it would feel like to actually hear a crowd of people rooting for you, he wondered if maybe he'd been wrong.

He snickered softly as he thought about what his friends would say if tomorrow, instead of going down to the A&W to hang out after school, he tried out for the football team.

Maybe, he decided, he'd just do it.

A few minutes later, half hoping the dream would come back so he could try the play again, Jeff drifted back to sleep.

Susan Paynter stood up and stretched. It had been a quiet night. The hospital was almost empty, and most of the patients were sleeping, except for old Mrs. Bosworth, who was lying in her bed staring up at the television on the wall of her room. Mrs. Bosworth barely slept at all, but it didn't seem to bother her, and as long as Susan left the TV on, she didn't complain about anything.

She wandered down the hall, glancing into each of the rooms as she went, then turned into the staff lounge at the end of the hall. The night orderly was sitting at the table leafing through a magazine. He glanced up, then went back to the magazine as Susan poured herself a cup of coffee. Wincing as she sipped at the stale and bitter brew, she reached for the sugar. But before she could pick it up, a scream shattered the quiet of the little hospital. Instantly, the orderly was on his feet.

"It's Frank," Susan said as they ran out of the lounge and headed down the hall. "Find Dr. Banning."

But from the other end of the hall, Bob Banning was already racing toward them.

Susan reached the room first, flinging the door open and snapping on the lights. When she'd stopped in no more than five minutes before, Frank had been lying peacefully in the bed, his breathing slow and regular, all his vital signs strong. Indeed, except for the abnormal patterns of his brain waves, he would have appeared merely to be asleep.

But now his eyes were wide open and he was once more struggling violently against the straps that held him to the bed. The veins on his neck and arms were standing out starkly against his flesh, and strangled sounds were bubbling from his throat.

"Jesus," the orderly whispered, his eyes widening as he stared at Frank. "Is he awake again?"

Bob Banning quickly surveyed the monitors on the wall. Frank's brain waves were going crazy now, forming a jagged line that bore no pattern at all. It was as if a storm were raging in his brain, sending stimuli to every muscle in his body at the same time.

Other monitors showed that his breathing and heartbeat had gone wild as well.

And then, as they watched, it stopped.

Frank went limp, his arms and legs dropping onto the bed, his head lolling on the pillow.

His eyes, staring up at the ceiling, remained open, but held a glassy, sightless look.

Susan Paynter gasped, her own heart pounding. She'd never seen anybody actually die before. Her eyes went to the monitors that tracked Frank's vital signs, and she saw that although the man's heartbeat had evened out, his breathing had all but stopped.

Though Frank Arnold wasn't dead yet, in a few more minutes he would be.

Without waiting to be told, Susan raced to get a respirator. In less than a minute she was back, wheeling the machine through the door and into the space that had been cleared for it next to the bed.

Almost silently, each of them knowing his job so well that few words were necessary, the three of them set to work.

Fifteen minutes later, Frank's condition had stabilized, and Bob Banning sighed heavily. "Get him into X ray," he told Susan. "Whatever happened in there must have been massive, and I want to see how bad it is."

Susan nodded. "Shall I call Jed?" she asked.

Banning hesitated. By rights, he supposed, Frank's son should be notified immediately of what had happened. But what good would it do, really? At the moment he could tell Jed nothing more than that his father had apparently suffered yet another stroke.

And what could he tell the boy when he asked about his father's condition?

Only that although his body was still alive, his brain was now, to all intents and purposes, dead.

"Let him sleep," he said. "There's nothing he can do for Frank, and

tomorrow he's going to have to make the hardest decision of his life." His
eyes drifted to the inert form in the bed. "He's going to have to decide
whether to keep his father this way, or let his body die too."

A few minutes later, as he prepared to take Frank, still in his bed, down
to the X ray room, he wondered if it wouldn't have been kinder for him to
have ignored the respirator when Susan had brought it in, and simply let
Frank go.

But that wasn't his decision.

That was a decision only Jed Arnold could make.

Then again, Jed might not have to make it at all. For it was quite possible
that Frank Arnold would have yet another stroke before the morning came,
and his suffering would be over.

But it was not to be: midnight had come, and now was gone.

Chapter 22

Jed stirred restlessly in his bed, then came abruptly awake. It wasn't a lingering waking, the kind of quiet emergence from sleep he usually enjoyed, reluctant to leave the comfort of his bed. Instead it was a sudden sharpening of all his senses, a tensing of his body, as if some unseen danger lurked nearby. He sat up, pushing aside the single blanket he had slept under, then rubbed at the ache in his right shoulder where his muscles had knotted from lying too long in one position.

He hadn't slept well. He'd gone to bed early, his mind confused with everything that had happened the day before. But as he'd lain awake, he'd remembered the strange sense of peace that had come over him the night he'd sat in the kiva with his grandfather. He'd begun to picture himself there, visualizing the glowing fire and the low roof, summoning from the depths of his memory every sensation he'd seen and heard and felt.

Slowly, as he lay in his bed, that strange trancelike state had come over him once more.

He still wasn't certain if he'd actually slept at all, for last night, in the end, had been another night spent with the spirits, and the memories of the things they had shown him were still fresh in his mind.

He had flown with Rakantoh again, soaring over the desert, seeing the world once more through the eyes of the spirit.

Everywhere, there had been evil. The earth below was scarred with the ravages of the white men, and from the sky he had been able to see them creeping through the darkness, feel the malevolence radiating from them.

For a time his vision had been filled with the brilliant yellow of flames, but after flaring up into a blinding radiance, they had quickly died away.

A little later—he had no idea how long, for time itself seemed to warp as he flew with the spirit—he had felt a strange vibration in the air and become disoriented. He'd felt himself tumbling through the sky, falling toward the earth, certain he was about to die. He had called out to Ra- kantoh, but the spirit was rolling and yawing in the air too, his enormous wings flapping uselessly. And then the curious vibrations suddenly stopped and he regained his bearings.

But from the earth below he felt a new sensation, a perception of pain such as he had never felt before. Rakantoh, screaming with rage, had wheeled on the wind, and they had soared away above the canyon, as the spirit searched in vain for his lost refuge beneath the lake.

Now, in the growing light of dawn, Jed lay motionless, his mind examin- ing what he had seen in the visions of the night, trying to fathom the meaning of his strange fantasies.

It was nearly six-thirty when Judith emerged from Frank's bedroom. Though Jed had insisted he didn't need her to spend the night in the house with him, she'd stayed anyway, knowing that if she'd be able to sleep at all that night, it would be easier in Frank's bed, where at least she would feel his presence. It had worked, for she had slept soundly, and when she awoke, felt herself oddly comforted by the faint smell of him that still clung to the sheet in which she was wrapped. Now she paused outside Jed's room, his door ajar. She tapped lightly, then pushed it farther open. He was lying on the bed, and though he seemed to be looking right at her, he didn't ac- knowledge her presence at all. "Jed?" she said. "Jed, are you all right?"

He stirred slightly, and then his eyes cleared. "I think we should call the hospital," he said quietly. "I think something else happened to dad during the night."

Judith felt a pang of fear pricking at her, but forced herself to reject it. What could Jed possibly know? If there had been a problem with Frank during the night, surely they would have called here. She said nothing, as she turned and walked through the small living room and into the kitchen, where she started a pot of coffee. But she kept eyeing the phone, the fear Jed had aroused in her growing by the minute. She remembered the other day, when he'd known it had been Randy Sparks who threw the rock through Rita's window.

At last, as Jed came in and sat down silently at the table, she picked up the phone and punched in the hospital's number.

As she listened to Dr. Banning's brief description of what had happened during the night, her legs weakened beneath her. Then she hung up and faced Jed.

"You were right," she said, her voice quavering.

Twenty minutes later, with Jed at her side, Judith entered the hospital. As soon as she saw the look on Bob Banning's face, she knew it was even worse than she'd thought.

Banning led them into Frank's room, standing quietly as Judith took Frank's hand in her own, her eyes flooding with tears. She gazed down at him, trying to see the vital man she'd come to love so much. But the man in the bed seemed a stranger.

His face was expressionless, his jaw sagging. Though his eyes were closed, he didn't look as if he were sleeping.

Despite the motion of his chest as the respirator forced him to breathe, he looked dead.

Though she was absolutely certain he was totally unaware of his surroundings now, Judith leaned over and kissed his cheek. Still holding his hand in her own, she whispered aloud the thought that was in her mind. "Oh, Frank, what do you want us to do?"

They stayed with him a few minutes, then finally left his room, following Bob Banning into his office.

"He—He could still come out of it, couldn't he?" Jed asked, his voice taking on a desperate tone. "I mean, people wake up from comas, don't they?"

Banning was silent for a moment. It would have been easier, he knew, if Frank had died during the night. Indeed, without the respirator he would have. But the respirator had been there, and it had been Banning's duty to use it. So now he had to explain the reality of Frank Arnold's condition to the two people who loved him most.

"I'm afraid he won't," he said, forcing himself to meet Jed's eyes as he spoke the words. The boy flinched as if he'd been struck, and his jaw tightened; but he said nothing, and managed to control the tears that glistened in his eyes. "Without the respirator," Banning went on, "I don't think he'd survive more than a few minutes."

He stood up and went to a light panel on the wall, where the latest X rays of Frank's brain were displayed. As his fingers pointed out large dark masses within Frank's skull, he resumed speaking. "The damage is very extensive. There are parts of his brain that are still functioning, but his mind is essentially dead. In fact, I don't think it's fair to say he's either asleep or awake. He isn't even in what I personally would call a coma. To me, a condition of coma implies that there is still a functioning mind within the brain, a mind that has a possibility, no matter how slim, of recovering." He took a deep breath, then went on. "But unfortunately, for Frank that just

isn't true anymore. What he's in is more like a state of suspended anima-
tion. Though his body is still alive, he has no control over it, let alone
awareness of it. He's conscious of nothing, and never will be." He paused
for a second, then forced himself to utter the words he knew he had to
speak. "I'm very sorry, Jed, but I'm afraid your father is dead."

Judith gasped, and reached out to clutch Jed's hand. "But there must be
something you can do," she pleaded. "His heart is still beating, and he's
breathing—"

Banning spread his hands helplessly. "Only because of the respirator," he
replied. "Without it . . ." He left the sentence hanging, and Judith nodded numbly, forcing herself to accept the unacceptable. At last, taking a
deep breath and unconsciously straightening herself on the sofa, she faced
the doctor again.

"What can we do?" she asked, her voice almost eerily calm.

Banning chose his words carefully. "I'm afraid there isn't much we *can*
do. Here—at the hospital—it's our policy to keep a . . . shall we say 'keep
a body viable' as long as we can."

Jed gazed uncertainly at the doctor, and Judith felt her eyes moisten.
Steeling herself, she forced the translation of Banning's words from her lips.
"You mean you won't let Frank die, even though he can no longer live on
his own," she said.

Banning nodded gratefully. It wasn't a policy he totally agreed with, but
he wasn't at liberty to suggest that perhaps the best thing for Frank, and Jed
too, was simply to turn off the respirator. But if one of them brought it up,
he was more than willing to discuss it with them. Now, to his relief, Judith
did just that.

"If we decided to move Frank," she said. "Is there a place where they
would allow us to turn off the respirator?"

An anguished wail erupted from Jed's throat. "Jude, I could never do
that—" he began, but Judith pressed his hand, silencing him.

"I didn't say that, Jed. I said *if.* We have to understand all the possibilities. And we have to do what's right for Frank, even if it's hard for us." Her
eyes shifted to Dr. Banning in a silent plea for help.

"She's right, Jed," Banning said. "I know how hard this is for you. Deciding what to do is going to be the hardest choice you've ever had to make.
It's possible that with the respirator and intravenous feeding your father
could live for years. Or he could die at any time. But as long as he's here,
we'll do whatever has to be done to keep him alive. On the other hand," he
went on, barely pausing, "if he were in a sanitarium, or a nursing home, you
would have the right to ask them to do nothing for Frank except make him

comfortable. And if you should change your mind about the respirator, there are places that would be willing to accommodate you."

Jed chewed at his lip for a moment, then faced the doctor, his eyes stormy. "If he were your father," he asked finally, his voice holding a note of challenge, "what would you do?"

Banning gazed steadily at the boy. "I'd let him go," he said, and saw Jed flinch away from the words. "I don't believe in keeping someone alive simply because I *can*. Here, I have to do it. It's the rule of the hospital. But if it were up to me . . . ." He shook his head. " 'There is a time to live, and a time to die,' " he quoted softly.

The words seemed to hang in the air, and then Jed spoke again. There was a new strength in his voice. "Can I do that?" he asked. "I'm only sixteen, but Dad doesn't have any other family. Can I make the decisions?"

Banning shifted uneasily. "I don't know," he finally admitted. "But it seems to me we'll have to find someone to act as your guardian, or trustee."

"Jude," Jed said instantly. His eyes shifted to meet hers. "Will you do it?" he asked, his eyes pleading. "You know it's what Dad would want."

Judith's eyes brimmed over and tears began to run down her cheeks. Jed reached out and gently brushed them away. "Hey," he said, his voice ineffably gentle. "It's gonna be all right. We'll make all the decisions together. Okay?"

Judith's whole body trembled for a moment, and then she regained her composure. "Is there a place we could move Frank to?" she asked.

Banning turned to Jed. Something in the boy had changed just now. His face was still pale and drawn, but in the depths of his eyes, Banning saw a new maturity. Quite suddenly, Jed had been forced to grow up. "There's a place up in the canyon," he began. "I don't know much about it, really—"

"The Cottonwoods?" Jed asked, his voice suddenly hard. Banning nodded.

"No," Jed said immediately.

Confused, Banning turned to Judith, but her expression had taken on the same look of determination as Jed's. "It's the only place I can think of right now—" Banning began, but Judith cut him off.

"Then we won't do anything for now," she said. "Frank can stay here, can't he?"

"Of course," Banning replied. Abruptly, the mood in the room had changed. Judith and Jed were looking at each other, and though neither said a word, Banning sensed that a communication was taking place between them.

Jed stood up. "I think we need to talk about this for a while," he said. "And then we'll decide what we have to do. Is that all right?"

Banning nodded, and a moment later watched helplessly as they left his office. Something, obviously, had happened, but he had no idea what it might have been.

Judith was sitting in the waiting room with Jed. They hadn't spoken for several minutes, each of them trying to absorb what the doctor had told them. They felt numb, their minds spinning helplessly as each tried to accept that Frank was now irretrievably gone.

A shadow passed over Judith, and she glanced up. A figure was silhouetted in the main doors, framed against the brilliant morning sky, but the glare from beyond the doors prevented her from seeing who it was. Then the doors opened and the person stepped into the lobby.

It was Greg Moreland.

He stopped, staring at Judith almost as if he'd seen a ghost. And then, seeming to recover himself, he came toward her. "Judith? Are you all right? Where have you been?"

There was an urgency in his voice that made Judith rise to her feet. "It's Frank—" she said, then broke off. Her eyes hardened, fixing on Greg. "But you already know what's happened, don't you?" she asked.

Greg hesitated, appearing confused. Then his expression dissolved into one of sympathy. "Oh, God," he said quietly. "You don't know, do you?"

Now it was Judith who looked confused. "F-Frank," she repeated, stammering. "He's had another stroke."

"Oh, Christ," Greg groaned. "No, it's Aunt Rita." He lowered himself into a chair and reached out to take Judith's hand. "I'm sorry." He felt Judith stiffen, then she jerked her hand away. "There was a fire last night," Greg went on, "out at her house. She—Well, I'm afraid she didn't get out."

Judith stared at him, stunned. "I don't believe it," she said, her voice hollow. But the words, she knew, were as hollow as her voice, for she could read the truth in Greg's eyes. "What happened?" she demanded, too shocked, too exhausted, too emotionally drained to hold back the cold fury that washed over her now. "What did you make it look like? A short in the wiring? A coal popping out of the fireplace?"

Greg paled and his jaw tightened. "My God," he breathed. "How can you even suggest such a thing? She was my aunt, Judith. She was almost as close to me as my own mother."

"Yes," Judith said, the word escaping her lips in a furious hiss. "And Max could have been your father. And what about Reba Tucker? Were you close to her too? What are you doing, Greg? Why?"

She buried her face in her hands, sobbing, and Greg gestured to Gloria Hernandez, who was just coming in for her shift. Gloria hurried over, and Greg spoke to her softly.

"She's hysterical, Gloria," he said. "There's a sedative in the cabinet in my office. If you'll just bring it."

At his words, Judith's wits returned to her. "No!" she exclaimed loudly. "It's all right, Gloria. I'm upset, that's all. But I'll be all right." She turned to Jed, grasping his hand tightly in her own. "Maybe you'd better take me home, Jed," she said. "I—I think I need to lie down for a while."

Instantly Jed rose to his feet, and with Judith leaning heavily on him, he led her out to her car. She fumbled in her purse, pulled out her keys and handed them to him. Then she collapsed into the front seat, once more burying her face in her hands. Only when she was certain that they were at least a block from the hospital did she straighten up in the seat again.

"Stupid!" she said out loud. "Stupid, stupid, stupid!"

Jed looked over at her, his eyes wide. "What the hell—" he began, but Judith shook her head impatiently.

"Not you. Me. How could I be so stupid as to sit there and accuse him like that?"

Jed glanced at her out of the corner of his eye. "You really think he killed Mrs. Moreland?" he asked.

Judith sank back in the seat. "Oh, God," she groaned. "I don't know. Maybe I'm crazy." They were in front of Jed's house now, but neither of them made a move to get out of the car. "What do you think, Jed? *Am* I crazy?"

Jed turned and looked at her. "I don't think so," he said. "But what can we do? We can't go to the cops—all they'd say is that we're both nuts. And everybody around here is crazy about Greg anyway. Shit, they think he's the next thing to God."

Judith's lips tightened into a hard line. "Wouldn't you think they'd notice that most of his patients are either dead or dying?"

Jed shrugged. "Even Heather Fredericks," he said. "Except I don't see how you can blame . . ." The words died on his lips as he remembered something. Starting the car again, he shoved it into reverse and shot back into the street. "We're going up to the mesa to see my grandfather," he said. "Remember the first time we went up there, when I said he was crazy?"

Judith nodded numbly.

"Well, I was wrong. He said someone made Heather jump into the canyon, remember? He said he'd seen it from the kiva, just like I saw Randy Sparks from the kiva. And if he saw what happened, maybe he knows *how* they did it too."

Chapter 23

Judith Sheffield stood at the doorway of her classroom on Monday morning, her eyes searching the hall for any sign of Jed. The first bell had already rung, but this morning the kids were slow in heading toward their classes, and Judith knew why. They, like the teachers in the lounge a few minutes ago, were talking among themselves about the fire in which Rita Moreland had died. Indeed, little else had been talked about in Borrego since the morning after the fire, when nearly everyone in town had gone out to the charred ruins of the house. There, they had gathered in small groups, murmuring quietly, speculating on what might have happened.

Judith herself had said little about it, either yesterday or this morning. Not that she hadn't wanted to tell them what she thought—that the fire had been deliberately set, and that perhaps she, as well as Rita Moreland, was supposed to have died. But as she listened to the talk, she realized that so far there wasn't even a rumor that the fire might have been arson. Indeed, according to Elliott Halvorson—who, as always, had stopped at the café that morning to pick up the latest gossip—the fire had apparently started in the basement, where the remains of a pile of oily rags had been found. She had imagined the looks on the teachers' faces if she'd told them what she suspected—that Greg Moreland himself had set the fire.

Frustration was building inside her. So far all she had were suspicions. But even those suspicions had grown stronger yesterday, when she'd listened to Brown Eagle describe what he'd "seen" the night Heather Fredericks died.

"There was someone with her," Brown Eagle had said. "He was talking to her, telling her what to do. And she did everything he wanted her to. When he told her to jump, she jumped." But when Judith had suggested that Brown Eagle tell the police about the vision he'd had, he'd shaken his head. "I was in the kiva, remember? I couldn't possibly have seen anything. I'm a Kokatí—an Indian." His voice had taken on a rare bitterness. "We all lie about everything, you know."

And so, in the end, she and Jed had found themselves with nothing to do but wait.

Wait until Peter Langston called, and told them what was in the syringe Judith had sent him; in the end, it was the only solid evidence they had. If, indeed, it turned out to be evidence at all. There was still a chance that she was wrong, she reminded herself.

Now, as the corridor began to clear and the bell rang signaling the beginning of the first period, she stepped inside, closing the door behind her. But Jed's absence preyed on her. He'd insisted he'd only stop at the hospital for a few minutes and would be at school in plenty of time. She decided if he didn't show up by the end of the hour, she would call the hospital.

She moved quickly up and down the aisles, collecting homework assignments, then went to the blackboard and raised the map to expose the morning quiz, a daily ritual always accompanied by groans of anguish from the class.

Today, however, there were no groans. Frowning, Judith ran her eyes over the class, doing a quick head count. Three people were absent, which was a little better than on Friday. So the lack of groaning wasn't simply a matter of fewer people. She tried to tell herself that they were just getting used to her ways.

The trouble was, she was used to their ways too, and she found she missed the loud complaint. It was almost as if they suddenly didn't care enough to protest. Still, they were all hunched over their papers, working diligently at the equation she'd put on the board. She began checking off names in her attendance book, then turned her attention to the stack of homework on her desk. She was about to begin correcting the first paper when the door at the back of the room opened and Jed stepped inside. Their eyes met, and she knew immediately that something had gone wrong. Signaling him back out into the hall, she walked quickly down the aisle to join him.

"They moved him out of the hospital," he said, his voice taut. "Gloria Hernandez told me."

Judith stared at him. It wasn't possible. "How?" she breathed. "Who authorized it?"

"Dr. Moreland," Jed replied, his voice cold, his eyes glittering with anger. "Gloria says he's always been Dad's primary physician—whatever the hell that's supposed to mean—and that when he came in this morning, he had Dad moved out to The Cottonwoods. He claimed it would be a lot cheaper, and that there wasn't any reason why Dad had to stay in the hospital."

Judith closed her eyes for a moment, cursing under her breath. Her mind raced, but she didn't have the slightest idea what she could do. "We have to get a lawyer," she finally said. "Look, why don't you skip school today. You've got to—"

But to her surprise, Jed shook his head. "I already thought about that," he said. "There isn't really anything I can do for Dad, is there? I mean, you heard what Dr. Banning said. And we both saw those monitors they had hooked up to him."

Judith bit her lip. "But to have him out there . . ." she said, remembering the terror she'd seen in Reba Tucker's eyes.

Once again Jed shook his head. "If we make a stink, it's only going to make Moreland more suspicious. And they can't hurt Dad, Jude," he added, his voice trembling now. "Remember? Dr. Banning says he can't feel anything at all. He—He's already dead."

"Then what are you going to do?"

Jed struggled with his emotions for a moment, then managed a trace of an almost wry smile. "I guess right now I'm gonna do what dad would want me to do. And that's stay in school. At least for today."

Judith took a deep breath, then let it out in a sigh of frustration. But Jed was right. For the moment there was absolutely nothing they could do that wouldn't make Greg more suspicious than he already was. "All right," she agreed. "But this afternoon we're going out there."

They went back into the classroom. When Judith returned to her desk, she found two of the quizzes waiting for her, already completed. She glanced at the names at the tops of the papers, then looked at them again.

Both of them belonged to students who only last week had hung onto their papers until the last possible moment, not out of any inability to do the work, but simply because they both preferred to daydream their time away. It wasn't, Judith knew, that they were stupid; they simply had no ability to concentrate on a task.

But today, both of them had finished, and their solutions were perfect. Surprised, Judith looked up and scanned the class until she found the two students. The two were sitting at their desks, their expressions serene, their eyes facing forward.

But they didn't seem to be looking at anything.

*   *   *

The bell rang at the end of the fourth period, and Jed picked up his books, wondering if he'd been right when he'd decided to stay at school that day. He couldn't concentrate on anything at all, and so far he hadn't taken a single note during any of his classes. His mind had been occupied with his father.

He kept seeing his father lying inert in the hospital bed, oblivious to everything around him. For some reason he didn't quite understand yet, he'd at last been able to accept the fact that his father was never going to wake up again. Perhaps it had happened last night, when he and Judith had stopped into the hospital one last time, late in the evening, and he'd hoped that something—anything—had changed. But as he'd stared at the flat lines running across the monitors displaying his father's brain activity, and looked once more into his father's expressionless face, he hadn't felt that he was seeing his father at all.

What he had seen was only a shell that his father had once lived in.

All morning he'd half expected to be called out of class to be told his father's body had finally died too.

But the call hadn't come, and by the fourth period he'd begun thinking about what he would do if his father *didn't* die. He had no idea how much it would cost to keep his father in a nursing home, but he suspected it didn't really matter. Whatever it was, he knew he couldn't afford it.

Nor, without his father working, would he be able to pay the mortgage on the house, or make the payments on the truck, or anything else.

He found himself wondering if his father had any insurance, and if so, what it might cover. Maybe, instead of going to the cafeteria for lunch, he should find a telephone and start hunting for answers to all his questions.

He stepped out of the room into the corridor and looked around for Gina, who almost always met him here on her way to the cafeteria. But she was nowhere to be seen.

In fact, now that he thought about it, she'd barely spoken to him during first period either. His brows furrowing into a puzzled frown, he started toward the cafeteria, stopping at his locker to drop off his books.

When he got to the lunchroom, he felt an immediate sense of relief when he spotted Gina sitting at their usual table with JoAnna Garcia, Randy Sparks, and Jeff Hankins.

He waved to them, then joined the line of kids waiting for food. But as he made his way through the line, instead of following his usual habit of taking double portions of everything, he caught himself looking at the prices of each item. Almost to his own surprise, he settled for a cheese sandwich and a glass of milk. It didn't look very good, but it cost a couple of dollars less than he usually spent. Taking his almost empty tray to the table, he set it down, then slid into the chair next to Gina's.

"Hi," he said. "I looked for you outside Mr. Moreno's room, but you weren't there."

Gina looked vaguely puzzled. "Was I supposed to be?" she asked.

Jed frowned slightly. "I—Well, I don't know," he said. "You just usually are, that's all." He turned to look at her, but she seemed to be concentrating on the food on her plate. Suddenly he thought he understood. "Hey, I'm sorry I didn't meet you on the way to school this morning."

She looked over at him, a half smile on her lips. "That's okay," she said, her voice carrying an odd, languid note. "I can walk by myself."

"I—I had to go to the hospital this morning," Jed said. "They moved my dad."

Gina's eyes gazed at him vacantly. "Is he going to be all right?" she asked.

Jed stared at her. She'd been at the hospital Saturday—she knew how bad he had been then. "No," he said, his voice shaking slightly. "He's not going to be all right. He—He's going to die, Gina."

Gina's eyes widened slightly and she looked vaguely confused. "Oh, Jed," she said. "I—I'm sorry. I didn't mean—it's just—" She faltered, then fell silent.

Jed was sure he understood. She just didn't know what to say, didn't have any idea how to handle the situation. "Hey, Gina, it's all right," he said. He took her hand and squeezed it. "And maybe something will happen," he went on. "Maybe he'll get better after all." Then, when Gina made no response, he looked at her again. "Gina? Are you sure you're okay? Is something wrong?"

Gina smiled at him and her eyes cleared. "I'm fine," she said. "I'm just eating my lunch. Isn't that what I'm supposed to be doing?"

Jed's eyes moved away from Gina then, flitting from one face to another.

Suddenly it occurred to him that Gina wasn't the only one at the table who looked strange.

JoAnna Garcia looked the way she always did, slouching comfortably in her chair, her feet sprawled out beneath the table so there wasn't much room for anyone else's, but uncharacteristically, she hadn't said a word since Jed had joined them.

Jeff Hankins was simply sitting there, his eyes focused only on the tray in front of him, slowly consuming the food on his plate.

And next to Jeff, Randy Sparks had the same faraway look, as if he was only barely aware of where he was or what he was doing.

Now Jed remembered bits and pieces of what Gina had told him about Randy on Saturday. *It was weird . . . he just did what I told him to.* He eyed Randy for a moment, then said, "Hey, Randy. Bet you can't hit the clock with a butter patty."

Ordinarily it was a challenge Randy would have risen to instantly. Today, he only looked at Jed curiously. "Why would I want to do that?" he asked.

Jed felt flustered. "J-Just to see if you *can*," he stammered. "Why do we ever do it?"

Randy's eyes fixed blankly on him for a moment, then he turned his attention back to his food.

Jed waited a few seconds, then spoke again. This time, though, the words were uttered as an order instead of a question. "Randy, hit the ceiling with a pat of butter."

Instantly, Randy placed a butter patty on the end of his knife and flicked it upward, where it stuck to the ceiling. But as he went back to his lunch, he seemed totally unaware of what he'd done.

Jed shifted his gaze to JoAnna Garcia. "What the hell's going on?" he asked.

JoAnna shrugged. "What's going on?" she repeated mildly. "Is something wrong?"

"What's the matter with you guys?" Jed was nearly shouting in his frustration now. "If you're all sick or something, why don't you go home?"

Randy, Jeff, JoAnna, and Gina all gazed blankly at him.

"But I'm not sick," Gina said. "I feel fine. There's nothing wrong at all."

"Well, you don't look fine," Jed told Gina. "You look weird. Maybe you'd better go see the nurse."

Without a word, Gina stood and started toward the cafeteria door. Jed hesitated a moment, then got up and quickly threaded his way through the tables. He caught up to her just as she reached the door.

"Hey," he said. "Are you mad at me?"

Gina gazed at him, her eyes expressionless. "No," she said. "I'm just going to the nurse's office. That's what you told me to do."

Without a flicker of emotion, she turned and walked out the door.

"I don't think you can wait for your friend to call you," Jed said as he got into Judith's car after school that day.

Judith, about to start the engine, paused, looking over at Jed. "Why?" she asked. "Has something else happened?"

Jed nodded, his eyes grim. "Didn't you notice it today? It's the kids—they're starting to act real weird." He began telling her what had happened in the cafeteria at lunchtime that day, and what had happened afterward.

When Gina left the cafeteria, Jed had gone along with her, trying to talk to her, but it had been difficult. Not that she'd acted as though she was mad at him—she just didn't seem to care at all. She'd answered all his questions, but her voice, usually filled with excitement about whatever she might be talking about, had sounded flat, taking on a listless quality Jed had never heard before.

She'd sat patiently in Ms. Sanders's office, answering the nurse's questions but volunteering nothing, only insisting in that strange lifeless voice that she felt just fine.

"Well," Laura Sanders had finally said after taking Gina's temperature, examining her throat, and checking her for swollen glands, "you certainly *seem* all right." But Jed had been able to tell from the nurse's expression that she too had noticed Gina's peculiar apathy. "Would you like to go home?" she asked.

"If you want me to," Gina replied.

The nurse frowned. "It's not what *I* want, Gina. It's what would be best for you."

Gina had said nothing. In the end she had walked back to the cafeteria with Jed and quietly finished her lunch. For the rest of the day, whenever Jed had seen her, she'd been the same: calm and placid, moving steadily from class to class, but never stopping to chat with her friends, speaking to them only if they spoke to her first.

"Jeff Hankins is acting the same way, and so is Randy Sparks," Jed finished. "Didn't you notice it? They're all wandering around like sleepwalkers."

She realized he was right—indeed, if she hadn't been so consumed with worry about Frank. . . . She abandoned the thought, concentrating instead on remembering her classes that day. Yes, there definitely *had* been a difference in some of her students. The two in her first period, for instance, who had suddenly managed to complete a quiz in the allotted ten minutes. And all her classes, she realized now, had been more subdued that day, almost as if the students had been given a tranquilizer.

The shots.

Could that have been what they were? But it seemed crazy. Why would they give a whole school sedatives?

And if the shots *were* some kind of sedative, why were many of the kids behaving perfectly normally?

Silently, she cursed Peter Langston—she'd tried to get through to him twice already, but had been told both times that he was in meetings. And no, he couldn't be disturbed, except for an emergency. She would have dreamed one up, but both calls had been made from the lounge, and she'd been certain that Elliott Halvorson, at least, was listening to her curiously. She ignored him, determined not to let him see how worried she was. Besides, she'd told herself, if Peter had anything to tell her, he knew how to reach her.

But Peter still didn't know how important the shot might be. Suddenly she knew what she would do. "I'm going down there," she said. Only as she spoke the words did she realize that Jed had been talking. She hadn't heard a word he'd said.

"I said I've decided to quit school," he repeated.

Judith stared at him. "You're what?" she repeated.

"I said I know Dad wouldn't want me to quit school, but I don't see how I can pay Dad's bills if I don't get a job."

Judith shook her head, confused. "But this morning you said—"

"I *know* what I said," Jed interrupted doggedly. "But I've been thinking about it all day, and there just doesn't seem to be any way out of it. Besides," he added, his voice hardening, and his eyes meeting hers for the first time since he'd suggested quitting school, "if I can get a job with the company—and I bet I can, even if they are laying people off," he added darkly—"maybe I can find out what they did to Dad. They're doing something, Jude. It's not just Dad and the Morelands and Mrs. Tucker. They're doing something to all of us."

Part of Judith wanted to argue with him, but another part of her knew he was right. "All right," she said tiredly. "Look. You go out and see your father. Don't act upset that he's there—don't do anything at all. Can you do that?"

Jed hesitated, then nodded. "Yeah," he said. "I can do it."

"Good. I'm going to drive down to Los Alamos right now, and light a fire under Peter Langston. Tonight, when I get back, we'll decide what to do. All right?"

For a moment Judith thought Jed was going to argue with her, but then he nodded. "Okay," he said. He opened the door of her car and slid out, then leaned down to stick his head in the window. "Be careful, huh?"

Judith managed a smile she hoped was reassuring, but Jed had already turned away, loping across the parking lot to his father's truck.

A moment later she pulled out of the parking lot, too preoccupied to notice the dark blue car that fell in behind her, following her closely as she drove through Borrego, but discreetly dropping back nearly half a mile as she headed south and east toward Los Alamos.

Chapter 24

The heat of the afternoon rippled over the desert. Ahead Judith could see a familiar mirage of water apparently lying across the road. But the shimmering image, as always, stayed far in the distance, hovering just below the horizon so the water seemed endless, merging finally with the sky itself.

She was forty minutes, and fifty miles, away from Borrego, driving fast, the speedometer hovering between seventy and eighty. The road was straight here, and though Judith ordinarily felt relaxed behind the wheel, today she was tense, the muscles of her back and shoulders already beginning to knot under the strain that seemed to make every nerve in her body tingle.

Now she frowned as she glanced in the rearview mirror. Behind her, maybe a quarter of a mile, was the dark blue car she'd first noticed ten minutes before. She told herself she was being paranoid, that there was no reason to think it might be following her. She hadn't, after all, noticed it as she'd left Borrego. And yet it seemed to her that if it had been coming down from farther north, and had only just now caught up with her, it ought to be passing her.

Instead, it seemed to linger behind her, almost as if it were deliberately keeping pace with her.

Frowning, she eased up on the accelerator, and the Honda began to slow. When she glanced into the mirror again, the blue car was closer.

Perhaps she ought to stop entirely. Would he simply pass, ignoring her completely? Or would he stop, asking her if she needed help?

And why do I keep thinking of the driver as *he*? Judith suddenly thought. It could just as easily be a woman.

Making up her mind, Judith braked the car, pulling off the road. A cloud of dust rose behind her as the tires struck the hard adobe shoulder, and then the Honda came to a stop.

The blue car zipped past her, and Judith frowned. She was positive that the man in the car—at least she was now certain it *was* a man—had seen her. But what had she learned by the fact that he hadn't stopped?

Either he thought she had a problem and didn't care, or he didn't want her to get a good look at him.

Feeling foolish, she put the car in gear again and moved back onto the road. Ahead, barely visible, she could just make out the blue car; every few seconds it seemed to disappear into the mirage, only to reappear a moment later.

She drove another thirty minutes and then, ahead, saw a gas station by the side of the road—one of those strange lonely-looking places stuck out in the middle of nowhere.

As she approached it, she saw the blue car pull off the road, and when she passed it a few seconds later, she could see the person in the car talking to a weathered old man who apparently owned the place. But this time the man in the blue car waved to her as she passed. Suddenly she felt better. At least he'd acknowledged her presence. Surely he wouldn't have done that if he'd been following her?

An hour later she was on the outskirts of Los Alamos. She hadn't seen the blue car again, and the simple fact of its absence had made her begin to relax.

As the traffic thickened and she began threading her way toward the Brandt Institute, where Peter worked, she didn't notice the beige sedan that had picked her up as she'd reached the edges of the town.

Judith pulled to a stop in front of a heavy chain-link gate. Beyond the gate there was a wide lawn, in the center of which stood a large two-story building. It was fairly new, constructed in a Spanish-Moorish style, its white plaster facade plain and unadorned, broken only by small windows covered with heavy wrought-iron gratings. It was capped by a gently sloping red tile roof, and the driveway, which cut straight across the lawn from the gates, ended abruptly at a pair of immense oaken doors, suspended from ornate iron hinges fastened to the wooden planks with large bolts. Except for that huge pair of doors, Judith couldn't see another entrance to the building. Nor was there much around it. She'd had to drive all the way through Los Alamos to find it; it wasn't even in the town itself. Around the high fence that surrounded the Brandt Institute, there was little to be seen except the desert itself, and Judith found the broad expanse of lawn to be faintly unsettling. It was as if whoever had designed the building and its landscaping had wished to separate it from its environment, but had instead succeeded only in making the building appear totally out of place.

The whole estate—for that was what it would have looked like, had it not been for the fence, the gate, and the guardhouse that sat in the center of the drive—was situated a quarter of a mile back from the road, and only a small sign at the main road identified it at all.

A guard stepped out of the shack, and Judith gave her name, asking for Peter Langston. The guard returned to his kiosk and picked up a telephone. A few seconds later he came back to the car and handed Judith a plastic badge. It had Judith's name embossed across the top. "I don't believe it," she murmured, staring at the badge.

The guard grinned. "Computer. Once you're okayed, I just type in your name and she spits the badge right out." When Judith remained puzzled, he added: "Yellow just means you're a visitor. Don't forget to turn it in before you leave. There's a magnetic strip on the back that can be detected from anywhere inside the fence. If you take the badge outside the fence, the computer knows it's missing and alarms go off."

Judith stared at the badge, then turned it over. It looked for all the world like a credit card, right down to the brown stripe across the back. "Am I supposed to sign it?" she asked, only half in jest.

The guard grinned again. "Only if you're permanent," he said. "Then you have to sign for it every day."

The guard watched as she clipped the badge to her blouse, then he stepped back into the kiosk. The gate rolled back, and Judith put the car into gear and drove onto the grounds of the institute.

The heavy chain-link gate swung closed behind her, and a moment later, as the car approached the wooden doors of the building itself, the huge portals began to swing outward, allowing the car to pass between them, through a short tunnel that ran below the second floor and into an enormous courtyard.

Judith's eyes opened in shock.

There was a parking lot at the near end of the courtyard, but beyond that a park had been constructed. Tropical foliage burgeoned everywhere, and there was an artificial brook meandering through the gardens, spanned here and there by low wooden bridges.

Peter Langston, a tall, angular man with hair that was grayer than Judith remembered it, was waiting for her, apparently bemused by her shock at the jungle contained within the building. "I don't believe this," Judith said as she got out of the car. "How on earth does it survive in the winter?"

Peter pointed upward. "There's a roof—see? It retracts when the weather's right."

"Incredible," Judith said.

"Isn't it just?" Peter replied dryly. He gave her an affectionate hug before holding her away from him, his eyes growing serious. "What's going on?" he asked. "I was going to call you tonight."

Judith shook her head. "I couldn't wait. There's too much going on, and I'm scared, Peter."

The last traces of his smile vanished. "Come on," he said. "Let's go up to my office." He led her up a flight of stairs to a broad loggia that ran around the entire second floor of the building's inner wall.

"I suppose there's no point in asking you what's going on out here, is there?" Judith asked. "From what happened out in front, I gather it's all pretty secret."

Langston shrugged. "Some of it is, I suppose. But a lot of it's only a secret if you have a financial interest in it, which Willard Brandt certainly does. We're doing a lot of work with superconductors here, and there's one group over in the east wing that's supposed to be working on a new computer that's going to make the best Cray look like a Model-T Ford." He turned into an office, then gestured to a comfortable-looking chair before folding himself up into a wooden rocker that looked oddly out of place to Judith. "Back problems," he said. "Now, what's this all about? And why the sudden rush?"

Judith explained what had happened in Borrego over the weekend and the odd behavior of some of her students that day. "I'm absolutely certain it has something to do with those shots," she concluded. "But until you tell me what they are, I can't prove anything."

"Well, as a matter of fact," Peter said, "I just managed to get some time on the electron microscope this afternoon. Let's go take a look."

He led Judith back out to the loggia, but this time they used an elevator instead of the stairs, descending to what was apparently the second of three underground levels. When the doors slid open, they emerged into a corridor tiled with glistening white porcelain and shadowlessly illuminated from fluorescent panels in the ceiling. All along the length of the corridor closed doors hid whatever activity was taking place down here from Judith's view. "Real space-age, huh?" Langston asked.

Judith made no reply, and at last Peter turned into one of the rooms and spoke to a technician who was studying a display on a computer monitor. "Is that my stuff?" he asked.

The technician nodded. "But I can't quite figure out what it is."

Judith stared at the image on the monitor. It looked like nothing she'd ever seen before, but at the same time it struck her as being vaguely familiar.

It was roughly rectangular, with two nibs, almost like the tips of ballpoint pens, protruding from one end. The body of the thing seemed to be wrapped in wire, and at what Judith assumed was the base of the object, there was another pair of points, these two mounted to the body in such a way that they appeared to be able to swing toward each other.

The technician, his expression as puzzled as Judith's own, finally spoke. "I give up," he said. "I can't tell you what it is, but I can tell you what it isn't. It isn't cellular, and it isn't organic. And it doesn't look like any molecule I've ever seen either."

Peter Langston nodded in agreement, his bushy brows knitting as he concentrated on the strange object the screen displayed. "It's definitely not a molecule," he said. "It's way too big. But it's too small to be anything organic. That thing could fit right into any cell in the human body, with plenty of room to spare."

Judith glanced at Peter. "Okay," she said, certain he already knew the answer. "What is it?"

"Off the top of my head," Peter replied, "I'd say it's some kind of a micromachine."

Judith's eyes left the display and fixed on Peter. "A what?" she asked.

Peter smiled at her. "A micromachine. If I'm right—and I'd give at least a hundred-to-one odds I am—it's a tiny mechanism, probably etched out of silicon."

Judith stared at him. "You mean it actually does something?" she asked.

Peter's finger moved to the screen and he traced along the twin protuberances at the object's base. "I'd be willing to swear that those two things swing on those pivots," he said, his finger stopping on what looked like the head of a tiny pin penetrating through the protuberance and fixed to the body of the object. "In fact," he said, "that looks like some kind of a switch. See?" he went on. "Look how the ends of those are beveled. If you brought them together, the two beveled faces would match perfectly, making a contact point."

Judith stared at him. "But how big is it? If it can actually work . . ." Her voice trailed off as Peter glanced inquiringly at the technician.

"A couple of microns," he said, "one point eighty-seven, to be exact."

Peter whistled. "Small, indeed," he said.

"But what does it do?" Judith asked.

Langston sighed heavily. "I'm going to have to get a lot of images of this thing, then have the computer put it together in three dimensions. At that point I should be able to get a pretty good sense of what it is."

Judith pulled her eyes away from the strange image on the screen to look worriedly at Peter. "How long will it take?" she asked.

Peter shook his head. "I wish I could tell you. A few hours, probably. But once I know what it is, I'll need more time to figure out how it works and exactly what it does."

"But I don't *have* time," Judith replied, fear sharpening her voice. "Peter, two people are already dead up in Borrego, and two more might as well be. And now something's happening to the children—"

Peter held up a restraining hand. "I understand," he said. "Look, I'll find someone to help me, and if I have to, I'll work all night, and all day tomorrow. Now, the best thing you can do is go find a hotel room and wait for me to call. All right?"

Judith shook her head. "I have to go home. Frank needs me, and Jed—"

Peter eyed her worriedly. "Look. Whatever's going on, it's got to be dangerous. And if anyone finds out you stole that syringe, it's going to be especially dangerous for you."

Judith took a deep breath and slowly let it out. It did nothing to relieve her fear. But she still knew she had to go back to Borrego today. "I can't stay," she said. "I just can't."

Peter started to argue with her, but knew by the look in her eye that it would do no good. "All right," he said, reluctantly giving in. "But be careful, okay?"

Judith nodded tightly. "I will," she replied. "But promise me, Peter. As soon as you know what that thing is, call me. No matter what time it is."

Ten minutes later, after Judith had left, Peter Langston set to work. Within an hour, as the truth of what the micromachines were began to dawn on him, a cold knot of fear began to form in his stomach.

The children of Borrego were in a lot more trouble than even Judith suspected.

Jed stared at the dark brick mass of the four-story building that stood at the corner of First and E streets and felt a twinge of doubt. The Borrego Building, still the largest in town, seemed to have taken on an ominous look this afternoon, but Jed knew that its foreboding air was only a figment of his own imagination. The building itself, with its vaguely Gothic facade, looked as it always had—faintly dingy, like the rest of the town, but with a feeling of solidity to it.

Still, as he pulled the pickup truck into an empty slot in front of the building, he hesitated. But he'd made his decision, and there didn't seem to be any point in waiting until tomorrow. Once he was working for the company, he might be able to find out the truth about what they had done to his father.

Jed swung out of the cab of the truck and walked through the door next to the bank that occupied the ground floor of the building, hurrying up the stairs to the second floor. At the top of the stairs there was a glass-fronted directory. Jed scanned it quickly, then studied the numbers on the doors on either side of him. Finally he turned left and made his way down the narrow corridor until he came to Room 201, its number emblazoned on the opaque glass panel in flaking gold leaf. Taking a deep breath, he turned the knob and stepped inside.

There were two desks in the room, but only one of them was occupied. Charlie Hodges, a gray-haired man of about fifty-five, whom Jed had known all his life, glanced idly up from his work, then smiled broadly as he rose to his feet and strode toward him, his hand out.

"Jed!" Charlie said. "This is a coincidence." His smile faded and his eyes grew somber. "I was just working on some of the forms regarding your father. Getting his insurance straightened out, and starting a disability claim." He shook his head sadly. "This is one of the worst things I've ever had to do. Every time I think of Frank . . ." His voice trailed off, then he seemed to recover himself. "How is he? Is there any change?"

Jed shook his head. "I went out to see him this afternoon. He's just the same. I—" His voice faltered, but then he managed to steady it. "I don't know what I'm going to do yet," he said, leaving it to Hodges to figure out what he meant. Though he'd already thought about it, and was going to talk to Jude about it tonight, he still couldn't accept the idea of deliberately letting his father die.

Hodges, though, understood immediately, and grasped his shoulder reassuringly. "It's hard," he said. "How's that girlfriend of his doing? The teacher."

"Okay," Jed replied. Then he gazed directly at Hodges. "I didn't really come down here about Dad," he said. "What I need to do is get a job."

Hodges looked at him in surprise, then repressed his automatic urge to ask Jed if he'd talked to his father about going to work. He nodded firmly. "Well, as you know, we've been laying men off all week, but I think maybe we can make an exception in your case. I mean, given the circumstances," he added, sounding flustered.

Waving to Jed to follow him, he returned to his desk, pulled a form from the bottom drawer and handed it to the boy. "You might start filling this out," he said. "Let me just call upstairs." He punched three digits into the phone on his desk, then waited.

"Mr. Kendall?" he said a moment later. "Charlie Hodges, downstairs. I have someone here looking for work." He was silent for a moment, nodding a couple of times as the other man spoke. "I know that," he said after Kendall had finished speaking. "But I think this may be a special case. It's Frank Arnold's boy—Jed." He listened again, then winked at Jed, and after a moment hung up. "Just as I thought," he said. "One thing around here hasn't changed this week. The company is still doing its best to look after its people."

Jed looked up from the application form he was filling out, his lips twisted in a wry grin. "How about the guys who are getting laid off?" he asked.

Hodges shrugged. "It's only temporary," he said. But as he read the doubt in Jed's eyes, he added, "Look, I know what your father thought about what's happened, but he's wrong. UniChem has big plans for this company. Within two years the refinery is going to be twice the size it is now, and there are plans to build a factory, as well."

"A factory?" Jed echoed. "Come on, Mr. Hodges. What kind of factory would they build out here?"

Hodges shrugged. "All I know is it's some kind of real high-tech deal. They're talking about new kinds of fusion, and that kind of thing. Three years from now there are going to be more jobs out here than we can fill."

The application form completed, Jed pushed it across the desk. Could what Hodges had just said really be true? Had his father been wrong? But then an image of his father flashed into his mind, followed by another, this time of Gina Alvarez.

His father, he decided, had not been wrong, but nothing in Jed's expression revealed his doubts as he faced the personnel director. "Sounds great," he said. "Maybe I'm getting in on the ground floor of something terrific."

Hodges's head bobbed enthusiastically, and he handed Jed a card. "Take this over to the hospital. Then report to Bill Watkins tomorrow morning, up at the dam."

Half an hour later, at the small hospital on the edge of Borrego, Jed sat uneasily facing Dr. Banning for the second time that day. This time, instead of studying Frank Arnold's tests, the doctor was looking at Jed's own.

Jed had already produced a urine sample, and the nurse had taken a blood
sample as well. Jed had felt uneasy as the needle had slipped into his vein,
and had had to fight down an urge to jerk away from the instrument in the
nurse's hand.

"Well, I guess that's it," Banning told him at last. "We've got all the
specimens we need, and you don't seem to have any problems at all. And
according to your records at school, you got your flu shot last week, so I
guess we're covered."

Almost automatically, Jed opened his mouth to correct the error in his
school records, but then quickly shut it again. If they thought he'd already
had his shot, he certainly wasn't about to tell them otherwise. "Then that's
it?" he asked, standing up.

Banning smiled. "That's it. Not too bad, was it?"

Jed shrugged, said good-bye, and hurried out of the hospital into the
warmth of the late afternoon. As he started home, he felt a twinge of
uneasy excitement.

The answers to all his questions were somewhere within the company he
now worked for.

And somehow he would find out what those answers were.

Chapter 25

The man in the dark blue Chevy parked across the street from Frank Arnold's house slouched low in the passenger seat as the glare of headlights swept his windshield. He hated having to sit by himself in a car in the middle of a residential neighborhood; he always had the feeling that eyes were watching him from every home. But his instructions had been explicit —as long as there was a light on in the Arnold house, he was to remain posted where he was, and he wasn't to leave for at least an hour after the last light in the house went off. Well, maybe the teacher and the kid were the kind who went to bed early.

The source of the headlights turned out to be the same pickup truck with the broken windshield that had left half an hour earlier, and the man in the car relaxed as he saw Jed Arnold, now accompanied by a girl he was sure must be Gina Alvarez, get out of the truck and disappear through the front door. When they were safely inside, he left his car and strolled up the street, glancing into the window of the house as he passed it. The two kids were talking to the Sheffield woman, but it didn't look like any big deal— they just seemed to be chatting. He wandered on up the street, crossed, then walked back along the other side until he was even with his car. Glancing around, still with the uneasy sense that he was being watched from every window on the block, he got back in his car and decided it was time to ignore his orders.

He turned on the engine and drove away. From now on, he would keep an eye on the house from a distance, driving by every half hour or so. But in a dumpy little town like Borrego, he didn't really think there was much likelihood that the Sheffield woman would be going anywhere that night.

* * *

The three of them were sitting in the small living room, Jed and Gina side by side on the sofa, Judith in Frank's big easy chair. Almost half an hour had gone by since Jed had brought Gina into the house, and as the minutes had ticked away, Judith had become more and more frightened.

Everything about Gina seemed to have changed. Gone were her expressive voice and animated gestures.

Her eyes, always sparkling with interest in everything around her, had lost their luster, as well as their movement. Her gaze seemed to fasten on objects from time to time, but Judith had a strange feeling that Gina wasn't truly seeing whatever she was looking at. It was as if her whole mind had simply gone into neutral. For the most part she sat silently next to Jed, answering questions only when they were directed specifically to her, seeming lost in some private world of her own.

Except Judith had the eerie feeling that there was nothing whatsoever in that world. The girl seemed to be existing in a void.

"Gina," Judith said, leaning forward in her chair, her voice rising, as if she were speaking to a deaf person. "I want you to tell me if anything happened Saturday night. Anything strange, or out of the ordinary."

Gina shook her head.

But what if she doesn't think whatever happened was strange? Judith suddenly thought.

"All right, let's try it another way. What time did you go to bed?"

Gina frowned. "About ten o'clock, I guess."

Judith nodded encouragingly. "All right. Now, did you go right to sleep or did you read for a while? Maybe listen to the radio?"

"I read," Gina said. "I was trying to read *The Deerslayer*, but I couldn't concentrate on it. And I fell asleep."

"Okay," Judith said. "And did you sleep all night?"

"No. I woke up when the fire truck went by, and I went to look out the window. Then I tried to read some more."

She fell silent again, and Judith began to feel like an inquisitor, painfully dragging information out of a subject, bit by bit. "How much longer did you read?"

Gina shrugged. "Not much. I kept sort of drifting off."

"But you didn't actually go back to sleep?"

There was a silence while Gina seemed to think. "No," she said finally. "That's when I started to smell something."

Judith cocked her head. "Smell something? Like what?"

"I—I'm not sure," Gina stammered. Then: "It smelled bad. Like garbage."

"And it woke you up?"

Gina nodded. Her nose screwed up as she remembered the odor. "It was really bad."

In her mind Judith heard an echo of Reba Tucker's voice, barely audible, croaking out words one by one: "Smells . . . bad. See things . . . bad."

"Gina," Judith said, her voice quavering, "I want you to think very carefully. When the smell came, did you see anything? Anything at all?"

Gina's eyes narrowed and her brows furrowed as she concentrated. Finally she nodded. "There were colors," she said. "And something else. There were things around me. I couldn't quite see them, but they were there."

Judith felt her heart beating faster. "All right. Anything else? Did you *feel* anything?"

Gina thought again, then slowly nodded. "Something funny. It was one of those spasms, you know? Like when you're just about to go to sleep, and your whole body jerks?"

Judith nodded. "That happened Saturday night too?"

"Just as I was going back to sleep. But it was funny. Usually when that happens to me, I'm wide awake again. But Saturday, after it happened, I just felt real relaxed and went right to sleep."

"Okay," Judith told her. "That's very good, Gina. And yesterday and this morning, you woke up feeling fine. Is that right?"

Gina nodded.

"Now, I want you to think once more, Gina. I want you to try to remember what time all this happened. We know it was after you heard the fire truck, which was around eleven-thirty."

"Well, it had to have happened before twelve-thirty, because that's what time Mom gets home. And it seemed like I tried to read for about half an hour after I heard the sirens."

Judith's whole body tensed.

Midnight.

Whatever had happened to Gina Saturday night had happened at the same time that Frank had had his stroke the night before.

And Reba Tucker had had her seizure.

An hour later, when Jed came back to the house after driving Gina home, he found Judith sitting pensively at the kitchen table, staring at a piece of paper. Jed slid into the chair opposite her, then turned the sheet around to look at it.

It was a list of names, starting with his father's and Reba Tucker's. Below that were more names.

Max Moreland
Gina Alvarez
Randy Sparks
JoAnna Garcia
Jeff Hankins
Heather Fredericks

There were three more names, but Jed skipped over them, for at the bottom of the list a single name jumped out at him.

His own.

And next to his name, Judith had placed a large question mark, underlined twice. After a few seconds his eyes left the sheet of paper and he looked questioningly at her.

"I'm trying to find a common denominator," Judith said. "There has to be a pattern."

Jed's eyes scanned the list again, and suddenly he thought he saw it. "It's the company," he said. "All these kids? Every one of them has a parent who works for Borrego Oil."

Judith frowned. "Gina? Her father's gone, and her mother works at the café."

"Her uncle," Jed replied. "Carlos."

"But what about Reba Tucker?"

Jed studied the list again, and then realized that there was something else the names on the list had in common. "Troublemakers," he breathed. "That's what it is!"

Judith stared at him quizzically. "Troublemakers?" she echoed.

Jed nodded. "That's got to be it—look. The kids? Christ, every one of them has been in trouble except Gina, and she hangs out with the rest of us. And you know what Greg Moreland and Otto Kruger think of Dad. Hell, he made life miserable for Kruger, and didn't want Max to sell the company."

"But what about Reba?" Judith said again. "I still don't know how she fits in."

"Oh, yeah?" Jed replied. "Well, I do. She was making all kinds of trouble at the school. She was always after them to fix the place up and get better equipment. She screamed about the books, the pay, everything. And last spring she got so mad she decided to try to get the teachers to form a union. Christ, she was over here all the time, talking to dad about it."

Judith stared at him. Could it possibly be true? It seemed so crazy, and yet . . .

And then she remembered something Frank had told her. *UniChem's put two of its companies into bankruptcy, just to bust the unions. They want everyone to shut up and do their jobs and not make trouble. But it won't work —they won't shut me up.*

But they had.

And then another thought struck her.

Jed.

As far as anyone except the two of them knew, Jed had had one of the shots too. If he was on their list . . .

And then she knew what had to be done. "You have to do something tomorrow, Jed," she said. She talked for almost five minutes, telling him what she had in mind. "Can you do it?" she asked at last.

Jed said nothing for a moment, then nodded slowly. "I guess I'll have to," he said. "If I don't, they might just kill me, like they did Dad."

Chapter 26

Jed negotiated the dirt track along the canyon's edge the next morning almost automatically, most of his mind occupied with what Judith Sheffield had told him the night before. After they'd gone to bed, he'd lain in the darkness, wide awake, wondering if he could actually pull it off. Despite what he'd told Judith, he wasn't sure he could. For a while he'd even considered not showing up for work at all.

Quitting the company now, on his very first day, would be like a red flag to Kendall—for Jed was certain that Paul Kendall was behind whatever was being done as much as Greg Moreland. But he managed to keep himself under control yesterday, about Greg Moreland sending his father to The Cottonwoods, and he'd do it again today, with Kendall watching him.

And so, all night, he'd thought about what he had to do. He remembered Gina, and Randy Sparks, and a few of the other kids he'd seen at school. And he kept in mind that he too was supposed to have gotten one of the murderous shots.

Now, as he parked the truck in the lot above the dam, he looked at himself in the rearview mirror. He let the muscles of his face go slack, making his features expressionless. Then he let his eyes lose their focus slightly, so they took on the strange, blank look he'd seen in Gina Alvarez's eyes last night and the night before.

Finally he got out of the truck, picked up his father's lunch bucket, and slammed the door. As he started down the trail to the dam, he kept his head down, staring only at the path in front of his feet. As he came to the operations office at the end of the dam itself, he paused, steeling himself to show no emotion, no reaction except cooperation, no matter what was said to him.

He stepped into the office. Bill Watkins, busy with some paperwork, glanced up at him. In the inner office, clearly visible through an open door, Otto Kruger was talking to someone on the phone.

"I'll send them down in groups of four," he heard Kruger saying. "It looks like everyone's here today, so there shouldn't be any problem." He was silent for a moment, then swung around as if he were about to speak to Bill Watkins, but stopped short when he saw Jed. His eyes narrowed, and Jed had to concentrate hard to keep himself from reacting to the man's stare. Then Kruger said, "Arnold just came in," his voice dropping, but still clearly audible. "He looks fine. He's just standing in Watkins's office, waiting for his orders."

He dropped the phone back on its hook, then stood up and came to lounge in the door to his office, his lips twisted in a quizzical half smile. "Hey, Jed," he said. "How you doing this morning?"

Jed let his head come up, but slowly. "Okay. I feel fine."

Kruger's brows rose a fraction of an inch. "Sleep okay last night? No problems?"

Jed shrugged. "I'm okay," he said again.

Kruger's eyes seemed to bore into him, but then he nodded. "Great," he said. "Well, don't just stand around here like an idiot—there's a lot to be done down below, and we're going to be shorthanded all day."

A twinge of anger plucked at Jed as the word "idiot" struck him, but he managed to shunt it aside. Nodding, he turned and walked out of the office, never even looking at Bill Watkins. But when he was gone, Watkins scratched his head pensively. "What's with Jed?" he asked.

Otto Kruger's lips twisted into an unpleasant grin. "Maybe he finally decided his old man had the wrong attitude," he said. "Looks to me like he figured out you're better off if you just shut up and do what you're told."

Watkins grunted. "Well, I wish all the men were like that," he said. "It'd sure make my job a lot easier."

Kruger said nothing, but as he went back into the inner office, he smiled to himself. Bill Watkins was going to get his wish a lot sooner than he ever could have imagined.

Jed moved steadily down the spiral staircase that led into the depths of the dam, his steps echoing in a regular rhythm on the metal risers, sending an eerie resonance through the shaft. Finally he reached the bottom and moved slowly along the tight confines of the corridor—lit only by bare bulbs in metal cages hung every twenty-five feet or so—toward the damaged power shaft. As he approached, the crew foreman's eyes fixed on him.

"You'll be working in the pipes today, Arnold," he said. "There's a min-er's light and probe waiting for you. All you got to do is look for cracks. When you find 'em, use the probe to open 'em up and clean 'em out as best you can."

Jed said nothing. He set his lunch bucket on a shelf, took one of the miner's hard hats off the rack, put it on, then found the probe. It was a piece of thick, hardened metal, its tip bent slightly, attached to a wooden handle. Finally he moved into the base of the power shaft itself.

A conveyor had been rigged up, a tall cranelike object that rose from the base of the shaft all the way to the top. A moving belt was already operat-ing, carrying an endless circle of scoops upward, where their contents would be dumped onto another conveyor that would carry them out and drop them into a chute leading down to a dump truck waiting at the base of the dam itself.

On scaffolding high above, men were already working, chipping away at the damaged concrete of the shaft, dropping pieces of debris into a tempo-rary chute that was designed to let men work at the bottom of the shaft in relative safety. Still, there was a steady rain of tiny fragments of concrete pattering down from above, and the air was thick with dust.

"Up here!" one of the men on the scaffolding called. Jed peered up, seeing the narrow opening of one of the intake pipes.

It might have been the same pipe from which his father had fallen on Friday morning. Taking a deep breath, he began climbing the scaffolding until he came to the platform where the man stood.

He stared into the black hole, no more than two feet in diameter.

A knot of fear formed in his stomach, but he forced it down, telling himself there was nothing to be afraid of.

"Headfirst," the man told him. "Turn on the light, and keep your head up. The beam'll give you enough light to work by." The man glanced down then, and when he spoke, his voice had dropped. "If you start to panic," he said, "just relax and give me a holler. I'm gonna tie a line around your ankle, and I'll be able to pull you right out."

Jed kept his eyes fixed on the hole in the side of the shaft. "I'll be okay," he said, doing his best to keep his voice clear of the fear he hadn't quite been able to rid himself of. "I'll be fine."

He reached up and switched on the tiny light fixed to his helmet, then, gripping the probe tightly in his right hand, ducked down and thrust his torso into the hole.

The first thing he noticed was the suffocating heaviness of the air in the pipe. Stale and musty, it threatened to choke him.

The fear in his belly blossomed, and he felt the first fingers of panic reaching out toward him. He closed his eyes for a moment, willing the panic to subside, making himself breathe in the dank air.

"You okay?" he heard a voice asking him.

Gritting his teeth, he forced himself to open his eyes again. The dim beam of light glowed softly ahead of him, disappearing quickly into the blackness of the pipe. But the panic had eased slightly. "I'm okay," he managed to say. "I'm fine."

He crept ahead, using his fingers to explore the concrete tube. A moment later he felt a rough spot and twisted his head slightly so that the light on the helmet shone on the wall. Using the probe, he dug at the crack, scraping mud and algae away from it. A piece of concrete broke loose, then another. He kept at it, chipping away, until finally the probe could pry no more fragments out of the break.

He moved on.

He came to another crack, this one in the top of the shaft.

He tipped his head up, but there wasn't enough room for the lantern to find the break.

He would have to roll over and lie on his back.

He began twisting his body, working it around in the narrow confines of the pipe.

A moment later he was looking at the top of the tube, only a few inches above his face.

Above it, he realized, were the thousands of tons of concrete of which the dam was made. And now, lying on his back, his belly exposed, he felt the full weight of the dam pressing down on him.

Once again panic closed in on him, and this time he couldn't put it aside.

Instinctively, he tried to sit up, and instantly hit the close confines of the pipe.

He felt it tightening around him, and suddenly he couldn't breathe. He wanted to scream, wanted to scramble to his feet and begin running.

His muscles contracted as he tried to draw his legs up, and then he felt them jam against the wall of the shaft.

He couldn't move, but he had to. He struggled for a moment, and the panic threatened to overwhelm him entirely.

A scream of unreasoning terror built in his throat.

And then, just as it was about to burst from his lips, he clamped his mouth closed.

He wouldn't do it—he wouldn't give in to the urge to scream, wouldn't give in to the panic that had seized him. He struggled again, but this time the battle took place within his own mind. He closed his eyes, then forced himself to imagine that he wasn't in the dam at all.

He was on the mesa, high up above the desert, with nothing around him except clean, dry air.

He imagined the air filling his lungs, washing away the dankness of the pipe.

Slowly the tension in his body eased, and at last he moved again, easing his torso forward to release his legs from the pressure of the pipe. He closed his eyes then and concentrated, as he had in the kiva with his grandfather; as he had alone in his room on Saturday night.

It worked.

Part of him stayed in the pipe, directing his body as it carried out the work he had been told to do.

But most of his mind moved elsewhere, traveling beyond the dam, breathing freely.

The panic—the terror of the pipe, which had overwhelmed his father— could no longer reach him.

After two hours he felt a tug on his ankle. "Take a break, kid," he heard a voice calling. "Nobody can keep that up all day."

Jed stopped working, and a moment later felt himself being pulled out of the pipe. The part of his mind that had been occupied with evading the terrible panic rejoined his body, and for a moment he felt another twinge of the paralyzing fear. Then he was free of the tunnel, back in the main shaft. He scrambled down the scaffolding, then stepped out of the shaft into the turbine room. There was a sudden silence as the conveyor belt stopped moving, and then the rest of the men who had been working on the scaffolding above began to appear.

Thermoses were opened and someone handed Jed a cup of steaming coffee. Around him he could hear the voices of the men, swapping jokes and casual insults, but Jed took no part in it. He sat still, staring at nothing, sipping with careful disinterest at his coffee.

When the allotted fifteen minutes was nearly up, the foreman spoke.

"Hey, Gomez. Take Harris, Sparks, and Hankins, and head down to the hospital, okay? Company's springing for flu shots."

Jed froze, but managed to say nothing, managed even to keep himself from looking up as Randy's and Jeff's fathers got up and, demanding to know if they were getting paid for their time away from the job, followed the other two men toward the stairs that would take them to the top of the dam. "Yes, you're getting paid," the foreman called after them. "If the company wants you to do something, the company pays you to do it."

A rowdy cheer erupted from the four men as they disappeared into the narrow corridor.

Jed wanted to yell after them, to warn them not to take the shots, but he knew he couldn't.

If he did, he would only give himself away.

Judith watched in silent dismay as her third-period class filed into the room and quietly took their seats. Randy Sparks, along with two others, was absent, but of the twenty-two students who were there, five had that strange glassy-eyed look that Gina, Randy, and the others had exhibited yesterday. The room was almost unnaturally silent, for in this class, as in her two previous classes of the day, it was the liveliest of the students who seemed to have been affected by whatever was being done to them.

Judith, like Jed, had done her best to betray nothing of what she suspected. During the just completed mid-morning break, she'd even managed to force a small laugh when Elliott Halvorson had joked that he wished that whatever kind of flu was going around this year would stay on. His classes seemed to have calmed down, and for the first time in years the students were actually paying attention to what he was saying.

Judith had felt like screaming at him that what was happening to the students had nothing at all to do with the flu, but she'd suppressed her words and coerced a smile from her lips instead.

It had been that way all morning.

She'd tried to tell herself that she was getting paranoid, just as she had yesterday when she'd thought that blue car was following her. Even on her way to work this morning she'd found herself glancing around, searching in every direction for something that might tell her she was indeed being watched.

There had been nothing.

No cars parked where they shouldn't have been; certainly no one who appeared to be following her. And yet, why should there have been? If anyone wanted to know where she was, it wouldn't be hard to locate her in Borrego. All anyone would have to do, really, was keep an eye on the main road leading north and south. Unless you had a four-wheel drive and were just a little bit crazy, there was no other way out of town. And as long as she was in town, anyone could find her in ten minutes.

She'd avoided the teachers' lounge entirely before classes that morning, certain she wouldn't be able to fake even an appearance of being relaxed, but by the time the break came, her paranoia had overcome her once more, and she'd decided that not to show up for a quick cup of coffee would look suspicious. Besides, if the rest of the classes were like hers, by then it must have been obvious that something was haywire.

Yet during the break none of the teachers seemed the least bit concerned. Most of them—like Elliott Halvorson—actually appeared to welcome the change. Their disciplinary problems had evaporated, and their classes actually seemed attentive.

But Judith wasn't certain exactly how attentive they really were. Now, as she looked at the class, an idea came to her.

She turned to the board and began quickly writing out a series of problems. Deliberately, she put some of the harder ones first, then scattered out the simpler ones toward the end.

Finally she turned to face the class. "You have five minutes to copy these," she said. "Copy them in order, please."

A few groans drifted up—groans Judith welcomed as at least a small sign that some of her students were still perfectly normal.

Judith watched carefully as they set to work. Most of the class kept glancing up at the blackboard, then turning their attention to the paper in front of them while they wrote in short bursts, only to look up at the blackboard once more a few seconds later.

The affected students—the sleepwalkers, as Judith had begun to think of them—seemed to look at the board less often, and their writing, though Judith couldn't actually see it, appeared to proceed at a much steadier pace.

At the end of the five minutes Judith reached up and pulled the map down to cover the board. "All right," she said. "Begin working on the problems. You have thirty minutes."

She sat down at her desk, apparently grading a stack of homework assignments, but glancing up every few seconds to study one student after another.

The seventeen unaffected students seemed to be working normally. Some of their faces screwed up in expressions that looked almost painful as they concentrated, and several of them tapped their pencils nervously on their desktops as they pondered their solutions. Others turned now and then to gaze out the window for a moment, or stared at the ceiling.

Three of them were surreptitiously trying to see what their classmates had already written.

The five sleepwalkers, however, all sat at their desks, their faces expressionless, their eyes fixed on the papers in front of them.

Their pencils moved steadily, except for two of them, who seemed to have frozen in place.

The minutes ticked by.

After twenty minutes three of the unaffected students had come up and placed their quiz sheets on her desk.

Two of the sleepwalkers had laid their pencils down and were now sitting quietly, their eyes staring straight ahead.

One of them was still working, while the last two were still staring at their papers, their pencils, unmoving, still in their hands.

At the end of the allotted thirty minutes, Judith stood up. "Time's up," she said.

Immediately, the fourteen unaffected students began passing their papers forward.

The five others didn't move.

"Please pass your papers forward," Judith said quietly.

The five students passed their papers forward.

Judith collected the papers, then glanced at the clock. There were still five minutes before the bell would ring. "All right," she said. "That's it for today. And there'll be no homework tonight. See you all tomorrow."

As the room began to empty, Judith began scanning the quizzes.

Seventeen of them seemed perfectly normal—most of the students had finished the quiz, or at least come close. All of them had finished the easiest of the problems, and there was a normal spread of right and wrong answers. Some of the harder problems, as Judith had expected, had simply been skipped entirely.

Then she turned to the quizzes turned in by the five strangely subdued students.

Two of them had finished the quiz, and both of them, not surprisingly, since they were her brightest students, had done the work perfectly. Their solutions were laid out neatly, with nothing either crossed out or erased.

The other three quizzes were strange. The work, as on the first two, was neatly written, with no changes having been made. And what was done had been done correctly.

But one of the students hadn't even finished the first problem; the second had gotten no more than halfway through the quiz; and the third had apparently given up on the next to the last problem.

The very last problem, which read simply $2 + 2 = x$, hadn't been touched by any of the three students.

Judith's throat tightened and a knot formed in her stomach as she realized what had happened.

The five students had, like Gina Alvarez night before last, done exactly as they had been told.

They had been told to "begin working on the problems," and they had. They had worked steadily and methodically, and they had not given up.

But when they had gotten stuck, they simply stopped.

And of course Judith knew why.

She hadn't told them to go through the quiz and solve the simplest equations first, then go back and work on the harder ones, solving them in the order of difficulty, which would have been the most efficient way to complete the test.

Instead she had simply told them to begin working on the problems, and they had followed her instructions to the letter.

What work they had done was perfect, until they got stuck. But when they got stuck, they were like robots that had walked into a wall.

They did nothing.

They just sat quietly, their gears spinning, and waited.

Chapter 27

Judith's nerves jangled as she approached the counseling office of Borrego High School. Despite herself, she kept glancing back over her shoulder to see if anyone was watching. But it was ridiculous—she was a teacher, and she had a perfect right to look at the records of any of her students at any time she chose. Still, she'd spent several minutes alone in her classroom after the fourth-period bell had sounded, devising a cover story should anyone ask her what she was doing. A review of her classes was what she'd finally settled on. She was thinking of advancing her lesson plans a bit, and wanted to see just how much preparation her students had had in the event she decided to introduce them to some of the intricacies of trigonometry.

She paused outside the office door, glancing up and down the corridor one more time, but there was no one there. Finally she pushed the door open and stepped inside. Carla Bergstrom, who served as the school's sole full-time student counselor, was just taking her purse out of the bottom drawer of her desk. "Judith," she said. "You just barely caught me."

Judith forced what she hoped was a disarming smile. "Actually, it isn't you I need at all," she said. "I just wanted to go over some of my kids' records."

Carla shrugged dismissively. "Be my guest," she said. "Do you know how to use the computer?"

Now Judith uttered a genuine laugh. "Is there anyone in the modern world who doesn't?" she asked. "But you could save me a little time by bringing up the right program."

Carla nodded, sat down at her desk and hit a few keys. "There it is," she said. "Just enter the names of the students you want, and your password, and go to it." She stood up, picked up her purse, and started toward the door. "If you get stuck, I'll be hiding out in the staff lounge with everyone else."

A moment later Judith was sitting at the desk, typing in the names of her students. The work went slowly at first, and after ten minutes she realized she was going at it the wrong way—at this rate, she wouldn't even finish getting the names in by the time the lunch hour was over.

Clearing the screen, she brought up a directory of the computer's hard drive, and almost immediately spotted what she was looking for.

A data management program, the same one the school in East Los Angeles had used. Breathing a sigh of relief, she brought up the program's main menu, then began making her selections, typing in specific words and phrases.

The computer itself would sort through the records, compiling a list of students whose records contained the key words. All she would have to do was look over the list it produced. If she and Jed had been right last night, she knew which names should be on the list. She thought carefully, finally constructing a program designed to dig from the records the names of every student who had a relative working for Borrego Oil and a history of disciplinary problems.

At last she pressed the Enter key, then stared at the screen as images flashed by. A few seconds later a report form generated itself on the screen and names began to appear.

The pattern was there.

The names of every one of her affected students, along with many others —some she recognized, and others she did not—appeared on the list.

She narrowed the focus of the search, linking several of the variables together.

A much shorter list appeared, but still, all the names of those strange, emotionless kids who had sat so quietly through her morning classes were still there.

Her mind in turmoil, Judith printed out a copy of the list of names, folded it carefully, and stuck it into her purse. Turning off the computer, she stepped out into the hall. She still had fifteen minutes left of her lunch hour, time at least to grab a snack from one of the machines outside the cafeteria door. But as she started down the hall, the sound of voices caught her attention. She glanced across the corridor to the open door to Laura Sanders's office. A man was standing in front of the nurse's desk. Even from the back, Judith recognized him.

Greg Moreland.

As Laura's voice, sounding furious now, erupted once more, Judith slipped silently across the corridor.

Laura Sanders knew she was losing her temper, but she wasn't sure she cared anymore. Though Greg Moreland had been perfectly polite when he'd appeared in her office ten minutes ago, his implication was clear—he was accusing her of incompetence. And if there was one thing that annoyed Laura more than anything else, it was to have the thoroughness with which she did her job questioned.

"I don't really care what you think, Greg," she said now, her voice rising as she fixed her eyes on him. "I administered every one of the inoculations myself. I kept the records precisely as Mr. Beckwith instructed me, and I cross-checked my work after every class was inoculated."

Greg's expression hardened. He'd been working all morning, ever since Kendall had called him at seven, demanding to know if one of the syringes could possibly have gotten away from them. Since the call, he'd reviewed the records again and again, but been unable to find a mistake.

Every one of the needles was accounted for in the records, either as having been administered to someone or as being in the safe in his office.

Indeed, more than an hour had been wasted in examining the contents of the safe itself, physically matching the syringes against the inventory lists.

Every needle appeared to have been accounted for.

"I'm not accusing you of anything, Laura," Greg said, deliberately keeping his own anger out of his voice. "I just want you to check these lists one more time. There seems to be a mistake somewhere, and all I want you to do is help me find it."

Laura's lips set angrily, but she picked up the lists and began scanning them one more time. Everything, just as she expected—in fact just as it had been the last time she'd looked at it, not two minutes ago—was in order. And then she glanced once more at the second name on the list of Judith Sheffield's first-period class.

Jed Arnold.

Her eyes focused on the number next to his name.

It was out of sequence; indeed, it wasn't even close to the numbers of the rest of his class, nor the class preceding.

And then she remembered.

"Well, there is one thing," she said, looking up. She paused as she saw Judith Sheffield herself, standing outside the office, apparently listening. She was about to nod a greeting to Judith, but when the other woman shook her head and held a finger to her lips, she changed her mind. "It's Jed Arnold," she said. "Actually, he missed his shot that morning. He was late that morning."

Laura saw Judith shaking her head violently. For a split second she didn't understand. And then she realized what must have happened. Her mind raced, and then, as she saw the anger in Greg Moreland's eyes, she decided what to do.

"That's why his number is out of sequence," she went on smoothly. "He came in after school and I gave him his shot then." She let her voice harden slightly. "In fact, if you remember, I was cross-checking the lists when you came to pick everything up."

Greg stared at Laura, trying to decide if she was telling the truth. But of course there was a way to find out—a call to the dam would tell him if Jed had become as compliant as the rest of them. But wherever the mistake had occurred—if, indeed, there had been one at all—it no longer mattered. If Jed was behaving as the rest of the teenagers were, all the syringes were accounted for.

He thanked Laura for her cooperation and turned to leave the office.

Judith Sheffield had disappeared around the corner toward the cafeteria only seconds before.

Peter Langston stared at the telephone.

Twenty-four hours.

That was all it had taken, but it seemed much longer. He and the technician had been in the second subterranean level of the Brandt Institute almost all night, and both of them had been back early this morning just a little after dawn. It hadn't taken too long to figure out what the micromachines were. That had been the simplest part.

They were nothing more than minute transformers. When the switch at the bottom was thrown, whatever electrical source was entering them from their base would be stepped up, and the protuberances at the top, made of a high-resistance ceramic, would heat up. Nor had the source of electricity been difficult to decipher.

He'd calculated the amount of electricity the machines would need to operate. Not surprisingly, it had matched the tiny amount of electricity the human body itself generated.

But there had been some anomalies too, and finally, this morning, he had called in Tom Patchell, a neurosurgeon who had often served as a consultant to the institute.

"There's some kind of coating on the things," Langston had told Patchell. "It's a protein of some kind, but I can't figure out why it's there or what it's for."

It had been Patchell's idea to inject a sample of the fluid in the syringe into a lab animal and see what happened. They'd selected a chimpanzee, and an hour after giving it the injection, had anesthetized it and strapped it to the bed on the institute's nuclear magnetic resonator.

A moment later images began to form on the screen as the machine bombarded the chimpanzee's body with incredibly brief bursts of powerful electromagnetic energy, then measured the reaction of the atomic nuclei within the animal, reconstructing in visual form the structures of the tissues themselves.

After some fine-tuning by the technician, the tiny micromachines began to show up as dark flecks in the bloodstream.

"I don't get it," Langston murmured almost under his breath. "They just seem to be floating around."

Tom Patchell frowned but said nothing, his mind already struggling to remember something he'd read several months earlier. Then it came back to him. "Let's wait a few minutes," he said, "then focus on the chimp's brain."

Fifteen minutes went by, and then, as Patchell issued instructions to the technician, images of the ape's brain began to take form, greatly magnified, only a few millimeters showing at any single moment.

The clock on the wall kept moving, and the minutes crawled by as they kept searching through the depths of the chimpanzee's brain, looking for anything out of the ordinary.

Finally, Tom Patchell thought he saw something.

"There!" he said.

He leaned forward to study the screen. Although most of the dark specks representing the micromachines were still surging through the capillary system like leaves floating in a swift-moving stream, a few of them seemed to have adhered to the walls of cells, almost as if some of the leaves had been caught in the exposed roots of trees along the stream's banks. "I don't get it," Langston said. But Tom Patchell wasn't listening to him.

"Blow that one up," he instructed the technician, using the tip of a pencil to touch one of the specks on the screen.

The technician's fingers flew over the control panel of the resonator, and a few seconds later a new image appeared. This time the image on the screen was of only a few molecules, enlarged millions of times, to the point where the molecular structure itself was visible.

The technician touched a button and the image froze on the screen. Patchell studied the images produced by the resonator for a few moments, then whistled softly. "For Chrissake," he muttered. "Someone's done it."

Langston was bouncing impatiently on the balls of his feet now. "Done what?" he demanded.

"Look at that," Patchell told him. "See those molecules there? The ones that are slightly intertwined?" Langston looked closely at the screen and nodded. "Well, what they've done is something that's supposed to be only in the early experimental stages," Patchell explained. "What you're seeing there are two different molecules, one of which is a part of a nerve cell, the other of which is part of the coating on one of those micromachines."

"So?" Langston asked.

"Every type of cell in the human body has a distinctive protein coating to it. Whoever made those micromachines has coated them with specific kinds of substances that will allow them to adhere only to specific kinds of cells. In other words, what the micromachines do is keep traveling through the bloodstream at random, until they come into contact with the type of cell they were designed to adhere to. When they do, they lock onto that cell. It's almost as if each of the machines has a unique set of fingers, and it's searching for a perfectly fitting glove."

Langston's eyes widened. "So what you're telling me is that there could be any number of different coatings on those things, and it doesn't matter how or where they're injected into the blood system. Once released, they'll sort themselves out all by themselves."

Patchell's expression set grimly. "You've got it," he said. "I think we ought to wait a couple of hours, then take another look and see what we've got. And in the meantime, let's see what we can do about figuring out the triggering method."

Leaving the still-unconscious chimpanzee under the watchful eye of the technician, Peter Langston and Tom Patchell had returned to the physics lab, where they'd been working most of the time since then. The answer had come to Peter quickly enough. "It has to be radio waves," he'd said. "From what Judith said, they have to be triggering these things by remote control." He'd tapped a tiny area near the base of the object displayed on the screen of the electron microscope. "That area right there looks as if it could be some kind of a simple receiver."

By early afternoon they'd been ready. Several slides had been prepared, each slide containing a drop of the saline solution from the hypodermic syringe. The syringe itself was sealed in a lead-lined container; the container was in a safe in Langston's office. Now they were in the microscopy lab, where Langston had jury-rigged a small transmitter capable of broadcasting a weak signal in a broad range of frequencies, and there were electrodes attached to the microscope slide itself.

The technician adjusted the electron microscope, and on the monitor images of half a dozen of the tiny devices appeared. Patchell touched a switch, and a tiny electrical charge, measurable only in millivolts, began coursing through the solution in which the micromachines floated. Finally Langston turned on the transmitter, chose a range of frequencies near the high end, then began turning a dial. For a few seconds nothing happened at all.

And then, so suddenly neither of them actually saw it happen, the image of one of the micromechanisms disappeared from the display screen.

"What the hell?" Tom Patchell muttered.

Patchell frowned, made a note of the exact frequency at which the transmitter had been broadcasting when the object suddenly disappeared, then readjusted it.

A moment later another of the objects disappeared.

"I want to get this on tape," Langston said, and the technician nodded.

"It's already done. If you want, I can play that last one back."

"Do it," Langston replied.

The monitor went blank, and then the images reappeared. At the top of the screen a chronometer displayed the lapse of time in microseconds, and another scale monitored the changing frequency of the radio waves to which the sample was being exposed.

As they watched, the switch at the base of one of the devices began to close, and a few microseconds later the contacts touched. Then the protuberances at the opposite end of the device began to change, and finally the whole device started to disintegrate.

"I was right," Langston breathed to himself. "As soon as the contact closes, the transformer begins drawing current out of the solution, and the whole thing heats up to the point where it burns."

Now it was Patchell who frowned. "But why didn't they all go?"

"They've tuned the switches to different frequencies," Langston explained. "It wouldn't surprise me if we find out that there's a correlation between the frequencies that activate the switches and the kinds of cells they attach themselves to."

A few minutes later they were back on the second level beneath the surface. The chimpanzee, still unconscious, lay inert on the bed of the resonator. The technician glanced up from the magazine he was reading. "Ready to take another look?"

Patchell nodded, and the technician set the magazine aside and began manipulating the controls of the machine in the next room. The scan began, and a greatly enhanced image of the chimpanzee's brain appeared on the screen.

Tom Patchell studied the screen carefully. Satisfied, he nodded. "They've clustered all right," he said. "See? There's a mass of them here in the hypothalamus region, and more here and here, in the area of the cortex."

They removed the chimpanzee from the resonator, transferred it to a gurney, and wheeled it back to its cage. By the time the two men had brought their small transmitter downstairs and set it up, the sedative had begun to wear off. The chimpanzee was beginning to stir.

Half an hour later the transmitter had been set up near the chimp's cage, and two syringes filled with a powerful tranquilizer were on a counter next to the lab sink. The chimpanzee, awake now but still lying on the gurney, watched them languidly.

At last Peter Langston turned on the transmitter and began broadcasting a sequence of frequencies, each of which had activated some of the micromechanisms in the lab.

As they watched, the chimpanzee's eyes suddenly widened and it sat up on the gurney, its head turning as if it was trying to focus on something invisible to either Langston or Patchell.

"Change the frequency," Patchell said.

Langston made a small adjustment on the transmitter. The chimp began to spit, wiping its mouth with its hands as if trying to rid itself of something bitterly distasteful. Then, as Langston once more readjusted the transmitter, the chimp began screaming with either rage or pain, and flung itself off the gurney, leaping up to grasp the bars of the cage.

"Shut it off!" Patchell yelled, but the order was unnecessary. Peter Langston had already cut the power to the transmitter.

Both men stared at the animal, which was now lying inert on the floor. Its face bore an oddly human expression, part frightened, part almost puzzled by what had just happened to it. Patchell hesitated a moment, then carefully opened the door to the cage, keeping a wary eye on the animal within.

The chimp watched him but made no move either to attack or to try to escape as the neurosurgeon slowly stepped inside the cage.

"Hand me one of the needles," Patchell said quietly, his body tense, his eyes never leaving the chimp.

Langston passed him one of the syringes, and Patchell approached the chimp slowly, making no sudden moves, talking quietly to it.

He tentatively touched the chimp's right arm, expecting the ape to jerk its limb away, but instead the chimp simply stared at him, its head cocked slightly. It flinched as the needle pierced its skin and slid into a vein, but made no move to try to pull away.

After a few minutes, it was asleep once more. Patchell lifted it back onto the gurney, and five minutes later they were back in the resonator lab.

"Jesus," Peter Langston breathed, whistling softly as the images of the chimpanzee's brain once more began to appear on the resonator screen. "Look at that."

Tom Patchell nodded, his lips compressing into a tight line.

Though many of the micromechanisms were still visible, others had disappeared entirely, to be replaced with the vivid lesions that were the physical evidence of a series of strokes the chimp had apparently suffered.

"It's horrible," Patchell said at last, shaking his head in awe. "If we'd set them all off, there'd be practically nothing left of the chimp's brain. And all you'd be able to find would be those lesions, without so much as a trace of what caused them."

Both men fell silent as they realized they were looking at the perfect tool for nuclear-age torture.

Or murder.

Peter Langston glanced at the clock on the wall. It was almost four o'clock. He started back to his office to call Judith Sheffield.

Chapter 28

Judith Sheffield felt as though the walls were closing in around her. All afternoon she had been telling herself she was being paranoid, that no one was following her, or watching her. Still, she kept finding herself drawn to the window. What did she expect to see out there? A man in a trench coat, a battered fedora pulled low on his forehead, his hands stuffed deep in his pockets as he lounged against a lamp post?

Well, there wasn't any lamp post, let alone a man in a trench coat and a fedora. And if she was being watched, she suspected that the methods would be far more sophisticated than those she was imagining.

Her eyes drifted up to the mesa, where there could be someone with high-powered binoculars—even a telescope—hiding in any one of a hundred crevices in the worn sandstone. There could even be high-tech listening devices directed at the house or tapping into the telephone.

Stop it! she commanded herself, then nearly jumped out of her skin as the phone in the kitchen suddenly rang, its bell jangling her nerves, making her almost run to snatch it up.

"Peter?" she asked, her voice quavering despite her determination not to let him know how nervous she was.

"Judith?" Peter replied, and almost immediately she felt some of the tension drain out of her body. "Are you okay?" Then: "Stupid question. Anyway, I've got it figured out. The micromachines are transformers with electrodes, and when we triggered some of them in a chimpanzee, they induced a series of what looks—after it's all over—exactly like strokes. But I've talked to a neurosurgeon, and he thinks the devices could induce hallucinations—both visual and olfactory. I won't go into all the details right now—hell, Tom and I don't even *have* most of the details yet—but it looks like they've got this thing down to the point where they can do damned

near anything they want to anybody who's got these things in their bodies.
Different ones seem to adhere to different parts of the brain, but in the end,
if there are enough of them tuned to enough different frequencies, you
could play a person like an organ. You could drive them insane, take away
their willpower—hell, if you set off enough of them, you could kill a person
almost instantly."

Judith felt weak as she thought of Reba Tucker and Frank Arnold. Neither was dead, but they had been punishing Frank Arnold, and experi-
menting with Reba Tucker.

And they'd killed Max Moreland outright.

"My God," she whispered, the words issuing from her throat in a strangled moan. "Wh-What can we do?"

"Right now, not much except find out how they're setting the things off,
and stop them. Then we'll start working on a way to flush the mechanisms
out of the brain. If we can find a way to dissolve the protein coating—"

The sound of the doorbell shattered what little concentration Judith had
been able to devote to Peter. Her mind numb, she tried to gather her wits
together. "J-Just a minute, Peter," she said. "There's someone at the door."

She laid the phone on the counter. Still preoccupied with what Peter had
told her, and the possible implications of it, she hurried to the front door
and opened it.

The moment it was open, she realized her mistake.

All the paranoid feelings that had been growing in her yesterday and
today, all the suspicions and intuitions that she was being watched or followed, had been right. For now, standing on her porch, were two men she'd
never seen before. They were dressed in a perfectly ordinary manner—both
of them in faded blue jeans and plaid western-cut shirts with mother-of-
pearl snaps. They wore scuffed cowboy boots, and one of them had a light
denim jacket draped over his right arm, covering his hand.

Instinctively, Judith knew the jacket was concealing a gun.

She gasped slightly, stepping backward as she tried to swing the door
closed again, but it was too late. One of the men simply stepped forward,
his left hand coming up to push against the door, and then he was inside.

His companion followed a split second later, gently closing the door
behind him.

Judith's mind lurched. It was all impossible. Two men—two strangers—
couldn't simply come barging in on her like this! And from outside, she
already knew, it would look exactly as if she had invited them in.

She opened her mouth to scream, but the first man, nearly six and a half
feet tall, with jet-black hair and broad shoulders that appeared even wider

because of the narrow cut of his shirt, reached out with an immense hand as if to grasp her neck.

Her training in karate and judo—the training that had allowed her to overpower Randy Sparks so easily that day in the lunchroom—came to the fore, and she quickly stepped aside, ready to twist the man's arm around behind him. But even as she made her move, he anticipated it, countering it with an instantaneous shift of his own that put him behind her. As his right arm snaked around her neck, choking off her scream so quickly it was no more than a tiny yelp, Judith understood with terrible clarity that his own first move had been nothing more than a feint, a trap she had instantly fallen into.

"Not a word," he said, his voice quiet but hard as steel. "If you try to scream, I'll kill you right here, right now." As if to prove his point his arm tightened around her neck while the fingers of his left hand found a nerve and applied just enough pressure to send a blinding pain screaming through her body. Her lungs automatically contracted as she tried to scream again, then she began choking as her windpipe closed tight.

The man holding her nodded to his companion, a sandy-haired man with cold blue eyes, who immediately went into the kitchen. Judith could hear the sound of the telephone being put gently back onto its hook.

"I'm going to let you breathe now," the black-haired man said in a tone so casually conversational that it sent chills through Judith's body. "But if you try to scream, or speak, or do anything else I don't tell you to do, it will be the last thing you do."

As he stopped speaking his right arm relaxed enough so that she could suck air into her aching lungs. A part of her mind focused on the fact that before allowing her to breathe he hadn't bothered to wait for any sign that she'd even heard his instructions, let alone agreed to them. That added to the terror that now threatened to overwhelm her, for she was certain he would do exactly as he had said, and didn't really care whether she agreed to his conditions or not.

The sandy-haired man was back in the living room now, and he casually lifted his jacket so she could see the gun in his hand. She hadn't the slightest idea what kind of gun it was, but it was small and compact, with a snub nose that made it look mean and ugly.

"It's a thirty-eight," Sandy-hair told her, his lips curling slightly. "And this," he went on, pulling a metal tube from a pocket of the jacket, "is a silencer. Actually, it doesn't really do the aim of this thing much good, and if you were to get away from us, I'd probably miss you from anything beyond ten or fifteen yards. But at close range, like if it's jammed into your

back, aim doesn't count for much, does it?" He smiled coldly, and neither
he nor Black-hair even seemed to notice the phone when it rang.

"What the neighbors are going to see," Sandy-hair continued, "if they're
looking at all, is us helping you out to the car. You're not feeling so good,
see? So that way, if I have to shoot you, you'll just look like you're feeling
even worse."

"Wh-Why?" Judith managed to ask. Her throat hurt where Black-hair
had crushed her larynx, and the word was no more than a croak.

Sandy-hair shrugged. "A man wants to talk to you," he said. "He sent us
to pick you up."

"I'll need your car keys," Black-hair said, his voice still carrying that eerily
conversational quality that made his request sound so ominous.

"M-My purse," Judith managed, nodding toward a small table next to
the sofa.

Black-hair moved to the table, picked up Judith's purse, then groped in it
until his hands closed on her keys. Then he handed her the purse and
opened the front door. "If you'll just take my arm," he said.

Numbly, Judith slipped her hand through his arm, and he led her outside
onto the porch. Sandy-hair pulled the door closed, almost shutting out the
sound of the still-ringing telephone, then fell in beside her, gripping her
other arm and letting her feel the pressure of the pistol against her rib cage.
Sitting outside, behind her own car, was the blue Chevy she'd seen the day
before.

Black-hair opened the passenger door for her, and as she climbed into the
front seat, Sandy-hair slid behind the wheel. "My friend here still has his
gun," Black-hair told her. "He'll be driving with one hand, and he'll be
holding the gun with the other. If you make any attempt to get out of the
car, or scream, or do anything else except sit there quietly, he'll kill you."

A moment later, after Sandy-hair had disappeared around the corner,
Black-hair ambled up the driveway, got into Judith's car, backed into the
street, and shifted the transmission into Drive.

Across the street and two houses up, a woman stood watering her front
lawn. As he passed her, Black-hair smiled and waved.

The woman seemed puzzled, but then she grinned uncertainly and returned his wave before going back to her watering.

Peter Langston stared at the receiver in his hand and rattled the button
on the phone. "Judith?" he said. He held the button down a moment, then
quickly redialed the number. He let the phone ring fifteen times, then

finally hung up. "Something's happened up there," he told Tom Patchell, who was looking at him, his head cocked worriedly to one side. "Someone came to the door, and then they hung up her phone."

Patchell's eyes narrowed. "Better call the police up there." But his words were unnecessary, for Peter was already dialing again. A few minutes later he began talking urgently to the Borrego police department.

"I'm telling you, something's gone wrong!" He repeated what had happened, then spoke again. "I don't know the address. She's living at her boyfriend's house." He searched his memory, but couldn't remember the name of Judith's new boyfriend. Possibly she had never told him the name. Then he had an idea. "Look, the guy's in the hospital. He had a stroke." A moment later he slammed the receiver down. "I'm driving up there," he told Patchell. "They knew who the guy was, but they said he's some kind of kook. I don't think they're even going to check his place out."

"You want me to go with you?" Patchell asked, but Peter shook his head. "Stay here and see what else you can find out about those damned machines. Like maybe a way to disable them."

Patchell looked at Peter, his eyes bleak. "I've already been thinking about that," he said. "I'm not sure there *is* a way to disable them, short of destroying them. And the only way I can think of to do that is to set them off."

Peter Langston's eyes turned to flint. "There has to be a way," he said. "If there isn't . . ."

But he left the sentence unfinished, unwilling to accept that for all the teenagers of Borrego, there might already be no means of escape from the bombs that had been planted inside their heads.

By the end of his shift Jed Arnold didn't have to pretend to move like a somnambulist. As he climbed the long circular staircase that led up to the top of the dam, his whole body felt numb. He'd spent the afternoon in the main shaft, shoveling debris into the conveyor belt, and his arms felt as if he could barely lift them. He took the stairs one by one, moving his legs stolidly, willing them to carry his weight upward. At last he reached the surface and emerged, blinking into the bright afternoon sunlight. He paused, sucking fresh air into his lungs, hacking and coughing in an attempt to dislodge the dust and grime of the power shaft from his throat. A moment later, realizing he was in full view of the operator's shack at the end of the dam, he let his head hang once more and started along the dam, as though unconscious of his surroundings.

"Arnold!" Otto Kruger's voice barked as he passed the open door to the control room.

He stopped, and slowly raised his head, keeping his expression carefully impassive. Kruger was holding a brown manila envelope out to him.

"Take this down to the communications center on your way home. Give it to the first person you see."

It wasn't a request; it was an order. From the way Kruger had spoken, it was clear to Jed that he anticipated no argument, no questions.

He expected that Jed would silently comply with his command.

Wordlessly, Jed held out his hand and took the thin package, then proceeded on his way to the truck, being careful not even to so much as look at the envelope.

Ignoring the rest of the crew, who had gathered around the bed of Carlos Alvarez's old pickup to enjoy an after-work beer, he climbed up into the cab of the truck, started the engine, and pulled out onto the road along the canyon's edge. Only when certain he was no longer within view of anyone at the dam did he pick up the envelope and look for any markings that might identify what was inside. There was nothing on it. No name, no address, not even a logo for either Borrego Oil or UniChem. It was simply a plain brown envelope.

Jed dropped the envelope on the seat beside him, then sped up, enjoying the wind in his face as it blew through the open window. He slowed the truck only when he came to the part of the road that switchbacked down the shoulder of the mesa, then sped up again as he started back up into the canyon itself.

Four hundred yards into the canyon, in the shelter of a thick stand of cottonwoods, he pulled the truck to a stop. He got out and stripped off his shirt, then splashed water from the stream over his face and torso. Finally he went back to the truck, pulled a ragged towel out from behind the passenger seat and wiped himself dry, removing the worst of the sweat and grime from his aching body. Only when he'd put his sticky work shirt back on did he finally pick up the brown envelope again, this time testing the flap to see if it was sealed.

To his surprise, it wasn't.

And yet, he reflected, why should it be? It was obvious they were certain he would simply do as he was told, and show no curiosity at all about what might be in the envelope.

Well, they were wrong.

Quickly he opened the envelope and slid the single sheet of paper out far enough so he could see what it was.

It was a list of the men he'd been working with all day, the men who had disappeared in groups of four at various times through the morning and afternoon, sent down to the hospital to receive their "flu" shots.

Beside each name there was a five-digit number.

Except for the list of names and numbers, the envelope was empty. Jed stared at the sheet for a few seconds, then rummaged in the glove compartment of the truck until he found a stub of a pencil and a crumpled paper bag.

He copied the names and their corresponding numbers, then shoved the bag and pencil back where he'd found them. He slid the sheet back into its envelope and carefully flattened the metal fastener.

Ten minutes later he pulled up in front of the communications center and climbed out of the truck.

He hesitated.

He wanted to see more of the building than simply whatever lay just inside the door. As he looked at the cars in the parking lot, an idea came to him. He hurried from car to car, until he found what he was looking for. Lying on the dashboard of a blue Buick was an envelope, addressed to someone named Stan Utley. He checked the other cars, but they were all locked, and he found nothing useful. He would have to gamble on the Utley envelope.

Making his face expressionless once more, he walked through the gate and into the building itself.

A girl he didn't recognize looked up at him. "Give me the envelope," she said, exactly as if she were talking to a robot rather than a human being.

Jed shook his head. "They said to give it to Utley," he said. "Stan Utley."

The girl stared at him for a moment, then nodded her head. "In the back," she said. "Go through the door into the transmitter room. He's in there."

Jed stifled a sigh of relief as he followed the girl's instructions. He stepped through the door, and almost immediately the temperature dropped as he came into the cavern that formed the back chamber of the building.

It looked to Jed like a control room. There seemed to be computer monitors everywhere, and at several of the monitors, blank-eyed, expressionless people sat tapping data into keyboards.

Jed stopped, his head down but his eyes darting everywhere, taking in everything he could. On a desk a few feet from him, propped up by one of the monitors, was a list of names and numbers. On the screen of the monitor, more numbers were flashing.

Suddenly a man in a technician's coat appeared in front of Jed. "I'm Stan Utley," he said. Nothing more.

Jed handed him the envelope.

"That's all," Utley said. "You can go home now."

Silently Jed turned and started out of the room, but as he reached the door, he heard Utley's voice speaking to someone else. "Get these entered, and have them matched to the Parameter B frequencies."

As he left the communications center a few seconds later and started driving back down the canyon, Jed was certain he'd found the source of what was being done to the people of Borrego.

The communications center wasn't broadcasting to other UniChem offices at all.

It was broadcasting to the town.

Chapter 29

Peter Langston hurried up the walk in front of the nondescript cinder-block
house and rapped sharply on the door. Darkness had already fallen, the first
stars beginning to glimmer in the sky, and Peter shivered, though he wasn't
sure if it was the chill of the evening that had brought on the sudden
tremor. He was about to knock again when the door opened and a teenage
boy, dark-complected, with fine planes in his face and startlingly blue eyes,
looked out at him. Despite his dusky complexion, the boy's face looked pale
and seemed almost expressionless, and as Peter remembered Judith's description of her "affected" students, he felt a pang of apprehension. But if
this was Jed Arnold, he couldn't possibly be feeling the effects of a shot he
hadn't had.

"Jed?" he asked. "Jed Arnold?" A hint of a frown creased the boy's brow
and he nodded warily. "I'm Peter Langston, Judith Sheffield's—"

Jed's face came to life, and he quickly pulled Langston into the house,
closing the door behind him. "Where's Jude?" he demanded. "Isn't she
with you? She wasn't here when I got home and—" His words faded away
as he saw the look on Langston's face. "Oh, Jesus," he breathed. "Something's happened to her, hasn't it?"

Peter nodded. "I think she's been kidnapped. I know it sounds crazy,
but—"

Jed shook his head. "Nothing sounds crazy around here anymore. What
happened?"

For a moment Peter hesitated. What, after all, could a teenage kid do?
He should go to the police, put the whole thing in the hands of people who
would know what to do. But as Jed's eyes fixed on him, Peter changed his
mind. There was a strength in Jed he'd never seen before in someone as
young. Quickly he told Jed what had happened.

"The antenna," Jed said as soon as Peter was finished. "That's where they're sending the transmissions from." His eyes darkened. "And I know where they've got Jude too."

"Then let's call the police," Peter said.

Jed seemed to think about it for a moment, then shook his head. "No," he said. "It'll take too much time. Even if they believe us, it'll be too late. We'll do it ourselves."

Without waiting for Peter to argue further, Jed grabbed his jacket and headed out the back door. A second later Peter followed him.

Judith strained against the heavy straps that held her to the bed, her wrists and ankles already abraded from her struggles against the thick leather bonds. From the chair a few feet away, Black-hair watched her indolently. "It won't do much good, you know," he said in that infuriatingly conversational tone. "You might just as well lie there and enjoy yourself until Mr. Kendall gets here."

Judith wanted to scream, but wasn't about to give Black-hair the satisfaction.

She didn't know how long it had been since the two men had appeared at her house and calmly taken her away, a gun in her back, with no one apparently either knowing or caring. She'd known where they were taking her as soon as they started up the road into the canyon. They'd brought her into one of the cabins at The Cottonwoods, tied her up and gagged her. A little while later an orderly had appeared, and, as Judith's heart pounded with terror, administered a shot to her. She'd expected to fall asleep then, but when nothing happened, her terror only grew as she realized that the shot could have been only one thing—a dose of the micromechanisms that had already been administered to nearly all the teenagers in town.

But finally, as the hours went on, her terror had given way to cold fury, and when Black-hair had at last removed the gag, she'd screamed out at him in rage, not fear.

He'd only chuckled quietly, settling himself back into a chair. "Scream all you want," he'd told her. "Around here, I guess that's what people are supposed to do, isn't it?"

Since then she'd remained silent, but still struggled against the bonds, knowing even as she did that she wasn't strong enough to break them.

Even if she were, Black-hair was still there, and she had no doubt that if it became necessary, he would kill her. Indeed, she was certain that he would even take pleasure in the act.

After a while the door opened and Greg Moreland entered the room. Nodding to Black-hair, he came over to the bed and looked down at Judith, his eyes glittering with cold anger.

Judith stopped struggling and glared up at him.

"Why?" she demanded. "Why are you doing this?"

Greg ignored the question. "I want to know where you got that sample of my flu inoculation."

Judith said nothing.

"Look, Judith," Greg told her, speaking exactly as if they were conversing at a cocktail party, rather than in a room where she was being held prisoner, "I don't know how much you've discovered about what I'm doing, but I can assure you that at this point, it won't make any difference. What I want to know from you is how you got your hands on one of our syringes. And you *did* get hold of one of them. There isn't any other reason why you'd have gone down to the Brandt Institute yesterday."

Judith's mind raced. He didn't *know*. So far, he was still just guessing. If she simply refused to speak—

It was as if Greg had read her mind. "You'll tell me, you know. The question is whether you tell me now or tomorrow morning."

Judith's eyes betrayed the sudden surge of panic that gripped her.

Moreland smiled. "I gather you figured out what was in that shot the orderly gave you a while ago. Actually, I considered having them put some sodium pentothal in it too, but the trouble with that is that you might have slept through the night. And I wouldn't want to deprive you of the experience of being realigned."

Judith stared balefully up at Moreland. "Is that what you call murdering people?" she asked, her voice trembling with both fear and anger. "Realigning them?"

Moreland's voice hardened. "Judith, you haven't the slightest idea of what it is we're doing here, but I can assure you that it has nothing whatever to do with killing people."

Anger overrode fear in Judith now. "Then what happened to Frank Arnold, and Max Moreland, and Reba Tucker?" she demanded.

Greg shrugged as if what Judith was saying had no importance. "You could call them victims of research, I suppose," he replied.

"Dear God," Judith breathed. "You're playing with people, just like you played with your puppy . . . ."

Greg's face paled. "So Aunt Rita told you about that, did she? She always hated me after that. She always looked at me as if I was some kind of freak.

And she wasn't the only one. She told everyone what I did, you know. That's why everyone's always hated me . . ."

His voice went on and on, but Judith had heard enough to understand the truth.

He was paranoid, certain that everyone in Borrego hated him. And it would have been the same anywhere he'd gone. Everywhere, he would have felt people watching him, listening to him, plotting against him.

But here in Borrego he'd found a way to vent his insane rage, to get even for the imagined hatred he'd felt.

Only when the stream of Greg's words died away did Judith speak again. "You don't even know what you're doing, do you?" she asked.

Greg's expression hardened, and Judith realized she'd struck a nerve. "You don't, do you?" she pressed. "You're just striking out blindly, seeing what will happen."

"Don't pretend to be stupid," Greg snapped. "You've already seen the beginnings of what we're doing. And if you think about it, you'll realize that it isn't so bad. Haven't you noticed that your classes have been better behaved the last couple of days? And don't some of your students concentrate on their work more than they used to?"

"They're like sleepwalkers!" Judith flared. "Whatever you're doing, it's destroying their minds."

"No," Greg replied. "That's where you're wrong. What we're doing is freeing their minds. By the time we get finished, we're going to be able to create a population such as the world has never seen before!"

Judith gasped, and suddenly thought she understood the whole thing. "Slaves," she breathed. "You're turning people into slaves, aren't you?"

Greg's features hardened. "That's an ugly word, Judith," he said. He began pacing the floor, then stopped and looked at her again. "You're a teacher, Judith. It seems to me you, of all people, would be able to see what's going on in this country. What we're faced with is economic ruin. It hasn't happened yet, but it's on the horizon. America simply can't compete. Our people aren't well enough educated, and they have no self-discipline. They spend half their time wanting things they can never have, and the other half being miserable about it. Christ, look at this town. Is anyone here really happy? No. They hate the town, they hate their jobs, they hate their whole lives. Well, I've figured out a way to change all that. It's simply a matter of making some adjustments to the brain itself. And what we're going to wind up with is a whole population that is going to have powers of concentration such as no one has ever seen before. They're going to be able to take orders from their managers, and then carry out their jobs with so few mistakes that even the Japanese will sit up and take notice."

Judith stared up at Greg, almost unable to believe what she was hearing. "But they're not people," she said. "For God's sake, haven't you even *seen* what you've done to them? Gina Alvarez was a bright, vivacious child three days ago. Now she doesn't speak unless she's asked a direct question. She doesn't seem to be interested in doing anything. She just sits and stares!"

Greg Moreland looked at her almost pityingly. "But if you asked her, she'd tell you she was feeling just fine, wouldn't she?" he demanded. "And that's the whole point—for the rest of her life, Gina—and all the others—will be happy."

"Happy?" Judith echoed. "My God, Greg, she won't be happy—she doesn't feel anything anymore. You've killed her, just like you killed Frank and Max and—" Her voice broke and her body was wracked with a sob she couldn't control.

Greg Moreland's lips twisted into a sardonic smile. "Well, that's a matter of opinion, isn't it?" he asked. "At any rate, it won't be much longer until you can experience a realignment for yourself." Judith shrank back on the bed, and Greg's smile broadened. "Don't worry about it," he said. "For most people, it doesn't seem to be too unpleasant. Nothing more than a bad dream. Except that I expect you'll be wide awake when it happens. And tomorrow, when I ask you where you got that syringe, you'll tell me. You'll *want* to tell me."

Nodding once more to Black-hair, he walked out into the night.

"That's it," Jed said quietly. He brought the truck to a stop a few yards from the antenna on the rim of the canyon. Jed's first impulse had been to go directly to The Cottonwoods, but Peter had talked him out of it. "If they've got Judith, they've probably already given her a shot. By now those things will have lodged in her brain, and they can activate them any time. Is there a way we can disable the antenna? If we can get it shut down for a while, at least it'll buy us some time."

Now Peter stared through the windshield at the chain-link fence surrounding the antenna. It had an ugly look to it in the silvery light of the moon, though for the moment it seemed totally inactive. Finally Jed opened the door of the truck and got out, Peter following him.

There was a large toolbox in the bed of the truck, and Jed immediately went to it, taking out a hacksaw and a large plastic-handled screwdriver. He and Peter approached the fence.

"Don't touch it," Peter warned, remembering the fence that surrounded the Brandt Institute. "It might be electrified."

Jed stepped forward, and making sure he was touching nothing of the screwdriver except its plastic handle, laid the tool against the fence.

Nothing happened.

Jed shook his head. "I don't get it," he said. "There's got to be an alarm system."

Peter frowned. "Maybe they figured an alarm would make it look too important," he suggested.

Jed shrugged. "Well, there's only one way to find out." Putting the screwdriver in his hip pocket and slipping his right arm through the frame of the hacksaw, he quickly climbed to the top of the fence, swung over the top, then dropped to the other side.

Instantly, a siren began to wail and four bright floodlights came on, wiping away the darkness with a brilliant artificial glare.

"Holy Christ," Peter swore. "Get out of there, Jed. They'll have guards up here in a minute!"

But Jed made no move to reclimb the fence. Instead, he moved to the antenna itself, where the PVC pipe that snaked up the canyon wall emerged from the concrete floor of the antenna pad. "We have some time," he yelled over the din of the sirens. "It'll take at least twenty minutes for anyone to get up here." Kneeling down, he began sawing at the PVC.

Peter, feeling almost naked in the glare of the floodlights, looked around for a way to turn them off, but it was impossible. They hung from the tops of metal posts, and the lamps were covered with thick Plexiglas, itself protected by heavy metal mesh.

For a moment he felt a twinge of panic, but inside the fence Jed, apparently unaffected by the lights and sirens, pumped steadily at the saw. The blade penetrated the top of the PVC pipe, then moved quickly as it cut downward. But then the blade struck the cables within the pipe and Jed paused.

One of the cables inside, he was sure, would be a power line. He pulled the saw from the kerf in the pipe, examining its handle carefully.

It was all metal. If he'd kept sawing and hit that power line, he would have electrocuted himself. "Peter!" he called out. "Look in the box. I need electrical tape."

Peter dashed to the truck and quickly rummaged through the tool chest. Finally, near the bottom, half buried under a confusion of wrenches, he felt a roll of plastic tape. He jerked it free of the tools, then tossed it over the fence.

Jed snagged the roll of tape in midair and quickly began binding the handle of the saw. After he'd covered it with five layers of tape, he began working again.

The blade bit into the cables once more, and now the work slowed down. But suddenly there was a shower of sparks, and then the lights went out and the wailing of the siren abruptly died away. Jed cursed softly as his eyes— their pupils constricted against the brilliance of the floodlights—failed him completely for a moment, but despite his blindness, he kept sawing.

A few moments later, as his eyes once more adjusted to the dim moonlight, the saw bit into the last centimeters of PVC, and then the pipe parted.

Jed jerked at the saw, trying to get it to come back up through the kerf it had left between the two ends of the pipe, but the cables within had shifted slightly, and the blade jammed firmly. Finally he gave it up, abandoning the saw as he quickly scaled the fence once more and dropped to the other side.

"I don't know how much time we have," he said. "But it's going to take them a while to get that back together again."

They rushed back to the truck, but Peter stopped short to stare at Jed. "Where do we go?" he asked. "If we go back the way we came, we're going to run right into them."

"We go the other way," Jed said.

Peter shook his head. "But the mouth of the canyon's behind us. If we're going to go after Judith—"

Jed was already in the truck. "Just do what I say, okay? Or do you want to wait around here and see what happens?"

Jed started the engine of the truck, and then, as they saw the first glow of headlights moving toward them along the canyon's rim, headed farther up the rutted road.

The track narrowed as it wound eastward, finally disappearing altogether. Peter glanced nervously over at Jed.

Jed kept going. What he was looking for was no more than a quarter of a mile up the canyon's rim.

Chapter 30

Greg Moreland was halfway between The Cottonwoods and the communications center when the quiet of the night was shattered by the high-pitched wailing of the siren. He leaned forward over the wheel and gazed upward at the brilliant white glow of the floodlights surrounding the antenna installation, then slammed his right foot down hard on the gas pedal. The car's rear wheels skidded on the loose dirt of the road, and the rear end fishtailed violently; a second later the tires caught and the car shot forward. Within less than a minute he braked to a sharp stop in front of the communications building and dashed inside. The front office was deserted, but in the cavern hollowed out of the cliff's wall he found Paul Kendall and Stan Utley huddled around a computer terminal.

"What the hell is going on?" Greg demanded.

Utley didn't even look up from the screen he was studying. "Not sure yet," he said. "Something tripped the alarm topside, but so far everything's working fine." He studied the display for a few more seconds, then glanced up at Paul Kendall. "Could have been a bird," he said. "If a mouse was poking around up there and an owl went for it, it could break the trip beam."

Moreland shook his head. Whatever had happened at the antenna had nothing to do with an owl, or any other kind of wild animal. If Judith Sheffield had discovered what was going on, then other people had too. "I want a crew up there," he ordered. "Right now!"

Utley shot him an irritated glance, but knew better than to argue. He picked up a phone and entered a number on the keypad, drumming his fingers impatiently on his desk until he recognized Otto Kruger's voice at the other end. Less than a minute later he hung up. "Kruger's going up there himself with a couple of the men from the dam," he said. "But if there's a real problem—"

Abruptly, the sirens stopped wailing. Utley started to smile, but as his eyes moved to the computer screen, the smile faded. "Shit," he muttered.

Paul Kendall, his fury mounting, shoved Utley aside and studied the display on the screen. It indicated clearly that not only was the signal cable to the antenna cut, but the power cable was broken as well. "I want that fixed," he said, his voice taking on a dangerous edge. "We've got a lot to do tonight, and none of it can wait."

Utley's tongue ran nervously across his lower lip. Until Kruger got to the antenna and assessed the damage, there was no way of telling how long it would take before the antenna would be functional again. But he'd worked for Kendall long enough to know better than to suggest the possibility that one of his orders might not be met. "I'll let you know when I've heard from Kruger," he said.

Kendall nodded curtly, his mind already on other things. He'd made his decision about what was to be done tonight much earlier, and there were preparations to be made. But instead of sitting down at one of the computers with Greg Moreland to begin designing the new program that would be broadcast out over Borrego as soon as the antenna was repaired, he found himself drawn out of the little building into the serene quiet of the canyon.

He glanced upward, but the lights around the antenna were out now, and all he could see were the black shadows of the canyon's northern wall. On the southern wall the pale light of the moon shone softly on the sandstone, its glorious daylight hues muted now to myriad shades of gray. Directly above, the sky glittered with stars, more stars than Paul Kendall ever remembered having seen before.

He moved away from the building, and a small breeze, redolent with sage, tweaked at him. Then, to the right, there was a flickering movement, nothing more than a shadow within a shadow, as a bat fluttered by.

The stream, running in its bed a few yards away, babbled softly in the darkness, and Kendall could hear the chirruping of frogs as they called out in an endless search for mates.

Kendall liked the canyon—even was beginning to appreciate the desert itself.

He hadn't wanted to come to Borrego at all. Indeed, his first choice for the experiment that was taking place here had been Alaska. Up there were towns with no roads leading in or out, towns that were all but cut off from the rest of the world during the long northern winter. But in the end he'd realized that the very isolation of those places could become a liability rather than an asset. While it was true that no one could get to those towns, neither could anyone leave them.

And Greg Moreland had assured him that Borrego would be perfect. "No one cares what happens there," he'd insisted five years ago when he'd brought his first sketchy ideas to Kendall. "No one will even notice what we're doing." But now, after all the years of research and planning, after all the experiments that had, in the end, proved the project to be completely feasible; now, when he was on the very verge of success, he was going to have to fold his tents, move on, and start over again.

Well, perhaps not completely over again. The mechanisms were perfected now, he was certain of that. If they'd had another month—maybe even as little as two weeks—they'd have been ready to unveil Greg's technique to the consortium of corporations that had funded the massive project he'd headed for the last five years.

And abandoning Borrego had its advantages. Before the successes of the past few days, there had been some failures.

Reba Tucker.

No one had meant for Reba to die, not really. But they'd had to have a subject for that first human experiment, and there had been compelling reasons for selecting Reba. The teacher, from the moment Greg had suggested her, had struck Kendall as one of those women who was devoted to her students, even sometimes capable of inspiring them. But she was also the kind who was overprotective of them, just as Frank Arnold had been overprotective of his men. And it wasn't protection anyone in the country needed. Americans, as far as Paul Kendall was concerned, had had entirely too much protection. And now, in the last decade of the century, they were paying for it.

The whole nation had become lazy, assuming that its forty years of economic supremacy was a permanent fixture on the planet's landscape. Too many people, inspired by other people like Reba Tucker, were taking the attitude that their own personal fulfillment was more important than carrying their economic weight. And the country was paying for it.

And then Greg Moreland had come to him with his plan to realign the minds of the nation's youth.

The most elegant aspect of the scheme—the aspect that had truly seized Kendall's imagination—was that by its very nature the realignment would allow subjects to be customized perfectly to suit whatever tasks society—or Paul Kendall—required of them.

People with unique talents could be provided with the personalities best suited to utilize those talents. Other people—the masses of individuals who would never stand out from the crowd—would simply have their minds adjusted so that, no matter what their station in life, they would feel a contentment that nature would never have allowed them.

That, of course, was still in the future. But in Borrego the final experimentation would have taken place over the next few weeks, possibly even months. Despite Greg Moreland's own eagerness to move forward as quickly as possible, Kendall had planned to move slowly, sending out only narrow ranges of frequencies at any given time, then monitoring the people who were affected. Already it was obvious that there were still areas in which the process needed refinement. Right now it appeared there were too many hypothalamus probes, and some of the subjects had already become almost too lethargic ever to be useful.

On the other hand, those extra probes could prove useful. Indeed, with Frank Arnold, they already had. Frank had gotten out of line, and he'd been punished.

Given time, it all could have been worked out. He and Greg Moreland would have been able to record the changes in each subject, and eventually devise perfect combinations of probes to affect any given subject's mind in almost any way imaginable.

That was why he'd insisted on keeping such meticulous records of who had received which shot. The probes were tuned to hundreds of frequencies. Until now they'd been very careful in their selection of subjects for realignment.

They'd started with the troublemakers, the kids who made life difficult not only for their teachers, but for everyone else as well. But now there had been a leak in the security of the project, long before they were willing to make it public. Until people could see the benefits of what they were doing, they could hardly expect them to approve. Right now, given the condition of the Alvarez girl, and the Sparks kid, they would surely be accused of "crimes against humanity."

Kendall had decided that he simply wouldn't let that happen.

Tonight he was going to eliminate the evidence.

Tonight, as soon as the antenna was repaired, he would send out powerful transmissions of the entire frequency spectrum to which the probes were tuned.

In the space of a few seconds every probe in the Borrego area would fire, burning itself away and leaving no trace whatever of its existence.

A lot of people would die.

Some of them might survive physically, of course, but Kendall knew there would be little left of their minds.

And then there would be the inevitable investigation, but in the end, with no evidence to show what had happened, none of the micromachines left in anyone's brain, there would be nothing left but questions.

Paul Kendall and Greg Moreland wouldn't be around to answer any of those questions. They would already be somewhere else, in some other small town in the middle of nowhere, preparing to repeat their experiments. But next time there would be no leaks.

As he started back to the communications center to begin putting together the program that would wreak havoc in the brains of nearly thirty percent of Borrego's population, Paul Kendall wondered how the town would react to what they would find in the morning.

It was a shame, really, that he wouldn't be able to stay here and study it. Aside from the sociological implications of the whole thing, he had come to like Borrego.

But not enough that he was unwilling to destroy it.

"We're here," Jed said quietly, braking the truck to a stop.

Peter Langston looked around. They were a few yards back from the edge of the canyon. The road had deteriorated into no more than a nearly invisible track winding through the scrub juniper on the top of the mesa, and Peter saw nothing unusual about the area. But Jed was already out of the truck. Peter followed him.

Jed was once more rummaging through the toolbox, finally sliding a rusty carpet knife under his belt and handing Peter a long screwdriver. "That's not much, but if you have to, at least you can shove it in someone's eye," he said.

Langston winced at the boy's words, telling himself they were nothing but adolescent bravado, but reluctantly took the screwdriver and secured it under his own belt. "Where are we?" he asked as Jed started toward the rim of the canyon.

"There's a trail," Jed replied.

A few minutes later the two of them stood on the edge of the precipice. The edge of the cliff dropped straight into the canyon. Peter, after glancing down, took a step backward, his groin tightening as the chasm seemed to draw him toward it, seemed to urge him to throw himself into its gaping maw. He looked away, following as Jed turned northward and trotted quickly along the brink of the cliff, apparently unaffected by the height. Twenty yards away there was a small cleft in the canyon's wall.

Peter peered doubtfully down into the rift. It notched no more than fifteen feet into the canyon's wall, and as it went down it seemed to get smaller, until it finally disappeared entirely. "Jesus, kid, that's not a trail."

Jed grinned in the moonlight. "Sure it is," he said. "My grandfather's been using it for years. He showed it to me when I was about ten." He didn't tell Peter that he'd never before attempted to use the trail, even in broad daylight.

He dropped down onto the edge of the cleft, rolled over onto his stomach, then lowered himself down until he was hanging only by his fingers. Closing his eyes and uttering a silent prayer, he let go, and dropped straight downward.

Peter froze. He couldn't believe what he'd just seen. The kid must be crazy. Then, from the darkness, he heard Jed's voice.

"Come on." The words drifted eerily up from the darkness of the cleft.

Peter approached the edge and reluctantly looked down. Jed was standing on a narrow ledge, his head five feet below Peter's feet.

Peter realized it was his turn.

He sat down gingerly, then let his legs drop over the edge. His groin tightened again, and for a moment he felt an almost uncontrollable urge to throw himself into the abyss. But the urge passed. Finally he rolled over and inched his way out until only his torso and arms were still on the mesa's surface.

"Good," he heard Jed encouraging him. "Now just a little more."

He inched outward, and then his whole body was hanging over the edge, his fingers clawing at the ground as if trying to dig into the rock itself.

He felt his fingers slip.

A scream rose up in his throat, but he choked it back. The instant during which he fell seemed to expand into an eternity, but then he felt hands grasping him, and suddenly his feet struck the ledge below. As the hands steadied him he pressed against the sandstone, his heart pounding, his breath coming in short gasps. "I knew there was a reason why I never wanted to climb mountains," he said, his voice trembling.

"It's not so bad," Jed said. "Just don't look down unless you have to." He was already sidling along the ledge, and a moment later he crouched down once more. This time, instead of lowering himself to another ledge directly below, he leaped across the gap itself, his feet coming to rest on another outcropping that was four feet farther down and as many across.

Peter stared down at the depths of the abyss, realizing that if he missed his footing, he would plunge down the wall into the canyon itself. Instantly, what was left of his nerve deserted him. "I—I'm not sure I can do it," he said, and his words seemed to bounce off the rock walls, echoing back to taunt him.

"You don't have a choice," Jed told him. "My grandfather told me this is a one-way trail. Without ropes, I can't get back to your ledge, and you can't get back up to the top without me."

Panic seized Peter. He pressed once more against the suddenly comforting stone behind him. But when he looked up, he realized that Jed was right. The only way out was down.

Steeling himself, he took the jump before he had enough time really to think about it.

"Yeah!" Jed exclaimed as he once more steadied Peter's landing. "It's not so bad, huh?"

They dropped farther into the cleft, moving as fast as they could. The lower they went, the darker it became, until Peter could barely see at all. But Jed moved quickly and steadily, using his inner senses to guide him along the invisible path.

The cleft finally dwindled away entirely, and they had to creep several yards along a narrow ledge that was more than three hundred feet above the canyon floor, until they came to another break in the wall. Peter negotiated it only by keeping his back flat against the cliff's facade, his eyes averted, and his feet moving only a few inches at a time.

Then they were into the second fissure. This one, only three feet wide, dropped away as vertically as a chimney, but all along it there were small fractures in the stone. Many of them appeared to have been deliberately hollowed out to provide hand and footholds, and when they finally came to the bottom of the crevice, Peter asked Jed about them.

"I think my grandfather did it," Jed replied. "But he only cut them where nobody could see them from above or below. He said sometimes it's good to have a path no one knows about."

Twenty minutes later they finally dropped from the lowest ledge down to the canyon floor. There was a turn in the canyon here, and the stream flowed next to the wall, so when they released their grips on the stone lip, they dropped into two feet of cold water.

Peter flinched in shock, then reached down and splashed water over his face, only now realizing that his whole body was drenched in sweat despite the chill of the night. He took a drink, then waded ashore, where Jed was waiting for him. Two hundred yards down the canyon there was a soft glow of lights from the buildings of The Cottonwoods. For the moment, though, the two of them, lost in the black shadows of the canyon, were totally invisible.

They moved quickly and quietly along the bank of the stream, then Jed seemed to melt away into the grove of cottonwoods.

Peter, suddenly finding himself alone in the darkness, froze. He strained his ears, trying to hear even the faintest sound that would tell him where Jed had gone, but there was nothing.

Jed glided through the cottonwood grove, his senses absorbing every vibration of the night. It was as if he could actually see the tiny creatures that scurried in the darkness, and smell the faint odors of animals that had long ago passed over the ground on which he trod.

He stopped. Though he couldn't see it yet, he knew there was a cabin close by.

The cabin his father was in.

He hesitated, knowing he should move on, find the right cabin, the one in which Judith Sheffield was being held. Yet even as he hesitated he knew why that strange spirit that seemed to have been guiding him from within had brought him here.

There was something he had to do.

He slipped silently through the darkness until he reached the deep shadow of the cabin. Only a faint light showed in the cabin's window—the glow of the screen on the monitors attached to his father.

His father was alone.

Jed moved around the cabin, coming to the front door like a shadow.

The door was unlocked.

He slipped inside.

He knew what it was that had to be done; indeed, he suspected he'd known it since yesterday, when he'd first seen his father here. He hadn't done it then; hadn't been able to summon up the courage. But now there was no other choice to be made. He gazed at his father in the dim light of the cathode tubes, trying once more to see some remnant of the man he'd known all his life.

There was none. All that lay in the bed were the ruined remains of what his father had once been.

His face, coldly pale even under the soft light, held no expression whatsoever.

Surrounding him were the machines that were keeping him alive, but now, as Jed watched his lifeless body being manipulated by the machinery, he finally grasped that his father wasn't truly alive at all.

He reached down for a moment, as if to touch his father's cheek, but then his hand trembled and he withdrew it. At last he drew a deep breath and straightened up. It was time for him to release his father's spirit from the body that had already died.

Steeling himself, Jed reached out and switched off the respirator that kept his father alive.

He stood perfectly still, watching in silence as his father's chest stopped moving.

Seconds ticked by.

Jed was about to turn away when he thought he saw something in the darkness.

A pale wraith of silvery light was drifting up from the bed where his father lay. It hovered in the air for a moment, and Jed felt a strange serenity come over him, as if the aura he beheld had reached out and touched him.

Then it was gone.

Jed glanced at the monitors: all the lines were flat now.

His father's body was truly dead, and his spirit was gone.

Turning away, Jed slipped out of the cabin as silently as he'd come, moving once more through the night until he was certain that what he'd come looking for was here.

At last he returned to the spot where Peter Langston waited.

"She's here," Jed said. "I can feel it."

Three pickup trucks, each of them carrying two men, pulled up to the antenna installation. They formed a crescent around the site, so their headlights flooded the area within the fence with a bright halogen glow. Otto Kruger jumped out of the first truck and hurried to the gate, a ring of keys jangling in his right hand. He flipped through the keys quickly, found the right one, and unlocked the gate. Once inside, it took him no time at all to discover the cut in the PVC pipe. "Hernandez," he called out. "Bring the toolbox in here and get to work. Briggs, you and Alvarez take your truck and keep on going."

"Shit, man," Joe Briggs complained. He had been almost ready to go home for the night when Kruger had commandeered him for this job. "They could be anywhere. If they had a four-wheel, they could've taken off cross-country."

"Maybe so," Kruger agreed. "But I'm sure not going to tell Kendall we didn't even look, and since we didn't see anyone coming down the road, maybe they went up. So quit bitching and move your ass."

Briggs, with Carlos Alvarez slouched in the seat beside him, backed the truck away from the chain-link enclosure, spun the wheel and jammed the transmission into low gear. Popping the clutch, he let the wheels spin in a gratifying release of his own anger. The truck skidded out of control and spun around, but Briggs steered into the curve, caught his traction, and sped off into the night.

Otto Kruger, watching him, shook his head dolefully. "Son of a bitch is going to kill himself at that rate."

Jesus Hernandez, carrying a large toolbox, came into the enclosure, frowned at the cut in the PVC, then pulled a hacksaw out and set to work. Within less than a minute a section of PVC a foot long came loose from the pipe. Jesus tossed it aside, then knelt down and, using a flashlight, peered into the tube itself. "God damn," he swore softly.

"What's wrong?" Kruger demanded.

Hernandez shrugged. "Lot of cable in there. Its own weight pulled it down. I can see the ends, but they're about five feet back from the opening."

"So? Fish 'em out."

Hernandez stared at his boss contemptuously. "Yeah?" he asked. "How you going to do that, huh? First off, unless you brought some tool I don't know about, I don't see how we're going to get hold of the ends of those cables. And even if we do, it don't matter. I don't know about you, but I can't lift a thousand feet of that stuff. It's too heavy."

The muscles in Kruger's neck knotted with anger. "Then what do we do?" he asked.

Hernandez shrugged. "Got to bust up the concrete," he said. "Only way to fix that tonight is break up the pad, get the pipe out of the way, and put in some jumpers."

Kruger nodded, his mind already made up. From Utley's tone earlier, he had been certain that Paul Kendall was standing at the man's elbow, listening to every word. And that meant it was Kendall who wanted the antenna repaired tonight.

Therefore, it would be done.

Kruger yelled at the two men who were leaning against the front fender of the third truck, smoking cigarettes. "There's a couple of sledgehammers and a wedge in the back of my truck. Bring 'em over here. We've got a lot of work to do."

The two men groaned, but tossed their cigarette butts away.

Twenty minutes later, as Kruger was pacing impatiently just outside the fence, Joe Briggs and Carlos Alvarez came back. Briggs swung out of the truck. "You were right," he said to Kruger. "We found a truck about a mile or so up."

"Did you recognize it?"

Briggs hesitated a split second, but nodded. "Oh, yeah. It's Frank Arnold's."

Kruger felt his temple throb with sudden fury. The man was as good as dead, for Chrissake—he was lying in a cabin up the canyon that very moment. Then he understood.

The kid.

"All right," he growled. "Where'd he go?"

Briggs shrugged. "How should I know? He wasn't around the truck, and there's no way he could have gotten down into the canyon from there, so he must be hiding up here somewhere. Hell, he could've hiked halfway back to town by now."

Kruger shook his head. "If he was going back to town, he'd have driven at least part of the way. But he wouldn't have gone in the exact opposite direction. So he's up here somewhere." He pulled a walkie-talkie out of its belt holster and snapped it on. Stan Utley's voice came through, scratchy but clear.

"Well, we know who did it," Kruger said, punching the button on the side of the unit in his hand. "A couple of my guys just found Frank Arnold's truck. I figure it had to be his kid, pissed off about what happened to his old man."

In the communications center below, Stan Utley glanced up at Paul Kendall. Kendall's face had gone scarlet with fury as he glared at Greg Moreland.

"That's where they got it," Kendall said, his voice shaking with rage. "That kid was supposed to have gotten his shot, and Watkins said he was doing just fine. Taking his orders, and keeping his mouth shut. But it was an act! The whole goddamned thing was an act!" His eyes went to the clock, then fixed on Stan Utley once more. "How much time have we got before that antenna's up again?" he asked.

"Half an hour, at least. Maybe an hour."

Kendall nodded tersely and began snapping orders to the technician.

Greg Moreland, filled with the same fury that had gripped Paul Kendall, turned and strode out of the room. He had half an hour, and there was something he wanted to do.

He wanted to watch Judith Sheffield suffer.

Indeed, he wanted to torture her himself.

Chapter 31

Jed froze, his whole body tensing as he heard the soft cracking of a twig. Someone was coming. He was alone again, having left Peter concealed in the deep shadows of the cottonwood grove while he himself moved out of the trees' shelter to get a closer look at the little cabin. He'd moved swiftly and silently, dodging between the boulders that lay scattered near the canyon's wall, finally waiting for several long minutes, crouched in the shadows, sensing danger even though nothing was visible.

Now, as a second twig cracked, he spotted the presence he had only felt before.

At first he could see nothing but the faint glow of a cigarette tip, brightening briefly as its bearer drew in on it, then fading away, almost disappearing into the inky blackness of the canyon's depths. But Jed's night vision still saw it clearly, bobbing slowly toward him.

Then the figure emerged from the shadows for a moment, and Jed saw that it was a woman—heavyset and walking slowly, as if she were tired. She paused, and Jed could hear her muttering to herself, but then she ground the cigarette under her foot and began walking again, more quickly this time.

She approached the cottage, rapped on the door a couple of times, and tried the knob. When it didn't open, she knocked again, more loudly. A moment later the door opened a couple of inches and a large figure loomed in the gap. Again there was the faint sound of voices, and then the door opened wider and the woman stepped inside.

The door closed.

Jed waited.

Time stood still.

After what seemed an eternity, but had actually been no more than a couple of minutes, the door opened again and the woman emerged. She was carrying a tray with what looked like a few dirty dishes on it. As soon as she was out the door, the man inside closed it again.

Jed heard the click of the lock being thrown. He stayed where he was, as still as one of the boulders he crouched among. When the woman started in his direction, he held his breath.

But the woman passed by him, no more than six feet away, never so much as sensing his presence. Jed began breathing again, but waited to make a move until the woman had disappeared completely into the darkness and his inner senses told him the danger was over.

At last, darting silently away from the protection of the boulders, he approached the bungalow itself. There were several windows, and he thought for a moment before deciding which one to risk peering into. Finally he chose the one in which the small table lamp was framed. Its light would turn the inner surface of the glass into a mirror. Still, he approached it warily, every nerve in his body tingling, ready to dodge away into the dark shadows at the first hint of danger.

He came to the window and peered inside.

Immediately he let his body relax, for the man inside was sitting in a chair next to the lamp, his back to the window.

Jed stole closer, then finally stood up to his full height. In the bed, strapped down, he saw Judith Sheffield. Her eyes were closed, but Jed was certain she wasn't asleep. Now she stirred and struggled to sit up, her eyes moving toward the window as if she sensed his presence there.

In response to her movement, the man in the chair stood up. He was a big man, much larger than Jed himself. Still, there would be two of them . . .

Satisfied, Jed faded back into the darkness. Within seconds he was back in the black shadows of the cottonwoods, whispering softly to Peter. A few moments later both of them moved out of the grove, this time making no effort to conceal their presence.

They approached the cabin quickly, Jed pressing his back to the wall next to the door. Peter stepped up to the door, knocked sharply, then rapped again, as if impatient at being kept waiting.

Peter heard movement inside the cabin. A moment later the door opened a couple of inches. A large man with black hair eyed Peter suspiciously, squinting at him.

"I'm Dr. Langston," Peter said, loudly enough so he hoped Judith would be able to hear him, but not so loudly as to alert the man whose body blocked the door. He prayed his voice would not betray his nervousness.

"Dr. Moreland wanted me to take a look at—" He hesitated, as if searching his memory. "Miss Sheffield, is it?"

The black-haired man's eyes narrowed still more. "He didn't call me," he said doubtfully.

Peter thought quickly, then decided a good offense was his best defense. "Well, that's not my problem, is it? And I didn't drive all the way up here from Santa Fe just to turn around and start back." He reached in his hip pocket, pulled out his wallet, then flipped it open to reveal an ID card from the institute. "Maybe you'd better give Moreland a call, if it'll make you feel any better," he suggested.

The big man's eyes flicked to Peter's ID, and his expression cleared as he remembered the scene earlier when Moreland had been there. He'd been furious, and it was possible he'd simply forgotten to mention the doctor. Still . . .

And then he saw the name on the card.

The Brandt Institute.

This guy hadn't been sent by Moreland at all! He was a friend of Sheffield's!

Peter saw the change in the big man's eyes. Instantly, as the door started to close, he launched himself against it, and the man, startled by the sudden move, reflexively took a step backward to catch his balance as the door smashed into him.

Peter shoved again and the door flew open, but the man was already recovering, crouching as he prepared to hurl a fist. Peter spun aside, and at the same moment Jed burst into the room. The rusted carpet knife already in his hand, Jed slammed the door closed behind him, then hurled himself at the man.

Judith, her eyes wide open now, choked back a scream as Black-hair's fist smashed into Jed. Jed fell back against the wall, but then Peter brandished the long screwdriver that had been concealed in his belt, now held tightly in his right hand. With no hesitation he hurled his whole weight at Black-hair, plunging the screwdriver into the man's stomach. Black-hair, eyes bulging with the shock of the sudden attack, grasped at the handle of the screwdriver, but before he could begin to pull it free from his guts, Jed was behind him.

As Judith watched, horrified, Jed's arm snaked around Black-hair's neck and he sank the curved blade of the carpet knife deep into the flesh and sinews of his throat just below his left ear. With a fast jerk he ripped the man's throat open, and blood began to spurt from his lacerated veins. His face twisting into a mask of fear and shock, Black-hair sank to his knees, his hands now grasping spasmodically at his neck. Then he toppled over and lay still.

Ignoring the dead man, Peter rushed to the bed and unfastened the straps that bound Judith to it. "Can you walk?" Peter asked.

Judith nodded, rubbing hard at the soreness in her ankles. She got off the bed and stood up, her head suddenly swimming. She lost her balance, falling heavily against Peter, who started to pick her up. She shook her head. "I can make it," she said. "I was just dizzy for a second."

Holding onto Peter's arm, she started toward the door, ducking her head away so she wouldn't have to look directly at the blood-sodden corpse of Black-hair, sprawled out next to the door. Jed, who had already jerked the screwdriver out of the dead man's belly, held the door open, and Judith, with Peter right behind her, lurched out into the night. She paused for a moment, filling her lungs with fresh air, then looked around in vain for the car or truck she had expected to be waiting for them.

"Jed—" she began, but her words were stifled as Jed's hand clamped over her mouth.

"Be quiet," he whispered. "Just keep quiet, and follow me."

He released her and darted toward the cottonwoods, Peter and Judith hurrying after him.

Just as they reached the shelter of the trees, headlights swept across the cabin, and then a car pulled up in front of it. But by the time Greg Moreland got out of his car and approached the bungalow's door, the three people in the cottonwood grove had already begun moving up the canyon.

Greg Moreland rapped sharply on the door of the cabin, then tried the knob.

It was locked.

He knocked again, louder this time. "Walters!"

There was no answer. Suddenly he had a presentiment that something had gone terribly wrong. He strode over to one of the windows and peered inside.

The bed was empty, and on the floor, so close to the window he could only see part of it, was Lamar Walters's body. But the part Greg could see —the wide-open, dead eyes, and the torn neck—told him as much as he needed to know. Cursing under his breath, he dashed to the main house, and burst in the front door.

Elsie Crampton, slouched on a chair with a romance novel open on the desk in front of her, looked up in surprise. As she recognized Greg, she got quickly to her feet. "Dr. Moreland," she stammered. "What are—"

"Where is she?" he demanded, glaring furiously at her. "What the hell is going on around here?"

Elsie looked at him blankly. "Where's who?"

"Sheffield, you idiot," Moreland snarled. He wanted to smash his fist into the woman's stupid, cowlike eyes. "She's gone, and Walters is dead!"

Elsie gasped, her face paling. "But I was just out there," she said. "I picked up the dinner trays, and everything was fine. It wasn't more than five minutes ago, ten at the most."

Moreland's fury got the better of him then. His hand came up, slapping Elsie's cheek so hard she reeled, then crumpled to the floor, sobbing. Moreland ignored her, snatching up the phone on the desk and dialing quickly. A moment later Paul Kendall's voice came on the line.

"The Arnold kid's in the canyon," Moreland said, not bothering to identify himself. "Somehow he managed to kill Lamar Walters, and Judith Sheffield is gone."

Kendall's voice crackled over the line. "I'll get some of Kruger's men down there right away," he said.

"Get the mouth of the canyon blocked," Moreland told him. "But don't take so many men that Kruger can't get that antenna fixed. I'll be there in a few minutes." He slammed the phone back on the hook, then, completely ignoring Elsie Crampton, left the house and sprinted back to his car.

Elsie, rubbing at her burning cheek, pulled herself to her feet and hobbled to the door. Her hip was hurting where it had slammed against the floor, and it was painful to walk. She leaned her weight against the doorjamb, her eyes narrowing angrily as Moreland's car shot past a few seconds later.

This, she decided, was it.

She didn't like this place—didn't like it at all. In fact, she'd been thinking about getting out of here all evening, ever since they'd brought that nice woman in—the one who'd come to visit Mrs. Tucker. Elsie had seen her twice now—once when she'd taken the two dinner trays out to the cabin, and again when she'd picked them up a few minutes ago—and to her, Judith Sheffield hadn't looked sick at all. She'd looked scared, and the man in the cabin had looked very much like the kind of tough that Elsie had once found attractive, until she learned, painfully, that men like that tended to talk with their fists instead of their mouths.

As Moreland's taillights disappeared, she started toward her room at the back of the house. She'd just throw her things in her suitcase, and in ten minutes she'd be gone. To hell with the last couple of weeks' pay—it just wasn't worth it.

But then her mind shifted gears and she remembered what Moreland had said about that man in Cabin Five being dead. Her mind still working, she left the house and trudged slowly across the lawn, rubbing her sore hip as she went. Finally she came to Cabin Five, knocked at the door, then used her key to unlock it.

She stared at the body for a moment, frowning, her mind working. If she left now—just took off—they might try to blame the murder on her.

She puzzled at the problem for a moment, then smiled as she figured out what to do. She'd get herself off the hook, and get even with Moreland at the same time.

Leaving the cabin door standing open, Elsie hurried back to the main building and rummaged in the drawers of the desk until she found the thin Borrego telephone directory.

The number she was looking for was printed in large red type on the inside of the front cover. She dialed it, settling herself into the chair behind the desk.

"Borrego police department," a bored-sounding voice said after the phone had rung several times.

Elsie smiled to herself. "My name is Elsie Crampton," she said. "I work at The Cottonwoods. You know, up in Mordida Canyon?"

"Uh-huh," the policeman said.

"Well, we've had some trouble," Elsie went on. "One of our patients is missing, and the man who was attending her is dead."

"Beg pardon, ma'am?" the man said, all traces of boredom suddenly gone. "What did you say your name is?"

Elsie patiently repeated her name. "The patient's name is Sheffield," she went on. "Judith Sheffield."

In the Borrego police department Billy Clark stiffened. What the hell was one of the high school teachers doing up there? "You say she's a *patient* there?" he asked, his voice reflecting his doubt.

Elsie briefly explained what had happened, then hung up the phone and went to her room to start packing.

She'd wait for the police, tell them everything she knew, and answer all their questions. By the time she left, Dr. Moreland would be in big trouble.

She wasn't absolutely certain, but she had a vague idea that not reporting a crime to the police was some kind of crime itself.

And if the crime you didn't report was murder . . .

She let the thought drift along, smiling happily. She'd teach Greg Moreland not to slap *her* around.

Judith slipped on a rock in the stream bed and stumbled, her ankle
twisting painfully. Instantly, Jed's hand grasped her arm, steadying her. She
tested her weight on her ankle and winced, suppressing the yelp that rose in
her throat.

"Are you all right?" Jed asked her.

Judith shook her head. "I—I'm sorry, but I have to sit down for a minute."

Jed's eyes bored into the darkness ahead. "A little farther," he said.
"There's a big rock in the middle of the stream. You can sit down there."

Judith considered arguing, but quickly thought better of it. When Greg's
men—and they were all certain that by now a search party had been formed
—discovered they hadn't gone toward the mouth of the canyon at all, they
would bring dogs up to find their trail, which meant the stream was their
only safety.

"Can you make it?" Jed asked, his voice low.

Judith nodded, leaning heavily on him as she hobbled through the water.

Twenty yards farther on they came to the rock and Judith gratefully
lowered herself onto its flat surface. She lifted her foot out of the water and
started to massage it.

Peter looked at her anxiously. "Is it broken?"

"I don't think so," Judith said, then prodded at it again. "In fact, I don't
think I even sprained it. It's just a twist. I'll be all right in a couple of
minutes." She fell silent for a few seconds, catching her breath. Since
they'd left the cottonwood grove, no one had said much, each of them
concentrating on putting as much distance between themselves and the
sanitarium as they could. But now, as the pain in her ankle began to ease
and she was certain they were not yet being followed, the other fear—
which had been growing within her since her arrival at the sanitarium—
came to the fore.

"They gave me a shot, Jed," she said.

Jed nodded. "We figured on that." He gazed back down the canyon and
up. High up on the canyon's rim he could see headlights. A crew was
already working on the antenna, putting it back into operating condition.
And when they did . . .

He slid off the rock, back into the stream. "We don't have much time."

Peter shook his head. "But it doesn't matter, does it? Where can we go?

Even if we can get out of the canyon, what good will it do? Once they get that antenna fixed—"

Judith stared at him through the darkness. "The antenna?" she asked, confused. "What does that have to do with it?"

His voice dulled by both his exhaustion and the certain knowledge that in the end, when the antenna was fixed, they would have failed, Peter explained to Judith how the tiny mechanisms were being triggered. "Jed cut the cables," he finished. "But they're up there now, fixing them."

Judith's eyes shifted upward, to the spot far down the canyon where a glow of lights created a bright splash in the darkness. "But there has to be something we can do," she said. "Can't we get up there?"

There was silence for a moment, then Jed spoke. "We don't have to get up there," he said. "There might be something else we can do." His eyes met Judith's. "Can you walk?"

Judith nodded, and as if to prove it to herself, she put her foot back in the water and stood up. A sharp spasm of pain shot up her leg, but it faded away a second or two later, and when she took a step, her limp was less pronounced than it had been just minutes ago.

They moved as quickly as they could, finally leaving the river when the bottom became too rocky for any of them to find a secure footing, and found a path that led along the riverbank, threading through the trees.

Ten minutes later they came to a dead stop. Twenty yards ahead of them the blank face of the dam rose up into the night, blocking their way.

Judith stared at the massive concrete structure, its surface looking almost glassily smooth in the moonlight. Then she heard Jed's voice.

"This way," he called out softly. He was moving quickly, heading off toward the north wall.

And then, finally, she realized where he was taking them.

Mounted in the concrete, starting about ten feet off the ground, were a series of metal bars—spaced about two feet apart—climbing up the face of the dam like a ladder. They ended at a small metal platform resembling a fire escape, a quarter of the way up.

"It's an emergency ladder," Jed explained. "We can climb up it, force that door, and get into the dam."

Peter gazed up doubtfully. "If we can get to that first bar."

"Take off your belt," Jed told him, removing his own even as he spoke. Peter hesitated, then did as he was told. Jed buckled the two belts together so they formed a loop more than two feet long. "Let's get me up there first, then Peter," he said.

Peter stood close to the dam and laced his fingers tightly together. A moment later Jed placed his foot in Peter's hands, and while Peter stood rigid, his back against the dam itself, Jed straightened himself up, keeping his balance by resting part of his weight against the concrete.

"A little higher," Jed said, and Peter strained to raise the boy's weight upward. "Got it," Peter heard Jed say, and a moment later Jed's weight lifted off him. Rubbing his hands, Peter stepped back and looked up.

Jed was hanging from the lowest rung. As Peter and Judith watched, he pulled himself up until his chin was level with the bar. Then, taking a deep breath, he let go of the bar with his right hand, which shot upward to grasp the second rung.

He repeated the action, and then managed to get his feet onto the bottom bar. "Easy," he said. "Now toss me up the belts."

Peter cupped his hands for Judith, while Jed waited, clinging to the second rung, the looped belt hanging down almost within reach. But Judith shook her head.

"You next," she said. "Someone's going to have to lift the last one, and I'm the lightest."

Peter felt an urge to argue with her, but then realized argument would only waste time. Besides, she was right.

Judith cupped her hands, and Peter bounced tentatively for a moment, then launched himself upward.

He missed the rung by nearly a foot, but Jed had anticipated him, and Peter's hand closed on the looped belts. He swung helplessly for a moment, but then, as Judith lifted and Jed pulled, he rose up until he could grasp the lowest rung. He hung there, then pulled himself up.

Jed's hand closed on the collar of his jacket, and a moment later Peter too was clinging to the ladder. Jed gestured upward. "Go ahead," he said. "I can handle Judith." Peter hesitated, then followed Jed's orders.

Jed crouched low on the bottom rung once again, his right hand gripping the one above. Stretching downward, he lowered the looped belts until they hovered just out of Judith's reach.

"Jump," he said, making the single word an urgent command.

Judith took a deep breath, then hurled herself upward, her hands closing on the leather band. Jed grunted slightly as he absorbed her weight. His body tensed and he began slowly straightening up. He paused for a moment, then swiftly released the second rung to grasp the third. Judith was able to transfer one of her hands to the lower rung. Jed kept lifting, and finally Judith's other hand came to the second rung. Releasing the belt entirely, she hauled herself up.

Less than a minute later they were on the balcony outside the door in the dam's face. Peter, with only the bloody screwdriver as a tool, was working at the doorjamb, prying at the wood, slowly splintering it away. At last he got a purchase on the lock itself, and as he leaned his weight against the hardened steel of the tool, the lock broke free from the wood and fell away.

They were inside the dam.

"That way," Jed said. There was a spiral staircase leading straight up, but Jed was pointing down a long, narrow corridor that curved away to the right, following the contour of the dam itself.

Jed began running along the corridor, and Peter and Judith followed him, Judith's ankle jarring painfully every time she put her weight on it. Finally they came to a branch in the corridor and Jed stopped. When the other two had caught up with him, he pointed down the corridor.

"Keep going," he said. "At the end, there's another staircase. It'll take you up to the top, near the south wall of the canyon. Then try to get to the pueblo."

Peter's eyes narrowed. "What about you?" he asked.

Jed took a deep breath. "I have an idea," he said. "It might not work, but I'm going to try it."

Now Peter did argue, but this time Judith intervened. "He knows what he's doing," she said. "He's gotten us this far, hasn't he?" She gazed at Jed for a moment, then turned away.

A moment later Jed was alone in the bowels of the dam.

Otto Kruger glared at Jesus Hernandez. A five-foot section of the PVC pipe had been cut away, and finally the ends of the cut cables were exposed. "How much longer?" Kruger demanded.

Hernandez shrugged. "Ten minutes. Maybe a little less."

Kruger's jaw tightened but he said nothing. As he turned away, something in the distance caught his attention.

Far away, off to the left beyond the mouth of the canyon, he saw a flashing red light moving across the desert.

A moment later he heard a faint siren.

Kendall, he decided, had finally called the police.

It wouldn't be long now before it was all over, and Jed Arnold got what was coming to him.

Chapter 32

Jed waited until Judith and Peter were out of sight, then moved quickly toward the main flume. He stopped dead as he came into the control area, for a man was sitting on a bench, chewing on a sandwich. The man looked at him, then frowned, as if searching his mind for some bit of information. Finally he got up and moved toward the intercom phone on the main control panel.

Jed's heart pounded. The man was much bigger than he was, and built like an ox. But as Jed watched the way the man moved, he thought he understood.

"Stop!" he said, his voice firm.

The watchman froze in his tracks as if some internal switch had been thrown.

"They sent me to relieve you," Jed said. "They want you to go home. Now."

Unhesitatingly, the man returned to the bench, closed his lunch bucket, and walked silently past Jed, leaving Jed alone in the control room.

He stared at the large board covered with gauges and switches, and for a moment nearly gave it up. But then he remembered Gina Alvarez and the strange, empty look in her eyes. If he failed, all his friends—almost everyone he knew—would soon look like that.

Eventually he too would be given one of the shots.

He shuddered, then put everything out of his mind except the problem at hand.

He moved to the main shaft and pulled the entry hatch closed, spinning the wheel in its center until it was dogged tight. Then he returned to the control panel.

To the left, mounted on the concrete wall, was another large wheel, nearly five feet in diameter, connected by a universal joint to a shaft that went straight up, disappearing into a pipe in the low ceiling. A thick chain had been run between two spokes of the wheel and attached to a heavy hasp mounted on the floor.

A padlock secured the two ends of the chain.

Jed tried the screwdriver first, sliding its blade through the hasp of the lock, then twisting. But he could get no leverage, and the lock simply twisted out of his grip.

He glanced around, then saw a toolbox sitting by the wall next to the flume's hatch. He darted over to it, opened it, and pulled out the top tray. Beneath the tray he found a hacksaw.

He went back to the lock, tested the saw's blade against the metal of its hasp, then set to work. After what seemed an eternity, the lock finally gave way, and he ripped the chain free from the wheel. Grasping the wheel with both hands, he applied his weight to it.

Nothing happened.

He climbed up onto the wheel itself, but even his entire weight resting on one of its spokes didn't budge it. Tears of anger and frustration welling in his eyes, he scanned the room for another tool.

He remembered.

He darted back to the flume's hatch, spun its wheel and pushed it open. Inside, the flume was pitch-black but Jed ignored the darkness, stepping into it and groping along the wall until he found what he was looking for.

It was the same shovel he'd been using most of that day, still where he'd left it, leaning against the wall of the shaft. Grabbing it, he hurried back out of the hatch, dogging it closed once more.

Back at the immense wheel, he stuck the blade of the shovel between two of the spokes, then jammed it beneath the wheel's axle. Now, with three more feet added to the radius of the wheel, his weight was enough to break it loose. It moved a few inches, and Jed readjusted the shovel, then applied his weight again.

A few more inches, but he was almost certain the wheel was moving more easily.

He abandoned the shovel, grasping one of the spokes of the wheel, and pulled down hard. The wheel began to turn, and far above, he heard a faint grinding sound. A few seconds later, as the floodgate forty feet below the lake's surface began to lift, opening the inlets to the power flume, Jed could hear the first trickling of water running into the huge chute.

He kept turning the wheel, and the trickling of water grew into a rumbling, then a steady roar. Finally the wheel came to a stop. The floodgates at the top would be wide open now.

The noise was deafening, battering at his ears, and Jed was about to start his own dash for the surface when he thought of one more thing he could do. Scanning the control board quickly, he finally found what he was looking for. There was a large lever, and when he pulled it, there was screech of protest before the enormous turbine at the base of the flume began to turn.

It emitted only a low growl at first, but as it began to pick up speed, its pitch quickly rose until it became a shrill scream floating above the roar of the moving water.

Suddenly there was a terrifying crash from somewhere within the flume. The sound galvanized Jed. Turning away from the control board, he raced out of the room and bolted down the corridor, turning left as he came to the main transverse that ran through the lower level of the dam.

His feet pounded on the concrete, but he could hear nothing except the roar of water, the scream of the turbine, and, increasingly, the terrible crashing sounds as chunks of concrete, torn loose from the damaged sides of the flume, struck the whirling blades of the turbine.

Jed knew what was happening—the turbine was flinging the concrete back, breaking some of it up, hurling fragments of stone and cement against the walls of the flume, damaging them even further.

Soon the turbine itself would begin to break up, and as its blades tore loose, the spinning monster would fall out of balance and begin tearing itself apart. And if it should come loose from its moorings before he'd reached the surface . . .

He blocked the thought out of his mind as he reached the base of the spiral staircase. His lungs already gasping for breath, his muscles worn first from the long day's labor in the dam, then abused further by the climb down the canyon wall, he started upward, his hands grasping the railing to pull himself up as his legs threatened to collapse beneath him.

Halfway up he tripped, pitching forward as his left foot missed one of the narrow steps, his head smashing against the sharp metal of one of the risers. Stunned, a wave of nausea swept over him and his vision blurred. He sank down on the steps, tears streaming from his eyes and mixing with the blood that was already running from a gash on his forehead.

Around him the cacophony built, battering at him.

He could feel the dam beginning to break up.

*   *   *

Judith stared in shock at the figure standing on top of the dam. She and Peter had emerged from the top of the spiral stairs only a few seconds earlier, and now she stood frozen, hardly able to believe her eyes.

"Brown Eagle," she whispered.

Jed's grandfather stepped forward. "I was in the kiva," he said. "I saw . . ." His words died on his lips as he saw Peter Langston, but then his gaze came back to Judith. "I know what Jed is doing," he said. Then he smiled. "I want to see it."

A puzzled frown formed on Peter Langston's face. He was about to ask the mysterious Indian who had appeared out of nowhere what he was talking about, when he heard a faint grinding sound.

It grew louder, and then Judith noticed it too. Instinctively she grasped Brown Eagle's arm. "What is it? What's happening?"

Brown Eagle's smile broadened. "I think Jed opened the main shaft," he said.

"The shaft?" Peter echoed. "Why?"

But Judith understood instantly. "They're repairing it, aren't they? If it's not ready—"

"If it's not ready, then it might tear the dam apart," Brown Eagle said, his voice placid. "I suspect that's what Jed is counting on."

Peter's eyes widened.

The roar of water into the flume was beginning to build, and as he looked over the edge of the dam, he could see water spurting out of the drainage spillway far below.

Suddenly lights came on, bathing the face of the dam, and at the other end, two hundred yards away, a man appeared, darting out of the control shack.

"Come," Brown Eagle said. "We'd better get away from here."

He started to move away, his hand on Judith's arm, but she planted herself firmly. "We have to wait for Jed."

Brown Eagle shook his head. "He didn't want you to wait," he said. "That's why he sent you ahead." But despite his words, he made no move to leave the dam. Instead, he looked over the railing, staring downward.

Water was roaring from the lower spillway. Then a piece of concrete broke loose, propelled nearly a hundred feet out by the force of the water before it plunged into the stream below.

The stream itself was already beginning to grow into a river.

Now they heard what sounded like a series of explosions coming from within the dam.

But still none of them made a move to leave the dam, their eyes fixed on the hatchway where Jed would appear.

If he appeared at all.

Jed's vision cleared slightly and he wiped the tears and blood from his eyes. His head was throbbing, and the roar from within the dam was hammering him with a force that was almost physical. But he struggled to his feet and once more began climbing upward.

The steps were trembling beneath his feet now, and he thought he could hear the rending sounds of metal being torn from metal. He pushed himself harder, scrabbling up the steps, his legs threatening to betray him at any moment.

And then, above him, he saw the hatch.

A surge of adrenaline coursed through his system and he sprang up the last few steps, throwing himself out of the hatchway and scrambling back to his feet even as he sprawled out on top of the dam.

He was almost blinded by the glare of the floodlights, but then, ahead of him, he saw three people. His grandfather was already starting toward him, followed by Peter Langston.

"No," he yelled. Then, when he realized they couldn't possibly hear him, he waved his arms frantically, gesturing to them to get off the dam.

Brown Eagle hesitated, and Jed began running. "It's breaking up," Jed yelled. "Let's go!"

At last the others turned toward the south wall and began to run, Jed pounding after them, his legs burning in protest. Now they came to the end of the dam, where a narrow trail led upward, switchbacking across the face of the canyon all the way to the top, two hundred feet above.

They started up, but paused to look back.

Below them a fissure in the dam was climbing steadily upward as the pressure in the damaged flume continued to tear away at the walls of the chute. Suddenly there was a crashing sound, then a hole appeared in the dam as the turbine tore loose from its huge anchoring bolts and exploded through the concrete facing. Then the dam seemed to split, the center section breaking away.

Judith instinctively shrank back against the stone wall of the canyon, her eyes fixed on the spectacle below as if she were hypnotized.

The lights on the dam went out as the force of the lake exploded the structure, and a deafening roar issued forth as a wall of water, nearly two hundred feet high, began to move down the canyon.

"Climb!" Brown Eagle shouted into her ear. "That water will tear this whole wall apart. The path's going to collapse under our feet."

Judith still stood frozen until Brown Eagle slapped her across the face—not hard enough to hurt her, but with just enough force to snap her out of her trance.

Nodding dumbly, she started scrambling up the steep path, Brown Eagle behind her, followed by Peter and Jed.

Elsie Crampton was standing near the window in Cabin Five. On the floor the body of Lamar Walters still lay exactly as they had found it a few minutes ago when she'd led the two officers, Billy Clark and Dan Rogers, along the path from the main building of the sanitarium. Rogers, the blond one who didn't look old enough to be a cop, had immediately checked the corpse for a pulse, and though she hadn't said anything, Elsie thought it was a waste of time. The man's head was half cut off from his neck, and there was blood all over the place. Couldn't have been more than a pint or two left in his body, from the look of things.

Billy Clark opened his notebook and began scribbling in it, asking Elsie questions every now and then. Elsie didn't mind the questions, since it was already obvious they didn't think she was involved in whatever had happened to Walters. Even sprawled out on the floor, his empty eyes staring up at the ceiling, he looked dangerous, and anyone could have seen right away that there was no way Elsie could have done this to him.

"What about Dr. Moreland?" Clark asked.

Elsie shrugged, ground out her cigarette on a plate on the lamp table, then immediately lit another. "I don't think so," she said finally. He'd be in enough trouble, and right now Elsie figured she'd better stick to the truth. "He wasn't hardly here long enough, and he sure didn't act like he'd done it. I mean, he wasn't even paying any attention to me, and he sounded real upset when he told the other guy Walters was dead. Besides, Walters was a lot bigger than Moreland, and he sure wouldn't have just stood there and let someone cut his throat. You ask me, it must have been at least two people, and they must have been waiting outside when I came out for the dinner tray." She shuddered slightly. "Guess I'm lucky to be alive, huh?"

"Guess so," Clark commented.

Then, in the distance, they both heard a sound. It was a low rumbling, almost like thunder. Elsie cocked her head, then looked out the window.

Her eyes widened as she gazed up the canyon, where a wall of water, towering up the chasm's walls and glinting strangely in the moonlight, was bearing down on them.

She uttered a choked scream and stepped backward. Now it was Clark who looked out the window, freezing as he instantly realized what had happened.

The wall of water was only a hundred yards away now, and even though a part of Billy Clark's mind knew it was already too late, he still bellowed a warning to his partner. "The dam!"

Dan Rogers, startled, looked up just as the raging flood hit the cabin. The walls burst instantly, the roof collapsed, and all three occupants of the cabin were crushed beneath a maelstrom of rubble, part broken concrete from the dam itself, part trees that had been jerked up by their very roots as the deluge roared down the canyon. In a split second the cabin and its occupants had vanished into the flood.

In her own cabin, Reba Tucker had been sitting in her chair by the window all evening, staring out into the night, waiting for the next attack of the demons that always seemed to come in the darkness.

When the first faint rumblings of the raging torrent drifted down the canyon ahead of the flood itself, Reba wasn't even aware of them. But as the noise built, it finally penetrated her failing consciousness, and in her lap, one of her hands twitched.

The rumbling rose to a thundering roar, and then Reba's dull eyes perceived the furious wave bearing down on her, its spume glittering silver in the moonlight.

For Reba those last instants of her life passed slowly, almost as if she were looking at old pictures, studying them one by one, savoring them.

She never understood precisely what had happened or knew how she was going to die.

But images burned into the remnants of her mind.

A tree, floating strangely, its roots up, its branches pointing toward the ground, flashed into her sight, then disappeared, lost forever in the roiling foam.

A block of concrete as big as the cabin suddenly rose up in front of her, and Reba gazed at it mutely.

It came closer, and then her window was filled by it, the foam suddenly gone.

She heard noises, worse noises than she'd ever heard during the times she'd been tortured here, and she felt the very floor shake beneath her feet.

Then the window exploded into her face, and her eyes, punctured by fragments of flying glass, failed her, but it didn't really matter.

The huge mass of concrete, propelled by the force of millions of tons of water, crushed her beneath its weight then moved on, reducing the cabin to little more than fragments of flotsam churning in the melee.

It was all over in a matter of seconds.

Where before there had been a frame house and several small cabins scattered through a peaceful grove of cottonwood trees, there now was nothing.

Not a scrap of vegetation survived the scouring of the flood's furious bore; not even a fragment of the building's foundations remained.

All that was left was the naked rock bottom of the canyon, scraped clean of everything, its sandstone gouged deep with the scars of an assault that nature itself had never designed.

The water rushed on.

Chapter 33

Jesus Hernandez began the last check of his work. The power was back on, and once more the concrete pad that supported the huge dish antenna was bathed in the white radiance of halogen floodlights. He examined the connections carefully, then finally nodded to Kruger. "Got it."

Kruger, who had been pacing nervously, urging Hernandez to work faster, punched a button on the walkie-talkie and spoke to Kendall. "Tell them to start testing."

Almost immediately the antenna came to life. The dish began to rotate, then tipped on its axis. "Okay," Kruger said. "Looks like it's good. It's just a jury rig, but it should hold up till morning."

In the control center Kendall felt a little of the tension drain out of his body. His eyes fixed on the screen of one of the computers as he quickly double-checked the codes once more, then he nodded to Stan Utley. "Send it," he said.

Utley glanced at the display, then whistled softly. "Jesus Christ—you'll blow every one of them." His gaze shifted uncertainly to Greg Moreland.

Moreland nodded curtly.

Utley hesitated, then shrugged his acceptance of the order. He made some adjustments to the controls of the transmitter, then prepared the machine to accept the codes from the computer. His finger hovered over the Enter key on his own computer and he looked questioningly at Kendall and Moreland one last time.

Both men nodded, and Utley pressed the button.

On the display screen numbers began flashing as the antenna above came to life and the first of the high-frequency waves radiated out over Borrego.

And then, abruptly, the lights went out. The cavern was plunged into total darkness.

Paul Kendall froze for a split second, then rage welled up in him. He groped in the darkness, then found the walkie-talkie. "What the hell's going on?" he shouted. "We've lost power down here!"

On the rim of the canyon Otto Kruger felt the same anger as Paul Kendall when the power went out again. He was about to yell an order at Jesus Hernandez when he heard a low rumble, almost like an explosion, drifting down from the eastern end of the canyon. He frowned, puzzled, but as the walkie-talkie in his hand came alive and he heard Kendall's voice —its fury evident despite the crackling of the transmission—he understood.

"The dam," he breathed, almost to himself. His whole body tensed, then he pressed the transmitting button on his own instrument. "The dam!" he shouted. "I think it's gone!"

The distant roar was getting louder now, and a moment later, as the wall of water hit a bend in the narrow chasm and shot a plume high above the canyon's rim, Kruger and his men saw it.

Churning out of the darkness, it roared down the canyon like a freight train gone out of control. The first enormous bore seemed almost like the head of some kind of reptilian monster, weaving back and forth across the canyon, smashing first against one wall and then the other. Behind it the body of the monster spread out to fill the canyon a hundred feet deep.

Trees, boulders, massive chunks of concrete churned on its surface, gouged up from the bottom by the force of the flood, only to sink once more, then reappear.

Kruger stared at the spectacle, every muscle in his body frozen by the sheer magnitude of it.

There was a bend in the canyon just above the antenna installation, and Jesus Hernandez, instinctively understanding what was about to happen, began to run, charging away from the edge of the chasm, stumbling through the sagebrush and juniper that spread across the plateau's surface. By the time the bore struck, he was a hundred yards away, but the force of the cascade of water that welled up from the canyon, overflowing its walls, flattened him to the ground. Then, as it began its backwash, the flood tried to drag him with it.

His hands grappled along the ground, then closed on the lower branches of a thick juniper.

The water, its force spent, released him. He scrambled to his feet and looked back toward the antenna.

It had been reduced to a mass of twisted wreckage. The chain-link fence had been flattened, and the one truck that had been left after the other four men had gone down to cordon off the canyon's mouth half an hour earlier now lay on its side, twenty yards in from the canyon's rim.

Of Otto Kruger there was no sign at all.

As Hernandez watched, the ground beneath his feet trembled, and suddenly fifty feet of the canyon's rim disappeared, dropping away, crumbling into the roiling water below. The antenna, the pad upon which it sat, and the truck were all gone forever.

Jesus Hernandez, stunned, crossed himself, then fell to his knees and for the first time in years began to pray.

Already the roar of the flood's charge down the canyon was beginning to fade into the distance.

In the cavern behind the old construction shack, Paul Kendall heard Otto Kruger's last words, though for a moment the full meaning of them didn't sink in. But a moment later, when he too heard the first ominous rumblings of the cataclysm that was hurtling toward him, he dropped the walkie-talkie and threw himself toward the door.

Kendall stumbled over a chair, lost his balance, and dropped to the floor. He scrambled to his feet, but felt disoriented in the pitch-blackness.

The roar was growing steadily, and panic began to overwhelm him. He groped in the darkness, his hands touching something hard.

A desk.

Which desk?

He didn't know.

"Utley!" he yelled. "Greg! Where are you?"

There was no answer, but he could hear the other men stumbling in the darkness, and tried to move toward the sounds.

Kendall's knee struck something hard and he recoiled, then tried another direction.

Greg Moreland, groping his way through the dark, fumbled with something that felt like a door. Then fingers reached out of the darkness and touched him. A second later he felt hands close around his neck, and then he was hurled to the floor as someone else—Kendall? Stan Utley?—tried to jerk the door open.

As the rumble of the flood grew, so also did Greg Moreland's own panic. Reason deserted him. He began thrashing in the darkness, stumbling first one way then another. But wherever he turned, something seemed to be in his way.

The roar was deafening now, and there was a crashing noise as the flimsy frame structure fronting the cavern was swept away. Then, as the inrushing water compressed the air in the cavern, he was struck by a blinding pain.

His eardrums, stressed beyond their capabilities, burst. Abruptly, Greg Moreland found himself in utter silence.

But even the silence lasted only a second before the water overcame him, knocking him to the floor, then picking him up again to hurl him against the rock wall of the cavern.

A fragment of concrete, carried from the dam on the pure force of the current, slammed into his head, crushing it like an egg against the rough sandstone wall.

The water swept on, scouring the cavern clean, gouging the bodies of Greg Moreland, Paul Kendall, and Stan Utley loose from the shelter of the cave, sweeping the transmitter and computers away, adding them to the great collection of debris the flood had gathered.

When the water finally ebbed a few minutes later, the cavern in the wall, like the rest of the canyon, had been swept clean of every trace that human beings had ever been there.

A moment later the wall of the canyon, undercut by the fury of the flood, collapsed, marking the spot with a pile of rubble that, if left undisturbed, would last for a millennium, slowly to be reshaped by rain and wind.

The four of them approached the rim of the canyon slowly. An eerie silence seemed to have fallen over the night. The roar of the flood had faded away completely, but the normal night sounds, the rustling of small animals, the flutter of the wings of bats as they hunted for prey, the chirping of insects calling for mates—all were gone.

It was as if every living thing on the plateau had been shocked into utter silence by the forces that had been unleashed when the dam crumbled.

Judith instinctively slipped her hand into Jed's as they crept toward the edge of the precipice.

The path they had come up a few minutes earlier was gone, and the verge of the canyon was twenty feet farther back than it had been before. The new face of the canyon, freshly exposed sandstone, was rough and uneven, like a gem waiting to be cut.

Far below them fragments of the great slab that had broken away from the heights lay shattered on what had once been the bed of the river but was now nothing more than the hard and wetly glittering surface of the bedrock beneath.

To their right was what had once been the bottom of the lake, a great layer of silt that had been carried downstream by the river over the course of half a century slowly sinking to the bottom of the lake, building up. Eventually, even if the dam had survived, the lake would have disappeared, the canyon filled by the silt. Now it lay gleaming in the moonlight, a huge mud slick thirty feet thick, its surface carved in strange patterns by the water that had left it behind.

Awestruck, they stood still, gazing out on the ruins of the reservoir and the canyon, each of them lost in his own private thoughts.

Jed stared down into the utter desolation below, the sheer magnitude of the fury he had unleashed threatening to overwhelm him. Finally he looked away, gazing up into the sky. The moon and stars overhead were comforting, for unlike the landscape below, they were unchanged, oblivious to the cataclysm that had swept through the canyon. As he watched, a shadow swept past the moon. Jed felt his grandfather's hand on his shoulder, squeezing gently.

"What is it?" Jed asked, murmuring the words softly, as if even his voice would defile the strangely reverent silence of the night.

The pressure on his shoulder increased. "Don't speak," Brown Eagle whispered. "Just watch."

Now Judith and Peter too were staring up into the sky. As if seeking the light of the moon, the shadow appeared again, silhouetted against the silver disk, and then began lazily spiraling downward.

It was a bird, its great wings set as it coasted on the air currents. As it came lower and lower, growing larger, the four people watching it gasped at its sheer size. It circled over them, then soared eastward, its huge wings pounding as it gained altitude and once more began riding the breezes, sweeping back and forth over the canyon. It disappeared into the distance, then, a moment later, reappeared, beating its way back to swoop low over the small cluster of people on the canyon's rim.

It screamed, a shrill sound that echoed off the canyon's walls, then began climbing, higher with every wing beat, silhouetted once more against the brilliance of the moon. Finally, when it was almost out of sight, it dove, sweeping its wings back, stretching its neck so that its enormous curved beak sliced through the air.

It was over the canyon now; and then, as it dropped below the rim, it screamed once more.

Its wings spread wide as it neared the canyon wall only a few feet above the great mud slick that covered the chasm's floor, and then it screamed a third time.

Its talons reached out, clutching at the naked rock, and in an instant it disappeared.

The four of them watched in silence, unsure whether they'd seen and heard the strange phantom bird at all. In the silence, Brown Eagle spoke.

"Rakantoh," he said softly. "He's come home."

They had been walking for nearly an hour, pausing now and then to look down into the canyon.

They'd stared in silence at the spot where the sanitarium had been.

Now, as on the rest of the canyon floor, there was nothing left: only a few boulders that the passing flood had almost whimsically dropped here and there.

Farther on they had paused again, and stared at the great slab of rubble where the ledge upon which the antenna had stood now lay shattered at the bottom, blocking the cavern that had been dug into the wall beneath.

At last they started down the gentle slope that led to the desert floor. In the distance they could see the town, a few of its windows glowing with candlelight.

Spread out across the desert, already disappearing quickly into the sands and gullies, draining down the myriad washes that cut through the flatlands, there was a sheen of water.

By morning it would be gone.

They paused, almost by common consent, and Judith turned to Jed Arnold.

"What do you want us to tell them?" she asked. Immediately, they all understood what she meant.

Jed was silent for a moment, but when he finally spoke, his voice was clear.

"We'll tell them the truth," he said. "They tried to kill us all. So I killed them first."

They started once more toward the town, with only the moon lighting their way.

But above them, high in the sky, the great bird soared.

Jed looked up at it, and smiled.

About the Author

In 1977 *Suffer the Children,* John Saul's first novel of psychological and supernatural suspense, became an immediate phenomenon, leaping onto national best-seller lists and selling more than one million copies. Each year since has seen the publication of a new bestselling novel of horror—among them *The God Project, Nathaniel, Brainchild, The Unloved, The Unwanted, Creature* and most recently, *Second Child,* published in hardcover in June, 1990. John Saul lives in Seattle, Washington, where he is at work on his next novel.